THE TURNAROUND

THE CREATORS PART 3

THE TURNAROUND

Colin Myerscough
as **J.M. COLLIN**

Copyright © 2017 J.M. Collin

The moral right of the author has been asserted.

Apart from any fair dealing for the purposes of research or private study, or criticism or review, as permitted under the Copyright, Designs and Patents Act 1988, this publication may only be reproduced, stored or transmitted, in any form or by any means, with the prior permission in writing of the publishers, or in the case of reprographic reproduction in accordance with the terms of licences issued by the Copyright Licensing Agency. Enquiries concerning reproduction outside those terms should be sent to the publishers.

Matador
9 Priory Business Park,
Wistow Road, Kibworth Beauchamp,
Leicestershire. LE8 0RX
Tel: 0116 279 2299
Email: books@troubador.co.uk
Web: www.troubador.co.uk/matador
Twitter: @matadorbooks

ISBN 978 1788033 138

British Library Cataloguing in Publication Data.
A catalogue record for this book is available from the British Library.

Printed by TJ International Ltd, Padstow, Cornwall
Typeset in 11pt Minion Pro by Troubador Publishing Ltd, Leicester, UK

Matador is an imprint of Troubador Publishing Ltd

To all those who have made our country better placed to face uncertainty than it was fifty years ago.

The Turnaround follows *Road to Nowhere* and *Flight to Destruction* in telling the story of a group of young people during the turbulent 'long 1970s'. They build their lives, and begin to build a world-beating business, while making a difference in some of the greatest crises of the time. The three novels are complete in themselves but form a whole.

J.M. Collin is the pen name of a man who lived through the times described and has many recollections.

Front Cover: *The Kiss* by Marta Galindo after Rodin, © Marta Galindo Artworks

Rear cover: 23rd February 1981 © EFE

Cover design by Rob Downer

CONTENTS

BOOK VI. STRUGGLE FOR SURVIVAL

1. Saturday, 15th September, 1979 — 1
2. Thursday, 27th September, 1979 — 32
3. Sunday, 28th October, 1979 — 62
4. Thursday, 8th November, 1979 — 89
5. Saturday, 1st December, 1979 — 115
6. Sunday, 2nd December, 1979 — 144

BOOK VII. JACK-KNIFED

7. Wednesday, 21st January, 1981 — 173
8. Monday, 16th February, 1981 — 200
9. Wednesday, 18th February, 1981 — 225
10. Monday, 23rd February, 1981 — 254
11. Tuesday, 24th February, 1981 — 278

BOOK VIII. THE DIFFERENCE MADE

12. Tuesday, 8th December, 1981 — 301
13. Friday, 18th December, 1981 — 327
14. Thursday, 7th January, 1982 — 354
15. Wednesday, 13th January, 1982 — 378
16. Friday, 15th January, 1982 — 400

EPILOGUE

Tuesday, 15th June, 1982 — 431
Transcript of *Musical Memories*, 22nd November, 2015 — 444
Creators Court – a guide to the new buildings — 465

PRINCIPAL CHARACTERS IN 'THE TURNAROUND'

*denotes a director of Creators Technology

NAME	AGE	DESCRIPTION
Douglas ARNOTT	51	Senior civil servant whose responsibilities include North Sea oil and gas policy.
Roberta BOOTH	68	(Formerly Strutt.) Aunt of Pete Bridford, living in Bellinghame, south London. Married to Frank.
Pete BRIDFORD* (*narrator*)	33	Head of Oil and Gas Sales Office, International Electronics plc.
Steph COOLIDGE	40	New Yorker. Corporate Director of Analysis at New Hampshire Realty Bank.
Melissa COPEHURST	32	Nurse in the medical practice the Woolleys use.
Ana GUZMAN	29	Daughter of Spanish noble and banking family. Married to second cousin, Carlos Casares.
Tony HIGGINS*	41	Lecturer in engineering at King's College, London. Pioneer of home computing.
Carol MILVERTON	31	Since May 1979, Labour MP for Holtcliffe, a Yorkshire mining constituency.
Paul MILVERTON*	31	Senior Analyst (Europe) at New Hampshire Realty Bank.
Brenda MURTON	31	Friend of Roberta and Frank Booth. Married to Alan.

NAME	AGE	DESCRIPTION
Morag NEWLANDS	34	Lecturer in maths at King's College, London. Partner of Sheila Yates
Sir Pat O'DONNELL	68	Chief Executive of International Electronics plc (IE), the company he founded in 1938.
Fred PERKINS	32	Formerly at Waterhouse College. Now a doctor in the medical practice the Woolleys use.
Dick SINCLAIR	34	Lecturer at the University of Surrey. Married to Jenny.
Jenny SINCLAIR*	31	Audit Manager at Plender Luckhurst, Chartered Accountants. Mother of David (8) and Katie (5).
Brian SMITHAM*	30	Moving up in management at Universal Assurance. Married to Susie, two children.
Liz WOOLLEY	34	(Formerly Partington.) Now married to Greg and mother of Jenny (2).
Greg WOOLLEY	36	Electrical engineer and hockey player.
Sheila YATES*	36	Lecturer in maths at Queen Mary College, London. Founder of the Pankhurst Centre. Partner of Morag Newlands.

BOOK VI
STRUGGLE FOR SURVIVAL

1. SATURDAY, 15TH SEPTEMBER, 1979[1]

"So, Peter, you've taken the Minister's seat – by the skin of your teeth. It's lucky for you we're late, I guess."

I pulled myself together quickly. For the next nine hours or so, I would be next to Douglas Arnott, the most senior official responsible for British Government policy on North Sea oil and gas. I had met him a few times at industry dinners and functions, but my main contacts with his department were a level or two further down, in the directorate responsible for promoting UK industry sales of offshore equipment.

Before being driven to Dallas/Fort Worth Airport, I had faced the usual early evening American business experience of the time – several shots of hard liquor, with very little to eat. Fortunately, I had time to compose myself whilst the usual safety announcements were made, and the typically Texan attendant brought us champagne 'to get us in the mood for dinner' as the Braniff 747 began to move, over two hours late.

It was quickly and reassuringly clear that Douglas Arnott had partaken of what Braniff offered to delayed first-class passengers. His post was renowned for the amount of senior level entertainment that it attracted. He was renowned for his

---

1 UK Time

strong head, and for clearly demonstrating that the hospitality assisted in communication but did not influence advice and decisions. I aspired to the same renown, on both counts.

I began my reply by saying where I had been for the afternoon – at the head office of one of the largest oilfield contractors in the world.

"When I said I was catching this plane, they regaled me with horror stories of the delays they'd had on it. These guys are practical engineers. They want Braniff to concentrate on running its flights efficiently, rather than kitting out its planes and attendants in gaudy colours. So they organised something practical. The Chief Exec's PA rang Braniff. She's a tall, middle-aged lady with winged spectacles, and she eats booking clerks for breakfast. They told her the usual story but offered an upgrade. So more time in the clubhouse, and here I am. What's happened to the Minister?"

"Invitation to Washington – political. Our people there will look after him. That's a relief for me. He isn't back until Wednesday, and then only for a day before the party conference. I've ten days to catch up. So I can relax now, especially as it's already Saturday at home. We have something of a lie-in, too. We'll reach Gatwick at 5 am current time, rather than 3 am."

This was the only occasion on which I had steak for dinner in-flight, but I guess that the 'national airline' of Texas[2] had to be able to do that for its first-class passengers. After disparaging the way the good Bordeaux had been chilled, we fell to comparing notes on our trips to the USA. I knew already from contacts along the way, that Arnott had been out with his Minister for a few days, calling on top people in oil companies to convince them that under the Conservatives led by Margaret Thatcher, the UK was open for business again. Not that they should have needed much convincing of that, as I pointed out. The North Sea had been very much open for business right through Labour's

---

2 Braniff International Airways ceased operations in 1982.

time in office. That was why, only four years after the start of production, we were producing two million barrels per day – more oil than we consumed. He had had a lot to do with that success.

"It wasn't as difficult with any of our ministers as you might have thought," he said, with a smile. "John Smith and then Dickson Mabon were very clear we had to work *with* business, not against it. All of them, without exception, were prepared to go along because of the clout it gave them in Cabinet. They were in charge of the only thing that was going really well, and don't you forget it. There were others in the Labour Party, too, saying that. Carol Milverton, for example – weren't you involved in her election campaign in 1974?"

"Yes, that came right for her then. It couldn't last, of course."

"In the few months she was in Parliament, she made quite a name for herself as a voice of sense on oil. Her column in the *Courier* is always worth reading. And now she's back in, rather surprisingly for a safe mining constituency in Yorkshire."

"That happened because the father of someone she knew in Cambridge is now on the Yorkshire NUM Area Executive."

"One of Arthur's boys, eh?"

"The father, yes, as long as Arthur[3] delivers the goods. The son is doing very nicely, thank you, at Universal Assurance. He's just been promoted out of computing services into a fairly senior management post."

"You're doing very nicely, thank you, yourself, from what I've heard. The bits man, as *Offshore Weekly* puts it."

"That's about it." I reeled off the names of a dozen or so electronic and instrumentation items. "All offshore platforms need lots of them. International Electronics is now the biggest supplier outside the USA."

"Now you're going for the US market, too."

---

[3] Arthur Scargill was then President of the Yorkshire Area of the National Union of Mineworkers (NUM).

"Not going for it, gone for it, and getting it. The last two and a half weeks have been hard work but I've seen the top design engineers in New York, Pittsburgh, Chicago, San Francisco, LA, Houston and Dallas. The IE brand carries weight with them now. People who've been rather complacent about their home market will find their gear isn't automatically specified any longer."

"There's no problem with the pound being well over two dollars again?"

"No. What matters offshore is durability, reliability and, particularly, ease and speed of installing replacements when something does go wrong. We've been in the North Sea long enough to have top reviews on all these. Enough oil company people have rotated back to the States that there's now a kind of critical mass of support for us there. It's time to build on that."

"I'm glad it's going so well for you. What do your colleagues in other parts of IE think about the pound?"

"Views are mixed but, in our industry, products change and prices fall so fast that the exchange rate fluctuations seem like a bit of noise, as Pat O'Donnell put it when I last saw him."

"I wish more people in British industry were like you people in IE. Just when North Sea oil has picked the country up off the floor, they're all moaning that they can't compete because the pound is too high. Then there are the types who are so used to failure that they don't believe anything can go well. They say that North Sea oil isn't actually good for us or even if it is we shouldn't be eating all the sweets at once. There's a whole lot of trouble ahead. God, I shouldn't be saying all this."

"Don't worry, we can't be heard here. It's well enough known round the industry that the government is considering depletion policy." [4]

I grinned to myself. Arnott had been trying to pump me but now he was worried that he had gone too far.

---

4 That is, holding back production so that the reserves last longer.

"I suppose that's right. What I hope isn't so well known is that people in my department who don't report to me, and also people in the Treasury and the DTI,[5] are pressing for an early announcement that we'll make cuts in production from 1982. They reckon that will bring the pound below two dollars again. We can order cuts but have to give two years' notice of them under the assurances Eric Varley gave in 1975 to provide some certainty for investors. His party isn't in power any longer but that doesn't mean we can ignore his assurances."

I already knew that senior civil servants had a grossly inflated idea of what was secret. In those days, there were four official classifications. 'Top secret' meant you knew last week if you read the right newsletter. 'Secret' meant you knew six weeks ago. 'Confidential' meant most people who were interested had known for months. 'Restricted' had a similar status to the speed limit in what were then sometimes described as 'restricted areas'. What Arnott had just said was somewhere between 'secret' and 'top secret', judging by what Steph Coolidge had told me two weeks before. I was able to respond to it on the basis of a little thought in odd moments.

"The higher pound is reducing the impact on the UK of the oil price doubling earlier this year. If the pound goes down below two dollars, that's at least a 10% increase in the price of oil and of lots of other commodities. That would feed through to inflation. In the Budget, the government has already taken a gamble on inflation. They must stop it going up further, else there'll be far more damage to industry than from the present exchange rate."

"You don't have to tell *me* that," he said, with a sigh. The Conservatives' first Budget had cut income tax, including through a reduction in the top rate from 83% to 60%. They had paid for this by increasing VAT, sending inflation from 10% to 15% 'at a stroke'.

---

5 Department of Trade and Industry – the title of the business department at the time.

"What's your Permanent Secretary doing about this disagreement in his department?"

"Nothing, as usual. It's very depressing. I could hold these people off if ministers could be assured that if the exchange rate goes much higher, production could be held back quickly, but these blasted assurances don't allow that."

"You've plenty of ways of cutting production without contravening the assurances."

"What do you mean?"

"To begin with, you could stop so much gas flaring. Everyone in Aberdeen knows that a lot of compressors on platforms aren't working properly yet. So a lot of gas is just being burnt off, when according to the companies' plans you approved it should go back into the reservoirs for recovery later when there's a pipeline available. You've been allowing this, in view of the shortage of oil since Iran came apart,[6] but now the situation is improving I guess you'll at least make an example of the worst cases. You'll always be able to do that. I've seen enough platforms to know that it always takes longer to get it all working right than the companies say it will. So if you want to, you can hold some production back by saying the plan isn't being fulfilled.

"You can hold back more by exploiting the unpredictability of oilfield reservoirs. At any time in Aberdeen, half the oilmen you meet are saying that production at their field is going better than expected and the other half are saying it's worse. But the levels of production from each field need your consent. There's nothing you can do about those that are below plan and so far you've allowed those that can go above plan to do so, for obvious reasons. But you *needn't* allow them to go above plan if you don't want to.

---

6 At the start of 1979, the Shah had been expelled and the fundamentalist government of Ayatollah Khomeini had taken power. This had led to Iranian oil production being much curtailed. Then the Organisation of Petroleum Exporting Countries (OPEC) made a further doubling of the oil price stick.

"And then you can use constructive inertia. You're always short of the specialised petroleum engineers you need to keep up with what the companies are doing, because the Treasury doesn't allow you to pay them the market rate and the companies keep offering them much more money. So, shortages of engineers can slow down approvals and consents, and it's the companies' own fault.

"I reckon that now or at any time in the future you could cut production by at least 10% within months through a combination of these measures. They wouldn't be caught by the Varley assurances because they're not officially cuts."

"But such behaviour would wreck our relationships with the companies. They would see what we were up to and cry foul. The trust built up over the last few years would be thrown away. Some of them would mount legal challenges."

"Of course that's right, if the government *actually did this*. But they're *not* going to do it. The important thing is that you can tell your ministers now that they *could* do it at some future date, if necessary. They don't need to give two years' notice."

"So our present ministers can leave the decision to whoever are doing their jobs after the next reshuffle."

"Precisely."

There was a pause. I wondered if I had become carried away, in telling this senior man how to do his job. Fortunately, I hadn't gone too far.

"You've given me some food for thought, there. I'd heard that you were a man with ideas. Perhaps I've more to do next week than I was expecting. Thank you, Peter."

"I hope it's helpful and, of course, it's between us. One other thought for your friends in the Treasury, which I'm sure they've heard from others. It's high time we got rid of all exchange controls. They were imposed at the start of the War[7] and

---

[7] Throughout this account, I adopt the universal usage of my generation, learnt from our parents. The 'War' means the 1939-45 conflict.

somehow never abolished. West Germany, which was supposed to have lost the War, abolished them in 1957. We certainly don't need them now. It's not just a question of having to fiddle about entering foreign exchange on your passport when you travel. With the exchange rate high, it's timely for companies to invest overseas. We need to rebuild Britain's capital position by converting some oil revenues into invisible earnings streams for the future. That's the right way to spread the benefits. Moving capital out will also keep the exchange rate from going up too much further."

"Do I detect a bit of self-interest, here?"

"It is true that my plans include a couple of acquisitions which will make our products look more American."

We talked on for a while over a couple of glasses of top bourbon and then let the lively attendant recline our seats and tuck us in. By ten o'clock Dallas time, Arnott was snoring away. He was better at long-distance travel than I was or ever would be. For some time I drowsed in the comfortable seat.

It had certainly been a successful trip, and not all work.

On the Wednesday two weeks before, I had flown to New York. Two busy working days were followed by a busy Labor Day long weekend, over which I was entertained by Ken Ankerman and his third wife Steph – Steph Coolidge, as she was still known at the New Hampshire Realty Bank, where she had been Corporate Director of Analysis for the last two years.

Ken was a few years older than Steph, and a finance vice-president of a large company. He did seem to have the strength and calmness she needed in a partner. He wasn't fazed by knowing that Steph and I had lived together for six months. At their colonial house in Connecticut, they looked very settled three years in. There were no children – 'don't seem it can happen' she said when Ken wasn't around, with a wistful look in her eye which may have had something to do with her having once wanted my children, on her terms.

She moved on quickly to tipping me off about British government thinking and reminding me of the stupidity of continuing exchange controls. She was interested in my aims for the US market and suggested that late in October, when she would be in London, we and Paul Milverton, Carol's husband, should meet up.

Paul had begun the transition from student activist to banker by joining International Electronics as Chief Economist. Then he had moved to New Hampshire Realty, in a way that did not bear too close an examination. Early in 1978, he had been promoted to be Steph's successor but one as Senior Analyst, Europe. I knew that he kept an interest in IE and consequently that New Hampshire had built up a portfolio of IE shareholders they advised, including various universities and colleges endowed by Sir Pat O'Donnell, IE's founder and Chief Executive.

My long weekend was my first experience of the wealthy East Coast at play. I made enough contacts for the weekend to be worthwhile in business terms, went on two yachts, and enjoyed countless cocktails with neighbours, accompanied by gloomy conversations about the performance of President Carter. Steph murmured to me that Ken took seriously being an old Yale man, as did Yale. So he had a slightly proprietorial air when he showed me round the place.

Four frantic days followed, of planes, taxis, meetings and hotels. Such days could have happened only in the USA even then and couldn't happen anywhere now. Only in the USA because whilst Monday had been a holiday, from Tuesday on everyone was at work and pleased to see you. Not now, for the days when you could turn up at a US airport twenty minutes before your domestic flight and get on, with your luggage, are apparently over for good. Then, though, another weekend break, a *very* pleasant break, before more of the same, culminating in the sultry heat of Texas, fortunately without interruption from hurricanes or tornadoes. I drifted off to sleep thinking of the previous Sunday afternoon.

I awoke to a light breakfast and the announcement that we would be landing at Gatwick in forty minutes. First-class passengers were off the plane first and our luggage was at the reclaim by the time we reached it. Soon we were passing through the 'Nothing to declare' channel.

"Just to say again, Peter, I'm pleased we had our conversation last night. We must keep in touch. I'm stepping on now. There's an Eastbourne train in ten minutes and our weekend place is near there. Are you going straight back to Aberdeen?"

"Not until tomorrow. I'm staying with my aunt tonight, in Bellinghame. Oh, oh… That's Pat O'Donnell's driver. Pat always works Saturdays. He must want an urgent report."

In the arrivals hall, there was a man with a card: 'PETER BRIDFORD'. This was an impressive way to leave Douglas Arnott. Whatever happened as a result of our conversation, I had made my number with someone who mattered.

I had the car divert via my Aunt Roberta's bungalow in the south London suburbs, so as to leave my luggage and put them in the picture. She and her husband, Frank Booth, were duly impressed.

"You've clearly done either very well or very badly, that Pat O'Donnell wants to see you straight away," observed Frank. "We'll expect you back here later, hopefully in one piece. You've probably guessed I'm out tonight for a Battle of Britain dinner at the club. In fact, Albert Simpson is presiding."

Frank had preceded his career as a solicitor with a good War in Fighter Command. His squadron leader, Albert Simpson, had retired as an air commodore and was now a non-executive director of IE, bringing to the table his extensive contacts in defence procurement.

"Yes, we'll have a quiet meal here, Pete," said Roberta. "I don't expect you'll mind that after your dash round the USA. Have you really been on fifteen flights in two and a half weeks?"

"Yes, including some little hops and a couple of helicopter rides."

"You've invited Brenda, too, Alan tells me," said Frank. "She'll be company of about your age, Pete, but don't be alarmed. Brenda and Alan have been happily married for over ten years. They live near here. Alan Murton is that unusual being: a teetotal former fighter pilot. He's kindly offered to drive me up and, more importantly, back."

"It seemed silly for Brenda to be on her own. She's a rather quiet woman but very nice."

I suspected that Roberta had some ulterior motive for her invitation but had no time to enquire further. I extricated myself and continued to IE's headquarters in the City. By now it was lunchtime, or second breakfast time for me, and I partook of a couple of the sandwiches offered me in Pat's outer office. Questions about what had been happening whilst I was away were met with guarded responses. I felt a little worried by the time I was called in and more worried when I saw Pat. He seemed to have aged ten years since I had last seen him, at the end of July. He began in a rather resigned voice, quite untypical of his usual manner.

"Pete, I'm glad to see you, and sorry to have brought you in after an overnight flight. First, cheer me up. Tell me about your trip. I'm sure it's gone well."

At least it was clear that I was not to be bawled out over something. I was indeed able to cheer him up. £5 million[8] of new business over there during the next year was a cautious assumption. That wasn't all gained on my trip, of course. It was the result of careful preparation, of cultivation of people I had met in Aberdeen and of visits and demonstrations by my staff. I had been able to confirm to senior management that what their staff were telling them about IE products was absolutely right. We could deliver to American specifications.

"So that's it in a nutshell. Nigel should have my full report by Wednesday, or Thursday at the latest. Shall I copy it to you?"

---

8 Multiply by four this and other sums of money mentioned in this Part, to estimate present-day (2017) values.

"Yes. Nigel is leaving at the end of the month. He's taking October as holiday, and from November 1st he'll be back at Consolidated Electrics doing very much what he's done here. Pleased?"

"I'm surprised, very surprised."

"So was I until I found out more. Before we get to that, I'll give you the good news. Effective October 1st, you're the acting Director of the Instrumentation Division. So you've a fortnight to sort things in Aberdeen, liaise with Nigel, and find somewhere to live in Leeds. It will be announced on Tuesday. You're to attend the Board meeting on the 27th, with Nigel."

"What does 'acting' mean?"

"It means that the post will be advertised but there's no point in anyone but you applying from within IE. It won't be advertised immediately and, for reasons I'll give you in a minute, the advertisement could well be irrelevant."

"I don't know what to say, Pat. I'm really most grateful. I realise there'll be quite a few senior managers rather put out, including at least two in the Instrumentation Division. I've never run a main factory."

"I know that. But in your first two years with IE, you did a great deal to make Sunderland a success. Since then, you've done more than anyone else to get IE stuff into the growing markets. Anyway, before you've been doing the job very long, people will have other things to worry about."

"What do you mean?"

"Why do you think Nigel is going back where he came from, at the same level?"

"Maybe he doesn't like being away from his family during the week. Also, Consolidated is a bigger company. He's a company man. He likes their way of doing things. As you know, I don't. That's why he and I haven't ever got on that well, though there's been mutual respect. I know that most of the changes he brought in were needed and have done IE good."

"If only it were just that, Pete. What do you think is Nigel's best quality?"

"He's very thorough and systematic. If he spots anything wrong, he doesn't rest until he finds out the full story."

"Quite right. Though the two of you are so different, you have that quality too, so I'm glad you recognised it. You weren't in a position to find out what's going to hit us, but Nigel was. I'm sure that's why he's bailing out. And though he's signing all the usual stuff about confidentiality, he'll know the score in his new job. To explain, he won't be the only director whose departure is announced at 3.30 pm on Tuesday. Henry is leaving 'by mutual agreement' as they say."

"You've sacked him. What's he done?"

"What's he *not* done? He didn't keep an eye on his treasury team. Last year, one of them tried to be clever by dealing in interest rate swaps. It went well for a while so he carried on and built up the business, effectively gambling on inflation and interest rates continuing to fall. Then the Shah was overthrown, the price of oil doubled, and inflation and rates took off. Our Treasury man was in trouble so he doubled up his bets. The head of the team says he didn't know but my guess is that he did and realised he had nothing to lose by going along. By the time they told Henry, we were £70 million down."

"*What?*"

"£70 million down. We've already said that last year's profit of £87 million might not be reached this year owing to difficult trading conditions. The market has taken that quite well; after all, everyone is saying it. You can imagine what will happen when we announce we're quite likely to make a *loss*."

"And Nigel will be placed to help pick up the pieces."

"That's right. I think I can trust him not to spill but I've a hunch that Consolidated has wind of this already and will be gearing up to pounce. After all, our loss on swaps is someone's gain. They'll have talked."

"Are we going to prosecute the people responsible for the loss?"

"What for? It probably wouldn't stick. They weren't breaking any rules. Henry hadn't made any rules. Not like George did when you and Paul Milverton took us into that adventure a few years back. We hadn't spotted Paul's political game at the end; but as far as this company was concerned, the financial risk was never more than half a million. We ended up with £19 million – nearly £50 million in current money."

"Has that all gone, now?"

"Yes, and well spent."

"Who's going to do the finance job?"

"Henry owned up three weeks ago, just before I went off on holiday. I'm glad I stuck with my plans because whilst away I met the senior partner of Plender Luckhurst and decided to confide. So, Tim Baldwin, one of their partners, is coming here as interim Finance Director. He's bringing one of the firm's best young stars to lead a support team. Or rather, he *hopes* to bring her. She's been away in the States with her husband who's an academic, so Tim could speak to her only last Wednesday. She was worried about taking the job because apparently she knows you."

"That must be Jenny Sinclair. She's risen fast at Plenders, whilst bringing up two kids. She was my girlfriend for a while but went instead for the man who's now her husband. That was just before I came to IE, you may remember. We've stayed good friends. Her husband spent the summer in California, and Jenny and the children went out for a holiday. I met up with them over last weekend. I'm surprised that she's worried. Presumably she expects me to be still in Aberdeen."

"Persuade her. Tell her about you, but nobody else before Tuesday. That's if you want the job, now you know the full story. I'll quite understand, Pete, if you think about it for a day or two. If you stay put in Aberdeen, and Consolidated takes us over, you'll end up with their North Sea operations merged into yours. Everyone knows that, thanks to you, we're streets ahead there. But you know who would take charge of a merged instrumentation business."

"It's an easy decision for me, Pat. I'm not interested in working for Consolidated. It's too managerial. There's no scope for individual initiative and flair. Its senior people aren't allowed to have other business interests. As you know, I have two. You've regarded that as good for my main job, and you're right. Incidentally, Jenny Sinclair is also involved in both of them."

"Frankly, Pete, I'm looking to you to front our fight back when it happens. You're a fast, calm thinker in a tight corner. This is the granddaddy of tight corners. Just when it was mostly going well, *this* happens. You're widely enough known as a big part of the future here. That must be part of the message to shareholders – sorry about the short-term hit but the long-term message is bright."

"I've learnt a lot from you, Pat, especially to focus on the task in hand. When you can't do more on that, focus on something else or relax. I guess the difference between you and Don Flitton accounts for much of the difference between IE and Consolidated."

Don Flitton was the Chief Executive of Consolidated. He symbolised their 'organisation man' culture. He was successful, but by relentless drive rather than flair.

"Don't be too hard on Don. His life hasn't been easy these last years. Now, there's a package for you outside. It's just about what's to be announced on Tuesday. There's absolutely nothing about the losses. No-one here knows about those yet except us, Tim, your chum Jenny and probably Nigel. There's a contract, which will give you some security. There's some stuff about the responsibilities of a director, which you'll know anyway. There's a pack of material Nigel has put together. You can call him at home this afternoon or later tomorrow. And there's a draft press release for Tuesday. Have a look at that before you go, and leave any comments. Apart from mentioning you and Tim, it says that in view of the current changes I'm staying till 1981 but definitely going then. Consultants will be looking for a Chief Executive on that timescale. That's meant to give a clear message. The new Chief Exec will come from outside the company and will have an established track record. So, Pete, he's likely to be someone round about the age of fifty. He probably won't be like me. He'll retire sometime in the early '90s, when you're forty-five or so."

"When do you think a bid from Consolidated might happen?" I said – rather flatly, being in some shock.

"That depends on when we have to come clean on the hit. Our half-year statement will be expected by the end of October. Tim will sort out the tactics."

"I've a pretty sure fire test of how much they know. If Colin Schofield has picked anything up, he'll try to pump me." Colin was Consolidated Electrics' man in Aberdeen. A takeover of IE would be good for him if I had left but bad if I stayed.

Pat and I talked for a little longer, though my mind was hardly in gear as the news spun round in it. At the end, I felt that at least I had cheered him up.

I collected the pack, to smiles from the secretaries now. The contract offered to me was very satisfactory, so I signed it and moved on to the press release. That followed what Pat had told me, with the additional information that the company would be looking to appoint a non-executive chairman. Pat still combined the roles of Chairman and Chief Executive. I put in more about how I had taken the company into new markets, including what I could say about my US visit. I wanted to convey the image of IE as the fleet-footed, adventurous company established by its founder, and to make a contrast with reliable but stolid Consolidated. I wasn't happy with some of what was said about Tim Baldwin – there was a hint of panic. I called Jenny Sinclair's home. There was no reply, but it was a fine day.

I looked through the material Nigel had left and called him at his family home near Colchester, the location of a substantial factory which he had managed before moving to IE. Given that he had two sons at the Royal Grammar School there, it wasn't surprising that he was on his own in Leeds during the week. He was friendly but gave no clue as to what he knew. I arranged to spend a day with him on the next Thursday and settled who should take my job in Aberdeen. That was easy but also innovative. I had full confidence in my deputy – Claire Macdougall, an Aberdonian who had joined the office in 1975. Nigel agreed and I left a note for Pat. She would be the first woman in IE to become a senior manager, reporting to a director.

That was enough for me at the office. If I was to be reasonably bright at dinner, I needed a rest. Other goodies, like sorting out a better company car, could wait.

On the train back to Bellinghame, I began to come to terms with events. In a sense, they were all predictable. I was rather remote from internal company politics, being greeted at gatherings as 'the man from the far North'; but I had seen and heard enough to know what had gone wrong.

Pat O'Donnell, for all his huge strengths and continuing energy, should have retired three years before, at the age of sixty-five. Then, there had been two strong internal candidates to succeed him. I had favoured George Armstrong, the Finance and Corporate Director. He believed as I did in making the company a more integrated operation but also recognised the need for individual initiative and flair. However, Ben Tyler, the Director of the Microelectronics Division, also had plenty of support. My then boss Terry McAvitt was nearing sixty and had no ambitions other than to enable a smooth transition to happen. Both George and Ben had told him that, if not selected

17

to succeed Pat, they would see the other in before moving on. They were both in their late forties, so still had prospects for a move.

But Pat hadn't retired. So, early in 1977, Ben had left to head up a consumer electronics company, and George had left for a good job in a bank. Neither could risk ending up on the shelf. Later that year, Terry had retired – a disappointed man.

The basic problem was that Pat was still interested in work. His recent one-week holiday at a luxurious and very expensive hotel in the Swiss Alps was typical. At least he had a comfortable home life. For over forty years, his wife had put up with him and calmed him down. By comparison, Don Flitton's home life was tragic. His wife had died three years before, after years of becoming increasingly unbalanced. It was said that he worked all the time to escape the memory.

The successor to Ben had been obvious within his team. I had known Mike Grimsey for ten years, ever since in my first job for IE I had reported to him at its semiconductor plant near Sunderland. In another ten years, it could be between me and him for the top job if IE survived. He would be just under fifty and would have the advantage of long experience in production management, if that was still important.

With Mike suited, there was no clear successor to Terry, and Nigel Thompson had come in from Consolidated Electrics. George's replacement had been delayed by arguments on the Board about whether the job specification should continue his corporate role or be limited to finance. Eventually, Henry Milsom had arrived from a finance company. It seemed that during the interregnum, bright ideas had flourished amongst those responsible for managing the company's cash and borrowings. Henry had not checked up, and here we were.

George had been worried that IE's decentralised structure made it vulnerable to a takeover, most likely by Consolidated. The parts could be worth more than the whole. Some could be sold off and others folded into Consolidated's rather similar organisational structure. A good run of results for IE, at least relative to the disastrous general performance of the economy in the mid-'70s, had made the threat recede. Although our stock market valuation had shown the same extraordinary swings as the market in general, we had moved from being a third to over half the value of Consolidated. My initiatives, and those of colleagues like Mike, had helped with that. The market liked the IE philosophy of encouraging initiative and accepting risk to find new business. Consolidated, whose tight corporate structure meant that senior people spent much of their time at committee meetings, seemed safe but stodgy.

Recently, though, there had been perceptions of drift, and worry as to whether IE was responding broadly enough to the opportunities and challenges arising from the new government. We had dropped a few percentage points in relative valuation. Now disaster loomed. The coming revelations could put us back to where we were ten years before. Consolidated might succeed with a bid at near the current share price.

I certainly hadn't expected to move up to the Board so soon. I would be responsible for about 7,000 employees, roughly half of them in West Yorkshire where there were several factories, at the largest of which the divisional head office was located. In my previous posts, I had not been responsible for more than about 150 staff, and that was at Sunderland. The North Sea Sales Office had grown to about eighty staff, of whom about half were in Aberdeen and the rest dotted around the principal factories.

Pat had given the real reason for my appointment. My greatest strength was my cool but fast reaction to crises. I had demonstrated that to him several times. It was needed now. If IE survived, my contribution would confirm my appointment and I would have the chance to be Chief Executive at around the age of forty-five. If IE didn't survive, I would be out. I was doubling up my bets.

When I arrived back, Roberta was in her fluffy mode.

"Pete, you must be tired, having to go to the office after your flight. Let me get you some tea. Jenny Sinclair called. Can you ring back at about 7.30? They'll have eaten by then."

Underneath her fluffy mode, Roberta was in her own way as smart as Pat, her contemporary. We had hardly met until I was in my twenties, for my parents in Dorset had not got on with her. In 1970 I had stayed with her for a few months whilst working in London, and we had found we liked each other. She had then been involved in the campaign which had led to Carol Milverton's sensational victory in the first general election of 1974. That had made her realise that, though widowed, she wasn't that old. She had also become close to Frank Booth, whose wartime marriage had not long survived peace. Late in 1974, they had married quietly. Since then there had been an element of mother and son in our relationship, for Roberta's own son disapproved of Frank. Fortunately, in the meantime, she and my parents had buried the hatchet.

I wasn't allowed a long rest, for Roberta had scheduled a dish which she knew I had the knack of preparing. As we worked on that, she became confiding.

"Brenda's keen to meet you, Pete. She's had a rather upsetting experience involving someone you might have known at Waterhouse College. I think it will help her to talk to you about it."

The Murtons arrived just before six o'clock, and Frank appeared, splendid in blazer and squadron tie. I was introduced as 'the man straight off the plane to see the boss'. I assured them that I hadn't been in trouble but that Pat liked personal reports. That was fine to get back to Albert Simpson.

Brenda looked a bit pensive as I chatted to her, while Roberta busied herself in the kitchen, but she livened up once we were on to the international situation, then dominated by events in Iran. She clearly had time to read the papers and watch TV, though it wasn't clear how much she thought about what she read and saw.

Roberta returned to pour drinks. Brenda accepted hers gratefully; this was a difference she and Alan lived with. Roberta said that dinner would be ready at a quarter to eight, so I could phone Jenny first. I closed the hallway door before dialling and was quickly at my conclusion.

"So I know why you were calling, Jenny, and I'm sure you'd worked out what you could say to me. But now you know that we would be working together. I very much want that to happen and so does Pat. We understand each other. You'll be totally honest but you're good at presentation, too. That will be needed."

"I very much want this job but I was worried about becoming involved in decisions that might affect you, without you knowing anything about it. Oh Pete, it's so marvellous we can talk, and such good news for you."

"It's good in parts – a tough assignment, but less tough with you to help."

Even down the line, I could sense Jenny's mood. I hoped that Dick wasn't nearby, not wholly or even mainly because our business was confidential.

Over dinner I talked about my trip to the USA, but then allowed Roberta to edge the conversation round so that Brenda said more about herself. She and Alan both had decent though unspectacular office jobs – he in the West End, she in Croydon, 'so I'm home before him and can get his meal ready'. They had a nice house in a nice road, went on nice holidays and had no money worries. That was, of course, because they had no children and, once on to that, things became emotional.

"Alan and I love each other so much. We have done ever since we met, when I was working at the base he flew from. We went all the way only a month after that and though we took precautions we were relieved nothing happened. Then we got married and still nothing happened. We've tried everything. Both of us have been to a clinic. There's nothing wrong with either of us but nothing happens. And after the horrible time I had in July, nothing will happen. I won't trust doctors again."

She burst into tears and Roberta put an arm round her.

"Now, Brenda, you tell Pete what happened in July. He may be able to help. It won't go beyond the three of us here. I've not said anything about this to Frank and I won't."

"It's my fault, I suppose. I saw this in a women's magazine." She showed me a small advertisement:

'STILL CHILDLESS?
There are many reasons. Even if you've tried others, try again. Experienced family doctor offers consultations and advice. Reasonable rates.'

"There's no harm in calling the number, I thought. A woman answered and asked a few questions, about my age, how long I'd been trying and who I'd already seen. Then she said the doctor could see me soon. The charge for a first consultation would be £15, which certainly seemed reasonable. The best time for an appointment was a week after my period, when I should be most fertile. Could I bring a copy of my marriage certificate? The doctor was most particular; he saw only married women. I asked whether I needed a letter from my GP. She said there was no need; the doctor was a GP not a specialist, which was why he could look more broadly at his patients.

"So I knew I was going to see a man but I was reassured that this woman seemed to be involved. I went along to the appointment, which was at some consulting rooms in Wimpole Street. I recognised the voice of the nurse who let me in and she remembered my call. She was a tall woman with short brown hair and eyes that looked as if they took everything in. It all seemed very friendly. She asked me to undress. As I did that, she had more questions about my general health and eating and drinking habits, and personal history, including whether I'd made love to anyone but my husband, and how recently with him. She wrote my answers down on a form. The last answer was easy – the night before. Then she measured and weighed me, and felt all over my breasts. Nothing untoward there, she said reassuringly. The doctor wanted all this information so as to offer the best advice. It still all seemed OK, though I'd not before had someone watching me as I undressed.

"Next she said that the doctor wanted her to insert a speculum. She guessed I'd had that done before. It was easier if the patient was quite relaxed and she'd found she could help patients with a few minutes' massage. Would I like that? It seemed a good idea so I lay down on a couch, she oiled me a little and massaged me all over for about ten minutes. It *was* relaxing; her hands felt nice and she said she could feel it was helping me. After that, I got into the examination chair. You lie back, legs apart and feet in stirrups. She slid the speculum in, opened it up and called for the doctor. It had been less of a shock than times before; in fact, I was feeling good.

"The doctor came in wearing a white coat; he was a tall and good-looking man of about your age, I guess, Pete. He read the form and talked as he looked in with a flashlight. He said that everything seemed quite normal. But he wanted to examine me with his hands; sometimes that gave him suggestions to make. So the nurse took out the speculum, he washed his hands and started feeling me, one hand inside and one out. He wasn't wearing gloves. He said this helped him know where to feel. His hands were nice and I began to feel really good. I suppose I must have smiled, for he kept it up for some time murmuring 'good' and things like that. Then he paused and said 'I don't think there's any reason why *you* can't have a baby'.

"After a bit he was fingering me, not just feeling. He looked very gentle and friendly, and I stopped thinking where this was going until I saw the look on the nurse's face. I'd already noticed her eyes. Now she was staring at me intently and her hand was inside her coat. There was no doubt what she was expecting to see and enjoy.

"That brought me back to earth. I saw, too, what was under the doctor's coat. My change in expression said it all. He took his hands away and went over to a desk where he wrote a note, facing away as I dressed. The nurse looked pretty sour, too. I took his note, which suggested relaxation before making love and being sure to go for the best time. I'd heard all that before. I paid my £15 in cash and left as quickly as possible. As soon as I was outside, I broke down. Oh, how could I have gone so far?"

Brenda began to cry again. Roberta came in, comfortingly.

"They both led you along, Brenda, but you knew to leave."

"Others won't know to leave. This horrible pair take advantage of women like me. We must stop them. Nowadays when I'm with Alan, I think of them and can't respond. He's beginning to notice. I won't be able to go properly with him till I know they've been stopped."

"Do you know who these two are?" I asked.

"No, there was nothing to say, and the note was just headed 'a family doctor's advice'. I noticed one thing. In the room where all this happened, there was a painted rowing oar on the wall. I had asked about it and he said it was a happy memory of his student days and there was no room for it at home. The words on the oar were Waterhouse College First Boat; I can't remember the date but it must have been around the time you were there, Roberta says."

"I do recall a medic student who rowed. I've not met him since I left Cambridge but I can look him up in the medical register."

"Could you go and see him, Pete?" asked Roberta. "His behaviour is quite unacceptable. He must stop. If Brenda complained, he would be struck off."

"No he wouldn't. He could just laugh it away. He had his nurse with him. He didn't do anything untoward. Brenda just imagined it. She walked out with his advice."

"What about waiting outside the surgery and warning people what to expect?"

"Brenda would be regarded as a nutter, quite possibly she would be moved on and it could generate publicity she doesn't want. If this is who I think it is, he's not stupid. He got firsts as well as being good at sports and taking his pick of the girls. My guess is that only women who've tried other doctors and sound pretty desperate are offered appointments in the first place. They only went as far as they did after you said you'd had sex with your husband the night before. So if a baby does come along, that's a happy event. How much gear was there in this room, Brenda?"

"There was the special chair but not much else apart from a desk, some chairs, a couch and the oar."

"So they could hire the room. Perhaps the special chair comes with it. The oar is a personal touch which gave confidence. It's probably been cut into sections to make it transportable."

"The hire would have cost them more than £15," said Roberta.

"That shows what they're in this for," I said. "Maybe other clients are charged more. What we must do is find a way to teach this pair a lesson they'll never forget. I've no ideas straight away but I'll think some more and let you know."

"Oh Pete, that is good of you," said Roberta. "Brenda, if Pete says that, you know something will happen. Now, tell us more about America, Pete."

That took us on to when the men returned and Alan took Brenda home. Then it was definitely UK bedtime, but I lay awake for a while, for it was still early evening on my clock.

I didn't think much more about what Brenda had told me. I didn't need to look at the medical register. I knew where the medic I recalled was currently based and how I could find out more of what he was doing now. And as I had given some description of my Labor Day weekend, an idea had sparked in my mind.

Nor did I think more about the risks I was taking by moving up in IE out of the North Sea role which I had carved so successfully. I was right to do so, just as I had been right to quit Cambridge in 1968, despite my academic success. A big opportunity beckoned for me, and I would be working with Jenny Sinclair.

Last Friday, it had been great to see Jenny waiting for me in the lobby of the office block where I had finished my last meeting in San Francisco. At thirty-one, she had not lost her youthful blonde beauty but her face showed more of the strength I had recognised in her years before. Soon I was with her whole family, enjoying the view of the sunset over the Golden Gate from the house in the Berkeley Hills that her husband had rented from someone at the university who was away.

Dick Sinclair's research had been in the doldrums until something of a breakthrough late in 1973. Three years later, he had at last obtained a tenured appointment at the University of Surrey. This had been convenient, since Jenny was set to move from Plender Luckhurst's Brighton office to its main UK office in London. Her astute timing of house moves at a time of rapid inflation had recently brought them to four bedrooms in Weybridge. Now, she worked four days a week, one of them from home. On some other days, Dick could collect eight-year-old David and nearly six-year-old Katie from school. Dick's parents, who lived not far away, also helped, especially when Jenny was visiting clients. This is all common enough now but was unusual then.

Dick's research breakthrough had also brought him the chance to spend most summers with a research group at the University of California, Berkeley. His earnings there had usually allowed Jenny and the children to join him for a holiday. This year they had been there for a month, since Jenny was between assignments and had spent a few days at her firm's San Francisco office. Whilst the children's school had agreed that being in San Francisco had some educational value, a week was the most they could lose. So the whole family had been about to return; their last weekend was with me.

On the Saturday, we covered sights that didn't pall even for the children. We went up and down on cable cars, and strolled through the Haight-Ashbury area, which was where 'hippiedom' had started in the 1960s but was now gentrified and full of expensive shops. We ended with a meal in Chinatown.

Sunday morning had been fine and still, a good time to sit in the garden admiring the view and to play with the children. I showed them how to work out the distance to the Golden Gate Bridge by placing two posts in the garden and aligning them with the towers of the bridge, whose length we knew. That had interested Katie more than it had David.

After an early lunch we set off to drop the children at a birthday party given by a colleague of Dick's. I had noticed Jenny picking up some used towels and sun oil so I was not too surprised at what she said on her return to the car. Indeed, already I had a pleasant feeling of anticipation.

"Pick-up is at 5.30 so we've plenty of time to show Pete the beach. We've not been there for three years, or is it four, Dick?"

"I've heard that since then it's rather changed."

Dick looked slightly uncomfortable as he replied but said nothing more. Half an hour's drive and a quarter of an hour's walk from the car park later, my anticipation was well rewarded.

The view of the Golden Gate Bridge in the distance was glorious, changing from time to time as small clouds drifted over. The view close at hand was even more glorious, changing from time to time as Jenny turned over. The view in mid-distance was not particularly glorious to my eye, though interesting. Even one slightly odd incident was forgotten quickly. We were pleasantly aglow when we returned to pick up the children.

I was also not too surprised when Jenny offered to run me to the airport early on Monday. She explained that it would give Dick a chance to pack and she could check where to leave the hire car later. Once we crossed the Bay Bridge and were through the worst of the traffic, she began a conversation I had been expecting.

"Thanks for being so smart yesterday, Pete."

"It was a win-win for me but I'm sorry it happened. The way I was looking at you, it wasn't surprising that he thought we were together and Dick was spare."

The interesting mid-distance view had been of men wandering up and down, singly or in groups, eyeing each other. Just after Jenny had asked Dick to oil her back, one of them had approached us, greeted Dick and suggested a stroll. I had invited Dick to go ahead; I could oil Jenny. Our visitor had taken the message and moved on.

"Dick said it was someone he'd met at the university. But in that case, why didn't he know about me? Also, he came up behind you, and Dick was looking out to sea. Only I saw the expression on the man's face. He knew Dick. He wanted Dick. Dick knew him and didn't want to go to the beach because he could be there."

"Dick is a darn sight more handsome than most we saw. I wonder what they find in each other."

"The beach *has* changed. When the children were little, we went there lots. There were single men but plenty of women, too, and families. We haven't been there since the children went to school because I wouldn't want them talking about it to their friends. Now there are ten men for every woman. It's clear what they want."

"You're all going home later today and Dick was saying he didn't expect to come here next year. It sounds like that's for the best. Anyway, I liked going to the beach and I think you did, too. Thanks, Jenny, and thanks for the whole weekend."

Our conversation paused as Jenny found her way into the airport and pulled up outside the terminal. Then she continued.

"Mmm yes, I liked looking at you, Pete, and I liked seeing that you enjoyed looking at me. You're still my brother."

"On the subject of brothers, how are things with John and Amanda?"

"There's not been much opportunity recently, my fault of course, but the worst is over. Imogen was three last June, and Louisa is one late next month. Amanda hopes to be back at work early next year, mostly on nights and at weekends."

"You arranged it all *very* well, Jenny."

"Yes, it's all worked out."

I licked my lips and so did she. Then we exchanged sibling kisses and wished each other safe journeys.

Eleven years before, Dick had tried to kill himself. Together, Jenny and I had saved his life. That had brought out her growing realisation that she wanted Dick rather than me. Since then, Jenny and I had always been friends. Indeed, Jenny had suggested that we should continue the mutual confidence of brother and sister. It had been quite right for me to be Best Man at her wedding, since I had known Dick for three years before either of us met Jenny. But for some years we had not met often. We were not trying to avoid each other, but there were too many memories.

After five years, I had returned to England and found again a circle of friends from Cambridge, which included Jenny and Dick. At the same time I met Steph Coolidge, who dubbed us 'The Creators' on account of our determination to make our way and to create something with our lives. Jenny and I had found it much easier to keep in touch within this circle. We had joined other Creators to set up a small company in the new business of home computing, and her accountancy skills had proved invaluable in another business venture of mine.

Jenny had developed, not only by qualifying as a chartered accountant but also by organising those around her 'in the loveliest sort of way', as Dick had put it. She had always been close to her real brother John. She had disposed of his unsuitable girlfriend by showing this closeness at secluded sunbaths. Then she had introduced him to Amanda Farquhar, a nurse who had helped Dick to recover. Amanda took to John and, just as important, being with him gave her opportunities to admire Jenny. She had followed John to Sheffield, where he was now a lecturer at the university.

Two weeks before Jenny married Dick, she had held a 'hen party' at a sauna. The literal climax was when Jenny laid Amanda on a couch which had already been well used but remained standing beside it herself. Jenny had smiled as she ran her hands over Amanda's body and felt adoration move to ecstatic submission. Then she had licked her lips in relish at her power, whilst the gentlest touch of her finger delivered the loudest orgasm of the day.

That story was well known in our circle, but only Dick and I knew of John's response and of what that led to from time to time. Indeed, Jenny's self-blame reflected that Imogen was quite likely to have been conceived during a family stay in Sheffield. After Jenny had warmed Amanda and John up by fingering and fondling, she would have pleasured herself whilst they did the job. Her pleasure was perhaps the same as the nurse's pleasure at the bogus clinic, but was obtained in a wholly honest, friendly and supportive way. Neither Amanda nor John touched her; that was reserved for Dick, and on that basis he accepted what happened.

Hearing of what happened had ended my misgivings about meeting Jenny more often. I knew how she was running her own life. Licking our lips was a sign to each other of our close and understanding friendship. Last Sunday afternoon had also been part of that friendship. It had made more vivid and pleasurable my imagination of her with Amanda and John.

If we had tried to do together what we had done separately, we would have failed and probably would no longer be friends. Now, we would be working together. There was no-one else whom I would rather have with me in facing the challenge. It was an exciting prospect for me and clearly the same for her.

2. THURSDAY, 27th SEPTEMBER, 1979

Tim Baldwin and I had been welcomed to our first IE Board meeting, though we would not be formal members until the next Monday. After we had dealt with some fairly routine business, Nigel had withdrawn, to thanks for his real contribution to the company during his short time with us. Then Tim had handed round his appreciation of the mess we were in, for which urgency and confidentiality had dictated a break in the strict rule of one week's notice. We took a twenty-minute break to read it. I did so carefully, though I had had some notice of its content during a long call from Jenny on the previous Monday evening. Once we resumed, Tim began.

"The facts speak for themselves. In November last year, MLR[9] had just been increased to 12.5%. On their own initiative, the corporate treasury team switched a lot of IE's borrowing to floating rates, since everyone thought the next move would be down. Because of Iran and the Winter of Discontent, it wasn't. In February, with MLR at 14%, they switched back to fixed rate, but then MLR fell back to 12%. If the team had stopped there, the loss would have been about £10 million. But then they assumed that the Conservatives would reduce rates further, and gambled to retrieve the situation using derivatives which meant they were effectively playing with far more capital than our total borrowings. Early last year, they'd made half a million or so using derivatives, which gave them exaggerated confidence in

---

9 Minimum Lending Rate – the term then used for the Bank of England base rate.

their own abilities. This time, the losses were multiplied when they got it wrong again. In June, MLR went back up to 14%. Furthermore, the losses are not capped against further increases in MLR. First, I ask you to agree to further switches that will have the effect of fixing the losses at a total of £67.8 million."

"Is there any chance that if we wait the losses will be reduced?" asked Pat.

"Very little, I'm afraid. If we do nothing, every percentage point increase in MLR will increase the loss by £16 million. Further increases are likely during the next months."

"You're effectively saying that you can get others to take over further losses from us. Why should they do that?" asked Albert Simpson.

"Because they're Arab banks full of cash. They don't really understand what they're doing."

We agreed the recommendation. I knew that it was based on some very hard work by Jenny and her team over the last week. Then, Tim continued.

"Now, the table on page 2 shows the timing of payments in settlement. Because most of the derivatives purchased in April look forward twelve months, about £55 million will have to be paid next April. The remaining £13 million is due sooner. I think the cash flow of the company is sufficiently good that these early payments can be made from it without disturbing operating or investment plans and without increasing long-term borrowings. I ask you to agree that the short-term financial targets of each division are adjusted, as set out at the bottom of page 2."

We agreed the adjustments. Then Mike Grimsey had an observation.

"So, the question is, how do we find £55 million within six months?"

"Yes, though let me emphasise that we are not insolvent. There are two practical possibilities, as set out on pages 3 and 4. We could find it all from current revenues, taking the whole hit on the current year's profits. There would then be either a small profit or a small loss for the financial year 1979/80 and we couldn't pay a dividend. If we take this route, we must announce it immediately as something directly impacting on the share price, and pass the interim dividend. Alternatively, we could, effectively, capitalise the loss as a one-off event. If we take that route, an announcement through the normal half-year statement, late in October, would be sufficient. We would have to state very clearly how we would ensure no repetition and how we would meet the cost – by increasing borrowings, disposing of some assets, or both. Increasing borrowings would be costly. We would be in some distress and would have to pay two or three points above MLR. My recommendation would be to fund at least £40 million through asset disposals. Here I am in your hands. You know your businesses. You can assess the practicalities."

Tim looked round at the five directors of IE's operating divisions, now including me. Pat responded before any of us could say anything.

"Thank you, Tim. This will have come as a great shock to you all, as it did to me. Once it goes public, if not before, the predators will circle, Consolidated in particular. Passing the dividend would bring them down on us in no time. As we've discussed in the past, there's no significant area where the combined businesses of IE and Consolidated dominate the market to the extent that the MMC[10] would rescue us. Therefore, I certainly prefer capitalisation, if it can be done. All we can do today is come to a view on that. We certainly cannot settle the detail of disposals. Let's break for lunch now and see how far we can get afterwards."

Sam Titchmarsh, the second non-executive director and a City man, broke in.

---

10 The Monopolies and Mergers Commission – replaced in 1999 by the Competition Commission, which was itself replaced in 2014 by the Competition and Markets Authority.

"Before we do, Pat, I must emphasise the need for a solution in accord with financial proprieties. We must not delude ourselves about the seriousness of the situation, let alone attempt to delude shareholders."

We all nodded assent and proceeded to a buffet laid out in Pat's office. As we ate, I looked round at my new colleagues. Reactions were clearly varying.

Alastair Heaton, the Director of Telecommunications Division, and Mark Dorney, Director of Defence Systems Division, were in their late fifties. They were talking quietly to each other and looking rather resigned. I could just imagine them saying 'not the company we grew up in...', 'too many youngsters with bright ideas...' Whatever happened, they would go on good packages. Mark would certainly welcome more time for golf.

The two externals were looking bemused as they spoke together. 'How did we get into this, it's not what I was expecting to face now?' perhaps from Sam. 'Tight corner but I've seen worse' might be Albert's reaction, judging from what Frank Booth had told me about him.

Pat and Tim were in their corner, maybe murmuring 'so far so bad...', 'no outright row yet'.

Mike Grimsey beckoned to me to join him and Neil Farnham, who was in his mid-forties and since 1975 had been Director of Control Systems Division.

"Well, Pete, are you still pleased you're here? What can you start off by selling?" asked Mike.

"I'll start off by buying. Neil, I think that later today the other shareholders in Creators Technology will agree to buy IE out, as we discussed last month. That won't go far to help, though."

"Can we talk about Sunderland?" said Mike. "Pete, you probably know that either we invest £50 million urgently or we get out."

In 1972 Mike had been promoted to manage the Sunderland semiconductor factory. He had then earned his place on the Board by leading its build-up as one of IE's flagship projects and a great commercial success. But in the semiconductor business, things didn't stand still. The plant was still profitable but literally the chips were down. The product was light, portable and durable, and hence easily exportable worldwide. Competition was growing fast from huge factories in the Far East. Either we invested to stay in the race or we closed the site in stages over the next few years. That would shrink the company by 10%. £80 million of annual business and 5,000 jobs would be lost, 3,000 of them at Sunderland and the others in linked businesses. There was no compromise choice.

After lunch, Pat showed his typical style by sitting down at his desk to sign a few letters. As a flying man, Albert liked a breath of fresh air. So Sam and Tim joined us. We went over the position again and then Neil summed up what the five of us were thinking.

"I'm sure you would defend your position strongly, Mike, but talking off the record, the most straightforward corporate solution would be to spend the £50 million we were going to spend on Sunderland on paying off these losses."

"I think that's right," said Tim.

"But if we do that, we're finished. We'll be seen as having no strategy and making a panic reaction to incompetence. Right?"

"Right."

"Publicly, it would be a disaster. The first big closure since Ham Lane in 1967 and, this time, of a well-run plant with a good workforce."

"Consolidated's bid would be written for them."

"Right; though they wouldn't keep Sunderland. They would close it and blame us."

My moment had arrived. I came in.

"So, it's not an answer. There's one idea you left off your list of possibilities, Tim. It's pretty wacky in present circumstances but perhaps it's the only hope." I explained, we discussed, and by the time Pat called us back in we knew what we would all say.

I soon learnt that Pat's normal practice for serious issues was to call on executive directors in order of seniority. Alistair and Mark still looked rather overwhelmed but each thought they could come up with two or three million. Then it was Neil's turn.

"Control Systems Division is struggling to meet orders, thanks to good efforts from sales teams, including Pete's Aberdeen office. Additionally, as we discussed at the June meeting, IE needs to be ready for when home computers become a mass product. I had been expecting to bring to next month's meeting proposals for acquiring small companies in the area, which could foster a product launch when we can deliver the right components. There's absolutely no scope to cut investment."

"You've not come up with much so far," Pat commented. "What about you, Mike?"

"I'd better summarise where I am on the business case for substantial further investment at Sunderland, following the discussion here in July."

He set it out and discussion followed the same course as half an hour earlier. "I need hardly say that, without this investment, the case for entering the home computer market is much less good," added Neil.

"We do seem rather boxed in," said Pat, gloomily. "Pete, I'll understand that you can't yet say much."

"With my separate interest in a small computer and software company, I fully agree with Neil and Mike that we need to invest if we want to stay in a market which is going to take off during the next few years. I certainly can't offer anything from Aberdeen. In fact, we could have been considering today my note about two US companies we could usefully acquire for about £5 million in total. Can I suggest another way? We make a rights issue, aiming to raise £100 million, which is around 8% of our current market value. So we offer one for ten, which we could do without an extraordinary general meeting."

"Eh? Why on earth should our shareholders want to put more money in when we've just lost a packet?" asked Pat.

"The issue would be at a discount on a share price which would have already fallen at the news of the loss. Shareholders would see a bargain if they were confident in our ability to take advantage of prospects for three or four years' time when short-term troubles were over."

Tim commented in a guarded but constructive manner. "We could only try a rights issue if we knew we could get it underwritten. We would first need to speak quietly to some of our big shareholders and have them on board."

Alastair clearly wanted out. "Consolidated would make hay. What's the choice, shareholders? An outfit that's lost your money but is coming back for more, or a reliable return?"

Mark nodded. Albert, who might have gone with them, didn't nod as Neil came in.

"If they smear us too much, Alastair, their own shareholders won't think buying us is such a good idea. Also, subject to proper examination by Tim's people, we'd be showing a clear strategy for developing Sunderland and going into home computers. We could challenge Consolidated directly. What would they do?"

"They've never been in the semiconductor business," said Mike.

"Just so. We could put them on the spot. Plenty of people would say, this is just a start to more Thatcher-era closures. I'm sure you know what the reaction in the North East would be, Mike. Public opposition would develop; MPs would get involved."

Tim moved the meeting back to the key issue.

"I'm looking at the list of major shareholdings as given with the Accounts for last year. Can we go through it and see how many of them we could sound out informally?"

"What would we say? That we're about to announce we've lost a packet?" asked Alastair.

"No, no," said Sam. "There are ways of doing these things. We can stress the big opportunities but mention that there are a few short-term difficulties to overcome. That goes, too, for possible underwriting banks."

We went down the list, beginning with Pat's own contacts. Again I was called last.

"I have contacts who could lead us to the decision-makers for over 8% of IE shares. I know a senior operations manager at Universal Assurance; it holds 3.4%. I also know the Corporate Director of Analysis at New Hampshire Realty, and its top UK analyst, who was our Chief Economist for a short time. New Hampshire advises many of the universities and colleges who've kept the shares you gave them, Pat."

I reeled off a list, which began with 'Carmarthen College, Cambridge, 0.53%', and totalled 4.7%.

"Will the beneficiaries of Pat's charity want to fork out for more shares?" asked Mark.

"I gave them the shares to finance new buildings and facilities," said Pat. "Many of them decided to keep our shares and sell other investments. They decided right. The total value of my gifts was £11 million but the shares are now worth over £50 million. In real terms that's nearly double. They could decide right, again. I've not met your Universal man, Pete, but I remember the other two *very* well. They're good people to have on your side if you're in a tight corner, but beware of their own agendas."

I forbore to mention that Pat had met Brian Smitham on the same evening as he had first met me. Tim summarised who could contact whom, and concluded.

"So we've informal ways to people who control over 70% of our shares. We'll need to use them, whatever we do."

"They'll need to understand that information we provide before an announcement is sensitive and not to be made use of in trading," said Sam.

"It's fanciful that we can swing them to favour a madcap scheme," said Mark.

"Of course not, but we can make sure they look carefully at any proposal we make, not just reject it out of hand," replied Sam.

That set off more argument, in which I deliberately played little part. At five to four, Pat summed up.

"I said we would finish at four and I think we've gone as far as we can today. I suggest this way ahead. Normally, our next meeting, on October 25th, would approve the half-year statement and it would be issued the next day. We stick with that timetable. Changes would attract comment that we can do without."

Sam and Tim looked at each other but neither objected as Pat continued.

"At that meeting, we must decide on our plan to deal with the loss so that that also can be announced the next day. A Friday announcement will at least prevent Consolidated from making an immediate riposte, and gives us time to brief the Sundays. Today's discussion means that we must choose between Plan A and Plan B. Plan A is a rights issue to raise enough capital by to finance both the loss and our investment needs, particularly at Sunderland and into home computers. You suggested this first, Pete, and thank you for doing so. Sam, Neil and Mike, you favour at least a careful examination of it. Alastair and Mark, you're more doubtful and want serious work on Plan B, which is to consolidate our position rather than expanding over the next few years. This probably involves closing Sunderland. Tim and Albert, you see the arguments for both plans but are quite rightly insisting that both are properly evaluated and the risks assessed."

Pat looked round the room, including at his two staffers in attendance.

"So, let's divide into two groups. Sam, Neil, Mike and Pete will form the Plan A group, with Jack as secretary. Albert, Alastair, Mark and I will form the Plan B group, with Chris as secretary. By two weeks today, that's Thursday 11th October, each group is to produce its plan and send it to the other group. Then each group will point out the holes in the other's plan by the next Tuesday, 16th October. Final versions of the plans will come to all of us by the Friday, 19th October, or if necessary by the Monday, 22nd October. Tim, you and your team will have to service both groups. Let me know by tomorrow whether you need to bring more people in for that. Finally, I suggest that you all travel here on the Wednesday afternoon, the 24th. I'll arrange a private dinner, so that there's a chance to talk things through informally before the meeting on the 25th. That will take other business in the morning and we'll decide on this in the afternoon. So, if questions come up on the Wednesday night, there'll be time to get them answered. Is all that clear? Then I suggest that the groups discuss their work plans. Plan A group stay here; Plan B group move to my office."

By five o'clock, I was on my way out of the building, feeling rather dazed but elated. Pat could still pull the stops out and run his Board in a pretty autocratic way. He had made everyone understand what they needed to do. By joining the Plan B group, rather than leaving it to the objectors to my idea, he was making sure that Plan B was properly worked up but equally that its risks were highlighted. Also, he would have noticed that Albert, whilst not professing to any expertise, was less of an objector to my idea than Alastair and Mark.

I had confirmed my reputation as an ideas man, whilst not being pushy at my first meeting. Unsurprisingly, and indeed as Pat had intended, I was to do much of Plan A group's work. But Tim was going to bring another audit manager in to support the Plan B group. I would have Jenny's full support on the finance. That was quite right, since Plan A had been her idea. Much of Monday's telephone call had been about it.

Now I had to focus on my second board meeting of the day. I would be chairing this one and Jenny would be there.

Back in 1974, five Creators had joined with Tony Higgins, then a lecturer in engineering at King's College, London, to set up Creators Technology Ltd, a supplier of kits from which enthusiasts could build their own computers or pay to have them assembled. IE supported my occasional involvement, seeing this as a means of keeping in touch with what was going on at very little cost and of finding out how IE products needed to be improved to keep up with developments. Also, at Paul Milverton's instigation, New Hampshire Realty Bank made a small grant to finance work on software which might eventually, when systems caught up, support commodity trading.

In 1976, Creators Technology had sold nearly 2,000 kits, half of them factory assembled. At premises on an industrial estate in Crawley, it had three permanent employees, and it took on temporary staff during university vacations. IE took an equity stake to finance expansion but let us get on with running it. As I could do little other than attend meetings arranged to coincide with my visits to London, I was made Chairman. Jenny Sinclair acted as Secretary and Finance Director, with a part-time finance clerk to support her. In May 1977 we declared a small dividend. The main UK entrepreneur then in this business was Clive Sinclair (no relation of Dick) but we had a respectable following.

This couldn't last. The heroic early age of home computing was coming to an end with the debut of the Apple II, followed quickly by machines from Commodore and Altair. Although more expensive than our kits, these were machines in a box, with a keyboard. You could connect them to an ordinary TV set to display your programs and results. The storage offered was no more than a few thousand bytes, which wasn't enough to do anything very useful, and it was a lot of fuss and bother to enter and run programs. However, 'Moore's Law' was already established; the computing power available on silicon chips was doubling roughly every eighteen months. We could see that, by the early '80s, machines would become available with sufficient storage to accommodate fair-sized programs. That capacity would also allow operating systems and software to be stored in the computer, so that it really would be 'switch on and go'. The market would expand rapidly and mass production would take over. Large companies would be able to enter the market seriously. There were hundreds of little companies like ours, mostly in the USA but several in the UK. Some would become big companies and a few would become very big companies. The rest would disappear.

Late in 1978, we had decided that we had little chance of being a winner at building computers but should instead concentrate on software development, where we seemed to be ahead of the field. So we should make as much money as possible selling kits whilst we could do so and use the profits to supplement the New Hampshire money. Now there was just one person putting together kits and we no longer offered to assemble them; but we had three people on software and were supplying this service for two other small companies. They were the problem for today.

The meeting was called for 5.30, and by 5.35 I had it underway, after some inevitable pauses for congratulations. Chris Rowan, our lead software designer and *de facto* Chief Executive, began.

"It looks as if Veriglen is going to fold, and Derwent isn't in much better shape. They're behind on royalty payments. People are putting off buying, knowing that in a year or two they'll be able to get something that's a quantum leap forward in convenience."

"What's our cash situation, Jenny?" asked Brian Smitham. Although he was now moving up the management ladder within Universal Assurance, he had begun in their computing department. We were meeting at the Universal offices in Holborn.

"Pretty good, apart from debtors. We've enough in the bank to pay wages for four months. Six if Derwent pay up."

"That assumes continuation of the grant from New Hampshire," said Paul Milverton. "By the end of the year, I need to put a case for that to be renewed. By the end of November, I must have your student's report on algorithm optimisation, Sheila."

For five minutes or so, they reviewed the work that the New Hampshire Realty Bank was financing at Queen Mary College, where Sheila Yates was a lecturer. At the end, Paul seemed satisfied and I used my chairman's powers.

"Order, you two, though it's fascinating. I can still understand about every other word."

"Don't be so modest, Pete," laughed Sheila. "Morag told me about the help you gave Laura."

Morag Newlands, whom I had known at Cambridge, was Sheila's partner, and a lecturer at King's College. It was through Morag that I had met Tony, who cut in now.

"I'm sorry to have to say it but it's clear to me that we should cease production of kits when present stocks of components are exhausted. At the current rate of sales, that's conveniently close to December 31st. What's Danny expecting to happen, Chris?" he asked, referring to our employee.

"He knows it. He can walk into another job, fixing video recorders for a rental company."

"Also, my own interests have moved on. I shall always be pleased to have been in on the early days of home computing, maybe I'll write a book about it sometime, but my present research on storage devices is opening up some very different possibilities and funding."

"So what are the prospects for software orders, Chris?" asked Jenny.

"People are hanging fire on software, in the same way as on hardware. They know that the capability to run software will increase hugely in the next few years. The big winners will be companies that put the effort in now, not just for next year's computers but for those of three or four years' time. That means they have to make some guesses about the system architecture, gamble on being right and have enough capital to carry expenditure for some years."

"And they have to decide what applications to specialise in," said Brian. "We need to do that, too. Paul, I can't see computerised commodity trading being feasible before about 1985. There has to be the beginning of a system giving fast interconnection, so that traders' computers can react in real time."

Paul nodded and I turned to Jenny.

"What's the continuing cost of Chris and his team?"

"Including overheads, about £90,000 per year."

"Chris, what's a realistic estimate of continuing business on current systems and anything else you can pick up?"

"Perhaps £40,000 per year."

"The New Hampshire grant is £20,000. Paul, what do you think the reaction would be if you asked for an increase in it?"

"Not good right now, especially as we're also funding Sheila's student."

"Whom Creators Technology should be employing after he gets his PhD, unless of course a post for him is going to materialise, Sheila."

"Not a hope, with Thatcher's funding cuts."

"If we employ him, and it would seem silly not to, that puts costs up to perhaps £110,000 per year, of which we'll have to find £70,000, plus inflation of course. I've a suggestion to make. This company has capital of £40,000, comprising £5,000 from each director and £10,000 from IE. We don't have any long-term borrowings. Jenny, I'm sure you agree that's a rather weird financial structure for a company which should now be targeting the future market."

"It's worked whilst our main business has been kits because buyers have paid upfront and most of the components have come from IE, which gives thirty days' credit. It doesn't suit where we're going now."

"As you've all said, and thanks, I've been doing pretty well, though only by working so hard that for some time I've not been able to spend my basic salary, let alone bonuses. Now I'll be getting a big rise. Also, I have a flat in Aberdeen to sell, which will fetch a lot more than I need to buy something very presentable in or near Leeds. So my suggestion is that we increase the authorised capital to £100,000. I'll put in £45,000 now, taking my stake up to £50,000. Each of you could have the right to subscribe when you wish for another £5,000, taking you up to £10,000. We'll buy out IE, as we won't interact with them anymore and there are various issues about my being a director of both companies if there are cross holdings. Now, Paul, that amount of equity can sustain borrowing of up to £200,000, can't it?"

"Yes, provided there's a clear business plan to justify the gearing."

"So, can we propose to New Hampshire that the grant terminates but we have a loan agreement allowing drawdown of up to £200,000 over, say, the next three years? We would then have a business structure on which to base a plan."

"I didn't know IE was such a good payer," said Brian, looking surprised.

"They are, to those who deliver results," I replied, avoiding looking at Jenny.

I had floated my suggestion during my long telephone conversation with her, and on Tuesday I had called Paul and Chris about it, since it would be for them to work out a detailed plan with Jenny; but for the rest of them it was something of a bombshell. However, after half an hour Brian seemed content, Sheila saw how my idea would allow her to stay involved without the student, and Tony saw how it suited his changed interests. All of them were accepting my dominant shareholding, knowing that I was taking the early risk, and that they could chip in if it turned out to be a winner.

"I've come back from California to find a lot on. Don't expect too much from me too quickly," said Jenny, avoiding looking at me.

"You must have a lot on, too, Pete," said Brian. "What do you think of Leeds? Have you any idea where you might live, yet?"

"I've been there quite often over the past two years. Nigel Thompson has held divisional meetings on the days after IE's Board meets. They move around the plant sites, so they've been in or near Leeds about half the time. I've found I can fly down to Manchester and take a taxi to the site. As to where I'll live, the immediate answer is that Nigel never moved his family from Colchester; he rented a flat. The contract runs to next June so it's convenient for both of us that I take it over. I guess I'll be looking for somewhere out of town, not too high up."

"You must come and see our place in Carol's constituency," said Paul. "In fact, at the end of next month, Steph is over here. We've thought to invite her up for the weekend of 27th and 28th October. Why don't you come along then, Pete?"

That prompted Brian. "Show him some proper Yorkshire, eh Paul? We need to visit my people around then. If I can fix it for that weekend, we could meet for a walk."

Jenny joined in. "If you're thinking of a Sunday morning walk, count us in. That weekend, we'll be in Sheffield. Louisa's first birthday is two days before."

"Mmm, I'll talk to Morag," said Sheila. "It's time the Pankhurst Centre ran without us for a weekend."

Morag and Sheila lived on the top floor of Sheila's large house in Stratford, the rest of which was the core of a refuge for victims of domestic violence. Over nearly ten years, Sheila had built this up into a substantial charitable enterprise.

"Sorry, Tony," I said. "This is cutting you out, but it seems that a Creators social is developing. I'm visiting Liz and Greg

Woolley this evening, as it happens. I'll find out if a trip to see Greg's parents that weekend is possible for them. It looks as if I'll be down here with my new car for much of that week, through to Saturday. I could bring Steph up, and you and Morag, too, Sheila."

"We'll be busy all day in the constituency. If you arrive about seven o'clock, that would suit," said Paul.

The meeting broke up with promises to keep in contact and I murmured separately to Brian and Paul that I would call them about lunch during the next week. I left the building with Jenny.

"Anything you can tell me?"

"We're on, for developing the rights issue. You're supporting me on it."

"Oh, *marvellous*."

For a few minutes we spoke of what was needed. Then I concluded. "So, whilst the last two weeks have been frantic, the next four will be worse. It's really great to have you with me, Jenny."

"Don't tell Tim that I spotted in the IE Articles that you could do it without an EGM. I should have talked to him before mentioning that. It's really great to be working with you, Pete. I just hope we can bring it off. I must dash now. I can just make the 7.10 from Waterloo."

I picked up the newly electrified 'Bedpan line'[11] at Farringdon. In those days the City was deserted by half past six, so the train was only a third full and I was able to spread out comfortably. As we rattled along, I recalled the last two weeks. 'Frantic' was a mild description for them.

Before setting off for the USA, I had visited my parents in Dorset for the English bank holiday weekend. So, after returning to Aberdeen, I needed to catch up on three weeks' backlog before the news broke. Then I was into a series of handover meetings

---

11 The colloquial name for the suburban service then running between Moorgate, St Pancras and Bedford – now part of Thameslink.

48

with Claire and key customers, interrupted only by my visit to Nigel. The day after that visit, I arranged for my flat to go on the market and for much of the contents to be taken into store, though the agent advised me to leave enough to look attractive to viewers. When I told Claire of this advice, she had news.

"That's great, Pete. All the people we've invited to your farewell party on Tuesday will fit in easily. Here's the list; have we forgotten anyone? Relax, you needn't do anything except let Jane have a key on Monday night."

That was largely true, though I did prepare some specialities of mine, such as various patés. And so my largest Aberdeen party ever had been judged a riotous success. My flat had a spacious living room and good views, and I had bought it with entertaining in mind, but I had gathered friends and business associates separately. Now, for the first time, they were all together, thanks to three women who had become good friends themselves through knowing me.

In 1974, Morag Newlands had introduced me to Laura Westlake, who was a lecturer in maths at the University of Aberdeen. She was very much into her work and knew of what I had done at Cambridge. She also liked a long walk on Sundays. Before very long we were going out or eating in most Saturday evenings and spending a comforting night before setting off into the hills. We had taken two holidays together, visiting old cities of Italy and my friends in Spain. Through her I had met others at the university; indeed, I had brought out my cello and joined their orchestra. But Laura wasn't interested in oil-related social life. She didn't fit in with the aggressive men and generally rather stupid women who populated that. At the end of 1977, she told me that she was becoming close to a colleague who needed looking after. A few months later, I was a guest at their wedding.

To partner me at oil gatherings, Jane Sandford, a flaming redhead, was just right. Two months after I had moved to Aberdeen, and some months after I had first met both her and

Steph, she had suddenly reappeared in my life. She had been providing massage and other services at clubs in London but wanted to run her own club now. She had some useful savings and clearly possessed a good head for business despite very limited education. I had already spotted that the growing number of expat personnel on their own in Aberdeen needed good-class rest and recreation services. Just outside the town there was an indoor swimming pool for sale. It needed updating.

To cut a long story short, Steph, Jane, I and several oilmen put up the money, Jane proved to be a good project manager with some advice from experienced shareholders, and 'Plain Jane's' had its grand opening on 18th June 1975, the same day as the first North Sea oil was landed. It took a little while for the message to go round but by the end of 1976 success was assured. For the last two years, before tax, my share of the profits had exceeded my pay as a senior manager in IE. Most of the shareholders had their dividends paid in the USA and linked to this were arrangements which were fully legal then and much reduced my tax bill. Fees for setting those arrangements up, and for other financial advice to 'Plain Jane's', had enabled Jenny to buy into Creators Technology.

So Brian had been right to wonder about my good fortune. Most of the money I could now put into Creators Technology had come from 'Plain Jane's'. My first stakes in both companies had come from the same source as IE's £19 million gain: profits on oil trading in the light of advance information about the 1973 Middle East War. In 1976 I had used a bonus from IE to buy the stake of someone who was returning to the USA and had not been confident of the prospects. Now I was selling this additional stake, for four times what I had paid, to someone whom Jane trusted and who had money to invest in a branch establishment near Invergordon. Because I was reinvesting the money, I would benefit from relief against capital gains tax.

Jane was always busy at weekends but if I had some oil executives round for drinks after work she had been a striking hostess in a gown that suited her hair. She had rarely left without some prospect of new business. Even her East End accent, grown a little more literate over the years, did not jar in a world of braw Scots and visitors mostly from Louisiana and Texas. Though our own relationship was largely business, sometimes early in the week she had called: 'It's quiet here – shall I come over?' This week, she had come over late on Monday evening and left on Wednesday morning at the same time as me.

And then there had been Claire, with whom my relationship had been very close, though totally professional, for she was happily married with two teenage children. My vision had been of an office through which IE's electrical, control and instrumentation gear could be marketed to the offshore oil industry, and rapid feedback obtained on how the products could be improved for their demanding duty. I had set this going but after a year or so, when we already had about thirty staff in Aberdeen and twenty spread around the main IE factories, more organisation was needed. Fortunately, Claire, a qualified engineer, was looking to return to work now her children were older. She had found it impossible to get a suitable post in any oil company. The rapid growth of sales and profits just wouldn't have happened without her.

At the party, I thanked the three, and all the others who had enriched my life in Aberdeen. Many of them had thanked me for *my* help. I knew that I had been a useful channel for all sorts of communications. Early on, Carol had given me plenty of insights into the thinking of the Labour Government, and contacts that I used later. As a non-political figure not part of the oil industry, I had been able to help the government and that industry to explain themselves to each other. Douglas Arnott had certainly realised that.

The party was a great end to my great time in Aberdeen. For nearly six years I had been where the action was, part of a project whose costs and technical challenges were comparable to those of putting men on the Moon but which would yield far greater benefits.[12] News from down South had seemed as from a different world. Financial crises, applications to the International Monetary Fund, and the Labour Government's expedients for clinging to power had all passed me by.

I had been wondering whether, from a career point of view, I was staying in Aberdeen for too long; but my reluctance to move had been matched by corporate reluctance to disturb something that was going so well. Now, the decision had been taken for me. When I set off south with as much as possible packed into my car, I had a sense that I was returning to reality.

I had been pretty tired when I arrived in Leeds, but a jovial dinner with Nigel Thompson at a local restaurant revived me. We had always respected each other, and with rivalries past got on much better. He certainly seemed interested in maintaining informal contact when he was back at Consolidated, and soon he was asking the guarded question I had been waiting for.

"So, does Pat know whether they're on to his little problem?"

I replied, truthfully enough: hunches do not count as knowing. "No. Last night, Colin Schofield didn't try to pump me, though he was pretty cheerful. If he thinks Claire will be a pushover, he's got another think coming."

That had taken us on to how to introduce Claire and also how to handle each of my erstwhile colleagues at his last divisional meeting, which would now be a handover meeting. I asked him how he thought he would find Don Flitton, to which it was his turn to say he didn't know.

That morning, a rather bleary pair had tumbled into the train. Fortunately we hadn't had to leave too early, since the best

---

[12] Expenditure by oil companies on developing UK North Sea oil and gas during the 1970s totalled around £75 billion at present-day (2017) prices. US Government expenditure on Project Apollo totalled around $110 billion at present-day prices.

trains on the Leeds–King's Cross run were already High Speed 125 diesels. By mid-afternoon Nigel would have been back in Leeds for *his* farewell party; and in the morning, he would set off in a full car for the divisional meeting. This one was at a site near Nottingham, and so on his way back to Essex.

I had a longstanding invitation to visit Liz and Greg Woolley in the commuter village near St Albans where they had settled to bring up a family. In the morning it would be easy to reach Nottingham, by changing trains at Luton. I had a special reason for meeting Liz now but that wasn't to intrude too much on a relaxing evening.

I had first met Liz fifteen years before, at Waterhouse College, Cambridge, of which her father had then been Master. A year later, she had become my first girlfriend and had taught me much about life. Our temperaments and interests had been too different for us to make it permanent but we regarded each other as the sister and brother neither of us had. Hearing of that had prompted Jenny to suggest the same regard, although she was close to her real brother.

Liz and Greg were in celebratory form, and not just because of the news about me, as Liz explained once we had said night-night to two-year-old Jenny and sat down.

"We can drink tonight, though not tomorrow night. Greg has a big match on Saturday. He's now captain of the first team at our club. They've won the first two matches in the Eastern League and want to stay at the top. The knock-out is going well, too."

Before replying, Greg ran his hand through Liz's brown hair and kissed her. Together, her head on his shoulder, they made a handsome couple and looked very happy. Another sign of that in Liz was that she appeared to have stopped smoking. It was so good that they had come together. During a weekend when we were all staying with Jenny and Dick, I had played a part in overcoming Greg's misgivings. That explained the naming of their daughter and would explain the naming of the son they hoped for in due course.

"What's more, Liz is playing again this season. The club has a crèche. I saw you in action last week. You'll soon be on your old form."

"You both look very fit," I said. "You're a contrast to Brian Smitham, Greg. I met him earlier this evening. He's definitely putting on weight."

"He had a good summer of cricket but he's given up football in favour of golf," said Liz. "So he's fully a slow sports man now. Dinner will be ready at eight. I'll sort the veg now. Greg, do tell Pete how you're getting on."

That was pretty well, by most standards. Greg was now responsible for planning and construction of most of the London electricity distribution network, with several teams of engineers responsible to him. We wondered whether, following some remarks made in Opposition, the Thatcher Government would move to put the electricity industry into private ownership, but concluded (correctly) that that would be some years off, since several problems needed to be solved first.

"Notably, of course, the miners," concluded Greg as we sat down to dinner. "How do you see it with them this year, Liz?"

"Joe Gormley is playing his usual clever game. Negotiations will run on and then they'll put an offer to ballot saying, accept it or go on strike. I don't think there'll be a strike this year. It would be too political so soon after the Tories are back."

"Isn't that what Mick McGahey wants, a political strike? The Scottish papers keep quoting him," I said. McGahey was the Vice-President of the NUM, the Scottish miners' leader and a lifelong communist.

"They'll be old quotes. He's on his best behaviour right now. He's still hoping against hope that Joe will retire before next May. Mick's fifty-fifth birthday is at the end of May and after that he's ineligible to stand for President. But Joe won't retire."

Liz sounded authoritative, with good reason. In 1974, she had left a job with the National Coal Board to work at the NUM head office, then located near Euston. Her move had reflected her abilities and also the personal interest of a very senior person there. Greg had accepted the consequences, which continued until she left in 1977 with Jenny on the way.

"I hope Joe Gormley has a succession plan," I said. "If he blocks McGahey, the field is left open for you-know-who." [13]

"There are others who are interested, Pete." Liz mentioned some names.

"Whoever has heard of any of them? Meanwhile, I hope the pay incentive scheme Gormley pushed for last year actually gets more coal dug. It's ludicrous that five years of massive investment have not lead to any increase in productivity at all. Right now, thanks to the Ayatollahs, we need more coal. If the industry can't deliver it, they'll be cut out of markets. Talking of miners, some of us look like meeting up at the Milverton constituency residence in four weeks' time."

That led to a discussion of arrangements. It would be the school half-term weekend, when no important matches were scheduled. Greg would call his parents the next day; his father was a Baptist minister in a village east of Leeds. Then they wanted to hear something of life as a director and about my visit to the States. By ten o'clock, I was yawning apologetically and pleading my busy times.

"Don't worry, Pete. We're early birds here anyway. I'll tidy up," said Greg.

"I need to settle with Liz what we're giving Katie for her sixth birthday, next week."

Liz and I were Katie's godparents. Once we had decided on a gift, Liz continued.

"It's really marvellous that you're getting on so well, Pete, but then you've always thrown yourself into things to the utmost."

---

[13] This was a reference to Arthur Scargill.

"So have you and Greg, Liz. It's true that for me the last two weeks have been amongst the toughest since the run-up to finals at Cambridge; and it will go on that way. Talking of Cambridge, someone Roberta knows told me a rather alarming story. I'm fairly certain it's about Fred Perkins."

As I had expected, Liz stiffened slightly. After me, she had had a brief relationship with Fred. On moving to the village, she and Greg had discovered that he was now a partner in the local general practice. Fortunately, they had been able to register with one of the other doctors.

Once I had recounted Brenda's story, I asked if Liz knew of anything like it happening to anyone she knew. Liz replied with the attractive pout I remembered.

"No, but I wouldn't. As soon as I stopped stopping it happening, it happened. It all fits with what I remember of Fred, though. He knew exactly how to take a girl but he didn't *care* about them at all. He just wanted them there and willing."

"And he got violent and had to be held back, at least twice; first by Dick and me when he went for Jerry Woodruff, and then by Brian when he attacked Paul."

"At least the second time made Brian and Paul friends. There's been no third time, so far as I know. Fred is very well thought of here, both as a doctor and as part of the community. He's a member of our sports club and quite often comes to the first team hockey games if he's not playing football himself. Injuries do happen in hockey and a couple of times he's been on the spot to deal. He's not married and doesn't make any effort amongst the single women at the club or around here."

"He must realise that his bad old ways don't suit his life as a family doctor."

"At parties he's often with the practice nurse but there doesn't seem to be anything between them. How did your friend describe the nurse who worked her over…? Yes, that sounds like Melissa Copehurst, who's quite an Amazon and a stalwart of the basketball team. She's also a dab hand at pencil sketches but her main interest is in amateur theatricals. We've seen her leading in several productions of the local dramatic society and she's roped Fred in to one or two."

"So Fred shows his good side here, and very good it is too, just like when he got the overbump for Waterhouse."

"Yes, and the efforts Melissa makes, over and above her duties, are also very well regarded. She's quite a persuasive woman, with eyes that look into you and make you ask yourself why you don't do what she suggests. That's good for persuading people to help out and for finding her subjects to sketch."

"Is that her work? It's rather good. I don't expect you and Greg needed much persuasion to allow her to do it." I pointed to a framed sketch of little Jenny sitting on her mother's lap, her father proudly beside.

"No, we didn't need persuasion for that one. We needed a little for the others she did later that same afternoon in June and then a week later. She's a fast worker."

Liz brought out a portfolio and opened it. I leafed through the contents, looking at each and back at her.

"Mmm, yes, you really *do* look fit, Liz. I like the way she's brought out the muscles in your belly. She obviously knows her anatomy. And Greg looks very relaxed and confident, like Dick on a few famous occasions."

"Yes, she is good at helping people to relax. She joked that my jungle of hair makes it almost look as if I'm wearing a brief."

"You both must have posed for some time for this one."

"The next week, we had someone looking after Jenny. Melissa posed us using a model she has of Rodin's *The Kiss*. She did several sketches from different angles. This is the best one."

"And is this Fred?"

"Yes. She knows I was once his girlfriend, so she gave me it for the memory."

"Does she sketch others around here like this?"

"Only when it's warm, she said. She has a thick folder of Fred, and several other folders. But it's all quite artistic and proper. We didn't strip in front of her; we went to the bathroom to change into wraps. I've heard a few people joke about being sketched but there's no bad gossip at the club or about her on the job. There's not even any real comment that she's les, though when I found myself in the shower with the basketball team, I noticed that she has a tattoo of a woman on her groin."

"I think the bogus clinic is her idea. She and Fred can enjoy their bad side together without causing problems in their jobs or life here. She has the skills and self-control to act the part, with only occasional slips such as happened with Brenda. She selects the women when they call that number, which must be on diversion to her home. Certainly anyone from near here wouldn't get in. She must be good at judging how they'll react. Some of them will be surprised but pleased. Others, like Brenda, will be too ashamed to talk."

"Pete, is there something we can do that stops their game but allows them to carry on the good they do here, and doesn't damage Fred's reputation at Waterhouse?"

"Talk of the Creators social has given me just one idea."

I explained, and Liz replied, pensively.

"I can't think of anything better. Pete, you're amazing, just amazing. In the midst of everything else you're doing, you've thought of this. You really do think you can sort out anything. One of these days you're going to come up against something you can't sort out. I hope it isn't yet."

Sir Pat's last throw

In an announcement which stunned the markets yesterday, International Electronics disclosed losses of £68 million through speculation in interest rate swaps but emphasised very good prospects. Accordingly, the company will be seeking to raise £100 million of new capital through a one-for-ten rights issue underwritten by New Hampshire Realty. This would finance entry into the home computer market and further development of IE's semiconductor factory near Sunderland, whilst allowing the loss to be capitalised.

A detailed prospectus will be pub lished on 8 November with IE's half-year financial statement. The offer price is expected to be between 250p and 270p. The announcement was made after close of trading, when IE shares stood at 346p. On Monday they are expected to open at around 320p.

The announcement opened immediate speculation over the long-rumoured intention of Consolidated Electrics to mount a takeover bid for IE (our business correspondent writes). It is very likely that the issue is an attempt to wrong-foot Consolidated. But that is a very high-risk strategy for IE. If the issue fails, then they will be wide open to takeover.

In many ways the announcement is typical of the audacious moves by which Sir Pat O'Donnell has built up his company over more than forty years. Less than two weeks ago, it was confirmed that he would step down in 1981, on reaching his 70th birthday. This is his last throw of the dice, an attempt to react positively to bad news and to end his long career still on top.

There was no immediate comment from any of IE's major shareholders. It is unlikely, though, that IE would have taken this step without some indications of readiness to consider taking up the rights. Shareholders' choice is effectively about how much risk they are prepared to take. Like all investors, they will consider the prospectus. It could well be very close to the closing date for applications of 29 November before it becomes clear to what extent the issue is taken up.

The decision to announce the issue in advance of publishing the prospectus is unusual but has been dictated by the need to disclose the speculative loss promptly. Assurance has been given that this loss is now controlled and cannot increase further. The timing also allows for final consideration of the offer price in the light of the reception of the Treasury's offer of shares in BP, to be made this Wednesday, 31 October.

The announcement perhaps explains recent changes in IE's senior management. On 18 September, IE announced the resignation of Henry Milsom, Finance Director, and the appointment of Tim Baldwin, a partner in Plender Luckhurst, as an interim replacement. It has now been confirmed that staff of Plender Luckhurst are assisting IE in resolving financial issues and handling the offer.

Also announced on 18 September was the departure from IE of Nigel Thompson to take up a board-level post with Consolidated Electrics. It is understood that he rejoins them during the coming week. His interim replacement helps to give IE's top team a more youthful look and is certainly consistent with the image Sir Pat wants to project. Thirty-three-year-old Peter Bridford gave up a promising academic career to join IE in 1968 and has since been very successful in building up IE's business in expanding markets – first in Spain and, since 1974, in offshore oil and gas. He has been much involved in the development of the rights issue during the last few weeks.

IE's strategy is targeted at the rapidly expanding market for personal computers. They see the next two years as the time to move into this business. They also wish to stay in the semiconductor business against the background of continuing rapid technical progress and increasing competition from the Far East. By linking the rights issue to this aggressive strategy and shrugging off the trading losses, IE has given a direct challenge to Consolidated. Industry analysts stress both the huge opportunities, as 'home computers' approach the point of real market viability, and also the scale of competition from huge new semiconductor plants in Singapore and Taiwan. If Consolidated was to launch a takeover bid, it would have to state whether or not it intended to stay in this business. If it did not do so, the Sunderland plant would close within a few years, with the loss of 5,000 jobs. Consolidated would need to consider the political implications of this.

Consolidated made no comment yesterday on whether it might bid for IE. If it did, before 8 November, the Takeover Code dictates that IE's rights issue could go ahead only with the consent of the shareholders at an extraordinary general meeting – effectively the issue would be placed on hold. The same would apply if Consolidated made a statement that it was seriously considering the possibility, or indeed if IE received privately some definite information of this. It is to be assumed that no such information has been received.

Consolidated therefore has three immediate options. The company could say nothing and see how the issue fares. That may be difficult if speculation pushes up IE's share price and thereby makes the issue more attractive. It could make a definite bid without the detailed information which study of the prospectus would give it. Or it could make a statement of intent, which would also delay the issue but would leave it under pressure to clarify its intentions urgently.

3. SUNDAY, 28TH OCTOBER, 1979

I awoke to the sound of somebody going out. I remembered Paul promising to buy all the Sundays. It was already light. I looked at my watch – nearly nine o'clock. It seemed cold in the room but I felt warm in bed. A murmur in my ear told me why.

"Mmm, wakies time, Pete. You've had a good rest. You really were dead beat last night."

"*Steph!* How long have you been here?"

"A couple of hours. I woke feeling cold. There was no point in getting up. How could I be warm? I've been lying here, looking at you and thinking nice thoughts about what we could do when you woke up. I've been *very* patient."

"Why are you here? And we must get up. We're setting off in half an hour."

"Relax, Pete. It's all clear with Ken. He goes to Asia quite often. His customers would be offended if he turned down the entertainment they arrange. Outside the USA, we're both open. And it's fallback[14] day, so we've an extra hour in bed. I need to tell you what happened when I went to see Dr Fred. That was on Thursday. I'd called the day before saying that a friend here had said how great he was but I was only in London for a few days. No-one can resist a quick buck. The charge for the urgent appointment was £150. So along I went. It was all as you said it would be. I kept up the mood by joking to the tall and sharp-eyed nurse as I undressed. I stooped a little on the height

---

14 The American term for the end of Daylight Saving Time.

gauge and sure enough she patted my butt to have me stand up straight. I laughed at that. So we can act it out, starting from there. Massage first like you know how... Mmm... *Mmmm*... I was being appreciative and opened my legs just a little. So she did a bit more – like that... *Oooooh*. I was enjoying it and so was she. Then it was time for fitting the gadget. Push two fingers in and spread them... That's nice... And now for Dr Fred's entry. The two-handed gyno job, outside and in... That's where he felt... Up a bit inside... Harder..."

"Did he really start feeling harder?"

"No, but let's leave the story for now. My cap is in; let's go for a 'Jenny'."

"Mmm, you're getting nicely wet."

"Harder... *Ooohhh... Harder... Ah... Aaaah... Aaaa-aaaaahh!.*"

Once she had hooked her feet over my shoulders, as Jenny had done with me all those years back, I had a very full load for her. After a few minutes of quiet contentment, I brought her back to the story.

"So what happened on Thursday?"

"I was smiling away, giving the impression I knew what was going on. When he said there wasn't any reason why *I* couldn't have a baby, I grinned and said, you're making me very happy so what do you suggest? Immediate treatment, he replied, rubbing me more. Let's see you, then, I said, and he took off his coat. He was bursting out of his pants. I laughed and motioned them down. It was a fine sight, one of the best I've seen. I reached out and fondled him gently. By now the nurse had her hand inside her coat. There was no doubt what *she* was doing to herself. My, I was tempted..."

"But..."

"I gripped and twisted, as hard as I could. Much harder and it would have come off. He went down screaming and was sick all over the floor. The nurse didn't move fast enough. I was out of the chair before she tried to grab me, I slapped her face hard and she went down. I pulled her coat up, knelt on her, pulled her pants right off, grabbed, pinched and twisted – as hard as possible, first one way then the other. There was that tattoo on her groin and I did get a look at that oar, by the way. It was for something called the Lents in 1968, and it had Fred Perkins' name on it. I'd come along in fairly pointy shoes. I slipped them on and scored a few kicks, including a great one, right up her crotch. *She* didn't scream but by the look she gave me I knew it hurt like hell. She won't be bringing herself off for quite a while. Then I dressed, and left saying that's what happens if you play this game."

"You must have been quite a sight, Steph, just as you are now. What a handsome forty you are."

"Oooh – *oooooh*... Don't harp on that, Pete. Yup, you can tell Roberta's pal they've had a lesson they won't forget. I'm really glad I got the bint so hard. She's the nastiest type – a lesbian sadist with one helluva will to power. She'd have loved being in the SS. It's bad luck on Dr Fred that he's met her. He's a repressed homosexual sado-masochist. She has him right where she wants him. He'll deliver just what she likes. I wonder what she does to him, some nights."

"Fred, a homosexual? At Cambridge he certainly wasn't that. Ask Liz."

"You say so, but the way he did girls sounds like an attempt to conceal what he really wanted, from himself as much as from everyone else. Twice that you know about he took his chance to show his real self with boys. When you're single in New York you meet these types. You need to deal with women as much as with men."

"Is there any chance they could catch up with you?"

"No chance. I showed my first certificate. I was Mrs Dunmore. So it's a job well done. Thanks for suggesting it, Pete. Mmmm, that's nice, but I guess I'd better return to my proper room and get dressed. I'm glad we've had this refresher."

"You'd packed your cap."

"Always be prepared. I was tempted to leave it off, you never know, but you don't look much like Ken. Anyway, it was nicer for us both than your using a condom. You would have burst that, anyway."

"I had six weeks' backlog for you. I still use them with Jane, though she's particular who she goes with now. She can afford to be."

"Mmm yup, great cheques keep arriving. She called me soon after she heard about you. Hopefully you'll be able to drop in on Aberdeen from time to time."

Carol's cheerful voice came from outside. "Don't keep Pete too long, Steph. Paul is back with the papers."

When I arrived downstairs, looking appropriately sheepish, Steph was already there, looking very content. "Slept well, Pete?" asked Morag with a grin.

"Yes, over ten hours straight through. That's not like me at all. For the last six weeks I've averaged about four. It'll be the same for the next few weeks. It's good to be able to take most of today off."

"I'm amazed you kept awake on the drive up here. I didn't, though that was to do with Friday night at the Centre," said Sheila.

"And with how comfortable your new car is, Pete. I wish we had them like that in the States," said Steph.

"You *can* buy them there. They're easier to park than your monsters. Will you people take more compact cars seriously now oil's over $30, I wonder? The answers I had on my trip were: in New York, probably; in California, maybe; in Texas, no way."

"Carter is meant to be serious about saving energy but it depends on getting legislation through," said Carol.

"Carter being serious about anything is the kiss of death," laughed Steph. "He was trying to make up to the new lot in Iran.

Now, he's let the Shah in for medical treatment.[15] He doesn't know what he's trying to do."

"So who's the right image for US energy policy, Steph?" I asked. "Jimmy Carter or Larry Hagman?"[16]

Before Steph could reply, Paul came in. "Who's the image of International Electronics right now, Pete? I assume you were expecting this."

He passed me the *Sunday Gatherer* business section. Its account of the rights issue was much the same as had appeared in the Saturday papers, but below was a section headed 'IE's new youthful face', with a photograph of me and a short account of my departure from Cambridge and subsequent business career.

"Yes, talking to them about that was half of yesterday morning. The other half was another meeting on the prospectus."

"Pretty selective on your outside interests, eh Pete?" joked Sheila. "Good music, and walking. I'm glad you mentioned Creators Technology, though."

"Thanks, Sheila, and you've reminded me to remind you all that my interest in 'Plain Jane's' is private, even amongst Creators. You know about it because of what happened in '74. The Smithams and the Woolleys have never heard of it. Jenny has given professional advice. She won't have said anything about it to Dick."

"Now you're a director of IE, you'll need to disclose the interest in the next IE Accounts," said Paul.

"No-one will notice," said Steph. "New Hampshire takes disclosure seriously. In our Accounts, listed against me is 'Plain Jane's', a provider of recreational services in Aberdeen, Scotland'. It sounds so innocent."

"Talking of Creators, we must be going," said Carol. "We're meeting the Sinclairs at ten o'clock, the other side of Stocksbridge, off the A616. Follow us, Pete; you can't miss it."

---

15 That happened on 25th October.
16 Star of the TV series *Dallas* which had just begun its third season.

"Oh yes I can. I've maps in the car. Show me or, better still, show Steph."

I had just time to check over the other newspapers before we left to arrive without incident at the café designated as the meeting point. From there, we set off for an hour's level walk round a reservoir, just right for the children on a fine still morning. I found myself talking to Dick, a little behind the rest of the party.

"It's nice to see how Carol gets on with Katie and David."

"She gets on well with everyone, as good MPs do. It's one of her qualities, inherited from both her parents. I don't think you've met them."

"No, I haven't. It's a break for me, not to be looking after the children. I've been doing a lot of that recently, Pete."

"So I can guess. IE has taken up a lot of Jenny's time, just as it's taken up a lot of my time. Now you know what she's doing. I expect she's told you that it will finish well before Christmas. She'll be entitled to a break then, as will you. I know I'll need one."

"She obviously likes working with you."

"I like working with her, too, Dick. We understand and trust each other as professional colleagues and friends."

"She reckons that if this share issue comes out right she'll be in line for senior audit manager. That could mean a partnership within five years."

"If that happens, she'll have earned it."

"So you and she are helping each other to get on, whilst I'm being left behind and regarded as some kind of useful accessory."

"I'm sure Jenny doesn't regard you in that way at all, Dick."

"The children are getting older. They're beginning to wonder why I'm doing lots of the things that other children's mothers do. So are the mothers. I'm being chaffed about it at the school gate."

"You've an answer, surely. In your job, you need to be there to give lectures and talk to students, and for lab work. There's also a lot of thinking and reading, which you can do anywhere. Have you explained to David and Katie what your work is about?"

"No. *I'm* wondering what it's about. Research has had its ups and downs for me, as you know, Pete. It seemed to be on the up a few years back, which is what put me in touch with Berkeley, but now it's stuck in a rut again. So here am I, going nowhere, while you help my wife to zoom on."

"To be clear, Dick, the decision to put Jenny onto this job had nothing at all to do with me. It happened while I was still out in the States. She wanted to be sure that I was happy about her working for IE, so that's why it wasn't settled until I was back. You've been married for nearly ten years to a very fine woman, who's borne you two children as well as taking her career forward. You've supported her and she's supported you. Look at it that way. Jenny is very busy now, so you're doing more, but think back a few months. When did you go out to Berkeley?"

"At the beginning of July."

"When did the others join you?"

"At the beginning of August."

"So who looked after the children for the month in between?"

"Jenny did, though my parents helped a lot."

"There you are. You help each other. That's the way things are going. More women are getting good jobs. It's a very welcome change."

"It's not affected you, though."

"Not directly, no, but I've been very pleased to hand over the job I was doing in Aberdeen to a married lady with two teenage children. Her husband is very proud of the way she's getting on, though it probably means that she's now paid quite a lot more than him. In fact, at my leaving party he was quite over the moon."

"Perhaps he was pleased you were going away."

"Dick, you're an old friend, so I'll say only that there was never any hint of what you're suggesting."

"It's not always like that with you, though, is it, Pete? And it certainly isn't like that with Jenny. It was perfectly clear why she wanted to go to that beach. You couldn't keep your eyes off each other."

"Jenny is a very attractive woman and you're a very handsome man. I liked looking at you, too, and you know me well enough not to read anything into that. You used to like being admired. I remember how you won Harry's famous beauty contest and then enjoyed showing yourself off with Gail. I also remember you telling Liz and me about the foursome sunbaths, which involved plenty of looking and more."

"They had a purpose, Pete. I'm sure you know that."

"Yes, Jenny had a purpose, you were pleased to play your part and it's worked out well. How are Amanda and John getting on?"

"It's like being back five years to when our children were their children's ages. Amanda can organise things now, just as Jenny could organise things then."

"Jenny is proud of her body and rightly so. She used that to organise Amanda and John in the loveliest sort of way, as I recall you putting it. But to her you're above all – above Amanda, above John and certainly above me. So, look as if you like being with her. On that beach you sat as if you had nothing to do with us. It's not surprising that the chap who greeted you thought that Jenny and I were the couple."

"Yes, thanks for getting me out of that one, Pete. Actually, during July I met that guy several times. I went out with him and some of his friends, to a bath house."

"Oh, what are they like?"

"On the face of it, rather like that club we went to near where Harry lived, but only for men. You can have the kind of massage we had there. But also there are cubicles with couches where you can do your own thing with anyone who takes your eye."

"Did you do your own thing?"

"There were four others in the party. They paired off. I told myself I couldn't refuse but I suppose I could have done if I'd wanted to. That afternoon on the beach I guess he was hoping to take me to some quiet place."

"It's good, then, that you're giving Berkeley a miss, for next year at least. Have you told Jenny about this man?"

"No, but I think she's guessed."

"When this IE business is done, and she's less stressed, perhaps you should tell her, and say it's over."

There wasn't more to say after that and we completed the circuit in silence. The groups had changed around ahead and Steph was now talking to Jenny and the children.

Dick had said nothing about Jenny's present relationship with John and Amanda. She had told me that she had told him. Either she had not told him that she had told me or he did not want to admit to knowing.

By the time we returned to the café, Brian was standing by my new car, talking admiringly and enviously about it to Susie. He clearly wanted a spin and deserved it for his help. I showed him all the luxurious new features on the dashboard, such as three-speed windscreen wipers, headlamp adjustment and a radio cassette system with several presets. Then he came to the point.

"I'm glad we can talk here, Pete. You haven't heard this but Consolidated is talking to our investments people."

"That doesn't surprise me but thanks for the tip. I don't suppose you have any feedback about the meeting Jenny and I had with your people."

"No, they're very tight on that."

"I wouldn't expect anything different. You had us in to see them quick but they must take their own view."

Brian had told me nothing definite that affected IE's position under the Takeover Code. Consolidated could have put the matter in many ways. Universal's 'investments people' were doubtless encouraging any action that would hype up investments. He changed the subject quickly, though, by referring to something that had been impending when we had had lunch three weeks before.

"I've not told you my news. I've been elected to the Down."

The 'Down' was then a fairly exclusive golf club located not far from Down House, where Charles Darwin had lived.

"Congratulations. How long were you on the waiting list?"

"Only three years, and that was time well spent, on public courses and driving ranges. I can play confidently off handicap twelve. That's a long way from your chum Mark but good enough to do my contact list something great."

"As yet I don't know Mark Dorney well. I believe he's been scratch or better for thirty years. I know he won an over fifties amateur championship last year."

"Yup, he had a feature in the golf magazine I read."

With Susie's encouragement, Brian had lost almost totally any accent which suggested that he was the son of a miner. Accordingly, he was able to use his natural bonhomie to advantage in presenting himself. As we pulled back into the car park I asked about his other recent initiative to this end.

"Is the Worshipful Company of Insurers in business yet?"

"It had its letters patent six weeks ago.[17] There are plans for the first banquet to be at the end of next April. By then I could be a Freeman of the City."

"Will the Company have its own livery hall by next April?"

"Pete, don't take the piss. There are plenty of places we can use."

We stepped into the café in good humour. Our coffees were at the table with Jenny, Sheila and Paul, and not yet too cold. An informal meeting followed. We lacked Chris Rowan and Tony Higgins but Jenny had checked they were happy with my ideas

---

17 This and several other livery companies were being set up to make the range of companies reflect better the range of services that the City of London provided.

of a month before. Also, Paul and Jenny had done a good job on the loan agreement, with the rate floating so that we were not locked in to high rates indefinitely.

"They'll go higher before they fall," observed Paul.

"Very likely," I commented, with a smile for which there was a reason.

The day after I had lunched Brian, I lunched Paul. Back in Leeds late in the evening of that day, I called Steph to describe what I hoped she could do to Fred Perkins and his nurse. As I had hoped she saw how this would combine a serious purpose with some fun. I took the opportunity to mention my lunch and its serious purpose. I noted that my mention of Paul did not bring Steph back to talking about Fred.

A few days later, Tim Baldwin had a welcome surprise in the shape of a call from Louis Demaire, Paul's boss, to suggest talks with New Hampshire Realty's investment arm about underwriting the rights issue. These had now progressed sufficiently to allow their intent to be announced but would go to the wire on the issue price. Changes in interest rates, and their impact on share prices, were a key factor. New Hampshire naturally took a more pessimistic line than IE, but we knew they were still going hard for a big foothold in the City. Walking away now would not help them to get further business.

Liz and Greg had now arrived and we emerged to the car park. Steph called us to gather round.

"Six years ago in Brighton, I described us as The Creators. It's great to see you all again. I'm so glad that Carol and Paul have found the time to make the arrangements. I'm saying this now, before Jenny, Dick, David and Katie leave us."

We waved the Sinclairs off and began another hour's walk, to a pub Carol knew. She and I started off together.

"This is very well planned, Carol. You've fixed it to suit everyone."

"It wasn't too hard to arrange. Jenny said she would like to bring the kids but they ought to lunch with her people before going home. Brian said they had better let his parents have a quiet breakfast before taking care of their two. Liz and Greg needed to go to the 9.30 service at which Greg's dad was preaching. So there were about twenty minutes when everyone could be together. I knew that Steph and Susie, at least, wouldn't want anything too arduous. We'll be back here by 3.30 at the latest, so you'll have no problem in running Steph to Manchester Airport."

"Good. Her flight to Paris should leave at 5.50."

"Last night she told us that she might pay you a visit this morning. We were saying how shattered you were and that there was no-one to look after you."

"Very nice it was to be looked after, but enough of that, Carol. There's no more consolation needed for you, I hope. You and Paul really do seem the well matched power couple these days, even more than before."

"Mmmm yes, and it's for real, Pete. It's all worked out as you'd hoped. Steph and you did help us to grow together. Even when we disagree we understand each other better than before."

"Yes, that was clear last night."

Over dinner, Steph, through lack of involvement, and I, through tiredness, had been left out of a left argument. Following defeat in May, Jim Callaghan was holding on as Leader of the Labour Party, hoping that Denis Healey would emerge as a clear successor. The Leader was then elected by MPs, but had to be acceptable to the trades unions, who remembered Healey for his pay restraint policies, and also credible to the electorate, who remembered him as the Chancellor who in 1976 brought the UK to begging for an IMF loan. Despite that, Morag was for Healey. As usual, Paul was rather difficult to pin down, but eventually he too plumped for Healey. Carol, however, preferred David Owen, and Sheila wanted Shirley Williams, to try a woman-to-woman confrontation. 'So none of you support Michael Foot or Tony Benn' had been one of my few interjections.

"I suppose the only thing we're losing out on is having children. Basically, we've not the temperament. If you look round the House now, the only women MPs with children are those with rich husbands, like Margaret Thatcher."

"You first told me about Margaret Thatcher and then she sent you that note. Has she noticed you, now?"

"She greeted me as we passed in the Central Lobby on my second day back. It's great to be on the way. Four years in the Opposition and then—"

"Optimist. Eight, if you're lucky. Meanwhile, you're one of the people on the left who can write; sorry to make a rather weak pun. Sorry, too, to be in the papers on a weekend you aren't. I buy the *Sunday Courier* for your fortnightly column."

"I could go weekly but fortnightly gives less risk of not having much to write about. Since I'm normally up here every other weekend I can write the column on the Fridays I'm in London. It's really great to see you again, Pete. I'll catch up with Brian and Liz now. I want to know what they've heard on the miners' pay negotiations. Brian's dad talks and Liz keeps up her contacts." Brian's father was NUM Branch Secretary at his pit, and a member of the NUM's Yorkshire Area Executive.

We were temporarily around a corner from the others. That allowed a quick kiss and a pat on her muscular swimmer's bottom before she dashed ahead, with tousled brown hair flapping around. Dressed in jeans and sweater, she didn't look very different from the girl I had met in Cambridge and with whom I had had an on-off affair over several years. She was chubbier and wore less heavy glasses. Her face was now more often relaxed and cheerful than tense. That day, her cheerfulness doubtless reflected relief that Steph's visit was proving uneventful.

In February 1974, Carol's electoral triumph had been marred by the discovery that Steph and Paul were having an affair. She had sought solace with me before going down to creditable but inevitable defeat in the October 1974 general election. Soon after that, Paul's job with New Hampshire Realty had taken him to the USA for two years. Carol had used the time there to develop her journalistic talents but it had been a great relief when Steph spotted Ken.

I dropped back, to join Morag, Paul and Sheila. They were talking maths, in particular about how the commodity trading software that we wanted Creators Technology to develop could actually work.

"Pete, the trouble is there's still a gap in the theory," said Sheila.

"I thought your student was aiming to plug that."

"He's perfectly good as they go, and will get his PhD fine, but he's not up to this job. Morag has reminded me that some of the work on automorphisms you did years ago might just possibly be relevant."

"Eh? I don't see how."

"Not the results, but the idea you had back then of generalising up from two dimensions."

"Let me explain," Morag continued. For ten minutes or so the conversation grew technical, and words and concepts I had almost forgotten came back to me. Then Sheila concluded.

"So, there's something there but it needs someone very good to get to it, someone at your level, Pete."

"Thanks for the compliment but it's over ten years since I did any serious maths, and right now I'm rather busy."

"I could set up a discussion early in the New Year, at a time when you're in London. You're still something of the missing, mystery man. Your name would bring people in. Laura would be interested in coming down, I'm sure."

"If this is eventually to be the basis of some proprietary software, do we want any work to be published before the software is available? I know that goes a bit against the grain but we need to think carefully."

"That's a good point, Pete," said Paul. "It's certainly how academics in the States do things when they have business involvement. I'd better catch up with Carol. I made the booking."

The group in front had broken up. Nearest to me, Steph and Liz were alone and laughing away. I could guess what that was about. I caught up with them at the tail end, and Greg joined us as we approached the pub. So we four were at one of the two tables Paul had booked – a wise precaution, for on that fine autumn day the place was packed.

The service was fairly quick because there was one choice for Sunday lunch. Nevertheless, Steph needed another glass of wine by the time we tucked into roast beef and Yorkshire pudding.

"How's that old College of yours?" she asked Liz.

"It wasn't really my College ever and certainly it isn't now. Father retired three years ago, though he still lives in Cambridge."

"A lot of the people we knew have retired," I added. "Arthur Gulliver could have been Master. He had the support but he and Miriam decided that they'd had enough. He went once Len Goodman was settled in. We keep in contact. I had a very nice note from him."

"That reminds me. To success and to Pete," said Steph, quite loudly.

I had already noticed a shortish bald-headed man staring in my direction. As three glasses were raised, he murmured to the woman next to him. She had a large pack over her shoulder. Clearly it contained something valuable and she did not want to put it down. I glanced towards our other table. Fortunately that was some yards away, so they hadn't heard or reacted to Steph. Carol wasn't there.

"Thanks. I'll be back in a moment."

I headed for the toilets. As I entered the corridor leading to them, Carol emerged from the ladies'. I stopped her, out of sight from the bar.

"There's a couple interested in me. Any idea who they are? I don't think they've noticed you."

She peered into the bar. "Damn. That's Dan Worsley, an industrial correspondent for the *Yorkshire Post*. The woman is his girlfriend and a photographer for the *Post*. They've been snapping the scenery, I guess. Now they've spotted another subject, matching your photo in the *Gatherer*. He won't try anything in here. If he did the landlord would throw him out. He'll wait for you outside."

"I can handle that. Thanks for the tip-off."

"We don't want him to spot me. That would put him on to Paul and there would be questions about what we're all saying to each other. So, your table leave first. While he tackles you, we'll follow with the crowd and head back the way we came, as if nothing to do with you."

She returned to her table, taking care not to face the couple. Fortunately, she was sitting with her back to them. I could see a quiet conversation developing. I could also see Worsley following me with his eye as I returned to my seat. I murmured an explanation and we continued to eat. Steph was now rather subdued.

At five to two, the couple left. We left just after two o'clock and had gone only a few yards from the pub when I was accosted.

"Peter Bridford? Dan Worsley, *Yorkshire Post*. Very many congratulations on your recent promotion, and welcome to Yorkshire."

"Thank you, Mr Worsley. I'm pleased to meet you; and I know you're interested in International Electronics, which employs over 5,000 people in Yorkshire."

"What brings you out here when I'm sure you're very busy with the rights issue announced on Friday?"

"The same as what I guess brings you out here. It's a fine day and I'm taking a short break with old friends. By six o'clock, though, I'll be back in Leeds getting ready for a very long day tomorrow."

"Can you tell me what benefits Yorkshire can expect from the rights issue?"

"I've come into this job from running IE's sales to the oil and gas industry, which will pass £40 million this year. Nearly half those sales are of products made in Yorkshire. With more capital we can purchase companies in the USA, through which we can sell more over there. Our semiconductor plant is near Sunderland but over 300 of its workforce live in North Yorkshire. Their jobs will be safeguarded."

I reeled off more like this. Eventually, Worsley got in again.

"Aren't you worried that the high pound will hit your sales?"

"We sell on quality and reliability. Customers want stuff that works. That's the challenge facing all of British industry for the '80s. Full sterling convertibility will help our business. Exchange controls were introduced as an emergency measure at the start of World War II. We won that thirty-four years ago."[18]

I could see the rest of our party leaving unnoticed amongst many others as the pub turned out. In those days, Sunday lunchtime licensing hours finished at 2 pm. All alcoholic drinks had to be consumed by 2.10 pm and you left very soon after that. Pubs re-opened at 7 pm.

I promised Worsley a full interview in a few weeks' time, and rejoined Liz, Greg and Steph, who were waiting a few yards away. The woman had taken a few shots of me and she took a couple of the four of us before they drove off. We caught up with Carol and Paul about ten minutes down the path back to the café.

"Phew. Thanks, Carol, for a good plan."

"I like that pub on Sundays because it's away from the constituency and there's less risk of being buttonholed. Sorry it

---

[18] On 23rd October, exchange controls were abolished and sterling thereby made fully convertible.

didn't turn out that way just now. I've certainly done *my* bit this weekend. I came up by train on Thursday evening, as there was a load of London stuff on, with no divisions. The constituency office had arranged a full Friday and into yesterday, and transport to get me around, including to the local pool first thing both mornings. Paul drove up yesterday, shopped and sorted out the house. A 15,000 majority is very nice but it means *more* local work, not less, because the people who vote for you are more likely to ask you for help."

"How do your miners react to having a woman MP?" asked Steph.

"For most of them, it's no problem. It's more of a problem for some of their wives but it won't make them vote Tory. My name from '74 and support from Brian's dad helped me into here but what really got me in is that there was no-one local who thought they had the right to the seat when Steve Barnes retired. Now there are enough people on the constituency committee who come to meetings that our friend Arthur's attempts to pack the Yorkshire committees with his men won't hit me."

"Good," I said. "He does have a plan. I'm not sure that Gormley has a plan, other than of keeping McGahey out."

"He'll find a way. He always does," said Liz.

"How do you find talking to the press, Pete?" asked Carol.

"It went well enough just now, and the briefings I gave on Friday and yesterday seem to have turned out OK. I'll be doing more. When we have a press conference for the prospectus, Pat wants me to take quite a lot of the questions."

"Good luck. You'll find it's different from talking to one reporter. They'll fire at you from all over the room. Have you had any practice in dealing with that?"

"Not really."

"Are you in London overnight any time this week?"

"Probably on Thursday night."

"That's good – Shipbuilding Bill, no division. Come to dinner at the flat, fairly late, say 8.30. Paul and I will shoot from both sides."

"How are you both finding the flat?" Liz asked.

The flat had been hers. At the same time as she and Greg were moving out of town, Carol and Paul had wanted a more central London base than their flat in Bellinghame. So they and Liz had saved on agents' fees and had managed to stay friends through the inevitable hassles.

"It suits me," said Carol. "I can be at the House in twenty minutes, so I don't need to stay there all the time if I know when divisions are expected. It's good for entertaining small groups, too, provided they can manage the four flights of stairs."

"The parking is getting more difficult," Paul grumbled. "Our permit allows us to park in any residents' bay in Kensington, which is helpful. It doesn't reserve us a place near the flat, which isn't so helpful."

A regrouping allowed Liz and Greg to catch up with Morag and Sheila. Steph and I found ourselves in the continuation of a discussion which had evidently begun over lunch at the other table. Brian weighed in.

"So, Steph, why are your companies like Ford and General Motors transferring all their production to the Continent?"

"They're not my companies just because they're American, Brian. Presumably their factories here aren't economic. They have had a reputation for strikes."

"When I joined IE, it had a reputation for strikes," I commented. "We sorted that out. Good management could sort Ford and GM out. Perhaps they've sent their good managers elsewhere."

"British industry was supposed to benefit from joining the EEC," said Brian. "Instead we're being closed down and relegated. More and more of the stuff in the shops is imported. It's got to even the Italians saying they're better off than us. For all this we're paying a billion a year to Brussels. Maggie Thatcher must say no."

"We still need to develop industries which dominate the European market and can compete worldwide," said Paul.

"Thanks to the North Sea, we've a chance to do that," I said. "With sterling fully convertible at last, the sky is the limit for the City and for financial services industries like insurance. IE's board discussed the implications on Thursday. No doubt New Hampshire will be doing so, too. There's a very positive message for Creators Technology. How's your company to react, Brian?"

"Universal should be able to expand on the Continent but we can't. The European Commission is run by the French. They use all sorts of piffling regulations to stop us. It's a swindle – heads they win, tails we lose."

"Margaret Thatcher needs to push for a market that's common and free for what we're good at, as well as for what the others are good at. For that, we need British people in the Commission who push our interests, hard, not people who keep a straight bat and think playing the game of Euro idealism is more important than winning for the UK. Your man Roy Jenkins has gone spectacularly native, Carol." [19]

"You people don't sound like those who voted two to one to stay in," said Steph.

"Wilson obtained some temporary concessions then and we were in such a mess that there seemed no alternative. Now the concessions are running out, the impact of membership is clearer, and we've got North Sea oil and a fully convertible currency."

---

19 Roy Jenkins had been the most senior Labour politician to favour joining the EEC. In 1976 he failed to become Prime Minister after Harold Wilson's resignation but in 1977 he was able to become President of the European Commission. In Brussels, he pressed on with attempts to secure 'Economic and Monetary Union'. Some concessions on access by UK companies to other members' service sectors were eventually obtained through the establishment of the single market from 1986.

We carried on like this all the way back to the café. I said that British industry could follow IE's lead in getting bits into goods assembled overseas. Even Carol didn't object to my analysis of the 1975 referendum, though I had perhaps minimised the impact of Euro idealism during the first years after we joined the EEC.

I had definitely exaggerated the extent of Thursday's discussion, which had been confined to agreement with my observation that convertibility would make New Hampshire Realty even more interested in being strong in London. However, on Friday I had been pleased to read Douglas Arnott's note, having received it more quickly than I would have done if he had known my home address.

> 'Very many congratulations, and thanks again for our talk on the plane. There's some fruit already and there'll be more very shortly.[20] I've a thought for you. The Department has an industrial advisor who spends one or two days a week with us. Barry Potton finishes his term in the middle of next year and is saying that his company will value his experience here. Clearly you're very busy now but keep the idea in mind.'

I could keep the idea in mind but I wondered whether he was expecting that by the next summer I would be out of a job or that I would be sufficiently proficient at the duties of an IE divisional Director that I could fulfil them part-time.

At the café, it was parting of the ways. Morag and I found ourselves alone for a moment. She passed me an envelope.

---

20 The next day, 29th October, restrictions on gas flaring at the largest North Sea oilfield, Brent, were announced. These resulted in some curtailment of production. The message was headline news in the following day's *Financial Times*.

"Look at this later, Pete. No-one knows that I've given it to you, not even Sheila. I know you won't use it unless you have to."

Morag and Sheila were returning to London with Carol and Paul. Steph and I set off for Manchester Airport, through the gathering twilight.

"Great day, great crowd. You're lucky to know 'em all, Pete. They have a lot to say about where your country is going."

"Just now, there's a lot to say and a lot to do."

"And, like you, most of them want to get on and do it. Carol told me this is the first reunion of the whole gang, even leaving me out, since that time in Cambridge."

"That was a 'Day to Remember'. Today has been slightly less exciting."

We were silent for a minute or so as we remembered the day of Katie Sinclair's christening and the news that had come in. Then I went on.

"Carol and Paul have settled down well together."

"They'll need to stay settled down. Paul doesn't always come up here with Carol. Sometimes she'll be lonesome and not far from you. What will you do then, Pete?"

"She has plenty to do here. We're lucky that she could take time out this weekend."

"You'll need someone, Pete. When you went off to Aberdeen, you were still seeing Carol and me. Morag introduced you to Laura, and there was Jane. There's no-one for you here."

"I don't think I'll have time for a while."

"I know you well enough, Pete. I know that when you're under pressure you like to relax with someone, and it helps your work. That happened in Aberdeen, it happened when we were together, it happened with Ana in Spain, it happened with Carol when you were working in Sunderland, and it happened with Liz and Jenny in Cambridge. I'm right, aren't I?"

"You've left Angela off your list. Someone will turn up, I'm sure, just as they have done before."

"You're right that the message will go round the Leeds moms with eligible daughters. An article in tomorrow's *Yorkshire Post* will help with that. Sorry if I caused Dan Worsley to tackle you, though."

"Don't worry. He was already staring at me when he may have heard you."

"When someone turns up, Pete, will it be the same as before? Not that there's anything wrong with that. Your relationships have all led to friendships, leastways those I know about. Will you go on with someone? I think I can ask. I gave you the chance to go on with me."

"I hope I'll go on. You're not the only one to ask that."

"You didn't talk to Jenny much today."

"We spent most of Friday talking to each other. I had a long talk with Dick, though."

"How did that go?"

"It was rather depressing. The rest of us have moved on but he hasn't. He's still wound up about Jenny doing so well. His research had a spurt which got him a permanent post and the chance to visit Berkeley in the summers but it's in the doldrums again. And in July something happened out there."

I elaborated and Steph sighed. "That's very much what to expect."

"Why? If more women are to progress, sometimes they will be in better jobs than their husbands."

"I said it before and I say it again, Pete. You destabilise that marriage."

"You said that six years ago but since then Jenny and I have found it easier to be close, understanding friends. Dick had his adventure at the bath house *before* I arrived in San Francisco. I hadn't met Jenny since June."

"When did you let them know you were coming through SF?"

"Like you, Jenny had said I should call in if I was ever over there. In June, I told you both I was planning a tour. Late in July, I let you both know the timings."

"Dick was already away, then."

"Yes, it was about a week before she and the children went over."

"So she told Dick when he next phoned. I bet Dick had his fling soon after that and just before Jenny joined him. He would have been feeling *very* frustrated."

"Dick is my oldest friend of everybody here today. I met him three years before either of us met Jenny. I met Liz through him. It would have been very odd not to visit."

"Well, I've gotten an idea of how it's seen from Jenny's end. There's sure that look in her eye when she talks about working with you."

"As I pointed out to Dick, our working together is a one-off. Once things settle down, I'll be based up here – not as far away as before but still quite a long way away."

"And that's what you want?"

"Yes, that's what I want," I replied, rather irritably.

"Are you sure, Pete? You've not gone on with anyone, including me, because in your eyes we don't match up to Jenny. Are you going to carry on like that for the rest of your life or are you going to get what you, and she, really want?"

We were approaching a lay-by and I pulled up in it.

"Jenny and I both made our decisions long ago, Steph. It's one thing for you, Paul or Carol to have a temporary change. It would be quite another to end the marriage at which I was Best Man, and which is bringing up two children. What about them?"

"What about them now? Katie, at least, is noticing Jenny's mood. I'm not suggesting you end the marriage but if Dick ends it, what then?"

"Steph, I know you're my friend and this morning you made me much less tense. I'll work better for that, which perhaps shows I need someone. I appreciate your directness as always but let's drop the subject now."

I leaned over and kissed her before we continued to the airport in silence. At least it was clear that she had forgotten all she had ever known about John and Amanda.

Back in Leeds, I was lucky to catch Brenda Murton alone. That allowed detailed repetition of Steph's graphic account, to overjoyed reaction. My next call was to Phil Harcombe, who had recently become IE's press officer. He made tut-tutting noises about meeting the press alone. I asked what I could possibly have done differently and promised that my next interview would have his full involvement.

Next, I opened the package of papers which had been on the doormat. At the head was my timetable for the forthcoming week: tomorrow, six meetings, but none over an hour; to London early on Tuesday for meetings with shareholders; back in Leeds on Wednesday; a visit to the Nottingham factory on Thursday morning and then more meetings in London on Thursday afternoon and Friday morning, mainly about the prospectus, before a 4 pm roundup back in Leeds. I could fit in dinner with the Milvertons. They might have more coaching to do than they expected if Jenny's ideas about presentation were agreed at one of Tuesday's meetings.

I had inherited a first-rate support office from Nigel. They were relishing the task of supporting my current life in the corporate stratosphere; for example, on Friday afternoon they had made sure that all 7,000 employees in the Instrumentation Division knew of the rights issue. Sometime, I would need to come down and meet some of my staff. How and when, I was not yet sure.

By nine o'clock I felt I was reasonably well prepared for the morrow. I made myself a plate of bread and cheese, poured a drink and opened letters. One had taken two weeks to arrive from Spain, via Aberdeen.

> 'Dear Pete,
> What marvellous news about you! Carlos has been away much recently so I have only just heard. Also, Father tells me that we may be working with New Hampshire to support your stock issue. Will you be visiting about that? Or perhaps you would like a break at some time in the future? As always, you would be very welcome to stay. It could be something of a 'busman's holiday', as is the phrase, I think. There is interest in translating my book into English. There is even a suggested title, The Lost World of Old Castile. If you visited, you could look at the translator's work and make sure it reads well.
> Carlos and Father send their congratulations, too. Now I must go. Young Pedro and Isabella both demand my attention. And I think there is another on the way; I know the signs now!
> Very best wishes, Ana'

Ana's two-week-old indiscretion about her father's bank, the Banco Navarrese, was useful and probably intentional. The official position of the bank was that participation in the underwriting consortium would be settled at a meeting the next Thursday.

I penned a reply suggesting that I might be able to visit next year and also mentioning the Creators' reunion, since she had met several of us. Her book was the result of our travels in 1972 and 1973, at a time when Carlos, her intended, was away in Argentina. We had visited towns, villages, monasteries and castles which had hardly changed for hundreds of years. Now, they were all changing very rapidly.

I was tidying up when I remembered that the envelope which Morag had given me was still in an inside pocket. I opened it, sat stock still for some minutes and was not to sleep as early as might have been.

4. THURSDAY, 8TH NOVEMBER, 1979

"We're here to launch our rights issue, but first, I want some of International Electronics' 50,000 employees to speak out."

Pat moved down from the platform, the lights dimmed slightly and he appeared again on screen to introduce the company he had founded in 1938 and which was, like him, going very strong. For ten minutes we toured the country. First, Claire showed us at the centre of the North Sea action in Aberdeen, next we journeyed south to Sunderland and Leeds, and then to Preston before crossing the water to Belfast. There, Pat appeared briefly to say that, as someone who grew up in Ireland, he was proud that IE was helping to create good employment for both communities. We moved on to Stafford, Cardiff, Andover, Chelmsford and finally Portsmouth. Finally, Pat was back on screen to conclude.

"You've seen what we are doing today and what we plan for the future. You as shareholders have the chance to join in."

Across the screen flashed the message:

ONE FOR TEN RIGHTS ISSUE. PRICE 275p.
CLOSING DATE – 12 NOON, 29 NOVEMBER.

Pat resumed his place on the platform and directors took seats around him.

"I apologise to people at the IE locations not shown. Clearly, in the time we couldn't show everything. There are VHS or Beta cassettes for you to take away. They are available to any shareholder on request. Next, I must introduce our Board of directors, who will be helping to answer your questions."

Once he had done that, firing commenced from the assembled reporters, who had had an hour to read the detailed prospectus in a locked room.

"Reg Swain, *Daily Telegraph*. You've set the price at the top of the anticipated range. Why?"

"We're aiming to raise as much as we can, as well as provide our shareholders with good value. The price is agreed with our underwriters, who bear the risk that not all shareholders will take up the offer. I'm pleased to welcome here Louis Demaire, Vice-President, Europe for the New Hampshire Realty Bank, which leads the underwriting consortium, and also Don Carlos Casares of the Banco Navarrese. Carlos knows IE well: his bank has been our partner in Spain for several years. Peter Bridford, who has recently joined our Board, started off our business there."

I picked up Pat's cue. "Yes, from almost nothing in 1971 IE's profits from business in Spain now exceed £5 million a year. If you buy a car made in Spain, it will have quite a few IE bits in its electricals. With Spain developing rapidly under its transition to democracy, and looking towards European Community membership, the way ahead is up."

I could see Carlos nodding and smiling, though he was rather lukewarm about democracy. Pat continued.

"That's just one example of how IE has found new markets. In our business, standing still isn't an option. We've kept up with developments in semiconductors and now look to marketing within a few years the kind of computers that will be possible for small business and the home."

"Mark Atherton, *The Guardian*. When do you expect to have a practical home computer for sale and how much will it cost?"

This was for Neil Farnham. "As Pat says, during the next few years. We expect the cost to be a few hundred pounds. The technology is changing so rapidly that it's not possible to be more precise. We'll produce something that's not a toy and which someone who isn't an enthusiast or expert can use easily. It will be switch on and go. That product is about two generations away; a generation in computer development being less than two years. We aim to market a successful machine, not what the Americans call a turkey. Pete has been keeping an eye on this for us, alongside our own R&D people."

I came in again. "Though this is a product area that falls to Neil's division, one of the good things about working for IE is that people are allowed, indeed encouraged, to have their own business interests if these don't clash with their job. For several years I've been involved in a small company which has marketed computer kits for enthusiasts. It's moving on to software development now, in other words towards providing the stored programs which will make a computer 'switch on and go.'"

"Jim Duthie, *Investors Chronicle*. Talking about avoiding turkeys is pretty rich when you've served up this great big steaming £68 million turkey of your own. How can you ask your shareholders for more when you've thrown all that away? Haven't you been rushing around with these bright ideas whilst not keeping enough tabs on your staff at the core?"

Pat was ready for this. "There are lessons to be learnt from what's happened and we've learnt them. I'll ask Tim to say more about that in a moment. I'll say quite clearly that I take responsibility for things that go wrong, just as much as over the years I've taken responsibility for things that go right. The rights have added up to a lot more than the wrongs. That's why IE is now a big company."

Tim Baldwin followed with an exposition of new financial controls, which seemed to satisfy the experts present.

"Brian Dursley, *Financial Times*. It's remarkable that you've gone ahead with this offer when a bid from Consolidated Electrics might be imminent. What do you think they will do now?"

Pat responded to this firmly. "I've no idea what they will do now. You'll need to ask them. We've acted in accord with the Takeover Code. Two weeks ago, your paper set out their three options. It appears that they've taken the first one."

"Dan Worsley, *Yorkshire Post*. What can you say definitely about the benefit to jobs from your plans?"

With a glance at Pat I took this one. "Ah, it's the man who scooped me a week back on Sunday up Stocksbridge way. Our plans will create hundreds of new jobs and safeguard thousands, particularly at Sunderland which Mike can tell you more about, but at other locations too. We expect that the firm's employment will go on increasing. IE employs 4,000 more people than it did ten years ago but at least half of our employees are in very different jobs from those they were in then. That's the way it will go on. In our business, products and technology change fast so jobs change fast. People can't expect to be doing the same thing for all of their lives."

"Brian Secombe, *The Journal*. Is it true that without this investment the Sunderland factory is doomed?"

This question from Newcastle's daily cued Mike Grimsey in nicely. "The semiconductor business is moving fast. If we didn't invest, we couldn't compete and we would lose market. So the answer to your question is yes, and within five years. However, we plan to invest in Sunderland and to compete effectively. The investment won't create many more jobs but it will increase the quality of many of the present jobs and hence the level of pay that will be possible if sales targets are met. It will be accompanied by opportunities for the present workforce to retrain and reskill for those jobs. Management there are already in talks with unions concerning how to bring this about."

"Albert Furniss, *The Economist*. I'm impressed by your video and that shareholders who have videocassette recorders will be able to watch it at home. This is a market which is expanding now but you're not in it. All the recorders are Japanese, even if they have British-sounding names. Why have you stayed out?"

Pat came back in. "That's a very good question. I mean that seriously, not because I'm playing for time. You could ask the same about other new products, such as the 'Space Invaders' game. It's a question for other companies than us though, including for one that's been mentioned here today. We're not a consumer electronics company. Our consumer electronics companies should have spotted this new market in time to meet it. We would have been pleased to supply them with components."

"Jim Lardon, *Wall Street Journal*. You're not a consumer electronics company but you're planning to market computers as a consumer product. Won't they be an untried area for you?"

Neil answered that promptly. "They will be an untried area for everyone. Initially at least, small businesses will be much of the customer base,"

"Joe Halton, *Evening Standard*. So how many jobs are at stake, here?"

Pat was clear enough. "Unless we make these investments, in total about 5,000 over the next few years."

After a few more questions, including one from the *Belfast Telegraph* which allowed Pat to repeat his message of support, Phil Harcombe brought the formal conference to a close. He took Pat and Tim off to another room for TV and radio interviews, leaving the rest of us to field the crowd. I dealt with a few more questions from Joe Halton, who made off quickly, and then from Jim Lardon, who was interested to hear of my visit to the States. By soon after midday it was all over.

Carlos Casares joined me. "That was a very good launch, Pete. I say so not just as an, er, interested party who does not wish to be left with too many of the shares. I believe you had a big hand in the arrangements."

"Yes, I suppose I did. It's very good of you to come over, Carlos."

"I needed to visit London. Now you have ended your exchange controls, it is the place to do business. We have the most cordial relationship with New Hampshire Realty but we need to open our own office here. I am also most grateful for your invitation to lunch, even at this very un-Spanish time; indeed, that suits me, too, since I have an appointment in Bishopsgate at fourteen thirty."

"Jenny Sinclair is joining us at the restaurant, which is close to there. She's been supporting Tim Baldwin on the financial side. I'll call her now to say we're on our way."

That done, we emerged into the Tottenham Court Road from the conference suite we had been using and took a taxi to the City. I asked after Ana.

"She is well and what she told you is now definite. She is expecting another. I am so proud of her, as is her father. He sends his regards and congratulations to you."

"Many thanks. You are both right to be proud. Please convey my felicitations. Ana told me that her book is being translated. Even if there is no convenient time for me to visit you, I can read and comment on any text she sends me. This will find me for the next few months." I passed him a card with my address in Leeds.

"It is pleasing that Jenny has been working with you. She and you were so helpful on that terrible day nearly six years ago. We had never met her then. Last year we met her, and her family, for the first time."

The year before, the Sinclairs had visited the large country house outside Pamplona which Ana and Carlos had taken over; Ana's father, Don Pedro, now preferred to live in town.

"We helped you both to reach the answer which has proved to be right. You reached it, not us. Ah, there she is now."

We passed Jenny a hundred yards away from the restaurant, so Carlos was able to greet her in formal Spanish style before we went in. Then I murmured to her.

"I'm in post Tripos mood, so it's over to you."

She knew what I meant. For the first time in nearly two months, there was nothing immediate for me to do. Although the outcome of the share issue was uncertain, we just had to wait for it, just as twelve years before I had had to wait for the results of the maths finals at Cambridge and then to find out whether I had topped the list. No longer was there the nervous pressure to keep me going. I could feel exhaustion closing in.

Jenny had suggested the idea of a video prospectus, to show how IE wasn't just about its directors but about the whole of its workforce. Phil Harcombe, who was a great improvement on his predecessor, had seen no difficulty in hiring a unit to make it and had given a good estimate of cost, which Tim had approved. Pat had said that it was a good idea if we could do it. So by the Tuesday nine days earlier, it was agreed that we were doing it.

That left me to consider locations, talk to the local managements and consult relevant trades unions at national level. I achieved all that by the end of Thursday through frantic phoning from Leeds or London. Indeed, I had the unit in Aberdeen that day, since I was sure of the ground there and it involved the most travel. Jenny joined in dinner with the Milvertons, which became an ideas session for the video. That evening wasn't all work, though. Paul had shown off his new hobby – a multiband radio which, with an aerial in the roof, was advantageously situated to receive almost anywhere.

Back in Leeds on Friday afternoon, I saw the video unit in action, but like all directors other than Pat, I did not appear myself. The video was about the management and staff who actually delivered the goods for IE, and their hopes for the future. Pat's decision to visit Belfast himself had attracted much coverage in both Northern Ireland and the Republic, coming as it did less than three months after the day in August when IRA terrorists had murdered Lord Mountbatten, some members of his family and eighteen soldiers.

By dint of frantic travel and taking advantage of the fact that several factories were working on the Saturday, the unit completed filming and was back in London late on Tuesday, just over thirty-six hours before the video was to be shown. By 2 am on Wednesday, we had a first rough cut, and I left the nightshift at the unit to tidy that. A viewing a few hours later had led to more changes, and at 5 pm it had been shown to all directors available. That had given more suggestions. At 10 pm, we had taken the final run-through and signoff at Pat's home. By then, Tim and Sam had finally settled the offer price with New Hampshire and its partners. Overnight, enough copies had been made for this morning, and here we were.

I relaxed whilst Jenny and Carlos compared notes about families. After a while, Carlos turned to me.

"Pete, we enjoyed your visit three years ago with your friend Laura. I believe she is married now?"

"Yes, that's right, a year ago."

"You could visit again next summer at the same time as Jenny and her family. There is plenty of room for you all. The little one will then be of three months."

"This year I've seen very little of my parents. I've said that I'll spend some time with them next summer. I could visit as part of a holiday in Spain in the autumn, though. I've never been to the Extremadura and down through Merida. That would be far too hot in the summer."

"When we were with you last year everything was changing under the new government," said Jenny. "I know you are cautious about this, Carlos. How is it going now, do you think?"

"You are right, I am cautious. Change must not risk the stability which the Generalissimo gave to us. Spain needed that stability, to repair the damage caused by atheism and communism. With others, I am keeping a very watchful eye."

The conversation drifted on to the main international news. Four days before, a mob had invaded the US Embassy in Teheran. They were holding the remaining staff there as hostages for the Shah's return for trial. The Ayatollahs had not sanctioned the mob action but were not protecting the staff in accord with international law. Carlos's views were plain and vehement.

"Carter's mistaken decision to admit the Shah has put his country into this impossible position. Do not forget that this occupation took place exactly twelve months before the election at which he will stand for a second term. It was not a spontaneous action. It was a carefully contrived plot."

"So what should Carter do?" asked Jenny.

"His forces must go in and rescue his people, and the sooner the better. The USA cannot afford to be humiliated in this way."

Carlos left for his meeting soon after. Jenny and I relaxed over the rest of our coffee.

"There's much in what Carlos said about Carter," I said. "He was putting it forward in a very assertive way, though. He'd had only two glasses of wine."

"Yes, he was assertive about Spain, too."

"Before I met him, Ana told me that his family were rather unreconstructed Falangists, whilst she and her father were 'progressive Francoists.'"

"During our time with them, they had several arguments over meals. Ana is becoming more interested in politics. She's for giving the elected government a chance, whilst recognising that it has a lot to learn."

The first elections to be held following Franco's death had produced no majority for any party. A centrist coalition was in power, but felt insecure.

"There was lots of table talk in English, then?"

"Yes, they aim to make their children bilingual. It will be good to see them all again. David and Katie were fascinated by their house. It's quite a castle, isn't it? There's room after room to explore. With the new swimming pool, they even preferred it to the beach. In California, they were asking whether we could go again. I'm glad at what you said about your visit, Pete."

"We must go back to where we were before September, but thanks so much for all your help, Jenny. Without you, I couldn't have done what I've done. I'll be telling Tim that, though I'm sure he knows it. Pat has made clear that from now on it's to be 'business as usual'. We must wait and see what shareholders do and indeed what Consolidated does. So I'll be where my real job is, in Leeds."

"It's nearly over for me, too. Some permanent recruits for the finance team will start next week. I've an assignment from the week after next, a company with a 31st December year end. The audit manager on the account is rather inexperienced and needs some, er, guidance."

"Well done, but you need some family time. You've worked way over full time, when you're meant to be part-time. Don't 31st December year ends mean no Christmas?"

"I've said that I must be out for the whole of the week before Christmas. Then they can have me from the Thursday, 27th, and all the New Year week if necessary. So thanks, Pete. It's been great to work with you on this job but, as you say, that's ending now."

Under the table, she put her hand on my knee and I put my hand on hers. Mine was at least mainly the hand of close, understanding friendship. Hers seemed to be more. She certainly had a look in her eyes. A few minutes later we got up and left quietly.

We were not quiet for long. Jenny saw it first.

"*Wow!*"

From a kiosk stared at us the headline of the early edition of the *Evening Standard*.

THE CHIPS ARE DOWN
Sir Pat goes for it – 5,000 jobs to be saved
Consolidated on the spot

Back at the office, 'business as usual' had commenced. Pat had told directors to fulfil any commitments they had for the afternoon. Those based nearer London were doing so. A brief wash-up meeting was for Tim, Phil and those of us who were not trying to return to their offices that day – Mike, Albert and me. Sight of the *Standard* helped to set Pat going on a cheerful note.

"From my conversations afterwards, and this, we've achieved our first objective. The issue isn't any longer our trading loss, but our plans for the future. As you say, Albert, attack has once again proved the best form of defence. The video is splendid. Well done, Pete."

There were murmurs of agreement and then Phil made an interesting observation.

"Luke Allnutt of the *Clarion* kept quiet. He's close to Consolidated. He knows Roy Delaval well. It's surprising he didn't come in after Dursley."

Roy Delaval was head of Consolidated's largest division and, at least in his own view, the Number Two there. He had the reputation of being a ruthless 'hirer and firer'.

"That suggests they're still wondering what to do," said Pat.

"Phil, will there be enough copies of the video to reach local authorities, MPs' constituency offices, and local papers by tomorrow morning?" I asked.

"Yes, that's all in hand by courier service."

"Why don't we send them over to the Houses of Parliament?" asked Pat.

"Carol Milverton told me not to try that," I replied. "Today's business goes on late and Members will leave quickly afterwards. Few will be in tomorrow for a Private Member's Bill. Even if the packages got through security in time to be collected, most of them would be left until Monday."

"It's particularly important my local people have them quickly," said Mike. "On Saturday morning I'm seeing at least ten

MPs, plus Durham County and the Districts. We'll run the video again but best if they've already had the chance to watch it."

"Send six round to the Aero Club for me," said Albert. "By Saturday will do. I'll be meeting people on Sunday."[21]

"How was Louis?" Pat asked Tim.

"Pretty happy, despite the surprisingly high price he agreed. Maybe like Sam he expects that Consolidated will offer to buy unsold shares."

"How much cash could they find for that?"

"About £40 million without too much strain on their balance sheet."

"So if there isn't full take-up they could have 4% of our equity. They would need 10% to demand an extraordinary general meeting, wouldn't they?"

"Yes, so they could do it if they had a couple of big investors with them, but it would be odd to use an EGM to challenge something most shareholders are likely to endorse. They could use the meeting to propose an alternative strategy or even to try to throw us out and have replacements elected who would accept a takeover. For any of that, though, they would do better to wait for the AGM next July."

"By then we'll have our investments underway. They really have missed the bus. Frankly, I'm surprised. I was expecting them to mount a bid or at least to express clear intention so as to stop us in our tracks, but it's their business. Was there anything from Carlos, Pete?"

"He was happy. He thought the launch went well. Most of the lunch was social."

"So far, so good, then. Our next Board meeting is on the 29th. By 2 pm that day, we should know what the acceptance level is. Phil, keep up the daily press summaries."

"Will do. Tim, can Jenny carry on helping with the assessments of shareholder comments?"

---

21 Remembrance Sunday.

"Yes, until the end of next week."

"She's been quite a star," said Pat. "Pete, I'm glad you overcame her reluctance."

"Without her, we'd have had much more trouble getting the prospectus through our auditors," said Tim. "Mike, a note from you and Pete about what she's done would be helpful."

"Heading for King's Cross, Pete?" asked Mike. "I can just make the Talisman.[22] In fact, you could come with me. The first stop is York at ten past six. There are plenty of trains to Leeds from there. You'll be back as soon as if you waited for the next direct train, which isn't a 125. We can do the note for Tim and talk through some plans for Sunderland that I'm not quite sure about. They affect particularly the part you ran ten years ago."

We were at King's Cross by five to four. Luckily, a pair of seats across a table were reserved but not taken, so we were able to spread papers out and talk quietly without being overheard, being interrupted only by a steward offering us tea and a ticket inspector who collected an extra fiver from me. We sorted out the note about Jenny. For Mike, she had dealt with several points on financing Sunderland.

"You took her to the lunch with the man from Banco Navarrese, I gather," said Mike.

"That was Tim's suggestion. Working with the underwriters is a Finance job, but he was tied up with Louis. Both of us had met Carlos before – me from my time in Spain, and Jenny via me, I suppose."

"She's an old friend of yours, I gather."

"Yes, a *very* old friend. That's why Tim asked you to send the note."

"You've certainly been thrown in the deep end these last two months."

"I hope I haven't rubbed too many people up the wrong way."

---

[22] The traditional name, still in use then, for the 4 pm departure to Edinburgh.

"Clearly you haven't rubbed up Pat, nor Tim, Neil or me. Alistair and Mark seemed taken aback by some of the things you said earlier on but they made sure that their sites' bits of the video turned out well. They both value Albert's opinion and he's been positive about you. I think you've made a very good start; better than I did."

"You didn't face what we've faced the last two months."

"True, fortunately. The really interesting thing is the effect on Pat. Earlier this year several of us thought that he was slowing down. This has brought him back to top form. Going to Belfast was a master publicity stroke."

"He really wanted to do that."

"And you gave him the opportunity. Letting others in, particularly your seniors, is a big skill of yours. You've ridden hard, and well, but remember that if you ride hard, you risk falling hard."

"You should know, Mike. My next big task is to find my way round the Instrumentation Division sites, and their people. Up in Aberdeen I was rather isolated from them. There will be some suspicion of me around, if not resentment. I suppose you didn't have that problem."

"No, I had the opposite one, and still have it sometimes. I've been man and boy at Sunderland, and know a lot about the site. It has nearly half of Microelectronics Division's workforce and it would be silly for my office to be anywhere else. But I'm not running it now. I have to remember that. So do the people who *are* running it. They shouldn't refer things to me just because I'm there. When there are tasks at home, Meg reminds me of that."

The Grimseys were certainly attached to County Durham. They owned stables and hired out horses. The Cheltenham Gold Cup was an immutable fixture in Mike's diary. I wondered what his, and Meg's, reaction would be if in some years' time the chance of the top job came up – in London. For me, being rootless could have advantages.

We went through Mike's plans and then I settled down and dozed until I felt the train slow down. As I woke up, some thoughts which had been at the back of my mind somehow came to the fore. They were not about anything that had happened in the last week but about my last conversation with Morag and Sheila.

"Gosh, is this York?" I mumbled to Mike.

"No, just the curves through Selby." He looked at his watch. "We're four minutes ahead of time. If we're not held up, there should be a train from Newcastle to Leeds across the platform, due out at 6.07. I use it sometimes."

"Isn't there a new line being built which will cut these curves out?"

"It will save five minutes or so. I suppose that's one benefit from spending a billion on developing the coalfield under Selby. If we spent as the Coal Board spends the taxpayer's money, we would have been bust long ago."

"They're developing the whole field in one project, rather than digging a series of pits, and finding out more about what's there as they go along."

"Yes. They say it's so that all the coal can be brought to the surface in one place. If that was at the power station where it's to be burnt there would be some sense. In fact, it will still need to be put on trains and trundled round to where it's to be used, so the railwaymen will still be able to stop it if they want."

"Oilfields need an integrated development plan. If you take some oil out of a reservoir, the rest starts to move around. But coal doesn't move around."

"There's only one reason why it's being done this way. The Coal Board and the unions wanted a scheme that a new government couldn't stop." We went on like this for the few minutes into York.

A dash across the platform brought me into Leeds twenty minutes before the direct train from London was due. There were no packages of work waiting at the flat. I had told my office that I would be in first thing to pick up the threads. A letter from my solicitor in Aberdeen confirmed the sale of my flat at the good price offered and suggested that I should clear it within a fortnight. There was also an invitation from various worthy charities to a pre-Christmas gala performance of Humperdinck's *Hansel and Gretel* at the Grand Theatre, to be followed by supper. I was thinking of the kinds of people who attended such events, and recalling Steph's predictions about 'Leeds moms', when the phone rang.

"Pete – Nigel Thompson. I'm staying at the Royal Yorkshire, room 207. Care to join me for a bite of room-service food?"

I gulped and it was some seconds before I responded, in a surprised tone. "I guess so. The freezer is bare here."

I arrived fifteen minutes later, to familiar pictures and sound on the room TV. A recorder was linked in and he was playing the IE video.

"That was a very good effort. I expect you had a lot to do with it, Pete."

"Maybe I did. So what brings you back up here, Nigel? The nearest Consolidated site is twenty miles away, and it's not in your division."

"Don't ask silly questions, and don't worry, there's no mole. A reporter gave us the tape. I rang the Gainsborough Hotel. You checked out this morning. Therefore you were coming back here. I must have missed seeing you on the 4.10."

"I went to York with Mike, and doubled back. We had a few things to talk about."

"Ah yes, timetable-expert Mike. I did that with him a couple of times."

"So, what have you to say to me, Nigel?"

"Quite a lot, and it's cleared with Don. What he's asked me to say to you, Pete, is that if, and I say if, the companies ended up together, there would be a big job for you. Consolidated can see that you're the kind of man we want."

"I don't know what you're planning that might bring the two companies together and I won't ask. But why do you want me to know what you've just said?"

"Isn't that obvious?"

"If you mean, don't fight too hard, then I'm surprised at you, Nigel. You know me well enough. You can't have briefed Don Flitton properly, if he thought it was worth your coming here just to give that message." I stood up to go.

"Sit down, Pete. Of course I've told Don about you, *all* about you, including *all* your business interests."

"So he knows that I don't fit into the Consolidated mould. Nor do most of my colleagues, as you know. Mike and his wife hire out horses. Neil's Portsmouth base suits his competitive sailing. Mark is one of the best amateur golfers of his age in the country. Pat likes his staff to have outside interests, though his are confined to philanthropy. He feels that as a result we have more business edge."

"We know that. We also know that Consolidated is too bureaucratic and slow. Certainly that's what I've said during the last week. Don and I admire the way that IE has responded to bad news. A single company would need a lot of IE in it."

"That's quite possibly so, Nigel; but since you've not said how 'a single company' might come about, there's no point in speculating."

"It would have plenty of room for you if you hadn't been damaged on the way."

"What *do* you mean by that?"

"What I mean, Pete, is something you must surely know yourself. You're having a lot of publicity in the papers. If things developed in a controversial way, there would be much more. Your link with the club in Aberdeen and the crowd who run it would come out."

"It will be declared anyway in the next Accounts. 'Plain Jane's' is no secret in Aberdeen. Jane Sandford runs it, very firmly. It provides services to people who are working very hard in the national interest. It does so wholly legally, in letter and in spirit; in particular, there are no drugs – none at all. The local police know that very well. You know that very well, too, Nigel, and so does Pat."

"That won't stop a good story. The headlines could be 'International Escorts' or perhaps, for you, 'Plain Fame'. Back in '74 the *Clarion* printed a picture of your friend Jane. They will still have the rights to it, and to others."

"You always do your homework, Nigel. Now, let's get this straight. Are you telling me that unless I accept whatever Consolidated might be cooking up, there will be trouble for me? This really isn't the way to persuade me that I could work with you all."

"The point is, Pete, that you're part of the story. I can see why that suits Pat. You're the sharp man on the Board, at a very early age. You fit very well with the story being IE's thrust for the future, not the cash losses. But as a result people *will* be looking for more news about you. It's very much in your own interests that they don't find out about 'Plain Jane's'. Now, have another drink and something to eat."

"That's a good idea, thanks Nigel. Whilst I do, you can look at this. In fact, you can take it away. I have another copy. I have no reason to doubt its authenticity."

I opened my wallet and passed Nigel what I had been keeping there for use if necessary. As he read it, I could see his face whitening. After a while, he managed to say something.

"Christ, this explains a lot."

"You mean, it explains why Don Flitton has been holding back from a bid. He knows that, with his name in the limelight, this letter would come out, for just the reasons you've given about me. The world would know that his wife killed herself because he made her life not worth living, with the brutal examples quoted."

"Who's Morag?"

"A university lecturer who does a lot of voluntary work at a refuge for women faced with abuse and violence. Linda Flitton was there for a while and then went on elsewhere but Don tracked her down and persuaded her back to him. We all know he doesn't stop until he gets what he wants. Because she went back the rest of the system lost interest. Morag was the only person left for her to talk to, and so the person she wrote to when she knew it was the end. Don Flitton knows all that. He doesn't know that Morag was at Cambridge with me."

"What do you expect me to do with this?" Nigel asked, rather weakly.

"You could show it to your Chairman, Lord Cunliffe, and leave the rest to him. Clearly, Don Flitton cannot be the Chief Executive of any 'single company'. I'll make one suggestion, quite informally of course, since no-one else in IE knows about this conversation or the letter, and it can and should stay that way."

"Go on."

"In principle, there's a good case for a single company. It's even possible to pencil in most of its board. Consolidated has six divisions, IE has five. Four of the divisions have much the same business area, so a single company could have seven divisions. On IE's board there are three of us with a future, and my assessment is that on Consolidated's board there are four with a future. I could leave Instrumentation to you and take Consumer Electronics to give the Japs a run. Your Finance Director is coming towards retirement and we're looking for a new one. I've heard that James Cunliffe is a very effective Chairman. Certainly he has clout, and contacts from his time in politics. That brings us to the Chief Executive. In eighteen months, Pat goes, and perhaps Don might go then, too. If in due course both companies put to their shareholders that they were discussing an agreed merger with effect from April 1981, candidates for either Chief Exec post would know that in practice it would be one post. There would be a lot of sense in the Chief Executive of the merged companies being from outside either company."

"You've got it worked out, haven't you, Pete?"

"Not really. These are just some wholly speculative thoughts, for later. Right now, this conversation suggests that we should all hold back on the rhetoric. That's what Pat wants. Earlier today his message to the Board was, back to our main jobs."

"I used to suspect that you were more of a shit than you seemed, Pete. Now I know."

"You started this, Nigel. You tried to blackmail me, no doubt aiming for an early feather in your cap back at Consolidated. Don't be sour because I've trumped your ace. The rule for shits is, don't get found out, or at least don't get found out on some stupid little thing. That's where Nixon went wrong. The game that brought him down was never necessary. He should have made sure that nothing like it could happen. Now the same will happen to Carter because he let in the Shah. That's incompetence rather than dishonesty, but at his level just as bad."

For the next hour our talk wandered around the world. I wanted to keep it going until I knew that on return to the flat I had a good chance of speaking quickly to two people. I was sure that Nigel would be on the phone as soon as I left him.

The first call was to Morag, who was alone since on Thursdays Sheila took the late evening shift at the Pankhurst Centre. I suggested that the original of the letter should be stored in a bank, and then changed the subject.

"On the train back here this afternoon I suddenly saw what you meant by saying that the techniques I developed at Cambridge could be applied to probabilistic analysis of trading." I explained briefly. "I realised there's someone who might have more insight and whom we could consult in confidence without it leaking back around the academic network in this country. I'm talking about Siegmund Kraftlein. I wonder where he is now."

"Retired and living near Stuttgart, I guess. He must be over seventy."

"Someone who might know is Professor Hunter. I'll contact him. Meanwhile, can you mention the idea to Sheila in whatever way is most tactful?"

It was quietening down in Aberdeen but Jane would be busy for another few minutes and would call me back. Five minutes later the phone rang. Fortunately I didn't answer 'Hello, Jane'.

"Hey, famous Brit boy, people clearly want you. It's lucky Leeds is on direct dial. I've a coupla things to tell you. For starters, your name's in the *New York Evening Post*. There's plenty about your time over here in September, under the headline, BRIT ELECTRICS SQUARE UP."

"How did they pick it up? They're Murdoch Group, aren't they? There was no-one from *The Sun* at the press conference. Someone called Jim Lardon from *The Wall Street Journal* asked a question and I talked to him afterwards."

"He's a freelance who feeds good London stories to any paper here. He uses the *Journal* title as no other New York paper is known in London. There's nothing New Yorkers like more than two companies having a scrap to the death, and it takes their minds off this jerk of a President of ours."

"They'll be disappointed this time. Consolidated won't play. That's a hunch, Steph, but I've reasons for it."

"Taken, but what this means is, if you did wanna come over, you could write the zeros on your pay check. Just remember that, Pete. A thirty-three-year-old hitting big time here ain't that great news. A thirty-three-year-old Brit hitting big time at home *is* news. To all over here, you've 'got something'. Don't be surprised if Jim wants more. Anyhow, that's the first thing; now the second thing. Liz may be in touch. She couldn't reach you so she called the office yesterday and I called her back."

"Oh dear, has something come up? I called her the day after seeing you off. I don't know what some of the words you used to describe Fred and the nurse really mean but they do suggest that she should keep a sharp lookout for untoward behaviour."

"She had that message from me but you were right to put it over, too, Pete. She didn't mention anything like that. Though I'd gotten her out of bed she was cheery to start because Greg's team had just won a floodlit match. Then she came to the point. Earlier yesterday she took Jenny in to the surgery with one of the ailments little ones get. They had to wait a while. Her doc was very busy because Dr Fred is sick."

"Surprise, surprise."

"While Liz was waiting, the nurse passed by. Clearly she's tougher than Dr Fred. She gave Liz a rather odd stare. Then Liz remembered that photographer who took some photos of you, and of all four of us. What got published? Could Dr Fred or the nurse have seen a picture of us all together which showed that I knew you and her?"

"There was a picture like that taken. I know because Dan sent me two complete sets. I passed one lot on to Carol, with my thanks note. But I'm sure that picture wasn't published. Let me check; hold on while I find the Monday's *Yorkshire Post*... Yes, here it is. There's a picture of me talking to Worsley, with Liz, not you, blurred in the background. Also, there's a picture of the four of us setting off. Someone who knew Liz or Greg might recognise them as with me, but your back is to the camera. There's no way to recognise you, even if Fred or the nurse had somehow seen the *Post*, which circulates in Yorkshire, not in St Albans."

"That's a relief. Can you call Liz? She must have been imagining it. The nurse does have those staring eyes."

"I'll do that tomorrow. It's a quarter past eleven here. I'll remind her, too, that Fred Perkins wasn't there when we all had dinner in Waterhouse, nor was he at Katie's christening the next day. There's absolutely no way he or the nurse could link you with any of us. That's why I put you onto the job."

A couple of minutes later, Jane was confirming that she was already being watchful and would step that up. Then we moved to business.

"So I'll drive up next Saturday, the 17th, and meet Claire and Jim that evening. The storage people can clear the flat on the morning of the 19th."

"Great, Pete. That gives a bit of 'us' time. I'll comes round 'bout five on Sunday. Yer cooks us a meal, after first things first, of course. Then I cin helps yer in the morning. Glad all's so super for yer. Met anyone?"

"I need a life down here but I've had no time for that, yet."

"Hopes yer do. Yer needs it to be happy. Missing yer here."

"I'm missing you too, Jane. I'm lonely at times."

"Yer'v the special book to helps you."

That was true enough, and in bed I started off by looking through her personal album. It began when she was younger and a false blonde, including shots of which, as Nigel had reminded me, the *Clarion* had published one from waist up. Even the incomplete picture had been 'very tasty' in Brian Smitham's view. It had shown just enough to suggest, correctly, that Jane had faced the camera fully and cheerfully naked. There were also some more recent shots showing her mature, redheaded character. But I could not obtain full relief that way, or by moving to the album Jenny had given me all those years ago when our friendship had begun to deepen. I compared her body at eighteen with my memories of her at thirty-one on the beach in California. Working together so intensely had been some emotional strain for me and clearly much more for her. That wasn't at all surprising, but it shouldn't last now that we would once again be seeing each other only from time to time. She had found a way to manage her life. We would go back to being close, understanding friends.

To obtain full relief I needed to look at a postcard of Rodin's *The Kiss* that I had spotted during the course of my travels, and to imagine Melissa Copehurst persuading Liz and Greg, and very likely other couples, to be sketched whilst locked in such an embrace. As she worked, she would conceal a mildly illicit version of Jenny's enjoyment of Imogen's creation. She would be satisfying her will to power in a fairly harmless manner. Provided that she was kept from much more illicit and harmful ways, she would be a fascinating if dangerous woman to know and handle. But there seemed no practical way in which I could meet her. When I called Liz, I wouldn't be floating any such suggestion.

I should have been elated by success but, whether through tiredness or a sudden feeling of emptiness, I wasn't. The loneliness of achievement could be borne for a while but I hoped not forever.

Qualified success of IE issue

International Electronics and its underwriters, led by New Hampshire Realty, have some reason to be pleased with the outcome of their one for ten rights issue. 78.4% of the shares on offer have been taken up. It is not expected that New Hampshire will have great difficulty in placing the remainder.

Whilst not the sell-out always aimed for, the outcome effectively confirms support in shareholder ballot for IE's bold strategy of expansion into new markets and maintenance of dividend, whilst financing losses of nearly £70 million through unauthorised trading in interest rate swaps. This success is despite setting an offer price which seemed high after the increase in MLR to 17% on 15 November. IE's effective communications strategy, including use of video, will have contributed to the success.

IE shares finished at 309p yesterday.

IE's own reaction to the outcome was low-key. "Our shareholders have accepted our strategy. Now, they expect us to deliver it. That's what I and everyone else in IE will be doing," said Sir Pat O'Donnell, the Chief Executive. He will certainly be relieved to be able to move towards retirement with the company he founded in 1938 going forward. It is understood that yesterday IE's Board of directors approved the placement of major contracts for developing and re-equipping its semiconductor plant near Sunderland to keep ahead of the competition. It also approved two acquisitions in the USA, which will further exports of offshore oil and gas equipment.

There was no comment from Consolidated Electrics, which had been expected to foil the issue by bidding for IE. The continuing and puzzling inaction there contrasts with the decisive action taken by Sir Pat O'Donnell and his Board. "There's life in the old lion yet," a commentator put it yesterday.

Voices in the City have already said that the two companies are in many ways a good fit, and this remains true. A combined company could bring together the buccaneering flair of IE with the cautious but effective management of Consolidated to create the strong second force that the British electrical and electronics industry needs. However, the events of recent weeks show that combination needs to arise through agreed merger rather than through a takeover battle. It would not be surprising if over the next year both companies put out discreet feelers towards each other. This could yet be the culmination of Sir Pat's long career.

5. SATURDAY, 1ST DECEMBER, 1979

"Thanks, Louis, for coming in to tell us," said Tim. "We'll put out a statement welcoming you both as shareholders."

The rest of us nodded. Louis Demaire had just said that New Hampshire and Banco Navarrese would be purchasing themselves the issue not taken up by shareholders. The price would be that applying at close of trading on Monday, which would probably be slightly up on Friday's close of 308p, since investors would know there was not to be a large block seeking a buyer. This being some 30p above the offer price, shareholders who hadn't taken up their rights could expect about 3p per existing share. The banks were paying approximately £25 million for a 2% equity in IE.

"It's the right thing for us because we get the shares without buying on the market. It's the right thing for shareholders because the unsold shares won't be a drag on the market. I think it's the right thing for IE because it shows our confidence that you and your team will deliver, Pat. That's what this press release for noon today says. I'm sorry to disturb you on a Saturday but this has to be out before the markets open again."

Louis passed round a draft. We didn't take long to agree it, and he left.

"Thanks, Pete, for coming down at such short notice," said Pat. "When Louis's office called yesterday asking to meet first thing today, they didn't give any reason. You know these people better than any of us, particularly Paul Milverton, whose hand I guessed would be in this. Fortunately you had the gist from him earlier this morning, so we were prepared. It's good news generally, I think."

"I think?" enquired Tim.

"It means they're expecting something to happen that will send our price up, and soon. There's no guesses needed what that might be."

"I don't think anything is going to happen quickly and nor does Paul," I said. "OPEC money is pouring in. It has to go somewhere."

"That's rather double-edged but let me be plain. I'll be pleased to bow out to a merger that leads to a larger company being run something like IE, with the improvements to financial management that you're making, Tim. I'll be pleased to see James Cunliffe as Chairman but I don't want Don Flitton as Chief Exec. If he were, that would be a takeover."

"Don hasn't covered himself in glory of late," said Sam. "I heard more gossip yesterday. Roy Delaval is putting around that he's totally hacked off."

"His hand is clear enough to anyone who reads the financial columns carefully," said Phil Harcombe. "Luke Allnutt's by-lines give not too subliminal a message that if Don went under a bus now, Roy would step up."

"I don't want that shit anywhere near IE, either," growled Pat. "Like Stalin, he believes in management by fear. People who are afraid have no initiative."

"Fortunately, James knows how long he would last if Roy stepped up," replied Sam. "I've not heard any suggestion of a boardroom coup. There would be no winner to that. This kind of visible disagreement will be telling people who matter, including James, that there's a need for someone new from outside, and on the timescale of your retirement, Pat."

Sam, Tim and Phil left but Pat kept me back.

"I hope I haven't messed up your weekend, Pete."

"Not very much. I'm actually going to Cambridge to meet, would you believe, Professor Kraftlein. That's in connection with my software company. Paul Milverton is coming, too. I've cadged a lift with him. He and Carol will be outside soon. I'm staying over at Waterhouse later."

"Good. You deserve a break, and if *I* say that, it means something. Just one thing, though. I think I see your hand in some of the stories going around about a merger. A lot of them seem to be coming back from the States, land of your former lady friend and of Jim Lardon. Phil tells me you've been talking to him. Maybe you've been talking to Nigel, too. No, don't say anything. You're one of those who will take this company forward but for now I'm still Chief Executive. You've heard what I want and what I don't want. Act on that."

"Be assured, Pat, that I wouldn't work for Don Flitton or Roy Delaval. If anything comes of these rumours it won't involve them if I can help it."

"How can you be sure? Don won't give up easily. Roy Delaval is too strong for him to break but if Nigel or anyone else over there gets across him, they won't last long. It's the same with me, though I'm not Don, thank God. Since September you've done everything I could possibly have hoped for, and more. You've shown again how you can be decisive in a crisis and you've taken others with you. Now, don't over-reach yourself. You'd better get along."

Paul was waiting in London Wall, as was easy on a Saturday in those days. He thrust a map in front of me and continued east. Carol was pleased to work quietly in the back and leave the navigation to me.

"Did it all go as expected?" asked Paul.

"Yes. We all agreed your press release, and our response will certainly be positive. Carol, to explain, last night I made the presentation at a leaving do in Leeds. Then I'd been expecting to have a quiet evening before driving to Cambridge this morning. But I had a message from Pat's office. He wanted me for an 8 am meeting with Louis Demaire. Left at the lights ahead, then second right. My only option was the last train, arriving at twenty to twelve. At least there was a room at the hotel where IE has a running account. So I'm sorry for the early call this morning but I knew you were picking Morag up at the Pankhurst Centre."

We were waiting for a few minutes outside the Centre, until Morag turned up with apologies and an explanation.

"It's been a rough night. Fridays are always the worst, of course. At about half past nine, a woman came in with the usual kind of story. We were settling her in when the bloke turned up and asked to see her. He wasn't threatening but he was insistent. Actually he wasn't the usual kind of bloke. He was really quite quiet and persuasive so we couldn't just call the police. While he doorstepped Sheila and me, three more turned up, two of them with kids. They had to be looked after by the others. Eventually the woman came out and wanted to talk. After another ten minutes they seemed calmer. The bloke really seemed rather shaken by her running off and was apologetic. He didn't make excuses. The woman was as tall as me and had tidy brown hair, not the usual mess which justifies our daily hairdresser. She looked able to give back anything she got. Off they went together, and we'll hope for the best. That left loads to do inside, and more this morning, but the day worker is there now. It's a great relief to have the funding for her on Saturdays. So I can stay on for the match. Thanks again, both." The Pankhurst Centre was on the corporate charitable list for both IE and New Hampshire.

Carol looked up from her work as I continued to map read the complicated approach to the new M11 and Paul concentrated on driving.

"I bet you're ready for a break, Pete. I know I am. This is the first week I've got in twice. That gave me plenty for my column but meant that nothing except that got done yesterday."

"I saw a report of you in the economy debate on Wednesday. I think I understand what you're saying. There's logic in matching interest rates to real inflation but our current inflation as measured by the Retail Price Index was artificially increased by the increase in VAT in June, so there's no case for linking to that. Did you or anyone else ask what the government plans to do next June? Inflation ought to come down sharply then because the VAT increase will drop out. Right at this roundabout."

"It's more complicated than that, Pete," said Paul. "You're right, though, that you must distinguish between endogenous and exogenous factors. Economists signed up to the New Cambridge School have a lot to say about this."

"Yes, I'm sure they have. Do they agree with Milton Friedman?"

"That depends on which work of Friedman's you're talking about."

We joined the motorway, heading north through blustery rain. Somewhere near Harlow, Morag changed the subject.

"What was the other debate you were in, Carol?"

"Yesterday, there was a Private Member's Bill to make the licensing laws more flexible. It's a pity some of my people didn't stay around. They were saying to me earlier that they supported the idea but wouldn't support a Tory Member's Bill, though a Labour Member was winding up for it. Someone forced a vote. It was 68-13 in favour but you can't decide business by vote on a Friday. So the Bill was effectively talked out. The time is not yet ripe, as they say where we're going."[23]

"Talking of Cambridge, were you at the Blunt debate[24] last week, Carol?" I asked.

"I dropped in and out. It was fascinating. Jim Callaghan tried to calm things down."

"I don't normally agree with the likes of Tony Benn and Dennis Skinner but they're right to ask why this guy was let off until now. Of course, he'd been to a posh school and not

---
23 A reference to *Microcosmographica Academica* by F.M. Cornford, a nineteenth-century text on academic politics.
24 That was on 21st November, following Mrs Thatcher's revelation of Blunt's treachery.

only worked for the royal family but is slightly related to them."

"To let him off was valuable in intelligence terms, I suppose," said Paul.

"Blunt was let off by the same kind of people as hounded Alan Turing as a security risk. Had Turing been left alone, we could still be ahead of the Americans in computers."

"True, of course," said Morag. "I hope you're saying that the law was wrong, not that Turing should have been above it, like Blunt."

I had to admit that she had a point, and we moved on to the biggest news of the morning. At the Council of Ministers' meeting in Dublin, Margaret Thatcher had firmly rejected an offer to rebate just one-third of our £1 billion net contribution to the European Communities. Despite criticism from other European leaders that her action was not *communitaire,* it had overwhelming national support, in which we all shared.[25] That first autumn of the new government, there was certainly much to discuss. As we approached Cambridge, Carol brought us back to our own business.

"Drop me off in Lensfield Road, Paul. I've sorted out our next priority, the Christmas list, and can start shopping. I'll meet you all at the hockey ground at one o'clock. Liz knows we can't stay. Though this isn't my constituency weekend, we're in the run-up to Christmas and there are two parties I need to show for tonight. There's nothing tomorrow, thank goodness. If the weather's still no good, we'll come back to London in the morning. We've both got loads to do."

"How do you think your constituents will take a miners' NO vote?" I asked.

"With relief. NO is right this time for both Joe and Arthur, too. Joe gives the members the opportunity but they don't take it. Arthur gets a big majority in Yorkshire but the rest let him

---

25 It took until 1984 to agree the rebate formula that has persisted to this day.

down. Neither of them wants a strike immediately the Tories take over." [26]

Today's visit had two purposes for me, or three if you included the chance to catch up with people at Waterhouse College. First, Professor Hunter had told me that Siegmund Kraftlein was visiting him over this weekend. He was sure that I would be a welcome caller. Second, when I had called Liz on Thursday, she had told me that the hockey team Greg captained had reached the final of the East of England championship, to take place in Cambridge that afternoon.

My call had been to give Liz some good news from Brenda Murton. Just over a month before, my account of what Steph had done to Fred Perkins and his nurse had really fired Brenda up. Her time had been ripe and she and Alan had not wasted it. Now, her period was definitely overdue. Hearing of that led Liz to say that Fred would be at the match and had been friendly to her recently. She had told Steph that she must have imagined what had happened at the surgery. I told her that the telephone number Brenda and Steph had called appeared to have been permanently disconnected. I observed that as we had hoped, a lesson had been learnt. I had not mentioned Melissa Copehurst by name.

The rain had stopped by the time we dropped Carol and continued to Professor Hunter's house in West Cambridge. This was familiar terrain to me from the past. Jenny's parents were still living only a few hundred yards away.

"I wonder if Kraftlein will recognise me as the organiser of the demo against his appointment, back in '68," said Paul.

"You're a smart man, driving an Audi. You weren't at the front of the demonstrators. Your name was mentioned in a couple of papers the day after, when he was back in Stuttgart. I wrote to him explaining what we wanted and gave both your

---

[26] The NUM had rejected a pay offer of about 20% and had sought authority for national strike action in the ballot required by the union's rules. Following rather half-hearted campaigning, the vote for a strike was about 49%, when 55% was required.

names and jobs. If he didn't want to meet you, Paul, we would know by now."

"How we've changed," said Morag. "I would have been in the demonstration but I wanted to hear your talk, Pete. Here we are now, come to see him."

I did not give my real reason for confidence. Four months after the demonstration directed at Kraftlein's Nazi past, I had met him again, over lunch. We had talked about the local newspaper's report of trouble at Waterhouse College, following the attack on Paul that had put him in hospital. Kraftlein had not connected Paul with the demonstration then, so there was no reason why he should do so now. There were good reasons why I had never mentioned this lunch to Paul or Carol.

Chris Hunter was giving a lecture but his wife Janet led us to the study where Kraftlein was in genial form. He had not aged much, being still the rather stereotypical fat, balding, older German.

Paul explained that we were after a clearer model of the fluctuations in commodity prices. Developments in computing could allow this to inform real-time buy and sell decisions. A trader who could make these decisions more quickly than other traders, and who had sufficient capital, would always win out eventually.

Morag explained the modelling work being done by Sheila's research student. This had confirmed that in the circumstances of, for example, the oil or foreign exchange markets, the amount of initial capital needed was not impossibly large. She apologised for her colleague not being available that day but did not mention that Sheila was half Jewish and had no desire whatever to meet Kraftlein. Morag suggested that the way fluctuations were determined by lots of separate variables, almost going round in circles, might create an analogy with the work on automorphisms that I had done in 1968. Then I concluded.

"I've hardly looked at any of this since writing my paper but Morag prompted me to go over it. I think I can see what needs to be done, though it's difficult."

"I am now retired. Your work has been continued in several university departments, Peter. Should you or Morag not be talking to them?"

"No. If we can work this out, we won't want to communicate or publish it straight away. We would release it only when a software package based on it is proven and ready to buy. Meanwhile, we want to be able to discuss our thinking, in confidence, with someone of your stature."

Ten minutes later, all necessary signatures were on the agreement Jenny had drawn up, and Kraftlein was a consultant to Creators Technology at 10,000 deutsche marks per year plus expenses. As we prepared to leave, Janet Hunter took Morag aside.

"There's a message for you to call Sheila urgently. You can use our phone."

Chris Hunter had returned from his lecture, and engaged me whilst Morag did so. "It's very good that you can find time for maths, despite all the other things you're doing. I saw your name in the papers. You must be very busy."

"I have been, though it's less frantic now. I've been able to bring my maths books and papers down from Aberdeen to where I'm living now in Leeds."

"You've cheered Siegmund up. I invited him over for old time's sake but he's not been interested in talking to people in the Statistics Department. I suppose he wouldn't know anyone there now that Charles Braithwaite has retired. In fact he asked me not to let them know he's here, so don't let it go round the academic grapevine."

I assured him that we had no intention of letting it go round. Morag looked rather distracted when she reappeared but concentrated on directing Paul to the sports ground.

When we arrived, Carol murmured something to Paul which persuaded him that they should stay for lunch before setting off north.

Brian and Susie arrived a few minutes later. We had cheerful assurance that Susie's parents were coping with their two children, plus little Jenny. Over drinks and snacks in the club bar, Liz explained some of the rules of outdoor or field hockey. I chatted to Brian and particularly to Susie. Five weeks before, I had ignored her completely, though this was partly because Brian had been so keen to ride in my car. Her talk was full of the joys of housewifery.

"Oooh, our new house is really nice. Well, not new but new to us. It's detached and has four bedrooms and three reception rooms. It's in such a good avenue in Chislehurst. When I invited the girls I used to work with, they were really envious. It's all because Brian is doing *so* well."

"Working for an insurance company helps with the mortgage," Brian added. "How's your house-hunting, Pete?"

That led to some talk with him and Greg about places in West Yorkshire, and then there was further approbation for Mrs Thatcher's stand in Dublin. At a quarter to two, we wished Greg luck as he went off to change, warm up and pep talk his team, and we saw Carol and Paul off.

"It's hard work being an MP, and being an MP's husband," said Brian. "You can't call much time your own. I guess it's been like that for you, too, Pete."

"Over the last three weeks, it's eased off. I've begun to learn my new day job. I've even had some free time. Once the issue was on sale, there wasn't much more to do. I'm glad that Universal was wise enough to take it up."

"I told my dad to look out for you in the *Post*. He was pretty chuffed to see it."

"On Thursday, I'm giving Dan Worsley a longer interview. Is your dad welcoming a peaceful Christmas ahead?"

"Oh yeah. It's all been games *this year*."

At twenty past two, we moved to the stand. There was plenty of room, since both teams were 'away'. Fortunately, the rain had largely stopped. Through the first half we yelled encouragement but to insufficient avail. At its end, Greg's team was 2-1 down. That didn't worry Liz.

"There's lots of time yet. They're playing better and the others were just a bit scrappy at the end. Oh good, there's Fred. He rang to say he was coming but might be late. After morning surgery there was something he had to do in central London but he said he would come on by train. We're giving him a lift back. Let's have a word."

Fred Perkins looked rather worried and distracted but was very friendly to Liz and seemed pleased to meet me again, having read about how I was getting on. We recalled our times at Waterhouse, which had culminated in his unofficial presence in the College First Boat when it had overbumped Carmarthen College's boat. It was noticeable that Brian and Susie did not join us.

For fifteen minutes into the second half, little happened. I had the impression that the other team was playing cautiously, so as to hold on to their lead. I found myself reflecting on what only Liz and I knew, out of those there. I had allowed Fred to continue his studies and become a doctor. I had ensured that he would not be brought to account for leaving Paul unconscious for two days and in hospital for a week. I had kept untarnished the example the overbump had set for people at Waterhouse. I had also saved Brian from punishment – rightly, since he had stopped Fred from hurting Paul even more. Brian did not want to talk to Fred now. Paul and Carol had stayed to lunch only because Liz had told them that Fred would be late.

Quite suddenly, Greg had the ball and knocked it in from a good distance. We screamed and cheered. It was two all, with twenty minutes to go.

Immediately, the game took off. The other team missed a chance and so did Greg's team. Ten minutes from the end, Greg had the ball again. This time, however, the other team was there to stop him. Somehow, several of them ended up on the ground. All but Greg got up quickly.

Fred went out to the group around Greg. I could see him feeling Greg's head. Greg first sat and then stood up and was led to a side bench. Liz joined him there. A substitute came on. Play resumed, noticeably less aggressively, though the fracas seemed to be accepted by the umpire as no-one's fault. I could see Liz, Greg and Fred talking. Five minutes later, Greg went back on. He looked all right.

With one minute to time, Greg had the ball. No-one tried very hard to stop him as he dashed for position and scored. He was the Man of the Match, and his team were the Champions.

Bedlam continued for some time whilst Greg accepted the cup from the Regional President's wife and then led his team off to change. Fred went with them. Liz returned, to Brian's greeting above the hubbub.

"What a game. I'm looking forward to patting Greg on the back."

"Not too hard, Brian. He took quite a knock from a stick and was stunned for a few seconds. I was worried about his going on again but he was keen. He knew they wouldn't go for him. I'm so glad Fred was here to say OK."

"I hope Greg is changed soon. We need to get back to tea with Granny."

Morag joined us. She was looking at me with a clear message.

"Do pass on my congratulations to Greg and his team. It was a great game. Sorry, Liz, but I need to go back to London now. I can just make the 4.36 train."

"I'll walk along with you, Morag. Before I knew about this match, I said I would meet someone at the Statistics Department. Do give my congrats to Greg, too, Liz."

We set off into the dusk and drizzle. Morag lost no time in coming to the point.

"That doctor – Fred, Liz said his name was. He's the bloke who turned up at the Centre last night."

"*What?* Are you sure?"

"I'm pretty certain. I had a good look at him when he was on the side bench."

"He's in the same practice as Liz's doctor. He was at Waterhouse in our time. He's not married and has no steady, so he doesn't fit with your bloke at all. Was there any sign he recognised you?"

"No, but he wasn't looking my way. In fact, he wasn't looking much at the match. He seemed lost in thought until Greg went down."

"Why on earth should Fred impersonate a violent husband? Why should the woman you told me about impersonate his victim? Could this be some kind of inspection?"

"I've never heard of anything like that. This has reminded me of Sheila's call. She's worried that someone has been into our files. She'd been working in the office and didn't lock up when she came out to help deal with this bloke. There's lots of confidential material there, including a copy of Linda Flitton's letter."

"How could they know anything about that? I'll call when you've had a chance to check, say at 6.30."

We parted and I headed for Waterhouse College, feeling rather worried. Morag's description of the woman at the Pankhurst Centre resembled what I had heard of Melissa Copehurst, who was good at amateur theatricals. If somehow Melissa and Fred had discovered that I had spoilt their game, they would want to spoil my game, and if they read the papers they would know how to do that. Perhaps they had offered their services to Consolidated Electrics. Perhaps Consolidated had thought that it might be able to obtain the original of the letter and that that would make my or any other copy less

127

incriminating. It was odd that no attempt had been made during the share offer period but perhaps Consolidated had once again been slowed down by its bureaucracy. In any case, the original was now in a bank. The most that Consolidated could have was another copy of what I had given to Nigel.

But what else might Melissa and Fred try?

Fortunately, the guest bedrooms at Waterhouse now had direct dial telephones. I was quickly dialling Aberdeen.

"Hi, Pete, how's things? Yer lucky to catch me. Gonna be a busy night here. And just hadda great bonus. Surprise job I likes doing as well as the money. 'Bout three, a tall dark gal, thirties, turns up. Sez she's *very* lonesome, wants to feel wanted, by a woman. I wan't busy then, so I takes her meself and glads I did. She's got a super body. She 'ad the works and I means the works. Full body, which she liked lots; seys she does some massage herself. Then deep fingering, round a spot where she was sore, praps 'ad a nasty a few weeks back. A good lick, tho' I sez its meself, and then the vibe. That makes her come and come and come, thrashing around like ter break the table. Gives me quite a kick, I cin tells yer, touchin' the right spot to set her off again. I wound her down real nice, sez 'nother time I'll strip and we cin gets to know each other if she likes."

"Jane, this woman, did she have a tattoo on her groin?"

"Yeh, athletic type, some previous gal, I guess."

"She's a plant. Positive."

"Gawd, and I leaves her in the room ter shower and get dressed. There's no-one else there yets. Call yer later. Wot's yer number?"

After I had calmed down slightly I picked up the local directory and found the number of Susie's parents. In those days that was easy enough, since I knew their surname and roughly where they lived. Brian answered the phone.

"I'm really sorry I missed seeing Greg after the match. How is he?"

"He seemed fine, bit of a headache, that's all. They've gone, with Liz driving. Fred was with them, because he came from London by train. It's a good thing he was there, I guess. They should be home soon after six. We'll be off shortly, to give Bill and Doris some peace. How did the meeting with Prof K go?"

I explained, and next called Phil Harcombe. In the morning I had missed giving him my contact number and this was a chance to discuss arrangements for my interview with Dan Worsley. It was also reassuring to hear that all was quiet. If anything had been brewing up for the Sundays, Phil would have been after me by now.

A few minutes later, the phone rang. I heard the sound of coins falling into a box.

"Blimey, Pete, you woz right. Stuff behind other bottles in the shower. It's in the sea now. I must gets back and be ready fer the raid. I'll calls yer later, praps half eleven – from a box again; bring more cash then. How does yer gets onto this?"

"I'll tell you then, Jane."

There was a knock at the door. The two people outside looked tidier than the typical undergraduates of my time and seemed very deferential.

"Mr Bridford? I'm Charles Spopporth, and this is Diana Hardwick. We're President and Secretary of the Waterhouse Business Club. We were wondering if it would be possible for you to talk to us and other members in the bar. Some people have gone down but there are still quite a few of us around."

"I'll be very pleased to do that. Can I be with you at a quarter to seven?"

No sooner had they left than the Porters' Lodge put a call through.

"Pete, it's Belinda Wingham. Chris told me you were in Cambridge this weekend."

"I'm here overnight but in the morning I'm going back to Leeds."

"I expect you're dining in Waterhouse but could you possibly come over afterwards? I'll be on my own. Harold is going to a Feast in Pembroke. I do want to talk to you."

I said that I would aim to be over at about nine o'clock, and then cleaned up and changed. After that, it was time to call Liz, who was cheerful.

"Greg still has a headache but he's good for a quiet evening. He's proud of what he did. Certainly I am. It will go down in the annals of the club. It's very good that Fred made the effort to be there. He kept us calm, though he seemed rather worried himself. We dropped him half an hour ago at the station where he'd left his car. He said he had to go out but he'd be back later. I think he's over that nasty game with Melissa. That's something else he owes to you, Pete, though he won't know it."

At 6.30 I called Morag. She was less cheerful.

"The copy I left when I took the original to a bank is still here but I don't think it's quite in the place I put it. Sheila had been using the photocopier, so the woman could have taken another copy. What would they be aiming to do with it? Could they be trying to expose Don Flitton? Could this Fred be a relative?"

"What was Linda Flitton's maiden name?"

"Judson. There were lots of them at the funeral. They all looked pretty sourly at Don, though they had never actually done much to help Linda. I never mentioned the letter to them. I don't remember seeing Fred there."

"I have a memory that Fred's mother is a doctor in Birmingham. I'll see if I can find out her maiden name. There must be a medical register in the library here. I'll call you tomorrow."

I visited the College library, which was unchanged from my time, when the scheme for an extension financed by Pat O'Donnell had fallen through. Dr Olivia Perkins, who practised in Edgbaston, was not born a Judson.

I could guess why Fred had to go out and why he had seemed worried. He had to meet a flight from Aberdeen. He was on another nasty game with Melissa. Although he had put on a good act of being friendly to me, they were working to do me down. So far, they had got nowhere, but they might do more.

Melissa and Fred had discovered that I was connected with 'Plain Jane's'. Nigel Thompson or someone else at Consolidated could have told them, though that seemed a very strange thing for them to do. Nigel knew that if I were hit I could retaliate by releasing the Linda Flitton letter. Should I have it out with him, just to make sure nothing else happened? But how would he respond? How would *I* respond in his position? He would stay on top, calmly. He would never have heard of Melissa or Fred and might suggest that I was over-stressed and needed a holiday.

No, I had done all I could, and should emulate Pat by switching off and relaxing. All might be clearer in the morning. As Mike Grimsey had said to me, if you rode hard, you fell hard. If you played in the big league, you had to take knocks and carry on, as Greg had done. But was it always going to be like this?

In the Crypt bar, about ten awaited me. After introductions, Charles Spopporth began.

"Mr Bridford–"

"Pete."

"Pete, we know you came here fifteen years ago and got a very good degree. Soon after that, you were elected a Fellow and made a big breakthrough in research, but then you left. Do you ever regret leaving and want to come back?"

"Those are two questions, Charles, and need two answers. No, I don't regret leaving. I feel I've achieved far more by working for IE than I would have done if I'd stayed here, and it seems that others think the same. On coming back, well, I sometimes look at the maths I did and I know roughly how it's gone on because I have some friends who are working on the subject.

That's certainly a way to spend a wet Sunday afternoon in Leeds, as I found last weekend. I've never had a definite career plan. I've taken opportunities as they arise."

"Is there anything in the stories that IE and Consolidated Electrics might merge?"

"Don't believe everything you read in the papers, Jim. They sell on good stories. IE in trouble and Consolidated about to pounce was a better story than IE getting shareholder support for a plan to develop markets and deal with a short-term difficulty. Consolidated hasn't pounced, so the papers have to make up some explanation."

Clive Salzburger, a beefy looking research student from Chicago, came in. "Isn't it true, though, that some City institutions, including the London office of New Hampshire Realty which underwrote your share issue, have been sounding out interest in a merger?"

"You've been doing your homework, Clive. It's hardly surprising that people are giving some thought to the idea but that's nothing to do with the press speculation."

Diana Hardwick fired in something a little more awkward. "Clive noticed that New Hampshire Realty's top economist in London is Paul Milverton, whom he met a few years ago. Paul was here at about the same time as you were. Did the connection help with the underwriting?"

"Paul came here a year before I left. He did maths in his first year and I supervised him. Since then, I've kept up with him, and with his wife Carol who's a Labour MP. However, New Hampshire saw a commercial opportunity and made its own commercial decisions."

We went on like this until I needed to find a spare gown and move to the Senior Combination Room, where Fellows were gathering. On a Saturday night almost out of term there were not many of us for High Table. Nick Castle was there to greet me. Len Goodman arrived briskly, two minutes before we went into

Hall. He placed me opposite him and next to James Harman. I decided to wind James up by asking how the Cambridge world was reacting to the disclosures about Anthony Blunt.

"It is so incredible, unbelievable, that amongst us all this time we had this man betraying his country whilst being so close to royalty. It makes one realise that we all have our secrets but some have bigger secrets than others. Can the young people here understand this failure of trust at the very top? Can they believe that their leaders act for the professed good—"

"Come off it, James. Blunt was never a leader. He's an art historian and critic," said Nick. That was rather unkind. James regarded himself as a literary critic.

"That means he was an influencer of opinion. So many people he has influenced must now feel betrayed."

"Isn't he a big expert on Poussin?" I asked. "How he behaved in the rest of his life can hardly be relevant to his views on an artist who lived over 300 years ago."

"You don't understand the nature of criticism, Pete. A critic reinterprets a work of art or literature and suffuses it with his own personality. Thus, for example, there can be a Marxist interpretation of works created long before Marx lived."

James's eyebrows were moving up and down in a way that was clearly familiar to everybody there. He didn't seem to have changed at all.

"Do you think Blunt is a Marxist?" asked Nick.

"He was certainly a communist," said Len. "Perhaps that was a good thing, too, considering that, at the time he was passing material to the Russians, we were supposed to be allied to them against the Nazis."

That remark drew others into a splendid free-for-all argument that occupied the rest of the meal. Afterwards, Len returned to the Master's Lodge and no-one else fancied a continuing dose of James over port and walnuts. So I had no difficulty in reaching the Wingham house soon after nine o'clock.

Belinda, too, seemed little changed since I had last met her nearly six years before. We soon reached the point that I was at least half expecting.

"Jenny has been calling me often, when Dick is out. Her working with you has been difficult with him."

"I know. A month ago, I had a long talk with Dick. It's the same old message. He resents Jenny racing ahead. It came up before at around the time Katie was born. Fortunately, he then got going in his research."

"Yes, I know there was that bad patch and then it went better. Now it's worse again – much worse. There's been another instance of Dick going back to his old ways."

"He told me. I encouraged him to talk it over with Jenny when things were less pressured for her. I'm glad to hear he's done so. When you talk about old ways, though, remember Dick had a girlfriend when he came here and then was with Liz Partington for two years. Only after that did he meet Harry Tamfield."

"And then he met Jenny because he knew you, Pete. You were so understanding and supportive. Jenny knows how much she owes you and so do I. I'm sure that it's because of you that she decided to make her own career. She's done so well. She's so different from Archie's daughters, though I shouldn't say such things."

"Prices for Angela's ceramics are going up. I say that as the owner of some. I believe that her interior design business is quite a success, too."

"Yes, Angela has done better since she met your friend Morag. Her business isn't helping her marriage, though. Hugh wants children but she doesn't. Only Penny and Donald are providing Archie and Jane with grandchildren."

"You and Harold have four grandchildren because Jenny introduced John to Amanda. That was another example of her ability to organise people in the loveliest sort of way, as Dick described it to me once. She's inherited that ability from you, Belinda. Recently, she showed it very fully during the time she was working with me."

"Jenny and John have always been close and supportive of each other. It's so good that Amanda can live with that."

"Dick has lived with it, too, and with Jenny's closeness to Amanda."

"You're right, I suppose. It's such a pity that Archie's children don't get on together."

"There's a good reason why they don't get on. Too much attention was lavished on Geoff and not enough on the girls. I was pleased to see Geoff got his FRS but I think the day will come when Angela is more famous than Geoff."

"I know you don't like Geoff, Pete. I know why, too, but actually, you and he have so much in common. Harold and I have never met anyone else who combines intellect and ruthlessness in the way you both do."

"I think you may be underestimating your daughter."

"Maybe you're right and maybe that's why she realises what she's missing. When you come near, you pull her away from Dick. I know you don't mean to but you do. At a party last week, an American astronomer told me how black holes in space can be detected because they pull apart stars that come too near. He made me think of you."

"Jenny and I worked closely together for about six weeks. We did very well and we both enjoyed it. That's over now, though. We've not met for the last three weeks. In future we'll meet as often as we met before September, mainly through Creators Technology. That's right for both of us and for Dick and the children."

"She knows that's right and hopes she can stick it. She's said to me that, but for the children, she would come to you, Pete."

"That's a very big 'but.'"

"I've said that Dick couldn't complain if she were to sleep with you occasionally and discreetly, perhaps when her work takes her near Leeds. That might help her to stay with Dick, and the children need never know. It happens all the time."

"Belinda, you're trying to help Jenny, and I understand what you're saying. Some enjoyable but manageable variety can help a couple to stay together. I've provided that for a couple Jenny and I both know, though it's not been needed recently. But if Jenny and I slept together, that would not be manageable variety. We would be together for good. It would end her marriage straight away."

"You know what you're saying, Pete. You're in love with her. She's certainly in love with you."

"I'm saying that I know and understand Jenny very well. Our friendship is very special but we both made the right choice. I'm sure Jenny will stick it. Have you told her you were going to speak to me?"

"No, and I won't be telling her we've spoken."

"We're having a frank discussion. Can I make a frank suggestion?"

"Please do."

"You're delightfully coy about Jenny's role in Amanda and John's marriage but I'm sure you know what happens sometimes, just as Dick knows. Incidentally, I'm the only other person who knows. Jenny told me about it several years ago; that's why I say I understand her. Dick's little lapse means that he couldn't complain if Jenny now went a little further. In January, Amanda is going back to doing some night shifts at the hospital. If Jenny's work takes her near Leeds, she'll also be not far from Sheffield. I think that Amanda would jump at the chance of an occasional and discreet night shift with Jenny."

"*What…?* What on earth would happen if John found out?"

"Like Dick, John would have to know. As you said, he and Jenny are close. He might have to persuade Dick that this was manageable variety, kept in-house and very different from any dangerous adventure with me."

"You're asking me to accept that my daughter and my daughter-in-law are–"

"They're the mothers of your grandchildren. I'm asking you to accept that Jenny knows how to get what she wants, in the loveliest sort of way. She relishes Amanda's crush on her. Now she can use it for the emotional release she needs."

"It would be good for Jenny if you were with someone again, Pete. During that last bad patch, you were with that talkative American lady. What happened to her?"

"She wasn't staying here and I wasn't going there. Her Mr Right turned up back in New York."

There wasn't much more to say and before long I was on the way back to Waterhouse that I knew so well. I reflected that Belinda was Jenny's mother and a Frampton. She, too, was used to getting what she wanted. I hoped that on reflection she would plant my idea in Jenny's mind.

Belinda had said much the same about me as Steph had said, and more recently Jane had said. I did need someone, despite occasional relief such as had happened two weeks before. My drive to Aberdeen and back had been well worth the effort, and not just for collecting maths books and other things and for making a rather triumphant call at the office. Jane and I had sorted out a lot of business as well as completing the hat trick of positions named after my Cambridge girls. Soon after she arrived, she rode me hard in a 'Liz'. After dinner, she crouched for a 'Carol'. Best of all, first thing in the morning she hooked her legs over my shoulders for a 'Jenny'. Afterwards, she asked me whether that was best because even with her natural hair she reminded me of Jenny. I had replied that I didn't know.

I did need someone – for me, not just for Jenny. I was a presentable bachelor, and the interview with Dan Worsley would put my name around in Leeds. Before the charity gala I could buy a new evening suit.

What Belinda had said about Angela Frampton turned my mind back to another successful combination of business and pleasure. When I had first met Angela, she had seemed rather stupid and conceited, perhaps through being spoilt by her mother, Lady Jane Frampton. But then she had knocked around, in particular through a two-year relationship with Morag. We had met again in 1974 and, until the man she was to marry returned from the USA, she had been my London girl. Then, her success as an artist in ceramics was beginning and she was receiving paid commissions for interior design. So I had invited her to Aberdeen. She'd hit it off with Jane through admitting that she was rather a plain girl herself and laughing at the contrast between Jane and her mother. At one of my first parties she had made a stylish impression, sold a few pieces and gained a clear understanding of her prospective customer base. Then she had come up with a distinctive but inexpensive scheme for giving 'Plain Jane's' a 'Wild West' look which would appeal to the Americans but which avoided the kitschy glitz that would put off more local customers. She was now doing the same job for the Invergordon branch.

It had been fun to fuck a Frampton, particularly in the light of my views on her father and brother. We had both enjoyed a discreet, friendly and uncomplicated affair. She hadn't been my only one and I was sure I hadn't been her only one. Maybe her marriage was coming apart. She certainly had her own life and career. I could ask Morag to keep me in touch with developments…

"Pete – want a nightcap?"

As I crossed Founder's Court towards my room, I turned to see Nick Castle. With him was Clive Salzburger, whom I had met before dinner.

"It will need to be fairly quick. I'm expecting a phone call at 11.30."

We settled in the Crypt bar and Nick explained that he was in College overnight because his actress wife's pantomime season had begun early, in Bath. Then he continued.

"This year, Clive is our Captain of Boats. He's the first postgrad ever in the job but it was no contest on his Montreal record.²⁷ We've been talking through plans for next term, which depend on how far Clive gets towards the Blue boat."

"Goodness, you must have a tolerant research supervisor," I observed.

"He's on message. I finish training before most people are up."

"What are you researching?"

"The development of food imports to the UK from the Great Lakes area, 1867-1892. I've access to the libraries in Chicago and over here I'm looking at the interaction of politics, economics and technology."

"What particular technology?"

"Your technology: the triple expansion compound steam engine, which made transoceanic steam freight economic. In the summer I went to Bristol to see the *Great Britain*. It's marvellous to see, but as built it was grossly uneconomic, like that more recent Bristol construction, the Concorde. The 3,000-ton ship needed 1,000 tons of coal to cross the Atlantic, so there wasn't much room for passengers or cargo."²⁸

Nick came from Bristol. I had the West Country man's admiration for Brunel. I also knew what cheap food imports had done to the economy of Dorset between the 1840s and 1850s, during which period Thomas Hardy set most of his novels, and the 1880s and 1890s, when he wrote them. So a good, friendly argument followed. Ten minutes later, Clive showed his appreciation.

"It's great that over here people from different disciplines come together and talk. We don't have enough of that in the States. Mind you, there are some here who talk as if they know everything, for example Dr Harman."

---

27 A reference to the 1976 Olympic Games.
28 The ship is displayed as it was refitted for successful commercial operation, as a 'steam clipper' using sails much of the time.

"You had a good dose of him tonight, Pete, but you started him off," Nick chuckled.

"I suppose I did, yes. After my grilling by the Business Club, I wanted to relax."

"Clive has a picture of James laughing. That's quite remarkable. James is far too fond of himself to laugh. It's also remarkable that the picture includes Paul Milverton. The only other time I can remember James laughing was at Paul's expense. Remember the joke you thought up about Macavity, Pete?"

It took me a moment to recall this incident.[29] Telling Clive of its context took us to how no-one was interested any longer in student power or radical action. "No doubt its time will come again," I concluded. "But, Clive, how on earth do you have a picture of Paul and James?"

"It was four years ago in the summer. I'd finished my sophomore year at Chicago and had a year's break scheduled for the Olympics. Meanwhile, I'd won an essay competition funded by New Hampshire Realty Bank. That got me to a conference they were running on the world in the '80s – three days in New York, all paid. There were some pretty good speakers, and James Harman. People were having a laugh at him when he was out of sight. The last evening, there was a drinks gathering with New Hampshire staffers. It was actually a local lady who cracked the joke that had gotten him laughing. I was just too far off to hear it but joined the group as a photographer took a shot. What was her name? She said she wasn't like the President. Coolidge, Steph Coolidge, that's it. I fell to talking with her and with another staffer, who was Paul Milverton. It turned out that he'd been here, and the lady had met Harman during a visit. Paul and I eventually got away from Harman and had some talk about Cambridge colleges. I was already interested in coming over to do a PhD and that prompted me to apply here."

---

29 See *Road to Nowhere*, Chapter 11.

"Nick, you'll remember Steph. She was my guest that evening lots of us were here, just after the first 1974 election. From later that year, Paul was posted to New York. Next time I speak to Steph, I'll ask what she said to make James laugh."

"Huh, it's a small world," said Clive. "Come round and look at the photo if you want, Pete. I'm in College, as Captain – C2 Cobden."

"First, I must take my call. I'll be round in twenty minutes."

"Work never stops, eh Pete?" remarked Nick. "Do you regret the quiet life here?"

"It wasn't that quiet for me."

I went back to my room and soon afterwards the phone rang. There was more clanking and clattering before Jane was through.

"They comes in at seven, turns the place over a bit, but thanks ter yer, Pete, we woz clean. Oi kept calm. Yer doing yer job, I know, I'm doing mine. There woz a coupla press with 'em, hacked off no story. Theys wot tipped 'em orf won't be poplar. They woz gorne by eight and we were tidied up by half eight. Clients took it; good evening since then. Now, how didz yer know?"

"The woman was up to no good down here, too. It looks as if there's a plan to discredit me through people I know. I'm sorry, Jane."

"It's not fer yer to be sorry. Sounds like yer needs cheering up."

A few minutes later I was viewing the photo, in its rather gaudy mount which commemorated the conference. It showed Steph enjoying the effect of what she had said, James Harman recovering from laughing and Paul looking his usual rather disinterested self. Clive, and also a man with a distinctive beard, seemed pleased to be in the group.

"I'm glad I have this back," said Clive. "I lent it to someone recently. In the summer, Harman got into *Varsity*[30] by saying

---

[30] The Cambridge University student newspaper.

that students were spending too much time on rowing. At the Bump Supper[31], we had a little sketch making fun of him. Someone said that at least he'd made us laugh, though he never laughed himself. Wrong, I said. I've evidence to the contrary. I was made to go get it and pass it around. Then a month back a guy wrote to me who'd been there as a guest. We invite one or two past members each year. This guy had quite a reputation from years ago. He'd been in a boat which made an overbump in the First Division but he couldn't be at the Supper that year because officially he'd been sent away following some punch-up. Eventually the overbump was disallowed, in fact."

"Yes, I remember that very well. I was on the bank. It was just before I left here."

"He'd known Harman and wanted to make a copy of the photo. He asked if I could lend it him for a few days, and enclosed a cheque for post and packing. So I sent it, and a week later he sent it back. You look thoughtful, Pete."

We talked for a little longer, whilst I tried not to seem too distracted. A huge chunk of the picture had fallen into place.

Fred Perkins would have noticed that Paul was in the photo. Although he had had only a fleeting and distracted glance of Steph dressed, he must have recalled her face vividly enough to be reminded of the woman in the photo. He sent for it, to check. He would have concluded that Paul had somehow found out about the bogus clinic and had put Steph up to wrecking it, presumably as revenge for being attacked by Fred those years ago. Any initial suspicion of Liz would have been overtaken.

So, he and Melissa had organised revenge on Steph, and Paul through her. In the New Hampshire Accounts, they had spotted Steph's holding in 'Plain Jane's'. Perhaps Fred had found out more about it from a medical contact in Aberdeen. He would

---

[31] This is the traditional drunken celebration on the Saturday evening at the end of inter-college boat races

have access to drugs. He would have no inkling that Liz or I knew Steph, or that I was involved in 'Plain Jane's'.

Fred and Melissa must also have thought that helping Consolidated Electrics would cause trouble for New Hampshire and thereby hit Steph and Paul. That had led to the business at the Pankhurst Centre. There was no reason for people at Consolidated to have told Fred that Morag knew me, and Morag didn't think that he had recognised her today. Nor was there any reason for people at Consolidated to have known about the attempt on 'Plain Jane's'.

Back in my room I wondered whether to call Steph but decided that there was no point. There was no way that Fred could get at her further. Cambridge didn't have direct international dialling then. It would be rather much to ask the duty porter to organise a transatlantic call at this time, and at seven o'clock on a Saturday in New York she was probably out. I would call her from Leeds.

Nor could I see any value in warning Paul straight away. Much was not clear, for example what Fred might have been doing in London before he came along to the match, but one thing was clear: I was not the target.

6. SUNDAY, 2ND DECEMBER, 1979

The phone woke me. I turned on the bedside light and looked at my watch. It was twenty-five past two. The duty porter put Liz through. Her tone woke me fully in an instant.

"Pete, oh Pete, you must help me. I'm at St Albans City Hospital. Greg is unconscious, hardly breathing. He went to bed early, still with a headache, and took the painkillers Fred had given him. He seemed to be sleeping peacefully when I went to bed. Soon after midnight, Jenny woke me. I settled her and then realised Greg was breathing very oddly. I kissed him, no response. I shook him gently, nothing. I called Fred. He got an ambulance quickly. We've been here an hour. Oh Pete, it's horrible. Why has this happened?"

"What can I do to help?"

"Bring Greg's parents down here as soon as possible. He's been X-rayed. There's an area of bleeding but it's probably stopped. They may operate to relieve the pressure on his brain. The doctor here says it's important for anyone in this state to have around them the people they love talking gently to them. That way the damaged brain responds and there's the best chance of recovery. The sooner Lorna and Timothy are here to help, the better. I know they'll want to be here but Lorna is full of arthritis. It's difficult for her to walk more than fifty yards and Timothy doesn't drive. It would take forever for them to get here by train on a Sunday."

"God, if only I had my car here… But I've an East Coast timetable in my wallet… Ah, a newspaper train has just left King's Cross. It leaves Huntingdon at 3.20 and is due into Leeds at 6.15. I'll get a taxi to Huntingdon. Give me their address and phone number, and the number of the hospital... Tell them I'll pick them up at 7.15. We ought to be with you by ten o'clock."

I called the duty porter. He would do his best to get a taxi. It was very urgent.

By a quarter to three I was at the Porters' Lodge, paying for my calls and scribbling a note to Len Goodman, apologising for no longer being able to have breakfast with him. A taxi was hoped for in five minutes.

At ten to three, there was no taxi. I was trying to keep calm.

Five to three... At two minutes to three the taxi arrived. Relax, what's the problem?

The Indian driver's confidence was borne out. The then A604[32] was a straight Roman road, with very little traffic in the middle of the night. Eighteen miles, including the built-up areas, in twenty minutes earned him a good tip. At 3.19 I was dashing onto the platform, waving my return ticket in case anyone was interested. They were just closing up one of the luggage vans. At 3.21 the train set off and I was stretching out, the only occupant of a first-class carriage.

As the train rumbled northward, punctuated by stops for unloading, I was reasonably successful in following Pat's strategy of switching off. All sorts of awful possibilities had flashed through my mind but my priority was to rest.

Whilst we were stopped at Newark, I recalled my conversation with Professor Kraftlein. More ideas about automorphisms and trading flashed into my mind. I took a pad of paper out of my overnight bag and jotted them down. They were probably nonsense but I could look at them later.

I drifted off to sleep and did not wake until we were in Leeds station, ten minutes late.

Back at the flat I had just time to shower and change before pulling out my West Yorkshire street atlas and setting off for the

---

32 Now part of the A14 and much busier.

manse outside Garforth where the senior Woolleys lived. They were ready to go, though not before giving me a couple of hefty slices of toast and a steaming mug of coffee. Liz had telephoned them at 5.30. There was no real change in Greg since her call to me but they weren't operating for now. Timothy had found a retired colleague to take Advent Sunday communion and a lay preacher for his other services.

I went for the A1 as a slightly shorter distance than the M1 and less likely to lead to encounters with police cars. Fortunately the morning was dry and clear, and my car well run-in by now and fuelled up. With little to delay us, by 9.35 we were on the outskirts of St Albans – 180 miles in 130 minutes.

"We're so grateful, Pete, and what a lovely car you have. But now I wonder what we shall find," said Lorna.

"I'm sure that Greg is having the best care possible and now it will include both of you being here."

"If only he'd had that care from the start; but I'm sure everyone acted for the best. We can only pray," said Timothy.

They did so in silence, whilst I followed signs to the hospital. By a quarter to ten, I was helping Lorna along the bleak corridors to the casualty ward. Greg was in a room off this, connected to various bits of gear on which I couldn't fail to notice the IE logo. He was breathing slowly. Liz was sitting beside him, white-faced as she greeted us.

"Oh Greg, here are your mother and father. Pete has brought them down here."

Further prayers and conversation followed, with no effect on Greg either visibly or on screen, where his heartbeat was for all to see. The door of the room opened. A cheerful West Indian nurse lifted little Jenny onto Liz's lap.

"Here you are, Jenny darling, back to your mummy and daddy; ooh and lots of new people."

"Thanks so much, Elspeth."

"No problem – it's a pleasure to be with such a lovely little girl. Greg, you must be very proud of her."

The room was now crowded and I was relieved when a few minutes later Liz suggested that we should take Jenny down to the canteen. There we found some cereal Jenny would eat, a play area and some fairly comfortable chairs. My arm round Liz was very welcome as she burst into tears. I knew what to do next. She cradled her head on my shoulder as I stroked her hair. Old memories came back to me, and perhaps to her – memories of an evening just before I left Cambridge when her happiness had been snatched away.

After a few minutes she sat up and lit a cigarette. That was discouraged but permitted then, and there were few people around us.

"Pete, I'm still wondering if this is some kind of nightmare. Shall I wake up soon and find Greg awake and cheerful, perhaps ready, beside me?"

"On the way here I was wondering that, too, but I'm afraid not."

"What makes it even more horrible is to wonder whether Fred *had* found out that we set Steph onto him. Perhaps he let this happen, for revenge."

"I can't believe that at all, Liz, and nor must you. Yesterday, Fred made sure to be there despite something else that had cropped up, and seemed genuinely pleased to meet me. I'm sure he did his best. You said yourself that he's an experienced doctor and well respected here."

"He was friendly and supportive on the journey back from Cambridge, though he seemed to be thinking about something else. He was clearly very shocked when I called him. He was here by the time we arrived and must have helped to stop any waiting around. But I noticed a hospital doctor looking at him pretty grimly."

"Anyone faced with this kind of emergency in the middle of the night would look pretty grim."

Jenny rushed up, crying.

"Oh, my little sweet, you're so tired," said Liz. "Tell you what. I'll say to Granny and Grandad that I'm asking Uncle Pete to take us home. Then you can go to bed and come back later to see Daddy."

Liz left me to keep an eye on Jenny. A moment later, a middle-aged man, in a suit rather than a white coat, approached me.

"You're a friend of Mrs Woolley's, I think? Haven't I seen your picture in the papers recently?"

"Yes, I'm Peter Bridford, of International Electronics. It's good to see some of our gear in use to help Greg."

"It's the best. I'm told you brought Mr Woolley's parents down, after finding your way up to Yorkshire by train. That's a very great help. You must be tired now."

"I am a bit but I'm used to crises. How is he doing?"

"Not well, I'm afraid. I'm Roy Brampton, consultant neurologist. I've come in to review the case. There's no sign of a real response to voices, so there's some damage, as if he's had a bad stroke. He's stable though, and it's not over, not over by any means."

"It's good that you and everyone else here are doing so much for Greg."

"That's what we're here for; but it brings me to something I want to say, in confidence, just between ourselves."

"Go on. I'm used to that, too."

"There will be questions asked about why he wasn't taken to hospital as soon as he took the blow."

"I was watching when he took it. He was very keen to get back in for the last few minutes. In that time he scored the winning goal. He was the Man of the Match."

"Even if he'd been taken to hospital as soon as the match had finished, it might well have been different. Can you note down as much as you can remember of what happened before he came here? You're not too directly involved so you can probably put it down objectively. That's going to be needed."

"I'll do that, but I left soon after the end of the match."

"Are there other spectators who could know more?"

"Perhaps there are. I expect I'll be making some calls to tell people what's happened. I'll gather what I can, without referring to your interest."

We exchanged contact details. Liz reappeared, and Brampton introduced himself to her with a slightly more hopeful line than he had given me. She looked a little better as she responded.

"Thank you so much for coming in. Pete is taking us home now but I'll be back in about half an hour."

I said nothing more as I drove to their home cautiously, for Liz was sitting in the back with Jenny on her lap. That was legal then, if not very advisable. Liz put Jenny to bed and showed me where to find materials for lunch and other essentials.

"I'm ready to look after Jenny all day if that helps, Liz. In fact, I've brought my Cambridge overnight bag with a clean shirt. Tomorrow morning I've no meetings so I could stay over and drive back up then – if that's convenient, of course. I would rather drive back when I'm fresh than tackle the drive later today."

"Great if you could, Pete. It shows the advantages of our house having four bedrooms. Lorna and Timothy clearly want to be at the hospital today. Though tomorrow and as long as they stay, they can take turns to look after Jenny. I've everything for a beef casserole. We were going to have it twice so there's enough for four. You can cook it."

"Do you want me to phone anyone?"

"Earlier on, I called the Minister at church. I expect they prayed for Greg. There's no point in anyone rushing over to visit today. I'll find out what they think best at the hospital and I'll call you with the latest news. Then if you can call people up that would help a lot. We should let some people at the club know –

these two from the team and also the Secretary, who will need to tell the club we were playing yesterday. Not that anyone there is to blame, of course. Here are their numbers. Keep Morag and Brian in touch. They both rang last night, soon after you did. And here's the home number of Greg's boss at work."

Liz drove off back to the hospital, looking almost happy. As so often happens during crises, talk of mundane arrangements had made everything seem slightly less horrible to her.

Over coffee I had much to think about. To distract, I pulled out the jottings I had made on the train. They *did* make sense. Still in my bag were my own paper of 1970 and a few other key papers I had brought along for the discussion with Kraftlein. I started to fit things together. After an hour I had three pages of notes, which amounted to the skeleton of the way the concepts of my earlier work might translate into commodity trading systems. I also had many questions for myself.

Might someone else have had the same ideas? Morag, Sheila or her student would surely have spotted anything that had been published, and Kraftlein was evidently still in touch with what was happening, but others might hold back for the same reasons as we might hold back. We needed to get on with developing my work.

I could see why Morag had said that to take this forward someone of my standard was needed; or rather, someone of the standard I had been at in 1968. Could insights gained through working in business make up for the decline in my mathematical acuity and knowledge? Was it remotely realistic to try to develop my work myself, whilst doing a very demanding full-time job? I would need to start by going through journals to bring myself fully up to date. When on earth could I do that? But if I didn't do it, who would?

I now knew more about my full-time job. It was quite different from anything I had done before. It was certainly demanding, and responsible. How much time did it actually need? I thought that I should spend more time than Nigel had done on developing Instrumentation Division for the future, and on looking out for wider markets. Perhaps through good use of my support office I need not spend as much time as Nigel had done on the day-to-day aspects, but I had to keep a close enough eye on issues which seemed routine, even boring, so as to spot potentially damaging mistakes in good time. Nigel had done that, whilst Henry Milsom had not done that. Furthermore, some of the day-to-day work involved public and staff relations. Friday evening's leaving presentation was an example. Such work could not be skimped or overly delegated, even if it seemed to be rather trivial. In the past, Pat had encouraged a rather casual approach to it and that had not promoted good industrial relations.

If I wanted to reach the top in IE, or in any merged company, my job there was my priority, and would definitely be full-time. Yet I was beginning to ask myself, *what kind of work do I actually want to do?*

A wail brought me back to earth. I plucked Jenny out of bed and headed for the toilet but she didn't quite make it. Then the doorbell rang.

At the door was a tall, well-built woman with dark brown hair. There was something in her eyes that demanded attention at once. I had no doubt who she was, even before she introduced herself over Jenny's cries.

"I'm Melissa Copehurst, the practice nurse. I was going to the hospital to talk to Mrs Woolley about what I can do to help. I've called here first because it's on my way."

"Do come in for a moment. I'm Pete Bridford, a friend of the Woolleys. I'm trying to look after Jenny and I'm not doing well."

That snapped her into action. In a very short time the mess was cleared up and Jenny was changed and happy. Then we found her some lunch and set her to play. Suddenly, the nurse seemed in no hurry to leave and frankly I was in no hurry for her to leave.

"I'm just going to make myself a sandwich. I'm sure Liz would like you to have something to eat, too. She'll call when there's some more news about Greg. Maybe you could speak to her then."

"I must talk to Liz, face to face. I'd better tell you, Pete. I heard about you from Fred. He said he'd been pleased to meet you again. That was last night; the last time I spoke to him face to face, the last time I'll *ever* speak to him face to face. He called me very early this morning. He knew he'd made a frightful mistake by not getting Greg into hospital straight away. Even if he wasn't struck off, he wouldn't be able to continue as a doctor. He reminded me that his mother is a doctor and that his family were so proud of him. Now what could he do? We talked for a while and I thought I'd calmed him down. I said I would go round after breakfast. When I did, I rang the bell but there was no reply. I have a key because we were close friends – never more than that but very close. We used to say that we were almost like the brother and sister neither of us had, as we were both only children. I went in. He was sitting in an armchair, seemingly asleep, but *he was dead*. He'd known what to take. There was plenty in the bag he kept at home for callouts. The police are there now. There's no note. I wanted to tell Liz before she found out another way, and to give her the apology that Fred can't give now."

She was obviously strained, though calm. I stood up, hardly thinking, and was about to put a comforting hand on her shoulder when the phone rang in the hall.

It was Liz. Roy Brampton had just spoken to her again. His report was little different from what he had told me before, though doubtless supported by more tests and observations. I gave some news.

"I've realised that we didn't move the child seat from your car so I can't bring Jenny over on my own. And Melissa Copehurst is here. She's being a great help in looking after Jenny. She wants to talk to you about what more she can do."

"I'll come over in an hour. You'll keep an eye?"
"Yes."

I made sandwiches and we were able to eat them quietly whilst Jenny amused herself with toys. After a few minutes I noticed how Melissa was looking at me with just the penetrating and persuasive eyes that Liz had described. She noticed that I noticed, and maybe her face was less strained.

"You have an interesting face, Pete. Would you mind if I sketched you? It would help me to work on something while I wait."

"Not at all, Melissa. Liz has shown me some of your work. It's really very good."

There was a vestige of a smile on her face as she took in that I wasn't just referring to the family group on the wall. She took a small pad and pencils out of her handbag, had me turn to catch the light better, and set to work. Her eyes seemed to be looking into me even more. I wondered how long it would have been in normal circumstances and warmer weather before she persuaded me to undress.

I had already been excited to imagine how Melissa sketched people, and had thought of her as a fascinating if dangerous woman to meet, but I had not expected that I would ever meet her. Now, I had met her.

It was clear why she was calm. She thought that no blame for what had happened could attach to her. Nobody would ever know what she and Fred had got up to some nights or, probably more accurately, what she had got up to with Fred some nights. She would have removed from Fred's house anything that she did not want to be found. Also, nobody would ever know exactly what had passed between Fred and her earlier that day, or the extent to which she had anticipated that Fred might take his own life and how hard she had actually tried to prevent him from doing so.

Unless I acted she could carry on unscathed. What might she do in the future? Should I prevent her from causing further harm?

Exposure of the bogus clinic would prevent harm by ending her career, but it would destroy Fred's posthumous reputation and with it an icon for generations of Waterhouse people. It would also cause upset to marriages whose infertility problems had been resolved in a way of which the husbands were unaware.

A wild idea was building on my previous imaginings of Melissa. If I came to know her well I could at least keep a watchful eye.

She was giving me signals. Her explanation for her visit sounded plausible enough but I wasn't convinced that it was real. She could have heard that I had brought Greg's parents here from Yorkshire. She could have guessed that the car outside was mine. But for Liz's call, her reference to the empathy of only children would have obtained an immediate response. It suggested that she knew something about me.

I could respond effectively but cautiously. Melissa would want to get away from here. There was a vacancy for a nurse in the practice in Leeds with which I was registered. I could suggest that she applied. Liz would understand. Morag, Sheila, Steph and Jane need not know, at least for a while. Once Melissa was up there, it would be quite natural and friendly for me to take her out. Then we could see what happened.

I felt some physical desire. She was sitting opposite me, with her legs crossed within a fairly short skirt, and was now looking quite relaxed as she completed her sketch. I could visualise her super body writhing with pleasure as Jane gave her 'the works'. Jane had taught me enough that I knew I could find genuine pleasure myself through pleasuring Melissa.

But I also felt something much more important. Evidently, Melissa was an extraordinary woman, in mind as well as in body. As Steph had said, she was possessed of a will to power. She had physical courage and grit, as evidenced by her being back at work while Fred was still off sick. She had intellect and ruthlessness. She could work out a plan, drive herself very hard to achieve it and ensure that others played their part.

The bogus clinic had allowed her to enjoy vicarious conquest. She could watch straight women strip, then use her hands on them, and finally pleasure herself to the sight of Fred taking them. She had not screamed when Steph had grabbed and kicked but her face had shown what she had wanted to do in response to being hurt and to her scheme being wrecked. Fred had spotted Steph with Paul in the conference photograph; but Melissa would have driven on plans for revenge, when Fred might have wanted just to forget the whole matter. Within the space of less than twenty-four hours, she had taken the main part of the business at the Pankhurst Centre and the whole of the action in Aberdeen. She had used her stage skills as the victimised wife and had ensured that Fred acted the errant husband. She had created no suspicion in Jane's watchful mind.

Belinda Wingham had identified intellect and ruthlessness as qualities in me and I had pointed out that Jenny had them, too. Indeed, most Creators had them, each in their own way, and mutual appreciation of that held us together. In another phrase of Steph's, we were as smart and as bad as each other. It could be said that we had a will to power – in the sense originated by Nietzsche in the 1880s, rather than as perverted in Nazi Germany.

Perhaps Melissa could be a Creator.

After fifteen minutes she had completed a very presentable sketch, and suggested that she try a different profile. I suggested a short break for me to make some calls and left the sitting room door open while I made these and she played with Jenny. Ten minutes later I was back with news.

"A couple of the people from the club know about the police at Fred's house. As we agreed, I didn't say anything about you being here, Melissa."

"Thanks, Pete. Oh, *well done*, Jenny. You are a clever girl, getting all the shapes through the right holes."

"Mummy... Daddy."

"Mummy will be back soon. Daddy isn't well but he's being cared for... One of the other people you called sounded quite angry."

"I think he was very surprised and shocked, as we all are. He was at the match yesterday."

I would be calling Brian again. I had left Morag until later. I settled down in a new pose and read Jenny a 'Little Spot' book whilst Melissa worked on. However, I was continuing to think, and this time about Fred.

As far as Liz and I knew, there had never been a repetition of his brutal behaviour at Cambridge. He had learnt to control himself. But then he had met Melissa, and became her mental prisoner, performing to her orders whether he liked it or not. He could well have regarded attending away matches as a break from captivity. He had clearly been determined to be at the match in Cambridge, but his worried and distracted behaviour showed that he hadn't escaped in mind. Greg's clear determination to play on and win the game had been persuasive but Fred could have insisted on precautionary checks immediately afterwards. Instead, he had decided to avoid being delayed, for if Melissa had been kept waiting at the airport, the consequences for him would doubtless have been unpleasant. The even more unpleasant consequences of his decision had been too much for him.

I had thought of Melissa's persuasive powers as like those of Jenny. But I could now see that her hold over Fred had been quite different from the relationship between Jenny and Amanda. Amanda was not Jenny's mental prisoner. Both of them had benefitted from their relationship, as had John and probably Dick too. That was why I had suggested to Belinda that Jenny could now go further with Amanda.

Nor was Melissa's version of will to power the same as what most Creators had in common. That was better described as the desire to achieve and make a difference. Long ago, Liz had said that was what drove people on. It had certainly driven her on.

If I didn't expose Melissa, it was very possible that she would take another mental prisoner. It was vain of me to pretend that I could prevent that. All I could do was minimise the possible consequences. Suddenly, I realised that I could begin exactly as I had been considering a few minutes before.

"What are you going to do now, Melissa?"

"I don't know, Pete. I don't want to stay here."

She put her pencil down and buried her head in her hands for a moment. It was very convincing, and confirmed what she was hoping I would say next. But I continued differently, though quite truthfully.

"Liz has told me how good you are on the stage. As it happens, several people I know have also seen you act."

"Goodness, you must know lots of people."

"You've been in lots of productions over the years and people remember you. Have you ever thought of going professional?"

"I'd really like to try, but how could I find the money to spend two years at drama school?"

"If all your sketches are as good as those I've seen, you could make a useful income from them. How many can you do in a session?"

"Oh, in three hours, perhaps six like those you've seen."

"I reckon you could sell them for £10 each or even £15. If you were at drama school, I'm sure you would meet plenty of suitable models. Liz told me you were good at persuading people to pose. To look at the economics, though, let's suppose you used a professional model. How much would that cost?"

"They charge £8 to £10 for a three-hour session, including expenses."

"For the Rodin or similar you would need two so, allowing something for materials and heating, your total costs could be £25. I assume you don't need a studio."

"No, there are lots of places where I can find the light."

"In principle, your six sketches could be sold for £60 to £90. But you won't always sell six sketches, and if you sell through a shop they'll want a big cut, so assume your average session revenue is £40. That gives a profit of £15 a session. You would earn £60 a week from four sessions, which you could fit round your training. If you're persuasive in obtaining models and produce sketches which buyers find particularly attractive, you might earn more."

"You're able to work these things out very quickly, Pete."

"Apart from my main job with International Electronics, I'm involved in two small businesses. I need to do this kind of financial analysis all the time. You need to go through it carefully and decide whether it would work out in the light of what fees you would be paying."

"I'll do that. Can I call you when I've thought about it more?"

"Of course you can, Melissa. I think you're worth a fresh start. You need to put this awful business right behind you. Here's my home number. Also, here's the number of a friend of mine, Angela Frampton. Have you heard of her?"

"I've seen her name in an art magazine I read. She looks to be quite successful."

"Not many years ago she was not far from where you are now. She does ceramics, not sketches, but she's learnt a lot about selling stuff into shops. She knows Liz, and I'll be calling her about what's happened. I'll tell her you would like her advice. Call her in a week or so."

"That's really good of you, Pete."

"You'd better finish your sketch."

Melissa worked on, and I reflected that her actions over the last two days amounted to a very full demonstration of her ability to succeed on the professional stage. But now there was something in her face that showed genuine relief at the prospect of being helped to set out on a new path.

It was time for me to consider the consequences of *my* actions. My thoughts moved to what that meant for me and began to tie in with what I had been thinking about earlier.

Two months before, I had discussed with Liz my plan for dealing with the bogus clinic. She had commented that one of these days I was going to come up against something I couldn't sort out. Precisely that had now happened. My plan had led to Greg's present state and to Fred's death. I needed to react accordingly, though only *I* knew the full story, and it could stay that way.

Liz knew that at the match Fred had been worried and distracted, and might conclude that his error arose from that, but she would see no link between Fred's state and what had happened when Steph had carried out my plan.

Nor need Steph be disturbed by being made aware of any link. There was no need for her to know that Fred had recognised her from the conference photo, or of events in Aberdeen. I could suggest that the stress of being Melissa's mental prisoner had led to Fred's error.

If Morag continued to believe that Fred was involved in the business at the Pankhurst Centre, she might assume that his distraction and error arose from that. If necessary, I could suggest that he must have known someone at Consolidated.

I could tell Jane that the attempt to incriminate her was part of some plot by Consolidated to do me down, but I could say confidently that there would be no more trouble.

I heard Liz pull up in the drive, and went to the door.

"I've heard about Fred, but I won't say," she murmured. There followed a scene of polite mutual sorrow, sympathy and dissimulation.

After ten minutes, Melissa made to go. "Fred's parents will be arriving soon. I must be there. Liz, if there is anything I can do to help, please let me know."

"That's so kind of you, Melissa. I think Greg's parents will be staying here for a few days so I'll be all right for the moment. Thank you so much, too, for what you said about Fred. I know how difficult it was for you to say it. We shall both have to carry on as best we can."

Melissa departed, leaving me with my choice of sketch. Jenny had some tender motherly care and, still tired, was put into bed for 'a short rest before we go to see Daddy again'.

Then Liz's restraint broke down. For ten minutes she sobbed in my arms. Mine were the first words, spoken after I had kissed her.

"I'm sorry, I shouldn't have done that."

"Yes you should have, Pete. You're doing everything a brother should do. You're making me feel there's someone I can rely on to care."

"You're still the sister I never had. I owe you a lot."

She unbuttoned her shirt. "Keep it up. Use your hands on my belly the way you've done so well before."

She lay across me and I found the spots where muscles were so tensed up. After a few minutes of gentle rubbing and kneading, they relaxed a bit. She sat up and managed an appreciative grin as she lit a cigarette and suggested a cup of tea before she took Jenny back to the hospital. That made, she continued.

"I've more to tell you. Just before I left, Roy Brampton asked for another word. To begin with, he told me about Fred and gave the impression that Fred had done the decent thing for the profession. He'll talk to Fred's parents. There won't be any investigation now, so there's no longer any need for you to get back to him."

"Won't there have to be an inquest?"

"Yes, but he says that it can be kept very low key. He expected that I would want to concentrate on what happens now."

"I guess that depends on what does happen now."

"He went on to that. Greg is stable and could be stable for days, weeks, months or even years. He could eventually go down. But equally he could recover and wake up, quite suddenly. Cases of that are known. So I mustn't lose hope, not at all. But he can't stay in the City Hospital for long. It's a hospital for acute cases and emergencies. If there's no change by late in the week, he will be moved to a hospital specialising in the long-term care of people with strokes and brain damage."

"Where would that be?"

"Normally somewhere not that far away but, and he wanted me to think about this, the best place he knows is round the other side of London, near Coulsdon in Surrey. That's not because it looks any better or has better gear than other places but because the staff are motivated and don't see it just as a dumping ground for hopeless cases. The lead consultant is an old friend of his and he's sure he could fix it. That's the best option for Greg, provided we visit him frequently and keep the unconscious stimulus going. But to get there from here, with Jenny, would be a frightful journey." [33]

"I see what you mean. Would you, and others from here, be able to keep it up? I've one idea, though. Coulsdon is only a few miles from Bellinghame, where Roberta and Frank still live in the bungalow you visited on the day Carol was elected. I'm sure that they would be prepared to put you both up sometimes so that you could make visits over two or three days without travelling back and forth. In fact, I think they would be ready to do some visiting themselves, and to be a splendid pair of surrogate, caring grandparents for Jenny. Also, some of our friends, for example Susie and Brian, could visit Coulsdon more easily than they could come over here. If Greg stayed near here, how many local people know him well enough that they would go on making the effort to visit?"

"Not that many. Of course, we know people at the club but otherwise it's not turned out as well around here as we

---

[33] The through route via the M25 was not completed until 1985 and Thameslink through rail services did not begin until 1988. In those days every suburb was separate.

had hoped. Perhaps that's because the local Baptist church is pretty hopeless, and we've gone on driving up to where we were married, in Hendon. At least there you usually get a sermon that means something. When I stopped working I expected to meet more mothers, but somehow I haven't. It's my fault, I suppose. I'm not that interested in talking about babies all the time. If Greg doesn't recover soon, and I guess that's what Roy Brampton was telling me, I would rather make a fresh start somewhere else, before Jenny goes to nursery. That way, I wouldn't have people continually asking after him but not doing anything helpful."

"Houses at Bishop's Park must be coming onto the market all the time. They're mostly not as big as here but they're not bad. Certainly Frank hasn't regretted selling his place and moving in with Roberta. It leaves them with no money worries."

"I'll have plenty of money worries. Though we sold Greg's place in Leeds as well as my flat, we stretched ourselves to come here on Greg's salary. That will go on for six months, then it will halve, and after another six months it will stop. I'll have to find a part-time job. God, *he* said call him if ever I needed to."

"You needn't rush into that, Liz, but it looks to me as if Roy Brampton has made you a suggestion that's worth accepting."

"You mean, he's offered a deal. I make no fuss and he looks after us."

"I suppose that's right. By the way, have you contacted your father?"

"You must be joking. What use would he be? Anyway, he's in Australia at the moment."

There was a little whimper from upstairs.

"It sounds like time for you to get Jenny up and go along to the hospital."

"It's *so* good having you here, Pete." Liz gave me a hug and quite a long kiss.

"I can put the casserole into the oven in half an hour or so, so it's ready at about half past seven."

"That's good. They want to keep up the idea of day and night for Greg, so we'll be back here by half past six. I think Jenny can last until then. Once she's in bed, the rest of us can eat – and drink. Lorna and Timothy don't drink often but they'll have a glass or two."

"How long are they staying?"

"They can stay the whole week but they need to be back in Garforth by lunchtime on Saturday. Timothy did well to find substitutes for today but as a result he has three services next Sunday."

"I can take Friday off. I'll drive down early. If Greg were moved by then, I could take you all over to Coulsdon. I know my way around south London. Maybe we could call in on Roberta and Frank for a cup of tea. Then I could take Lorna and Timothy home on Saturday morning. I need to be in Leeds on Saturday evening."

"You can do all this? You're so busy, Pete."

"I can't always work flat out, and I don't need to. Give me a key. Once the casserole is in I may go out but I'll be back by seven o'clock."

After Liz and Jenny had left, I collected my thoughts for a few minutes whilst preparing the casserole. It was clear that today my life was changed but it was not at all clear how things would develop. Eventually I decided that most possibilities sent me the same way. So I called Pat O'Donnell at home.

"Pat, I'm sorry to bother you on a Sunday."

"If you bother me on a Sunday, Pete, I know it's important. Where are you? Phil was trying to call you. The Waterhouse College porters said you'd gone back to Leeds in the middle of the night. But you weren't there earlier today."

"I'm near St Albans now. I want to come and see you for a few minutes."

"Come along in an hour. Call Phil first. It's not urgent anymore but he was worried."

"What's happened?"

"It was pretty odd. Early today, Phil had calls, first from the *Clarion* and then from other papers. They were asking what we thought of the idea that Don Flitton might eventually become the Chief Executive of a merged company. How might we all work with him? It did cross my mind that you'd been up to something."

"I hadn't."

"I believe you because Phil had a tip-off that a big story was to break about Don. They were all fishing to see if we knew anything about it."

"We don't."

"Once that was clear, they lost interest in us. Phil did find out that this wasn't being stirred up by Consolidated's press people. Luke Allnutt was pushing it. So there's the hand of Roy Delaval, I guess. An hour ago, Phil called me to say the story has folded. That's a good thing. Don has had a rough time in his life. Perhaps he has a good lawyer. It's certainly good for us if Roy has over-reached himself."

I touched base with Phil, and put the casserole into the oven. Next, I gave an update to Brian, who didn't bother to show any sympathy for Fred. More important was my call to Morag. She was still clear that she had recognised Fred, but she accepted my explanation of what had then happened and was relieved that nothing more was likely to be heard of Linda Flitton's letter, provided we kept the story to ourselves.

Twenty minutes took me down the M1 to Pat's house. It didn't take long to say what I had to say.

"Pat, I want you to know first because I owe you so much. I assume that my job will be advertised sometime in the New Year. I won't apply. Of course I'll carry on until whoever takes the job is available, and I'll help them in. I hope that I can leave, in a sensible way, by April or May."

Pat was silent for several seconds and then took a long pull of his whiskey.

"What are your reasons, Pete? I hope there's nothing wrong with you and that there's nothing I've missed that's wrong in IE."

"No, there's nothing wrong with me or in IE. There are four reasons. First, you know about the software company I'm in, with Paul Milverton, Jenny Sinclair and others. It's now clear to me that this could turn into something big and I'm the man to lead it there. I have a lot of experience and reputation in market development. My name should raise capital."

"So that's the public reason. What are the other three reasons?"

"The second reason is an extension of the first but is private. The reason the software company could turn into something big is that some of the maths I did in Cambridge can be applied to probabilistic analysis of commodity trading and can form the basis of very marketable software for the kinds of computers that will be in traders' offices in a few years' time. The quickest way to deliver the software involves my having a few quiet months to work out the theory and to talk privately about it with Professor Kraftlein. Yesterday, we signed him up as a consultant."

"Are the other reasons more personal? You don't need to tell me them if you don't want to."

"The third reason is both personal and business. I think an equal terms merger with Consolidated is the right way ahead for IE but I don't think that I would do my best in the merged company. All my big contributions to IE have been about getting something new going rather than running an established operation. I began the moves towards better working arrangements at Sunderland. Then I developed new markets, in Spain and the North Sea. Most recently, the rights issue has been a new challenge. You've given me all these opportunities."

"And you've taken them, Pete, along with others presented to you, such as happened when you and young Ana overheard said Kraftlein. That's all been to the immense benefit of IE."

"Yes, but none of them have involved running the kind of big operation I'm running now. It's only over the last three weeks that I've been doing just that. I'm already seeing that I can do it perfectly well, but it doesn't excite me very much. There's a risk that I'll become bored with it and lose concentration. That would take the edge off my performance. I've been promoted very young, so everyone inside and outside IE will be watching me very carefully. Anything short of brilliance will be regarded as failure."

"You're saying that you're not like Nigel, Pete. I know that, as I told you before. I wouldn't have promoted you if I'd had any doubts at all about your ability to run the Instrumentation Division."

"Run, yes. Do more than run, I'm not sure. The last three weeks have given me much more understanding of why Nigel worked the way he did. He left me excellent systems for running a big company organisation, but using them has shown me that I'm a new and growing company man, not a big company organisation man."

"That makes you rather like me, Pete. Frankly, my most satisfying days were before IE was called IE, when it was my company and was grabbing market share in the forefront of technology. I can smell new markets. I've always aimed to find good people to understand the technology and to look after the detail and chores."

"Perhaps I am like you, Pat. I've started out with far more advantages than you had but your approach has rubbed off."

"I meant it to. All those years ago, I could see that you were like me, not just from what I'd seen of you myself but from the way you kept turning up in Andrew Grover's diary. You had huge academic ability and you were a schemer but you applied both to a vision. That's where you have the edge on people like Milverton, and don't you forget that in your enterprises with him. Well, you've proved a good bet for IE.

You've amply justified my pushing you forward. We'll be very sorry to lose you but I understand what you say. What's your fourth reason?"

"That is more personal but it isn't private and you should know it. Yesterday the husband of a very close friend of mine was hit on the head when he was playing hockey. At the time he didn't seem to be seriously hurt but now he's unconscious in hospital and no-one has any idea whether he'll wake up. They live near St Albans, which is why I'm there today. So my friend, and her young daughter, will need a lot of support. I don't think I'll be spending many weekends in Leeds and I want to be living down here fairly soon."

"This isn't Jenny?"

"No. Actually, you met her on the same day as you first met me. You thought well of her, as I recall. Then, she was Liz Partington, the Master's daughter. Now, she's Liz Woolley."

"Yes, I remember her. You do take these things on yourself, Pete, but that's another part of your character. Look, if this is the real reason why you want to leave, I could agree that you're only in Leeds two or three days a week. You've already shown you can run Instrumentation Division well without being in the office."

"No, Pat, this personal issue has brought into focus the other reasons I've given. It's like what happened when I took up your offer and left Cambridge, but I'm not saying I'll walk out next week, as you had me do then. When the job is advertised, I guess it will be best to announce that I'm leaving to develop my own business interests. That will make for more good applications."

"Anyone applying won't know what the future is for IE but that shouldn't put them off if they've got something. Let me have some details of your company. I could put in some money of my own."

So the official story of why I was leaving IE would be part of the truth, just as the official story of why I had left Cambridge had been part of the truth. In 1974, I had told that story on TV.

As I drove back to Liz's house, I wondered if I would ever tell this further story on TV.

When I had called Pat, I had almost made my mind up about what to say to him. My conversation with Phil had removed any doubts by giving an explanation of Friday evening's events at the Pankhurst Centre. It was an explanation that sounded improbable but, as Sherlock Holmes said several times, eliminate other possibilities and whatever remains, however improbable, must be the truth.

Melissa and Fred would have seen Luke Allnutt's by-lines. They would have picked up the message that Roy Delaval favoured an aggressive stance. IE, and through them New Hampshire Realty, would have a rougher time if he were in charge at Consolidated. So they had contacted Roy, perhaps via Luke Allnutt, and asked what they could do to help him. Roy would have reacted according to what he knew, or rather what he knew he didn't know.

Nigel would have shown the Linda Flitton letter to Lord Cunliffe, who would be discussing it with Don Flitton and coming to an agreement about the future. Neither Nigel nor Lord Cunliffe would have shown the letter to Roy. They would know that nothing would suit Roy better than Don having to resign, for reasons unconnected with Consolidated and certainly unconnected with him.

However, Roy or Luke could well have picked up that there was something going on which involved a letter from Linda Flitton. They could well have known that she had used the Pankhurst Centre. So, the idea of the raid on the Centre had been born – Melissa's idea, though she would have had to leave contact with the *Clarion* to Fred, for tabloid journalism was then still very much a man's world. There had been no need to obtain the original of the letter. A copy passed to the *Clarion* would finish Don. Roy's hands would be clean when the story burst.

The story had not burst. That might be because Fred had never passed the letter to the *Clarion*, because Fred's suicide made the story unusable, or because Roy had realised that without Fred he would have to be overtly involved. I didn't know which reason was correct but that no longer mattered. I was certain that if Melissa still had the letter she would destroy it as part of moving on. Don Flitton would survive for the moment, and the path to an agreed merger of IE and Consolidated would be smoother. But I wasn't going to work alongside Roy Delaval – ever.

So today would be a day of fresh starts, for Melissa, for Liz and for me, though not for Fred.

I came in to find Timothy on the phone.

"Yes, it's been the most terrible shock for us all. We're going to have to trust in God and live with it as best we can. It's been a huge help that Liz's friend Pete was able to drive us down so quickly this morning. Ah, he's back here now... Yes, you can speak to him. Pete, it's Jenny Sinclair."

"Pete, I was calling Liz to invite them over before Christmas, but now – *this*. I just can't believe it."

"Nor can I, but it's happened."

"Fred Perkins – don't I remember his name?"

"He was the man who shouldn't have been in the winning Waterhouse boat."

"What an awful day for you all. Have you spoken to others?"

"So far, just Brian and Morag, who were at the match. I'll call Paul and Carol later."

"They've had a rough day, though nothing like yours. Half an hour ago, I called Carol. They were only just back from Yorkshire. They were delayed in setting off because all the morning she was a target for the press, particularly the *Clarion*. They had stories about the student riots she was in years ago. She managed to put the lid on and it all died down around lunchtime so hopefully there won't be any more problems for her. Now, when do you think I should come and see Greg?"

"His parents are here this week so it's best to leave it until next week. I'll be down again on Friday. I'll keep you in touch."

"Oh Pete, you're dashing up and down, on top of everything else you do."

"This, and some other things, will make a difference to me. Not to talk now, but I'll send a note round Creators Technology during the next few days. Paul probably told you that we signed up Kraftlein yesterday."

Carol's experience put more pieces into a picture that now seemed fairly complete, though there were still some puzzling points. At Cambridge, Carol had known a girl who was with Fred for some time. Therefore, Fred would have had some memory of Carol as a student activist. Research in newspaper files would have provided material to rake up, though the most potentially damaging story, of how I had rescued her from the police, had never emerged.

Fred's business in London on the Saturday morning was explained. He had delivered to Luke Allnutt a dossier on Carol. I still didn't know whether at the same time he had delivered the copy letter but that didn't matter anymore.

Paul kept a low profile. Melissa and Fred had not found a way to get at him directly. So, they had made three separate attacks, on New Hampshire Realty, Steph and Carol. All had failed in their actual objective but they had had an effect. They had focussed me onto the need to move again.

And after saying night-night to little Jenny, I needed to be on the move to preparing the vegetables. I poured myself a drink and set to.

PRINCIPAL NEW CHARACTERS IN 'THE TURNAROUND' BOOKS VII and VIII

NAME	AGE	DESCRIPTION
Ronald CLARKSON	45	Civil servant responsible for energy finance issues.
Howard LARKIN	41	From March 1981, successor to Martin Turner.
Ed PLUNKETT	35	Leader of a small team of civil servants dealing with coal industrial relations issues.
Jean SIMMONDS	28	Pete Bridford's civil service secretary.
Alan SMITHAM	53	Father of Brian. National Union of Mineworkers branch secretary.
Julian STREET	57	Senior civil servant whose responsibilities include coal and energy finance.
Martin TURNER	46	Civil servant, in January 1981 head of the directorate advising on coal policy.
John WILLIS	50	Director of Information – in charge of press and publicity on energy issues

BOOK VII
JACK-KNIFED

7. WEDNESDAY, 21ST JANUARY, 1981

I looked hard at Douglas Arnott as I spelt it out, again.

"The strategy of hiding behind the National Coal Board simply isn't going to work, for two reasons. First, when this hits, no-one will believe that the government can just stand aside. There'll be an expectation that you should do something. Second, the Board won't let you stand aside. Why on earth should it?"

Martin Turner, the head of the Coal Directorate, replied in his usual detached way.

"They have the statutory duty laid on them by the Coal Industry Act 1980 to break even by the financial year 1983/84 after social grants."

"They've had statutory duties under umpteen Acts. Most have been supposed to set a permanent framework for the future in terms of grants and so-called loans from the government. A few years later there's been another Act. Either it's added a zero to most of the limits on grants and loans or, if the resultant numbers are absurdly large, it's clocked the loans back to zero – written the money off, given a chance for a fresh start. Why do you think it will be different this time?"

"Ministers have made the importance of the financial targets very clear as part of their overall strategy for the nationalised industries," said Ronald Clarkson. He was in what was then called the 'Establishments Directorate', which dealt with both finance and personnel.

"I know they have," said Douglas. "But Pete has a point. If you were running the Coal Board, what would you want? More money from the government, of course. And how would you get it? Do little to stop the NUM from making a fuss. Let's ask ourselves why the Board wants to tell the unions that there has to be a national-level plan for closing uneconomic pits.[34] It's closed hundreds without one. There's an established procedure whereby the Board's Area Directors discuss the position with the unions locally. I'm told that what happens then depends on the circumstances. A pit will be making a big loss because it's difficult to get the coal out and so because working conditions are horrible and dangerous. The men will be crawling through seams three feet thick or less. If there's a way out for them, they will take it. Older men might take redundancy on the government-financed terms introduced by Labour in 1968. Younger men could move to a better pit, where older men take redundancy to make room for them. Why can't things continue in that way?"

Julian Street, the man at Douglas's level to whom the coal and finance people reported, joined in. "There isn't time, Douglas."

"There isn't time if you want to close all these pits within three months, Julian, but there is time to get most of them closed within a year, particularly if you improve the redundancy terms."

Martin was peering at us through his heavy spectacles, which reminded me of what Carol Milverton had worn when I had first met her. She had moved her appearance on, whilst Martin hadn't. Once again he came in, blandly.

"As you know, we're looking at that possibility but we're not ready to seek Treasury agreement to it."

---

34 'Pit' was the universally used colloquial term for a coal mine or colliery.

"I think we're ready enough, Martin," I said. "I know that the Board sent us detailed proposals only a week ago but since then your people have been going all out to put them into a form that could be cleared quickly. Though there's a lot of detail, the key point of the proposals is simple to understand. At present, any miner made redundant at over the age of fifty-five gets weekly payments amounting to half to two-thirds of their previous pay until they become eligible for their pension at age sixty. But the Board's staff, including deputies,[35] can usually get the same level of benefit from age fifty through their pension scheme. The government already meets the cost of that. The proposals are more or less to provide for miners what deputies already have."

"That makes them very expensive," said Ronald Clarkson. "It will be difficult to get the Treasury to agree. As Martin says, we'll need to prepare the case very carefully."

"The case doesn't depend on the detail. The cost of extracting coal from these pits is twice, or even three times, what it can be sold for. It would actually be cheaper to give their miners full pay to stay at home. Anything less than that is a bargain."

"We don't have information about the costs of these pits. That's for the Board," said Julian Street.

Richard Seymour, an economist, came in, having been uncharacteristically quiet.

"The financial figures the Board is now giving us don't make sense unless there are about fifty wildly uneconomic pits. Those I know in the Treasury would accept Pete's argument about the economics. The problem over there is with the policy people. They believe that the costs of redundancies should be met by the Board, as they are in a private company. There shouldn't be a separate government scheme. Also, they don't want more money to go into redundancy payments, and into the social grants which are mostly about the pensions costs Pete

---

35 First-line supervisors in coal mines.

describes, until we have proper financial controls agreed with the Board."

"The practical argument for a separate redundancy scheme is just that it is separate," I said. "If the Treasury agrees, we can get more men out without changing the Board's financial targets. We need to plug that point hard, and soon."

Martin looked unhappy but Douglas changed the subject before the argument became too heated.

"I've been looking at the briefing pack for today's debate. I'm struck by the way it advises slapping down any suggestion of a tripartite meeting of the government, the Coal Board and the mining unions."

"Foot and Benn will certainly suggest a meeting. They invented them," said Martin, with obvious distaste. "Ministers, and No. 10, are very clear that they don't want it. The Board can't want it either."

"It's clear what the Board wants. Ministers may not want a tripartite meeting but, supposing it's forced on them, do we have a Plan B, Julian?"

It was now Julian's turn to look unhappy because he had been in his present post right through the Labour Government; and it was the turn of John Willis, the Director of Information, to change the subject.

"Is there some substance in this plan to close fifty pits story that's in all the papers today, then? The Board is denying it, of course."

"It's not come from here," said Martin, with a sigh. "The only figure that's been suggested to me is about twenty-five to be proposed for closure during the next few months."

"So the Board's aiming for a sense of relief that it's only half as bad as expected. That's a dangerous game which hasn't been discussed with me or, it seems, with anyone else here. Bernard[36]

---

36 Bernard Ingham, Mrs Thatcher's press secretary, who had formerly worked in the department. On his role in these events, see Thatcher, *The Downing Street Years*, p. 140, and his own *Kill the Messenger*, p. 233.

called me about it at home, first thing. The only bit of relief is that the *Guardian* has shown its usual form."

John passed round a cutting of an article rumouring that the Coal Board was to close fifty pubs.[37] That prompted Douglas.

"Well, Julian, we'd better close on that. We all look like having a busy day. Indeed, we look like having a busy few weeks if, as Martin's note suggests, the Board plans a national-level discussion with the unions during the second week of February. I called this meeting because today's parliamentary debate is on energy policy, and so briefing for it falls to my side. It's now clear there will be plenty about coal and that's reflected in the briefing and arrangements for the Box.[38] I'd hoped that Ministers could say something about measures appropriate to the situation, for example improved redundancy terms, but now I know that's not on for today. Taking on arrangements with the Board is for you, of course. I'm ready for my people to support yours in any way that would be helpful during what looks to be a very tricky time. In particular, can Pete be kept in touch please?"

The meeting broke up and I was left with Douglas and the expostulations of an incandescent John Willis.

"Thanks, Douglas, for actually getting me into a meeting about this. They're sleepwalking. They don't realise what's going to happen and why. You hit it on the nail, Pete. We're being set up. If I can meet the Secretary of State on his own, I'll tell him that, and I might just talk to Bernard."

"The improvements in redundancy terms could have been sorted for announcement by now," I said. "Apparently, they were presented at a lunch Martin had with the Board before Christmas. He should have asked for details straight away. The Board didn't provide those until last week, which shows that they don't want

---

[37] In those days, the *Guardian* was known for its frequent misprints – hence *Private Eye*'s references to the *Grauniad*.
[38] The Officials' Box in the Commons Chamber, from which parliamentary private secretaries can collect extra briefing for their ministers on issues arising in the debate.

the unions calmed down quickly. Martin doesn't realise that but his staff do, which is why they're working all hours developing the case for improved terms. They're also trying to sort out the financial controls. There should be detailed agreements setting out what the Board can claim in grants. There won't be those agreements any time soon unless the legal team is told to give their drafting high priority."

"You've been talking to Martin's staff, then," said Douglas.

"Of course I have; not to take up their time but to understand what they're facing. They haven't been given any coherent priorities for action or the support they need."

"I hope Martin hasn't spotted you. He doesn't like his staff talking to people."

"Perhaps that explains why we're heading nowhere. If there's a big problem I'm used to people talking to each other and working out how to deal with it – fast. That's what happened in IE, it's what happens in my company, it's what I've seen happening in oil companies and certainly it's what happens in your teams, Douglas. So why isn't it happening now?"

"I'll call on Julian and say that. I'll also emphasise to him that you're needed on this. Keep stirring, Pete. You can't make it worse."

"I'll stay out of the way for the rest of today. Thanks for getting me a seat in the gallery for the debate. I'll be keeping my eyes and ears open."

I returned to my office, where Jean Simmonds, the secretary I shared with the Scientific Advisor, had stacked up an alluring pile of paper received during the morning. I focussed on the essentials to get through it. At half past twelve I left the department's offices on Millbank with only a few items in my briefcase, whilst Jean had plenty of memos and messages to put round during the rest of the day. In particular, I wanted another talk with Ed Plunkett, the man on Martin's staff who led on the redundancy terms issue. That should be the next morning, if he could spare the time, though not too early since he would be at the Houses of Parliament all the evening.

I had taken up Douglas Arnott's suggestion. After leaving IE at the end of April 1980, I became Industrial Advisor to his department, paid for one and a half days per week. A retirement had led to Douglas's responsibilities being extended to cover energy policy, and he found my help on that very welcome.

Years of government influence on the prices charged by the electricity and gas industries had left a muddle, which allowed many businesses to claim they were being charged much more than their rivals overseas, especially with the successful development of North Sea oil pushing the pound up 50% compared to three years before. I had made the point that the use of coal at the prices the National Coal Board charged was adding nearly £1 billion annually to the costs of generating electricity. That was on top of a subsidy to the coal industry of over £800 million through grants and 'borrowing' that would never be repaid. So the policies the government had inherited on coal were costing the public not far short of £2 billion annually.[39]

Initially I had kept out of direct involvement in the problems of coal, since my 'contacts' were considered a potential embarrassment in such a sensitive area. Then, on my first day in after Christmas, Douglas told me that the new Permanent Secretary had agreed that I should be involved, since my 'contacts' could be valuable. This decision was not universally popular but I could see that for a while I would be spending more than a day and a half per week on advisory duties.

I was at the Universal Assurance offices in good time for a board meeting of Creators Technology, of which I was now the Chief Executive. With the growth of the company, the meetings had settled into a cycle. Every two months, we spent the whole afternoon at the premises in Crawley where our staff, now up to ten, worked and I spent about two days a week. In other months,

---

39 I.e. some £7 billion in present-day money.

as now, we met briefly in London, usually over a sandwich lunch hosted by Brian Smitham.

Today's agenda, though short, was important. Just like the Coal Board, we needed more money. By one o'clock, Tony Higgins had called the meeting to order and I was setting out the problem.

"To remind ourselves of the three big pluses we have. First, I've cracked the maths to my, Sheila and Morag's satisfaction. I visited Stuttgart in November and worked through it with Kraftlein. He said that he would go over it carefully on his own. You've all seen the letter he sent me three weeks ago. He's satisfied that it's right. We have the theoretical basis for our trading algorithms. As far as we know no-one else has it, though there's nothing to stop anyone else from working it out. We can't patent it. Secondly, Tony's note suggests that, by the end of 1984, there will be small computers on the market with at least 256 kilobytes of memory, and at least 10 million bytes of hard disk storage. Those should be able to run the algorithms as we see them developing. Finally, Paul's note makes clear that by then banks and traders here and in the USA will be installing the networks which will allow fast and reliable communication of data. So, if we can launch packages in 1983 for introduction in 1984, we're on to a winner.

"But then we have the big minus. To push the work on, we've needed more specialist staff than we thought. Costs have built up to roughly £250,000 per year, despite my working without salary. Thanks to Chris, we won the Datex contract, which is bringing in £70,000. So, we've £180,000 a year to cover. At the end of 1979 we ourselves subscribed to bring capital up to £100,000. We've also had investments totalling £60,000 from Sir Pat O'Donnell, Waterhouse College and Frank Booth. Staff options have picked up another £50,000. The loan facility with New Hampshire is for up to £200,000. Thus a year ago we had about £400,000 available. Currently, we have about £290,000 available. At £180,000 per year, we'll run out of money around September 1982. Right, Jenny?"

"Yes," she responded, curtly.

"Also, Tony, what's your estimate for the demonstration equipment we need to launch?"

"It's difficult to be precise because the equipment doesn't exist yet. My guess is £40,000. That's for a minicomputer that can emulate the micros to be available in 1984. We'll need it by mid-1982."

"That brings the date we run out of money forward to around June next year. We've plenty of cash available now. Indeed, we won't need to start drawing down the loan facility seriously until the summer. But there's a gap of a year's funding yawning in front of us. In practice, it's worse than that. If our staff realise that we're running out of money, their stock options won't keep them with us. They'll find other jobs and the whole thing will come to a halt – curtains. To be secure, we need assured access soon to at least another £250,000, and preferably £300,000 so as to allow for inflation and contingencies."

"Is there scope for cutting staff?" asked Brian.

"Not really," said Sheila. "We need the different kinds of expertise."

"For a reliable product, each component needs to be checked thoroughly," added Tony. "Effectively, it must be worked through again from scratch by at least one separate person, preferably two."

"Can we find more revenue from other business?" asked Jenny. "We *have* ended up with most of our eggs in one basket."

"Chris reckons that in the present economic climate the prospects are not good," I responded. "Also, there's no spare staff time. Our costs would go up, too. Chris will look out but it would have to be very much a cert to be worth going for."

"What about more capital, from us or from other shareholders?" asked Sheila.

"We can all think about how much more we can put in but

we won't find anywhere near £300,000 unless we do something dramatic, like all sell our houses. Even that depends on how much of the value of your house is mortgaged."

I looked round the room but could see that there was no scope to pursue this suggestion further. Nor was there any point in saying anything now about how much more I might be able to put in.

"And the loan facility, Paul?" asked Tony.

"I don't think I could persuade New Hampshire to extend it. My colleagues would be aware that once you started drawing down you would have a very large interest bill, larger than was expected in 1979. I doubt that if you were requesting the facility now such a large amount would be agreed, despite the widening of the capital base. Certainly you couldn't get any further facility from another bank except at quite penal rates. It's with some diffidence that I have to put forward what seems to me the only way out. That's to see if a risk capital provider is willing to subscribe. New Hampshire has an arm dealing with small company financing but of course there are others."

"You're right to be diffident, Paul," said Brian. "The amount of new capital would be more than our present capital. We would lose control."

"There's the position of other shareholders to consider, too," said Jenny. "I can't see Pat O'Donnell, for one, being pleased if the value of his holding is effectively halved overnight."

We had elected Tony Higgins as Chairman, partly to maintain his interest and partly to ensure continued valuable input from an expert now working outside the company's business. He made such input now.

"I agreed with Pete that we should have this meeting of just the six of us, without anyone else, even Chris, because the issues are so important and confidential. Each of us needs to consider them so that we can discuss them more fully and formally at our next meeting, which is at Crawley on the afternoon of

24th February. I've just one other point to make which is very speculative and on which I'll look out for any further news. There's a rumour going round that IBM is planning to produce a microcomputer."

"IBM – you must be joking," said Brian. "Or maybe if you're talking 1990?" In the 1960s IBM had dominated the commercial computer market but since then had developed a reputation for being very slow to innovate.

"Apparently they've set up several in-house groups and something might appear this year. This would be the first move by a really large, established manufacturer and others would follow. It wouldn't be what we need to run our software but people would know that improved models would appear quickly. So we would be in a much better position to trail our product as capable of running on relatively inexpensive machines only a generation or so away. If we could do that by the middle of next year, I assume the finance to fill the gap would become available, Paul."

"Yes, it would, provided there are prospects for a network to be there, too."

"If the machines happen, networks will happen, and quickly."

"A summer '82 launch is a tall order, bearing in mind the need for checking, but it could be our best opportunity," I said. "It would make the short-term financial problem worse, though. Accelerated development would mean more staff and more costs, very soon. I'll talk it through, just with Chris for now, and let you have some thoughts, Jenny."

"Thank you."

"Much will depend on how fully the team understands my work. They've had it since November, and I've had several seminars with them, but for someone without the mathematical background it's difficult to get round. An expert voice, other than that of the author, could be helpful. Sheila, could you come down to Crawley for half a day sometime next week?"

"Not with my teaching load this term and what's happening at the Pankhurst Centre. I'll ask Morag if she can."

"Thanks. Meanwhile, I'll see if anyone at Crawley has heard anything about IBM's plans and I'll ask Neil Farnham, too. I'll provide a paper for our meeting on 24th February. Can we meet at 3.30 rather than 2.30 that day? I've something on in London which may not finish until around two o'clock."

"Is it definite that Neil Farnham is leading on computers, post-merger?" asked Brian.

"Yes, but it's less clear what International Consolidated will actually be doing."

"Sorry, must dash," said Jenny. "I'll circulate a short note, just to us."

"Message from Carol – Strangers' Bar at 7.30, Pete," said Paul.

"Does she reckon she'll get in tonight?" asked Brian.

"She hopes to – later on and keeping it short."

I had nearly an hour before my next appointment and the afternoon was fine and mild, so I walked there, collecting my thoughts.

My fellow directors were right to be worried. Had I not rather neglected my responsibilities as Chief Executive in favour of getting the maths sorted out, had Chris Rowan been as good at finance as he was at software design or had Jenny and I been working together effectively, we could have spotted the cash problem earlier. We had all been over-optimistic on the scale of effort needed to deliver the package and on the revenue we could obtain from other contracts. I personally had been over-optimistic as to the value of my reputation in obtaining more loan finance if necessary. Paul had echoed what I had been told by Sam Titchmarsh and Steph Coolidge. In these difficult times, old working relationships counted for little. We needed to have something deliverable. We hadn't got that, yet. Once again, I faced a 'credibility gap'.

I was at the Spanish Embassy with ten minutes to spare for my appointment but soon tasted the old Spain which had motivated my meeting there. Whilst waiting, I reread part of the letter that had accompanied a Christmas card from Ana.

> 'It is so good that all your help has borne fruit and that my book is to be published next month.
>
> Our Embassy in London is ready to hold a reception to mark this event. It is thought that publication will encourage tourism to those parts of Spain which have very few visitors compared to the Mediterranean coast. The date that the Embassy has agreed with the publishers is Tuesday, 24th February, to take place at your lunchtime. They would like your help in drawing up a list of invitations, to include people in the travel industry, travel writers in the newspapers, authors of English books about Spain, and so on. They are making a list but you may have some suggestions. What about Paul's wife, Carol? About a hundred people can be invited.
>
> I am looking forward to seeing you again, Pete. We have not met for so long. It is such a pity that you were not able to visit us last autumn but I understand how tragedy has changed your life. I am looking forward to meeting Liz at last, having heard about her from you so long ago. I have also asked that Jenny and Dick be invited to the reception. When they were here in the summer, Jenny did not say much about Liz, or about you. Is there anything wrong between you all?'

The delay in starting the meeting mattered little, for the business was quite brief. The Embassy and the publishers had done their homework and I could suggest only a few additions to the guest list. I had asked Carol to contact the fledgling British-Spanish Parliamentary Group, and the Embassy people were pleased to invite some of them.

The publisher's representative departed quickly for another meeting. I followed more usual and appreciated custom by strolling gently back to the door with the most senior of the Spaniards we had met. He was very affable.

"It is very good that the lady Ana Guzman[40] can visit us. She comes from an aristocratic family which supported General Franco but she has spoken out to say that all must now support the transition to democracy. You know this, Mr Bridford, from your time in Spain."

"My time there was near the end of General Franco's rule. To my mind the transition had already begun then, as was his desire. It has been assisted by industrial development. I can see from what I read how important just now is the support of people like the lady Ana. I had hoped to visit her and her husband last year but circumstances prevented me."

"Ah yes, her husband. He is not so sure in his support for the transition."

"Yes, I know. That is a pity."

"I believe that you are a business associate of his, Mr Bridford."

"In the past I was his associate but I expect you know that I have now left International Electronics, to develop my own business."

"I read that International Electronics and Consolidated Electrics are to merge on the first of April. It is described in the press as a merger of equals and a last triumph for Sir Pat O'Donnell."

---

40 This is the English translation of '*la doña Ana*', as she would then have been referred to formally.

"That's right. It certainly lets Pat go out well. Though I know nothing of current plans, I think that the combined company will build on IE's involvement in Spain. With European Community membership in prospect, you are not a market or manufacturing location to ignore."

"Ah yes, you realised that ten years ago. You are remembered as a friend of Spain, in private and public ways. It is good, therefore, that the Ambassador, who is a friend of the lady Ana's father, wishes to mark her visit by giving a small dinner on the evening before the reception, that is on Monday 23rd February. He would be honoured if you could join us, and your companion also."

Memories flashed through my mind. Thanks to Ana and me, Spain had been prepared for the oil crisis of 1973, and a financial killing had been made by IE, New Hampshire Realty Bank and the Banco Navarrese, of which Ana's father Don Pedro was a director. High officials 'in the know' had, like me, joined in the killing. The man I was talking to might have been one of those officials and a Franco-era man who had made the transition. He certainly seemed more senior than I had expected for a meeting like this.

"Thank you, I am most grateful. I will need to discuss it with her but I am sure she will be pleased to come, too. You may be aware of our circumstances."

"I am informed, yes, and so is the Ambassador. The lady Ana has asked that two English friends who have helped her much should also be invited – Dr and Mrs Richard Sinclair. I believe that you know them also."

I nodded, and we parted with mutual salutations. As I walked east, I felt that my long call to wish Ana a happy New Year had been very worthwhile. Just before the next Board meeting I would now have two opportunities to break the ice with Jenny, and something Ana had said to me suggested a fair chance of success.

I was into the Houses of Parliament with remarkably little fuss by present-day standards, considering that Airey Neave had been within the building when he was murdered by Irish terrorists less than two years before. I found my gallery seat just as my department's Secretary of State was finishing a protracted response to Merlyn Rees's opening speech. The debate continued with much about coal but few original observations. Then it moved on to industrial energy prices and I spotted some good points which could be made in response on these.

Just after 7.30 I entered the Strangers' Bar, which was then the haunt of moderate Labour MPs. Carol was there with several fairly elderly men, two of whom I recognised as having already spoken at length. To describe them as weather-beaten would not have been fully accurate, unless it were accepted that there is 'weather' underground – hot and dirty.

"So this is your civil servant friend, Carol," said one of them.

"I'm not a civil servant. Most of the time I run a small business," I said.

"Ah, you're here under false pretences," said another. "This bar is for MPs and for civil servants in attendance for debates."

"And MPs' guests," said Carol. "Enough banter, we've not much time. Grab a roll and join us over there, Pete. I've bought you a drink."

"So what do you make of us so far, then?" I was asked when I sat down.

"Here's my view as Industrial Advisor. This is not any official view; we are off the record. Everyone is missing the main point, and I mean everyone. Everyone says the Plan for Coal should be followed. What does that mean? There's a document called the Plan for Coal, dating from 1974. It's what people signed up to then. I've had a look at it. It says that, based on experience during the few years before 1974, productivity, that is output per man shift, should go up by about 4% per year. So now it should be about 30% higher than it was in 1974. But actually, it's around the same as it was in 1974. So the Plan for Coal *hasn't* been followed. If it had been followed, then with the bonus of higher oil prices the industry would be selling more, investing more, paying higher wages *and* making a profit."

"But..." said Carol.

"Quite right, but, employing fewer people – not necessarily 30% fewer, though. That would depend on what extra sales had been achieved."

"The industry has been held back by the legacy of years of low investment," objected someone.

"There are about 230 pits. 30% of 230 is seventy-seven. Are you talking about seventy-seven pit closures?" said another man, angrily.

"I'm not talking about any number of closures. Some of the improvement might have come from closing pits that are difficult and unpleasant to work in, and some might have come from new pits planned for high productivity, but a lot of it would have come from making existing pits work better."

"Have you ever been down a pit?" another asked.

"No, I haven't, but I have worked at senior levels in a big company. I know that improving productivity isn't so much about grand declarations as about involving the workforce in lots of individual ideas. That's clearly been missing in coal during these last few years. There *is* a legacy holding the industry back, a legacy of complacent, bad management. If anything like what's happened in coal had happened where I worked we would have been bust. But that wouldn't have been allowed to happen. It would have been prevented by sacking people – not the workforce, the management."

"You *are* talking about job losses, though, Pete," said Carol.

"I'm talking about bringing the workforce to a level which provides secure, continuing, well-paid jobs in decent working conditions. If men leave before normal retirement, perhaps after many years of service, they need to be looked after."

"Is there anything in the rumours about improving the redundancy terms?"

"It is odd that deputies can usually get good benefits if they leave at age fifty, whilst the men they manage have to wait until age fifty-five."

"God, the redundancy scheme," said another weather-beaten figure. "It's a good idea to improve it, and to simplify it, too. Have you looked at the rules? People keep contacting me because some rule turns out to cut their benefit. I call the Board's office in Sheffield that runs the scheme but the people there can't sort it out because the rules are made by the government. I write to the Minister but nothing happens."

"The rules are set out in an Order approved by this House. Next month there'll be a debate on an amending Order to update the scheme. It's normally on late in the evening. Any of you can say your piece there. There's time to draft the Order so as to tidy up the rules. So, all of you, send me a list of the problems you know about, as soon as possible. Tell your colleagues to do the same. I'm only in the office two days a week so write to me at my home address. Here's my card."

"We must get back," said the man who had been angry. "You've a lot to learn about coal, laddie, but at least you're talking to us. That's a change from the way it's been since *she* got in. Thanks, Carol, for suggesting this."

"And thanks from me, too, Carol," I said as we walked back to the Central Lobby. "Encourage them to call me at home if there's any other message they want to get through. Tell them who might answer their call if I'm not there. At the department, all we hear about the attitude of the men is what the Board chooses to tell us. I'm already placed to make a direct input, of course, but the more information I have, the better. Well, good luck. I'm sorry this has kept you out of the Chamber longer than it should have done, if you wanted to speak."

"No worries, Pete. I'm not going to try to speak tonight. There are too many more senior people who think they have first pick. Lots of things have changed over the last few months. I'm no longer the star of '74, triumphantly back. I'm a youngster who has to know *her* place, work *her* passage and mind what *she* says. That was made *so* clear to me earlier today."

"The people we were talking to just now seemed friendly enough."

"Oh yes, on the outside. I'm talking about what they say to the whips behind my back, and what the whips then say to me. The main reason that that guy just now hates Margaret Thatcher is that she's a woman doing a man's job. I'm not looking forward to Wembley except that it gives me an extra weekend down here, so Liz and I can swim on Sunday."

"They can't stop you writing your column. That's as good as ever, this week."

"No, they can't."

"How are your US contacts? I expect they're mostly Gerald Ford era."

"Reagan has brought in mostly new people but there'll be some I know. Paul has been talking to Steph. New Hampshire is organising a big reception in Washington early in April. We can both go over, so there's a chance for more writing about the US scene and a chance for some work over there, too. Meanwhile, *back I go*."

The papers were full of Ronald Reagan's inauguration the day before and of the release of hostages by Iran. At least that was giving Carol something to look forward to. Otherwise she was obviously disappointed, and rather upset. Over the last year much had changed in the Labour Party, including the leadership. In November, following Jim Callaghan's resignation, Michael Foot had narrowly beaten Denis Healey in a run-off. Carol's preference, David Owen, had not stood, and had left the Shadow Cabinet. The next Saturday there was to be a Party conference at Wembley Arena, to consider whether the Leader should be elected by a procedure including union block votes, rather than just by Labour MPs. This wasn't expected to become a live issue for a while but it was a totem for the direction of policy.

Labour had already adopted policies which might have some justification in principle but no justification in terms of the reasons given. Abandoning the nuclear deterrent had some support, since the alternative was substantial expenditure on the Trident submarine missile system. It was being suggested that the money would be better spent on other equipment for the armed forces; I had heard Frank Booth on the needs of the RAF. However, there was no sign that Labour would apply any savings in that way. Withdrawal from the EEC had fairly wide support, in view of the high cost and low benefit from membership. However, Labour viewed the European Communities as a capitalist conspiracy, which did not suggest that their version of withdrawal would benefit business. Their policy was also unhelpful through the political equivalent of Newton's Third Law of Motion; it had made the government move to a more pro-European line. I shared Brian Smitham's disappointment at the consequent slowing in action to obtain more benefit from membership.[41]

The Labour Party was heading leftward but Carol wasn't. She was also disconcerted by moves towards mandatory re-selection of parliamentary candidates.

I spent another half an hour in the gallery while the debate meandered on. Then I found my way round to the passage behind the Speaker's Chair, from which access is gained to the Box. Clustered around were various officials who were feeding material to their colleagues inside. I passed my suggestions

---

[41] As already noted, it took several more years for the Thatcher Government to obtain some improvements in terms of membership. Newton's Third Law, 'Every action has an equal and opposite reaction', applied again in 1988 when the Labour Party was attracted by Commission President Delors' vision of a socialised Community over-ruling national governments, and Mrs Thatcher responded with her Bruges address.

to the man co-ordinating the briefing on energy prices. I had noticed John Willis coming and going from the Press Gallery and now he joined us. A few minutes later, as the last Conservative backbencher spoke, Norman Lamont came out from the Commons Chamber. He was then the Parliamentary Under-Secretary responsible for energy policy issues.

That was the signal for Martin Turner to appear from the Box, and a last briefing meeting took place in the corridor. Martin made sure that no-one else from his team spoke to Lamont. The people there from Douglas's side were less senior but knew their jobs. I just nodded, with the occasional interjection. Just after nine o'clock, Lamont and Martin were back in place as Alex Eadie began to wind up for Labour. I hung around outside in case anything else came up.

"Have you heard about Martin's latest bombshell?" John murmured to me.

"I don't think I can imagine Martin firing a bombshell."

"He'd booked a holiday in Italy for the second week in February. He's not planning to change it just because the Board has this meeting with the unions."

"It's up to him and Julian but he'd better make sure that his staff can do things when he's not here. It would be a start if he let them do things when he *is* here."

"He said to me that he was sure that Derek could handle the matter."

"I hope he's right."

Once Lamont was speaking, I hurried to Victoria, and was pleased to find that the train I was aiming for was not cancelled because of 'staff shortage'. Changes of government had not solved the problems created by Treasury control of train drivers' and guards' pay.

As we rattled along, I reflected that it was useful to know about Martin's holiday before the talk I hoped to have with Ed Plunkett the next morning. Ed reported to Derek Morris, who reported to Martin. Derek was at a meeting in Brussels that day. His main interest was international policy on coal, which was a high-profile subject at the time. The previous June, a G7 meeting in Venice had committed to doubling coal production and use by 1990 so as to reduce the pressure on oil demand and to compensate for delays in nuclear power programmes following the Three Mile Island accident.[42] At this time, few people had heard of global warming; or if they had, they thought that it would delay the onset of the next Ice Age, whose imminence was authoritatively predicted.

Derek had only about eighteen months to go before the then compulsory retirement of civil servants at age sixty. He knew that a year or so before, Ed had taken the coal job in the hope of promotion to succeed him. Accordingly, he was pleased to give Ed his head on the detailed work on industrial relations and redundancy terms. He made sure that he knew enough to answer Martin's questions, since when he was there Martin would not speak directly to Ed. So, with Martin away, the onus would be on Ed during what would clearly be a busy week. It was all such an odd set-up and hardly the best way to face a crisis.

---

42 In Pennsylvania, on 28th March 1979. There were no casualties but a written-off reactor and a great deal of public concern.

HOUSE OF COMMONS, 10th FEBRUARY, 1981

Mr Foot. Will the Right Honourable lady reconsider her answer? This is a matter for the nation to consider. Will she give an undertaking that no steps will be taken along that road until the House has had an opportunity to discuss the matter? Will she not reinstitute the tripartite system of discussions for the coal industry, which produced 'Plan for Coal' – which the government said they would carry forward for a period? Does she not agree that it would be better for industry and for the country as a whole if an agreement were reached between the National Coal Board, the miners and the government about a plan for the industry, rather than the Right Honourable lady condemning it to the disaster of quarrels between all three?

The Prime Minister. It would be quite wrong for the government to attempt to manage every nationalised industry. It is for the government, in conjunction with the Coal Board, to fix the amount of finance that is available. We have done so, and the figure I gave to the Right Honourable gentleman is considerable. That money will have to be found either from taxation or from borrowing, and will go to the Coal Board for its operations next year. That is in addition to the price that we shall pay for coal and the increased price that we shall pay for electricity because the price of coal is high.

Mr Foot. Since the future of the nation is involved in this matter and since we shall never recover from the recession if the Right Honourable lady and her friends allow the coal industry to sink, may we have an absolute undertaking that all the proposals will be discussed in the House of Commons before the procedure under which she is directing that industry proceeds?

The Prime Minister. No, Mr Speaker. I am not directing that industry. We have fixed the amount available for the industry. It is for the management of the National Coal Board to make the arrangements and we shall stand by those arrangements.

12th FEBRUARY, 1981

Mr Foot. Is the Right Honourable lady seriously saying that in this critical situation she will refuse to call the tripartite meetings which we had on the coal industry and which saved the coal industry following the experiences of 1974? When we came in then, we had to call those tripartite discussions to deal with the matter. That is what the Right Honourable lady will have to do on this occasion. Will she not decide to do it now instead of being forced to do it later?

The Prime Minister. No, sir, and I am not forced to do many things.

Sunday Courier 15 February 1981
Pit closures: what the heck's going on?

asks **Carol Milverton MP**

The trouble with doing a fortnightly column is that sometimes it's difficult to decide what to write. Not this week, though. The antics of the government and the National Coal Board make it easy.

Indeed, very easy. I can start by quoting what I heard the Secretary of State say less than eight months ago, in introducing the Coal Industry Bill.

"It must be recognised that in the past there was undoubtedly a feeling that the coal industry was no more than a survival, doomed to irreversible decline and early extinction. This view is utter rubbish. Nothing could be further from the truth. Coal is our greatest single natural resource. Our total coal resources are about 200 billion tonnes and the National Coal Board's estimate of operating reserves at existing mines and those in the planning stage totals about 10 billion tonnes. Over time, about 45 billion tonnes are thought to be suited to extraction by existing technology and its developments – that is, over 300 years' worth of production at current rates. By any standards, this is a secure, indigenous source of energy.

As oil becomes dearer and supplies more vulnerable and less reliable worldwide, and as our own offshore oil and gas resources decline in the 1990s, as they are bound to do, I am confident that there must be new opportunities and a new demand for coal. That is the reason why we have put coal, along with higher energy efficiency through conservation, and with nuclear energy, at the centre of our energy policy."

That's all absolutely right, of course. But even eight months ago, the financial targets set out in the Bill were impossible for the industry to reach in the face of the recession brought about by the government's policies. For Labour, David Owen made that very clear. And then the first Conservative MP to speak in the debate agreed with him![43] That wasn't so surprising. Everyone knew that the targets had been

---

43 See the speech of Patrick McNair-Wilson in *Hansard* for 17th June 1980.

worked out before the end of 1979. The Bill should have been brought to Parliament then but it was held up until after the steel strike.[44] It was out of date even before we had the chance to consider it.

Since then, the recession has got worse and it's going on getting worse. During 1980 the economy shrank by a staggering 4%. Three million unemployed suffer the greatest cost of this Tory mismanagement. Many of them were employed in industry which used British coal but has given up the struggle against foreign competition arising from the high pound. Just one recent example – the Bowater paper mill in Ellesmere Port has closed with the loss of 1,500 jobs, and the loss of a market for thousands of tons of coal per year.

So, faced with these impossible targets, what has the National Coal Board done? Until last Tuesday, NOTHING. At the time the Bill was before Parliament, its Chairman, Sir Derek Ezra, could have said the targets were impossible. He didn't say that. Now, he's trying to catch up by replacing with centralised diktat the well-tried procedures for handling pit closures by local discussion with the unions.

Because pit closures aren't new. They go on all the time. Every pit has to close eventually – because its reserves run out or because it becomes so difficult or dangerous to work that the men should move to a better pit or retire on terms which reflect their long and arduous service. The existing local procedures reflect this. Indeed, several of the twenty-three pits the Coal Board has now proposed for closure are already being discussed locally and are likely to close anyway.

So why has the top management of the Board made this sudden change in policy? No-one knows. Not the unions, including the union which represents the people who manage pits. Not the men. Everyone's saying, what the heck's going on, or words to that effect which can't be printed here.

Perhaps someone thought that having accepted two pay offers in a row the men would accept this tearing up of agreed procedures. Perhaps they thought that, as happened in 1979, the

---

44 A strike in the steel industry lasted from January to early April 1980.

NUM would ballot for a national strike and then the men wouldn't give the 55% majority needed for that. Or if they did, the strike wouldn't begin until next month, or even April, and then the days are longer, the demand for electricity is lower and the power cuts of 1972 or the three-day week of 1974 wouldn't happen. It would be the right time for a strike.

That ain't so. The Board has created a separate dispute in each NUM Area. In a climate of total bewilderment and anger, the response is fast. Wales, Scotland and Kent are coming out this week. Judging by what I'm hearing from my constituents, Yorkshire will be out next week and other Areas, too. I'm told that the NUM HQ is trying to figure out how to conduct a pithead ballot on a national strike, when the men are already on strike. And once they're out on strike, how do you get them back in? It's the nightmare of anyone who knows anything about industrial relations.

What to do? No-one can have wanted to be here but that's where we are. As Michael Foot has pointed out, there are established procedures for government, Coal Board and unions to get together and thrash out the problems facing them all. They need to meet as soon as possible this week and before all this gets worse – a lot worse.

8. MONDAY, 16TH FEBRUARY, 1981

I awoke to the sounds of the dawn chorus and to the comforting feeling of Liz's head on my shoulder, just as when we had eventually fallen asleep after a frantic day. I slid my right arm round and ran my hand through her hair. She kissed me, whilst hardly stirring.

There were a few minutes before we needed to get up and face the present. Memories came back of how we had come here. They began with the Friday after that dreadful Sunday, over a year before.

I had driven down from Leeds early and taken Liz, little Jenny and Greg's parents Lorna and Timothy across London to Coulsdon. On the way we stopped with Roberta and Frank, who insisted on providing lunch and were particularly charming to Lorna and Timothy. Then for a while we talked to Greg and wondered if we were obtaining some response. One could see that Roy Brampton was right. Though the hospital was full of those in the same comatose state as Greg, the surroundings and staff were cheerful.

Back near St Albans, Lorna and Timothy had gone to bed early so as to be ready to set off with me in the morning. Liz had been calm and organised all day but once snuggled up with me on the sofa, she broke down. After a few minutes of tears, she unbuttoned her shirt for the belly treatment. A few minutes of that and she loosened the belt of her trousers.

"Move your hand down, go on, you know where… That's lovely, Pete… In a bit further… Harder now… Just there…

Harder... Aaah – *aaahhh* – *aaaahhhh!*... That was great, Pete; just what I needed. I hope I've not left you too frustrated."

We had exchanged a few fat kisses and made our separate ways to bed. I was more shocked than frustrated but perhaps not totally surprised.

Three days later she was back in practical mode when she called, first to tell me that the inquest on Fred Perkins had indeed been short and low key, and then to describe how she had felt uncomfortable at church. Everyone had been very kind, perhaps too kind. She had been too much the focus of attention. People had said that they would try to visit Greg, though they would call her first.

Meanwhile, a kind of rota was emerging. Brian, Morag, Carol and Jenny would all be there at times, and she and little Jenny would be staying overnight with Roberta and Frank later in the week.

That brought her to the real point of her call. During the next weekend I had engagements that I couldn't miss, but the weekend after that was the start of the Christmas break. She wanted to be near Greg then. She didn't want to be on her own with Jenny, let alone to be pressed to join in some Baptist Christmas lunch. She knew that my parents and I would be staying with Roberta and Frank. Was there any way in which she and Jenny could be there, too, though she knew there were only three bedrooms. I promised to see if there was a way.

There was a way. Roberta and Frank knew well a couple living nearby who were going away for Christmas. My parents arrived in time to meet them.

Everyone showed the right degree of sympathy, without constantly reminding Liz of what had happened. That included my mother, who had not got on well with Liz during their previous encounter many years before. As for little Jenny – what bliss, with six adults to make a fuss of her.

I had Christmas lunch ready for when Liz and Jenny returned from Coulsdon, and the afternoon was filled with the usual drowsy fun. Later that evening, after my parents had resumed 'house-sitting', Roberta sat down beside me on the sofa, put her hand on my knee and murmured.

"Frank and I are sound sleepers. We won't notice any unusual sounds. It's so nice that you're looking after Liz, who's such an old friend of yours, Pete. She deserves to be looked after and I know how she wants to be looked after tonight."

Earlier, Liz had been very ready to help Roberta clear up, and perhaps that had allowed some private chat. So a little later I was unsurprised, even anticipatory, when my bedroom door opened quietly. Liz lifted her nightdress over her head and squeezed in beside me.

"Time for some incest... Ooh, that feels encouraging, but a nice belly rub to start. Don't worry, I'm still on the pill."

She rode me much as she had done years before. Then we dozed in each other's arms, forgetting everything else, until a whimper from Jenny took Liz away.

On Boxing Day we set off for Coulsdon without Jenny, but on the way pulled into a car park and turned off the radio, over which had been coming news of the Soviet invasion of Afghanistan. We were both feeling some shock, guilt and shame. It took a little time for either of us to know what to say. Finally, we both got it out.

First her: I would find Greg unchanged from when I had seen him last, more than two weeks before. The nurses were keeping up her spirits and she had met the consultant. Greg wasn't going downhill. He was taking nutrition and his body systems were working. They thought that he was hearing people talking to him. At least he was aware of their presence, so frequent visitors were important. But as to when he might wake up, if he ever did, they just did not know. So her whole life was on hold. It was almost – horrible thought, followed by some minutes of tears – worse than if he were dead. She couldn't stand waiting alone. The people at church had suggested that prayer would help her. She doubted that. Meeting people from the sports club just reminded her of her loss. Now, she definitely wanted a fresh start, with fresh people.

And she needed to have someone special. She had not been out of a relationship for more than a few weeks since she was eighteen. She needed one now. I was the only possibility. I had shown once again that I was her best friend, the brother she had never had. Could we once again have an occasional relationship of the kind we had had at times before; could we be 'best friends plus' again?

Then me: I knew her well enough to understand what she needed. It could end as soon as Greg recovered. But in the meantime, what would be the impact on Jenny? How would you describe me to her? She had agreed that those were questions we would have to answer, but one step at a time; we were finding our way. I explained that I was leaving IE and that wasn't wholly or even mainly about her, but it did mean I would move to somewhere near Crawley and hence south of London.

That was almost a rehearsal for the somewhat frigid time I had the next day, after Liz and Jenny had returned home and I told my parents that so as to develop my own business, I would be quitting the top job I had obtained only three months before. As often, Roberta and Frank were more understanding and soon asked if they could make an investment in Creators Technology.

Things developed a step at a time but quite quickly, in a direction reinforced by there being no change in Greg. Liz wanted and needed me, and gradually I realised that it couldn't just be occasional. I wanted and needed her, to end my loneliness.

By late March 1980, my offer had been accepted for a house on the Bishop's Park Estate, only 200 yards from where Roberta and Frank lived in Bellinghame. We took up permanent residence during the sweltering bank holiday weekend at the start of May, just in time to see on live TV the successful consequences of Mrs Thatcher's decision to send the SAS in to clear the Iranian Embassy of Iraqi-sponsored terrorists. That result had been as good for her prestige as the failure of an attempt to rescue the hostages taken in Teheran had been bad for that of President Carter.

Liz kept the house near St Albans so that if Greg did recover he could return to its familiar environment, but from the beginning of June it was let furnished. Some complicated removals split furniture between the two houses. The third bedroom at our house was full of things that Greg would want back near him and things I would want if alone again. It just had room for a desk for me.

In the meantime, Liz and I were filling the gap in each other's lives. It was an amazing change to be together again. Nearly fifteen years before, we had enjoyed my first serious relationship, and her second. But then and later, we had found it impossible to be together for long, since our interests were so different. Even a holiday together had been a disaster. Now, we had two major interests in common – little Jenny, and Greg. Jenny was accepting me. We had told Greg what we were doing. No reaction was observed, though the nurses thought he was happy for us.

We had developed as much of a social life as a couple with a young child could expect. Liz was a member, and I an associate, at a local sports club where she had had a good first season of tennis and was now concentrating on squash rather than hockey. I had brought out my cello again and joined an amateur orchestra. Their concert a week before had culminated with the Tchaikovsky 1812 Overture and had been a great success despite taking place literally in a swimming bath. In the winter the pool was emptied and boarded over and seating fitted above.

Brenda and Alan Murton were now blessed with little Stephanie and were not expecting to stop there. Though they knew of the tragic error that had led to Greg's state, they did not know that it had been made by the man whom Steph had put down so well. I had wondered how Liz would react to meeting the Murtons but she welcomed their efforts to introduce us to local people, as Liz and Pete, with little Jenny who was now meeting other children at a playgroup. Liz wore a wedding ring. Those we met made the obvious assumption, unless we trusted them enough to say otherwise.

Some people we met recalled my appearance on TV in February 1974 or the more recent coverage I had received during the IE share issue. Questions as to why I had left IE were helpfully reticent and polite. No doubt some people suspected that I had left under a cloud.

The Bellinghame house was as expensive to buy as the property near Leeds that I had budgeted for when committing £45,000 to Creators Technology. Given my reduced income the mortgage I could obtain was less. Fortunately, Jane wanted to increase her own holding in 'Plain Jane's' and had saved enough to buy half of my original holding at five times its cost to me in 1974. By juggling the cash around I had obtained more tax relief without needing more advice from Jenny Sinclair.

Income from my remaining holding, my part-time salary, and rental from St Albans allowed us to pay two mortgages and live in a modest suburban style. It helped that Liz was not smoking too much and that holidays were limited to a few day trips to the South Coast in her car, though that was a consequence more of limited time and a poor summer than of limited cash.

Through the early summer of 1980 I had usually spent three days per week either as Industrial Advisor or at the Creators Technology offices in Crawley. The rest of the time, I worked away at home on the maths problem and looked after little Jenny whilst Liz was out. She often visited Greg. On sunny days patients were moved out into the grounds and the nurses thought that Greg responded to the stimulus of bright light.

There were two periods of a few months in my life when I made major mathematical breakthroughs. In the first, back at Cambridge, I had been buoyed along through ups and downs by my growing relationship with Jenny. Now, my grown relationship with Liz was having the same effect. Late in July I told both the department and Creators Technology that I wouldn't be in for some weeks, and Liz, Roberta and Frank that they would need to look after little Jenny almost all of the time. I rarely emerged from the third bedroom except to eat. Twice I worked through most of the night and unwound with Liz in the dawn. By early September I had cracked the problem Morag had identified a year before. It just needed to be written up and checked. The way through to the trading software was clear. As far as we knew it was a private way for Creators Technology.

"Phone's ringing," I murmured into Liz's right ear.

"It must be *him*."

She jumped out of bed, pulled on a dressing gown and ran downstairs. The light caught the muscles in her body, as athletic now as ever. Jenny was now demanding attention. By the time I brought her down, Liz had a simple message.

"There'll be an emergency Executive meeting on Thursday. Unless there's some give before then, it will formally authorise the Area strikes."

I added to the extensive notes I had made already from calls over the weekend – she from members of the NUM National Executive, I from some of the MPs I had met with Carol, from others they had put on to me, and also from Brian Smitham's father.

News of Greg's state had led to sympathetic suggestions that Liz should return to her job in the NUM head office; she was missed. Once we were settled in Bellinghame she took up the invitation, for one day a week. Then, either I was at home, or Roberta and Frank played at being doting grandparents. Recently, it had been mainly the latter. So far, Liz's job had been strictly daytime; but there had been calls to a private telephone number, especially during the last few weeks. One such call had just been returned.

By seven o'clock, I was on my way out of the house. On the train in I had a good view of the outsides of most newspapers. They all looked much the same.

Jean arrived at my office a few minutes after me and was full of enthusiasm as she sat down to type out my notes.

"It's worth getting in early to be on a story like this, Pete. I'm so glad you warned me on Friday. Gosh, you have had a busy weekend. What's this word?"

"Exhaustion."

"What you were feeling, I guess."

"Here, it's when a colliery runs out of useful coal."

While she was taking copies round, I answered the phone. At ten o'clock there would be an urgent meeting with Julian Street. Yes, John Willis and Ed Plunkett were both invited. I called Ed in.

On the previous Tuesday, Derek Morris had fallen sick, just as the Coal Board began to tell the unions of plans for pit closures. Martin Thomas was away in Italy, so there was something of a vacuum above Ed. By dint of working all hours, he was filling most of it, but with at least the acquiescence of Julian I was lending a hand. We settled our line and Jean typed out one sheet of paper. Armed with copies, we picked up John on the way to Julian's office.

"I've just had a message from the Secretary of State's office," Julian began. "The Prime Minister wants to see him, Jim Prior[45] and John Biffen[46] at 12.30. I'm seeing the Secretary of State at 11.30 and going over with him. On Friday I advised him that he should call a tripartite meeting for Wednesday next week – the

---

45 Then Secretary of State for Employment.
46 Then Chief Secretary to the Treasury.

25th. That's the day after the E Committee[47] meeting. Provided our paper is round by Thursday, the Committee will have discussed it. So he can go into the meeting with agreed proposals. It's also the day before the strike ballot we're expecting the NUM to arrange. A constructive result from the tripartite could swing the ballot."

"On Friday I was doubtful about that timing and so was Bernard," said John. "Now, I'm certain it's no good, for two reasons. First, look at the headlines in the papers today. Dammit, yesterday Prince Charles fell off his polo horse and Lady Diana Spencer burst into tears. That's on the inside pages, repeat, *the inside pages*. And then we have the information in Pete's note. It's darn useful that you have all these contacts, Pete. We don't just have what the Board gets round to telling us. From next Monday most, if not all, of the industry will be on strike. Even coalfields where no closures have so far been suggested are likely to join in. They reckon that unless this is stopped now, they'll be next."

"Hmm yes, and perhaps a third reason," said Julian. "Have you seen the note from No. 10 to the Parliamentary Branch, Ed?"

"No, I was talking to Pete before we came here."

"To quote: 'It is anticipated that the bulk of proceedings at tomorrow's Prime Minister's Questions will be on this topic.' I agree that the tripartite must come forward, but we can't go into it with nothing to say. We must have time to reach some agreement to our proposals on redundancy terms, on reducing coal imports and on building a plant to demonstrate synthesis of oil fuel from coal. Martin called me. He arrived home very late last night and had not expected to come in today but having heard the news he'll be here about lunchtime. I'm going to ask him to have a paper ready by close of tomorrow. Ed, perhaps when you return to your desk you can warn your colleagues that he'll need urgent help. Pete, can you discuss with the DTI what we can say about imports and oil from coal? I'll suggest to the

---

47 The Cabinet committee on energy matters.

Secretary of State that he presses for a ministerial meeting to be arranged for Thursday or Friday. Then we can set up the tripartite for Monday. With that done, at least the more moderate Areas of the NUM will surely wait a day to hear what happens before precipitating strike action. I've spoken to Ezra. He thinks the prospects for that timetable are good."

I replied firmly to this. "Based on what I've heard and put down in my note, I think the prospects for that timetable are *not* good. I'll do my best but there is no possibility of agreeing definite proposals on coal imports during this week. Cutting imports is not just about persuading the British Steel Corporation to pay more for British coking coal. It's about ensuring that British coal can meet the standards of consistency that are needed for reliable high-quality steel production. That needs technical discussions and trials, taking several weeks if not months. Also, the DTI won't pay for making oil from coal. Why should it? If we think it's important, we can find the money ourselves. In any case, oil from coal is not going to swing any key player. The only way we can swing key players is by improving the redundancy terms. I think we should go all out to get the principle of improvements agreed in time to announce at a tripartite meeting on Wednesday, before the NUM Executive meets."

"How can we possibly do that? The Treasury isn't convinced on the cost. The DTI is worried that the Board's proposals will create pressures to improve the terms for steel workers. Everyone wants some assurance that improved terms will lead to more closures. Then there are all the suggestions from the Cabinet Office that the introduction of the terms should be phased and that the terms should be time-limited to encourage quick departures."

"We can't sort the detail in two days from now, that's for sure. The Board's proposals arrived late and have been thrown together. There are all sorts of inconsistencies in them. Nor is there any way we can link them to any level of closures. Instead,

I suggest that the Secretary of State uses what Ed and I have put down on this sheet."

I passed it round, and continued.

"The Coal Board is overmanned compared with what the Plan for Coal envisaged. Productivity is static, when it should have increased by 30% since 1974. They should be producing as much coal as they do now with about 60,000 fewer men. That would reduce their costs by nearly £400 million a year and more in the future. So to get back to Plan for Coal, we need to help 60,000 men to leave over the next three or four years. It doesn't really matter whether this happens through closures or by making continuing pits run more efficiently. We can see from the Board's figures that a very attractive package has an average cost for the age mix of around £20,000. Add a bit for luck and make it £25,000. So the total cost for 60,000 men is £1,500 million. That includes £300 million already earmarked, so the extra cost is perhaps around £1,200 million, spread over some years. The maximum extra cost in any year is about £250 million. That's big money but it leads quickly to bigger savings. It's spending to solve the big problem. From what I've heard of the Prime Minister, she should find that attractive. Giving the Board more money in grants and so-called loans just puts off solving the big problem."

Ronald Clarkson came in, helpfully.

"So, Pete, you're suggesting that the Secretary of State tells the Prime Minister and the Chancellor what they're letting themselves in for, but that it should be a one-off. I think that has a chance, Julian. It's a realistic response to where we find ourselves now. The Treasury is desperate to avoid a commitment to pour more and more money in indefinitely. In principle the terms are time-limited because the legislation authorising payments is time-limited. Currently it runs until the end of March 1984."

"Pete's suggestion gives us a good public line," said John. "We recognise that the industry needs to restructure further in accord with the Plan for Coal. To that end, we'll bring before Parliament proposals for further improvements in the redundancy scheme introduced under Labour in 1968 and carried through by all governments since then. We could have those improvements apply to anyone leaving from now on."

"I think you've persuaded me," said Julian. "I'll put it to the Secretary of State when I see him. John, you'd better come with me, but otherwise, it's best to keep the meeting small."

"It's important that the meeting is aware of what's in my note about coalfield reactions," I responded. "John can quote it as 'information coming in'. The rest of us have lots to do. Julian, there are two ways in which you can make things easier, particularly for Ed. When you tell the Board what's decided this morning, ask them to talk detail of the redundancy terms directly with him. They've said that they want a meeting with Martin first. Then tell the lawyers here that defining exactly what the Board can claim under the various grants is now the top departmental priority. With that priority, we can show the Treasury we're serious about improving the financial controls. Also, the parliamentary Order due next month can include the right package of improvements and can make some detailed changes which are inexpensive but will reduce the volume of complaints coming in to miners' MPs. That will make them feel we're listening. MPs are very receptive to anything that gets constituents off their backs."

The meeting broke up and I walked back with John to the press office, where he could get the latest news before meeting with the Secretary of State.

"You push it hard, Pete, but you seem to have swung Julian," he observed.

"I had a pretty narrow window of opportunity, just as we all have right now. Where I worked for twelve years, if you were in a tight corner you thought carefully about what to do, discussed it with whoever you needed to and then did it, fast. This isn't an academic exercise. Good luck, anyway. I have to say I hoped to be at the meeting with the Secretary of State. Do you think I should ask Douglas to weigh in on that?"

"Best not. Julian is right about keeping it small. You would be an unexpected face at a difficult meeting. We'll need the luck, but thanks, Pete. At least you've provided a coherent plan."

"That's what Sir Pat O'Donnell used to say to me when we were in a spot."

I spent the rest of the morning learning more about coking coal as I called various people in the Coal Board, and in the DTI which then sponsored British Steel. I had just dictated a note to Julian, which more or less confirmed what I had already said, when John looked in.

"Sorry, Pete, we went through the position and I used your note but the Secretary of State wants to stick to Wednesday week. At most, he'll come forward to Monday. He actually said that he wanted to give Martin a chance to catch up with the position and then talk it through tomorrow morning."

"Why the hell does he trust Martin so much?"

"Because Martin gives the air of having thought about it and is really very good at the reassuring, elegant phrase."

"Elegant phrases won't save us now. What are we doing about redundancy terms?"

"He wants to keep those in reserve, the message to the NUM being that he'll look at them if they calm down. He thinks they're reacting irrationally at the moment and things will improve if the Board puts over a better message about the level of investment in the industry."

"What planet is he *on*?"

"I don't know, Pete, and nor does Julian, who keeps his cool, as you've seen, but was pretty near the edge. I called Bernard. Perhaps that will help. Come and have lunch."

We went downstairs to the canteen and crowded round a table, with others understandably keen to know the latest crisis news. Lunchtime socialising was a good feature of life at the department; without taking up much time, it kept people informed outside their immediate work area and allowed informal contributions to thinking. Most of the senior people joined in but there were exceptions.

"When's Martin back?" someone asked.

"This afternoon, apparently," said John.

"How would we know? He never comes in here. His only break from sitting in his office or talking to Ministers is when he wanders around the building on his own, ignoring anyone he passes."

"Don't you know why he wanders around?" said someone else.

"No."

"At a Christmas party his secretary told mine. There's a special toilet, for which anyone at his level or above can have a key. Most don't bother, but he never uses the ordinary toilets. When he's wandering around, he's on his way there, or back."

"I've some sympathy for Martin on that," I commented. "Doubtless one gets used to toilets that look as if they haven't been cleaned since this place was built fifty years ago but for someone coming in from outside they're a shock. Who *is* responsible for cleaning them, anyway?"

"Supervising the cleaners is one of the jobs in Establishments reserved for people who can't do anything else."

"So it's more of the plain living, fine thinking ideas that too many civil servants have. All I can say is that if people at any IE plant came in to find the toilets in the state we put up with here, they would all be out straight away."

That was the way it was in the days before contracting out.

After lunch, I moved on to making oil from coal. Fortunately, the Scientific Advisor was in that day. I began my meeting with him and his staff by apologising for using so much of Jean's time, whilst pointing out that I would not be in for most of the next day. Then we looked at the facts, which were simple enough.

The main reason for interest in building a 'demonstration plant' was that its proposed site was in the constituency of a prominent maverick Tory backbencher and in a small coalfield where the local NUM was led by 'moderates' whose position would thereby be strengthened. However, the only countries to have made oil from coal on any scale were Nazi Germany and South Africa. They had their reasons. Some improved processes were now available but it would take at least another doubling of the oil price to make them anything like economic.

Meanwhile, however, there were other ways to replace oil by coal. For example, oil refineries needed fuel to boil the crude oil. Unsurprisingly, they usually burnt some of the less saleable oil fractions but there was no reason why they shouldn't burn coal. Substitution would be straightforward in two or three modern refineries which were tuned to produce wholly saleable products. The result was equivalent to making oil from coal, the economics didn't look too bad and it could be happening in a year or so. The Coal Board should be talking to oil companies about initiatives of this kind.

The door opened and Jean put her head in. "Pete, message from Julian Street's office – meeting in five minutes."

My scientific colleagues offered to draft a note. They were rather excited to be asked to do something within an hour. The cast of the morning's meeting reassembled, and Martin joined us, to hear Julian's debrief. It didn't take long.

"Basically the outcome is what I expected. The Secretary of State wanted to stick with next Wednesday. The No. 10 and Cabinet Office people there wanted to go for this Wednesday, though there was no taste for saying anything definite then about redundancy terms or anything else. The Prime Minister was clearly of the view that things should go faster. So Monday is the compromise, with our paper to E Committee by Thursday. Meanwhile we're to press the Board to take a more positive line and you, John, are to liaise with No. 10 about presentation, starting with what's to be announced straight away. I think that's all. Martin, can we have a word?"

John hurried off to the press office. "So that's that," I said to Ed. "We'll see."

"I'd better finish off the briefing for Prime Minister's Questions tomorrow. I've a couple of thoughts on lines, Pete."

We discussed for a few minutes and arranged to meet early the next day. Then I returned to my office and made a few amendments to the scientists' draft on oil from coal. Jean had nearly finished typing a final version, for signature by both her bosses, when she took a call.

"Martin Turner wants to see you, Pete."

My equivalent rank in the Civil Service was not clear but Martin evidently thought he was senior, so did his secretary, and arguments about status did not interest me just then. A few minutes later I was in his office.

"Pete, thank you for coming down. I won't detain you long."

"How was your holiday, Martin?"

"It was very pleasant but already a receding memory. I wanted to say, Pete, how grateful Julian and I are that you helped out during the unexpected sickness of Derek Morris and my perhaps not most felicitously timed absence. Julian will be conveying that to Douglas."

"No problem. It's part of the job to help out in a crisis."

"Yes," he sighed. "The mineworkers' leaders are behaving so irrationally."

"They aren't behaving at all irrationally. They know what they want and see how to get it. So does the Coal Board."

"Yes, it's important that the Board be more positive. I've already warned the Secretary that the Secretary of State wishes to speak to the Chairman this evening. As to the NUM, I had hoped that Gormley would bring about some sense but he's missed the opportunity."

"He hasn't missed anything, Martin. He may have left school at fourteen but he's as smart as they come."

"It's fortunate that you have these contacts with him and his supporters. Julian thinks the information you get is valuable in judging what to do. He hopes that you can go on providing it."

"I'll certainly do so, though I'm not sure right now how valuable it's found to be."

"It can be only part of the picture, Pete – the *big* picture. Now, if you will excuse me, I must complete drafting the brief for Prime Minister's Questions tomorrow."

"Ed's draft will be ready for you very soon. I don't expect you'll need to make many changes."

"Oh, I think it's a mistake to deal with briefs as important as this at a junior level. I know the style that is preferred."

"You should at least look at what he's done, Martin. These last weeks he's been working very hard, against the odds. You need him to sort out the redundancy terms and the financial problems around grants. I've already suggested to Julian that he makes sure Ed has the legal support he needs. Ed also needs more people in his team, very urgently. You'll remember that a month ago Douglas offered to provide help if needed. Take him up on that."

"I'll consider it, Pete."

Martin looked more nonplussed than resentful at my suggestion that he should actually manage his staff. As soon as I returned, Jean was dialling.

"Liz wants an urgent word. Nothing wrong with Jenny, I hope?"

There wasn't, but the calls were stacking up at home. And was I going to be back in time that she could play squash at 7.15? I said yes before turning back to Jean.

"So, nothing more today once that note is around, and many thanks. Tomorrow I'll be in early again so it would be great if you can make it like today, but at 10.30 I'm off to Crawley."

"No probs, Pete. It's great to be in on this. You make everyone feel they're involved. That's not like some of the others here."

I spent an hour going through the day's papers on oil and on energy policy. Fortunately nothing needed much input from me and I was trying to avoid the civil servant's habit of making marginal comments on everything which then had to be photocopied and dropped into others' in trays.

Soon after 5.30 I was amidst the crowds heading for Victoria. The newsstands there were busy. The final edition of the *Evening Standard* was selling well, on its arresting headline:

DOWNING STREET DITHERERS

Below, there were pungent views on the afternoon's announcement that there would be no meeting with the NUM for another week, by which time most miners were expected to be on strike. Inside, there were pen portraits and mugshots of some of the principal players, all under the banner heading.

COUNTDOWN TO CRISIS.

That heading was also over another double-page spread which recalled 1972 and 1974, and carried some rather ill-informed speculation about the impact of a strike.

My train was cancelled – 'no guard' – but by dint of cramming onto a train going to a station two miles away and running most of the way from there, I was back home at five past seven. Liz was already changed.

"Here's Daddy to read you another story. Night-night, Jenny."

After a kiss, she drove off. I was still panting as I read the story and settled Jenny. Downstairs again, I read Liz's note.

'Casserole in oven, ready about 9. Back 8.30ish. Calls…'

I returned some calls and began notes for my morning bulletin. I suspected, though, that I would be adding nothing to what would be very clear by then. Just before half past eight the phone rang.

"Is Liz there?" I recognised the voice.

"I'm sorry, no, she isn't. Can she call you later?"

"Is that Pete?"

"Yes, it is."

"She's told me a lot about you and what you're doing. I guess you've had a bugger of a day."

"Yes, rather."

"So have I. There's only one way out of this. I'll tell you now." He went into detail, which I noted down. Then he continued. "And one other thing – your chum Carol's column yesterday was mostly fine but she needs to watch her back."

"How come?"

"She praised David Owen. The knives are out. I've another meeting now but can Liz call at about 10.30?"

He rang off as I heard Liz pull up outside. She took off her coat and pushed into my arms. I kissed her and slid my hand under her sports dress and round her bottom.

"Mmm, that's nice. Gosh, I just won, but I'm thrashed. You've not met Mary. She's nearly as tall as Morag so I was giving her eight inches. It's half an hour till we eat so just time for a shower. You look as if you need one, too, Pete. Great you made it. We've lots to talk about but first things first."

Showering together and soaping each other's bodies had been part of our relationship fifteen years before and it certainly was now. Liz still got a great kick out of having her ample breasts caressed and bounced up and down. Afterwards was familiar ground too but none the worse for that. First Liz lay face down across me, her breasts cupped into my left hand as my right ran over her back and bottom. After a few minutes she turned over for a really good de-tensing of the knotted-up muscles in her belly.

"Mmmmm.... I'm very wet." That was confirmed by the very pleasant squelching sound as my finger went in. "Ooh... There, harder... *Oooh*... Up a bit... *Harder*... Ready, you drive."

Ten minutes later we were both very satisfied.

We didn't exchange news until we were eating. Liz's reaction to mine was understandable.

"What a ghastly mess. How on earth did Martin Turner get to where he is now? He seems a complete disaster."

"He has a very good degree."

"So have you."

"I'm told that he could have been a fine historian. He wrote a well-regarded book on why the UK shouldn't have entered World War I but rather should have let Germany win it."

"Big deal."

"He's very good at saying nothing elegantly. He's not made any mistakes, so far."

"He's made one hell of a mistake now."

"Yes, the only cheering thing about his ignoring Ed Plunkett's work is that it will all have to be totally redone in the morning anyway."

"He really sounds like someone out of *Yes, Minister*.[48] Are they all like that?"

"No, but they're too good at avoiding decisions."

"Talking of *Yes, Minister*, it's lucky that Roberta and Frank have splashed out on their video recorder. We can ask them to record it next week, as well as looking after Jenny while we're at this dinner for Ana."

---

48 The second series of which was to begin on 23rd February.

"It's good that Jenny doesn't mind staying over with them. The dinner starts very early for Spain. Drinks are at 6.30 and dinner at 7.30. We'll still be back late, though. Talking of Jenny, you called me daddy in front of her for the first time."

We were sitting at the table side by side and I gave her a hug.

"Yes, for the first time but not for the last, Pete. I went over to the hospital today, as usual. The consultant was there and he asked for a word. He thought it was so good that I, you, and others were still coming in so often and talking to Greg. But he had to say, and he was sorry to say, that there's very little hope now. We need to make our own lives, as we've been doing, I guess."

I kissed her gently as the tears came and it was a few minutes before I replied.

"I guess that decides something for us. We should keep up with Brenda and Alan. Jenny needs a little brother or sister."

We kissed harder, before Liz returned to practical mode.

"Mmm yes, and before then some changes around the house. My time with Greg is part of my life and I'm proud of it. In the lounge, we'll have Melissa Copehurst's sketch of him, me and Jenny."

"People will ask about it. We'll have to be open with them."

"We'll need to be open anyway once Jenny starts at nursery in the summer. The other kids will ask her about her mummy and daddy. Enough people know about us that it shouldn't be a problem anymore."

"I like the sketch Melissa did of me. We'll put that up, too."

"And would you mind if we had the two of Rodin's *Kiss* in our bedroom?"

"That's a good idea. Perhaps downstairs we could risk pairing that sketch of Fred with Angela's Christmas present. They're both done very artistically."

"So we have two exes facing each other."

"Yes, though I was thinking that they would be on opposite sides of the display of Angela's work."

"She was a good sport to pose for Melissa."

"Long ago she told me that artists like posing for each other. And as you said long ago, below her plain but characterful face she has a good body. She's grown out of being an Ugly Sister, thanks to Morag. She's also been a good sport to give Melissa so much help in finding places to take stuff for sale. She did say that Melissa seems to be good at persuading some of her drama school friends into *very* saleable poses."

"Surprise, surprise! No doubt they get a cut. I'm glad you encouraged Angela to keep an eye, though."

"I said nothing at all definite, but Angela has knocked around enough to have sized Melissa up. She said that when the sketching was done there was a 'come on' moment, but she doesn't want anything to detract from the memory of her time with Morag."

"The important thing is that Melissa is on track to show her good side, in a role that doesn't involve caring for people. And the important thing for us now is that we're here for good. The tenancy at St Albans expires at the end of May. I'll sell it then. There could be £40,000 after paying off the mortgage, certainly £35,000. I know what I want to do with it, Pete."

"That depends on sorting out one thing, or rather one person, Liz."

"I know. Maybe the Spanish dinner will give us a chance to rebuild."

"Ana knows that's what I hope we can do."

"Gosh, it's a quarter past ten. You'd better make any calls you want before I make mine."

I called John Willis to give him my latest information before the early morning call he was likely to receive from Bernard Ingham. Then I called Douglas Arnott. He had been in Paris all day and was grateful for the chance to think overnight about how he should weigh in in the morning, at least by speaking to the Permanent Secretary. I also gave my view of Martin's approach to using and supporting his staff.

Then it was over to Liz, as I finished clearing up; but not for long. She returned, looking quite tense.

"Stop that and sit down. He wants me twice."

"What do you mean?"

"First, he knows I'll be in on Thursday for the National Executive, but he wants me to be ready to go in on Wednesday as well, for the tripartite. He says I know how to put the right piece of paper in front of the right man."

"That's fair enough. You could be on the attendance list as Mrs E.J. Woolley."

"The Coal Board people would spot me."

"Do they know we're together?"

"I've not been in touch with any of them recently."

"Let's hope that Roberta and Frank are around. By about lunchtime tomorrow you'll know for sure whether to ask them for Wednesday. I should tell a few people that you'll be there. I needn't tell Martin."

"That's the first way he wants me, the easy one, but now for the second way. He'll have a difficult job managing his end of the meeting and the Exec on Thursday may be very tough. He knows what he needs in between. So on Wednesday night he'll want me at the same place as before. Oh, Pete, *this*, and after what we were just saying."

She was referring to a small club near St James's Square which provided private dining facilities, rooms upstairs and total discretion. During Liz's earlier time with the NUM, visits there had never been part of her formal terms of employment; but Liz had gone into the job knowingly, and had enjoyed them. There were some more kisses before I replied.

"Liz, it's your decision. It won't affect us, except that Jenny's little brother or sister may have to wait until he retires. Before you married I helped to persuade Greg to accept this arrangement. I can hardly say no to it myself. I remember you saying that it was a chance for you to make a difference. Whether or not it was a chance then, it certainly is now."

HOUSE OF COMMONS, 17th FEBRUARY, 1981

Mr Foot. Has the Right Honourable lady had the chance today to apply her mind to the question of the growing coal crisis? While we are extremely grateful for the fact that the government has abandoned the stance that it appeared to be taking on Tuesday and Thursday last week, against having the tripartite meeting for which I asked, does she not think it absurd that the country should have to wait until next Monday for that meeting to take place? Will she give orders that it should take place at once?

The Prime Minister. My Right Honourable friend the Secretary of State for Energy will be having a meeting with the National Coal Board and the National Union of Mineworkers. It was at first fixed for next Monday because it was thought that that date was convenient to everyone. Since then, a message has come in with a request for a much earlier meeting. My Right Honourable friend will be making a statement about it after questions. It is expected to take place tomorrow.

Mr Foot. I thank the Right Honourable lady once again for having agreed to the proposal which the National Union of Mineworkers put forward this morning, which it put forward yesterday, and to which the government could have agreed. I thank the Right Honourable lady. Will she now agree that all proposals from the National Coal Board or the government will be held up until those conversations have taken place?

The Prime Minister. I imagine that tomorrow morning the area boards will carry on with their meetings with the unions. As one would expect, they took place yesterday, this morning, and are due to take place on Wednesday. They will need to do so to get the facts out about what their proposals are. I understand from the advice that I have received that there are far fewer pits to be closed than has been rumoured and, similarly, far fewer jobs to be lost than has been rumoured. It is absolutely vital that any talks should be conducted on the basis of the facts. I thank the Right Honourable gentleman for his thanks. It is a rare treat.

9. WEDNESDAY, 18ᵀᴴ FEBRUARY, 1981

"It's total surrender, I'm afraid. I told her that this would cost £500 million but she wasn't listening. It was very upsetting indeed."[49]

So Martin Turner concluded his dispirited account of a meeting at No. 10 late the day before. Julian Street seemed more nonplussed than dispirited. He didn't actually ask for any ideas but that was his implication.

"We're not where we wanted to be but where do we go next? There's another meeting at No. 10 at 12.30 to discuss what to say at the tripartite. Thank you for your latest information, Pete. At least we know the worst. When I called the Chairman earlier, he didn't seem to have a clue about what was happening, or if he did he didn't let on."

Ronald Clarkson had a few ideas. He knew the words to use, because he had been in the Coal Directorate a few years before.

"I take it that the aim is still to minimise the commitments but it looks as if we'll have to make some. Pete, I was interested in the two notes you did on Monday. Do you think we can get away with a promise to examine the scope for reducing imports?"

"We'll have to be more positive than that but I think we can avoid any numbers. Obviously the NUM's bottom line is a bit better than the message to me. We should be able to say that British Steel will have to discuss with its unions what would be the implications for jobs of any switch back to British coking coal. The steel unions say they support the miners but they won't

---

49 For Margaret Thatcher's description of this encounter and of other events narrated here, see *The Downing Street Years*, p. 141.

give any support that hurts them. Last year they went on strike for three months but had no useful support from the NUM at all."

"That's a good idea. Martin, speak to DTI about the words that can be used. They'll need to speak to Ian MacGregor[50] urgently," said Julian.

"The word is 'discuss', which MacGregor should agree, not 'consult', which he certainly won't agree," I said. "If necessary, I can weigh in with my oppo in DTI."

"Also, Julian, I was thinking about this coal liquefaction demonstration plant," said Ronald. "I gather that the British Association of Colliery Management is particularly keen on it. Could we set up a tripartite sub-group to look at the possibilities? That would get one of the three unions at this afternoon's meeting into a better mood."

"See if you can sell that to the Treasury, then, Ronald," Julian responded.

"Neither of those will be the clincher," I said. "I wasn't around for the discussions yesterday afternoon but I presume the aim is to end the tripartite with the proposed closures still in play at local level within the established procedures. The people who've talked to me over the last few days know the position at most of the twenty-three pits announced for closure. If there's some extension of the redundancy terms, at least half of them will close quietly, within a year or so. We don't yet need the whole of the Board's package. Ed has listed out the improvements which look most attractive and form a coherent package. He's also spoken to the Board's office which manages the steel and shipbuilding redundancy schemes as well as the Board's own scheme. As a result, he has a table which compares payments under the three schemes to men of various ages. It shows that these improvements can

---

50 He had become Chairman of the British Steel Corporation after the 1980 strike.

be presented as not going radically beyond what's available to steel or shipbuilding workers. Can he run through all this for a moment?"

Martin looked displeased while Ed did that, but Julian, Ronald and John were certainly interested. Then Ed moved to what he and I saw as the clincher.

"Martin, I think your £500 million extra cost is the total over the next three years. It comes from what the Board told us yesterday would be the costs of not going ahead with the closures they've announced. That's between £150 million and £200 million a year. The total extra costs of improved redundancy terms over the next three years are rather lower, at about £300 million."

Ed passed round another sheet of paper but Ronald objected.

"The £300 million is on top of the £500 million, not an alternative to it."

"As Pete says, with these terms the Board ought to be able to get at least half of its proposals. That would be over double the recent rate of closures. Assuming proportionality, the £500 million cost of no closures comes down to £250 million. So there would be an extra spend of around £550 million. That's not much different from the £500 million, but over half of it is about solving the problem, rather than prolonging it. The Prime Minister should like that."

"It's now five past ten," I said. "The tripartite meeting begins at five o'clock. By then we need Treasury and DTI agreement to the following. The Coal Board should say that there isn't a national closure list but there are twenty-three proposed closures to enter discussion with the unions under the established local procedures. Ministers should accept the principle of improved redundancy terms. Those should be detailed next month when the parliamentary Order is published for approval but should apply to anybody leaving after today. Ministers should also say anything they can say about imports, and oil from coal. That adds up to a coherent first response. It would give a good chance that tomorrow the NUM Executive will recommend suspension of local strikes while there are further talks, and won't yet call a national strike ballot."

"Pete, we can't do that in the time," said Martin. "Before we approached the other departments formally, we would need to clear our lines with the Board."

"After the mess they've got us into they can damn well do as we say and like it," said John, who had been silent so far. "I'm with Pete and Ed. For the first time this week we've a chance of being seen as offering a sensible response, not just dithering about. I can sell that to Bernard. He's been wondering how effective improved redundancy terms would be, but coupled with a return to normal procedures it all makes sense."

"I'm ready to go to the Treasury with it," said Ronald. "We'll also be able to say that we're doing something about the financial controls. Following your word with the lawyers, Julian, I've a meeting with them at 10.30. I'm sticking with it, despite all else that's going on."

Julian was calling his secretary and waved us to be quiet.

"Get me John Moore's[51] office... Is he free for an urgent word?... Due to go out in five minutes? We'll be down straight away."

We arrived to find John Moore talking to his private secretary[52] in a rather agitated way.

"Alan, I simply can't go to this energy conservation event right now. Call them and apologise. They know there's a crisis in coal."

So we had a little longer than five minutes to calm him down and explain. He seemed relieved that there might actually be some kind of plan for the afternoon.

---

51 Then the Parliamentary Under-Secretary whose responsibilities included coal. Now Lord Moore of Lower Marsh.
52 A middle grade civil servant whose task was to support the Minister within his private office.

"This looks to be the best we can do. Alan, get me in to see the Secretary of State as soon as possible, and make more copies of these two very useful notes. Julian, John, you had better be with me when I speak to him. He wants to take this first tripartite meeting as purely exploratory."

I spoke slowly and clearly.

"If he does that, tomorrow the NUM National Executive Committee will authorise the strikes in its Areas and call a national strike ballot for next Thursday."

Julian looked firmly at Martin and continued.

"I can see why you want to keep the meeting with the Secretary of State small, but can you bring the Permanent Secretary in? Pete, Ed and Ronald can go round and brief him now."

Martin kept quiet. Luckily the Permanent Secretary was free, and ten minutes later the three of us had signed him up. By then his office had been told of a meeting with the Secretary of State at eleven o'clock.

"That was a very good start to the day by both of you," said Ronald as we went back to his office.

"It followed a very good day's work yesterday whilst I was in Crawley," I replied. "Did you actually go home last night, Ed?"

"For about six hours. Fortunately, I'm near the District Line. The two people Douglas Arnott has provided were useful straight away and stayed on, too. They were pretty excited to be in on all this. One of them picked up very quickly the task of telling people where the tripartite meeting is being held, providing attendance lists and a seating plan, and so on. I would have suggested that they come to Julian's meeting but Martin doesn't yet know that they're here."

At Ronald's office, the department's senior lawyer and two of his team were waiting. Ronald apologised for the delay and invited Ed to explain where we were.

"The pension-based redundancy terms for the more senior people in the coal industry, and the costs of transferring men from one pit to another, are paid for through government grants which were introduced in the late '60s. Since then the aim has been to define precisely the amounts that the Board can claim but no-one has given any priority to doing that. The excuse was that if the money were not paid as one of these grants then it would be paid to the Board through another grant. However, just before I moved to this post, E & AD[53] noticed the lack of financial control. They asked some questions which were actually quite wrong, but in the course of answering we discovered and had to admit to a different overpayment of grant. So they realised that we were a soft target, offering plenty of bangs per buck. Anything they lobbed in was likely to hit something, however ill-prepared or misconceived it was. Fortunately, they haven't yet hit the worst error."

"What's that?" asked Ronald.

"All these grants are supposed to be for costs relating to pit closures. That's what the legislation has said since 1965. However, the Board has been claiming the costs of all staff early retirements and transfers, irrespective of whether they have anything to do with pit closures. Over the past ten years, about £15 million has been paid out without any statutory authority."

"The Board's auditors are supposed to have confirmed that the claims are correct. Have they done so?"

"Yes, but when I asked to see what checks they had actually made, the Board's finance people got very angry and complained to Martin."

"What did Martin do?"

"He's refusing to authorise some of the grant payments until there are clearer rules."

"Coming in from outside, I find this complicated framework of grants rather bewildering," I said. "Ideally there would be something much simpler to administer, with less scope for

---

[53] The Exchequer and Audit Department, predecessor of the National Audit Office.

mistakes. We're landed with it, though, and Ministers have emphasised that these grants will continue. Indeed, they will increase if more men leave."

"So we must get it right," said Ronald. "We'll have no credibility with the Treasury unless they see us on the way to that. You've made a very good start, Ed. What support do you need to finish the job and give us clearer rules?"

"There need to be proper legal agreements with the Coal Board that define what can be claimed. We need a lawyer full time to draw them up."

I added that there was also likely to be a lot of urgent work on the parliamentary Order which would define improved redundancy terms and deal with my 'sweetener list' of queries from miners' MPs. Soon we had agreement that by the next day the legal team would set out changed priorities to its customers. Those whose work was delayed would have to accept that. Crises have their value.

The lawyers had just left when John turned up. He advised us to sit comfortably before he began.

"When I arrived at the Secretary of State's office, Martin was already there. He said that the Secretary of State had specifically asked that he be at the meeting. When we got in Martin was asked for his views first. He trotted out more or less what he had said on Monday evening – he was sure that the Secretary of State could hold the situation without saying anything definite tonight. Julian should have intervened but he didn't. The Perm Sec followed Julian. John Moore looked rather confused. All I could say was that I thought we would be pressed hard for definite concessions, and I read out parts of your reports, Pete. The Secretary of State wasn't listening any more. He had heard from Martin what he wanted to hear. Now, he and John Moore have gone off to No. 10, with Julian – and with Martin."

It was some seconds before any of us could say anything. Eventually, Ronald managed to open his mouth.

"So he kept fairly quiet at the meetings with all of us. Then, once we'd gone off to see the Perm Sec, he makes a beeline for the Secretary of State's office. He knows the people there. He tells them who's coming to the eleven o'clock meeting, in a way that leaves them no option but to invite him in, too. Then, and only then, does he come out with his line. John, I'm sure that he was very soft-talking and persuasive."

"Yes, he was."

"This is ridiculous," I said. "I thought that once civil servants had an agreed line, they put it collectively. How did Julian allow this to happen?"

"Martin isn't a man to underestimate, Pete," said Ronald. "He does know how to get his way. That's why he's where he is, now. I did wonder why he took Julian's comments about a small meeting so quietly. He got in to see the Secretary of State and you didn't."

"I'd been expecting to have to call off an important meeting that I have this afternoon in the City. It seems now that I needn't call it off, but I'll be back here well before five o'clock. Make sure I'm somewhere at the back, Ed."

"Martin said that he wants the numbers of officials kept down."

"I bet he does. However, Douglas has asked me to attend on his behalf because he will be on his way to Brussels. I'm not missing this. We could have focussed on a sensible plan a month ago, on Monday or even this morning. We haven't done that, because of Martin's smooth talk. This evening he's going to be found out."

I returned to my office. Jean grinned as she handed me a list of messages.

"It's popular boy Pete, again. Are things going OK?"

"No," I said, tersely. "Sorry, I'm fuming."

"Oh dear, I'll make you a coffee. Who's Carol? Does Liz know about her?"

"Yes. Carol Milverton MP is an old friend. We both met her in Cambridge."

I read her message. 'Can we have a bite at 1.15 in the Two Chairmen? Reply only if you can't.'

"The last caller, Brian, said it was very urgent."

"Get him, first."

Despite the urgency, I was put through only after the usual tussle of secretaries, each wanting to stop their boss having to speak to the other.

"Where's the best fair-sized pub near your office, Pete? Good if it serves northern beers."

"Hmm, there aren't many around here. Your best bet is probably the Morpeth Arms. That's along Millbank, between the Tate and Vauxhall Bridge. Why?"

He explained. I asked a few questions and suggested that he alert the Morpeth to this unexpected custom. As soon as we had finished, I called Jean in.

"Right, Jean, before anything else, take the following minute.[54] URGENT. To: Mr Willis. Copies: PS/Secretary of State, PS/Mr Moore, PS/Permanent Secretary, Mr Arnott, Mr Street, Mr Turner, Mr Clarkson, Mr Plunkett. I am told that parties of miners are setting off from Yorkshire, South Wales, Kent and possibly elsewhere. They will be outside this building from 4 pm onwards, to encourage the NUM leadership on its arrival here for the tripartite meeting. They will be expecting to be told of the conclusions of the meeting once it finishes. The leadership is aware of this. Local reporters are travelling with the parties, and some of the coaches used may have been paid for by the local press. Miners' MPs may join them, though this depends on timings of the evening's business. Total numbers may be several hundred. There is no intention to obstruct normal traffic in and out of the building or along Millbank, and the width of the pavement should allow that."

---

[54] Then the Civil Service term for note or memorandum. PS was short for private secretary.

After some practice, I was getting the civil service style right. Whilst Jean typed and circulated that, I attended to another message.

This time, my oppo in DTI wanted my help. The Commons had two substantial motions for debate that evening. He was concerned with the second, which was to increase the powers of the British Steel Corporation to 'borrow' from the government, pending implementation of Ian MacGregor's rationalisation plan. Labour was not opposing this, or the first motion which was to increase the amounts that could be paid out in rebates to employers towards statutory redundancy pay. However, they wanted full debates so as to make the most of the government's difficulties, especially as it was expected that several Conservative backbenchers would want to contrast the huge assistance to British Steel with the lack of support to that part of the steel industry which was still in the private sector. It looked to be a long night. Could I join a Box conference at ten o'clock?

I supposed so. At least this would be a favour remembered when we were able to sort something out on imports. As I put the phone down, I had an idea. I dialled a number I knew and was promised a call back in ten minutes. I had just time to dash down to the library before Pat O'Donnell came on.

"Well, Pete, how's the department? You're in the thick of it, I guess."

"You could say that."

"I hope you're not responsible for this prize cock-up in coal."

"I'm trying to help pick up the pieces but doing other things, too. Late tonight there's a debate about steel. DTI reckon there'll be lots on industrial energy costs. I'm looking at your article in last month's *Business Today*. You give figures on energy costs for Sunderland, and the reductions to be achieved at the new plant there. People tend to forget that these costs are high for new industries, as well as for old. Your message is to stop moaning and find ways to improve efficiency. Can you be quoted?"

"Yes, of course."

"I'll draft something out and have it read over to your office."

"It's good to hear from you, Pete. I hope you're finding enough time for Creators Technology. Your autumn report looked good."

"We're facing some decisions. There's something I had in mind to ask you."

I explained briefly and arranged to see him on Saturday. By the time I rang off, Jean was back. I dictated another note.

"I need to take that with me in half an hour. Then you'll need to read it over to Sir Pat O'Donnell's office, on this number."

Half an hour later I set off for the Two Chairmen – then, as now, a quiet pub to the south of St James's Park. On my way, I left the note at the DTI building in Victoria Street and called my oppo from their reception so that he could collect it. Neither my department nor the DTI had a document transmission machine of the kind that I had used in IE for several years.

Carol arrived at the pub a few minutes after me, looking rather worried under her usual cheerful face. I could guess why.

"Pete, it's great that we can meet. Paul told me you had a meeting with him scheduled so I guessed you would be on your way if you could be. I hope this means it will be sensible this evening."

"It means I've done everything I can. Have you heard about the miners coming down here?" I explained.

"That just about does it, Pete. The constituency office should have called me."

"Perhaps no-one from Holtcliffe is coming. Brian's people are about three constituencies away."

"They should have let me know. I'm being cut out. I suppose I asked for it on Sunday."

"You mean by referring to David Owen."

"Yes, but last summer he *was* the energy spokesman. If he's treated as a non-person, he'll break away completely. So, Pete, you're one of the people whose judgement I admire and trust. Should I come out?"

Late in January, on the day after the Wembley conference had changed the leadership election rules in favour of trades unions, Roy Jenkins, Bill Rodgers and Shirley Williams had met with David Owen at his house. In the 'Limehouse Declaration', they had said that they would set up a 'Council for Social Democracy'. They had not at this stage formed a separate party but this was on the cards. Several Labour MPs had already declared their support.

"I don't know, Carol, I really don't know. My only advice is to do what you're most comfortable with and what suits best where you think you're going. Do you actually want to be a politician or a journalist?"

"I've been trying to be both."

"Plenty have been both, like your new leader who was a big name in the maverick Conservative *Daily Express*. That was before he became frontline, though."

"Paul thinks I should toe the line enough to avoid being deselected and write more while I wait for the tide to turn. There's a lot of sense in that, I know, but if Thatcher holds on I could be waiting a long time and I wouldn't be making my name in Opposition. Alternatively, if Labour win on anything like their present programme, I'm nowhere, particularly as a woman."

"As Pat O'Donnell once said on TV, don't believe the manifestos. I can't advise you about being a woman but I remember your being an admirer of Barbara Castle. Do you know her well enough to talk to her, if you can find a time when she's here?" [55]

"That's a good idea, Pete. I think I can."

"My guess, just a guess, is that any new party won't break through. If it does, there'll be years of fighting with Labour whilst

---

[55] Despite being opposed to membership of the European Communities, she had become a Member of the European Parliament after losing her Commons seat in 1979.

the Conservatives stay on top, as they did while the Liberals went down in the '20s."

"Yes, and just as Baldwin did then they would encourage the new party until it became stronger than the old one. I think you're telling me to stay in for the moment."

"Yes, because if you come out you're out of Parliament at the next election. No new party will have a spare, winnable seat for you. More immediately, even if you haven't been told about these miners, come and join them. They'll be good for an article somewhere, I'm sure. You can say hi to Brian, too."

"That fits well, Pete. I know some miners' MPs want to speak in the redundancy fund debate, so they won't be there. I can show my face and then get back for the steel debate. I can speak in that. They need people to match the Tory backbenchers. There's no steel plant in Holtcliffe but about 400 constituents work in the industry."

"I've been roped in for a Box conference at ten o'clock. I expect I'll look in at the Morpeth beforehand."

"The steel debate will go on very late. I can put you up afterwards, in the spare room, of course, though Paul will be away." She grinned.

"Thanks, but I'm hoping I'm there just for the conference. I do need to get home tonight. The NUM has called Liz in, and Roberta and Frank are looking after Jenny today. Tomorrow it's down to me, for Liz's regular work day."

"The department is getting a good day and a half a week from you."

"It is just now. You're not exactly idle yourself, Carol. New Hampshire keeps Paul busy. Brian is moving up in Universal Assurance and doing a lot for the new insurance livery company. The Pankhurst Centre devours time for Sheila and Morag. Most of the Creators are busy. We're all aiming to do something with our lives and make a difference."

"Talking of Creators, is Jenny – big Jenny, I mean – still being silly about you and Liz?"

"She's still very cool, though not as icy as she was last March. In October, we visited them for Katie's birthday and then in November they came to us for little Jenny's birthday. Children are great healers."

Carol made a slight grimace at my perhaps tactless reference to children.

"I had quite a row with her. I reminded her of how she threw you over for Dick. That made her pretty upset."

"I hope we're moving on. Jenny will be at my meeting with Paul and we'll both be at a dinner the Spanish Ambassador is giving for Ana next Monday evening."

"I'm looking forward to meeting Ana on Tuesday. She's becoming quite a politician herself. Spain is one of Paul's responsibilities at the bank. He says there's plenty in their papers about her as the aristocrat who believes in democracy. Look, thanks for meeting up when you're so busy, Pete. You've helped lots. You need to get to your meeting. See you later at the Morpeth Arms."

The meeting at New Hampshire Realty's offices was to go over the latest financial projections for Creators Technology and to see what we could do both to fill the financing gap and to be ready to accelerate development if the stories about IBM were substantiated. I hoped that we could make progress, but without a full team it was going to be difficult. Paul had observed that like the Coal Board, we had no realistic financial strategy. We were definitely between a rock and a hard place and missing something we needed. He didn't actually say that we needed other financial advice unless Jenny was ready to make the creative input of which she was capable, but he implied that.

The day had given me one useful idea, as I explained to Paul's two colleagues who dealt with credit control.

"I've arranged to see Sir Pat O'Donnell on Saturday. He retires at the end of March and I might be able to persuade him to become our Chairman. I hope that having someone of Pat's stature on board would increase your confidence in Creators Technology. He may be ready to invest more, too."

"Mmm, we might be able to lend you another £50,000 but it would cost you. Interest would be fixed for three years, with a penalty for early repayment."

"That doesn't worry me. We're on track to have this product on the market before anyone else. It will become the industry standard. Every trading organisation will want it once they understand how it works. To make sure they understand that, I'll write the manual myself. Jenny can check its readability. She began as a reporter and publisher's sub-editor."

Jenny nodded. She had little choice but to do so. I went on.

"We just need the capital to develop the reliable product. Once it's developed the production cost will be under £500 for a few copy protected floppy discs, the manual and a nice box. Our dummy simulations set out here show what profit can be made from using it. Trading organisations should be prepared to pay £10,000 for it. Paul, you're clear that there's a market for at least 500 copies in the year after announcement, perhaps 1,000. Our entire costs will be recovered within months."

"And then someone bigger than you puts out a better product."

"No, we put out a better product, with some discount for existing users to upgrade."

"What happens when everyone has it?"

"Once people are aware of the profits that can be made from arbitrage using it, more and more copies can be sold," said Paul. "As networks develop and become interlinked, the potential increases hugely. Look at the predictions in this article in *Computing Weekly*. By 1990 a world network will be developing. It will link everyone and everything."

"1990 is a long time away. We'll have a word with Jim."

"Who's Jim?" asked Jenny, after Paul's two colleagues had gone out.

"Jim Schurman is the Head of Credit Control," responded Paul. "It's a good sign. You're being taken seriously."

To pass the time, I referred to Ana's forthcoming visit. That prompted Paul to say more about the Spanish political scene.

"It's a pretty confusing picture there right now. The centrist UCD party is still in government but its leader, Adolfo Suárez, resigned at the end of last month. There is now a new leader, Leopoldo Calvo Sotelo, but to be Prime Minister he needs the approval of the Congress of Deputies, the Spanish parliament. That's supposed to be happening on Friday."

The name rang a bell for me. "There's an Avenida Calvo Sotelo in most Spanish towns, named after a man who was assassinated just before the start of the Civil War."

"That was José Calvo Sotelo. Leopoldo is his nephew. He was quite a big man under Franco but is very firm that now is the time for democracy."

"He sounds like Ana's man."

"Ana supports him strongly and may have swung some votes for him to succeed Suárez. But now there's a clear split in her family. Carlos has come out in public for *Fuerza Nueva*, the Francoist party."

"Ana also supports Franco, the Franco who knew things had to change after him."

We carried on until the credit control team returned. I had been hoping that Jenny would refer to some conversation with Ana, but she didn't.

The team's message was about as good as we could expect.

"We can lend another £75,000, on the fixed interest terms I said. That will be subject to your finding at least another £100,000 of equity. There's to be no drawdown on any of our lending before the start of 1982. Your equity will need to cover your costs for the rest of this year."

After they had left again, I summed up.

"So, there it is. With that loan available, we need assurance of at least another £175,000, and much preferably something like £225,000. I can put in another £25,000, so we need another £200,000, some of it this year."

Paul had a plane to catch and Jenny wasn't being communicative. In any case, there was no point in discussing it further. I didn't want questions about my £25,000, though both Jenny and Paul would guess its source. I was selling my remaining stake in 'Plain Jane's' to a very satisfied customer whom a disappointed but realistic Jane had sent my way.

I returned to find groups of burly men standing around outside the department and coaches pulling in to drop off more. There were also a few police and, I suspected, others out of sight round the corner; but it seemed clear that people knew to avoid obstruction. A TV crew was setting up. At my office, Jean was excited.

"Oooh Pete, the girls are all worried about these miners. Will we be able to get out of the building? But I told them you said there won't be a problem. It's super to be involved in things which are all over the papers and TV."

"Super isn't quite the word for where we are now, Jean, but I'm very grateful for all you've done recently. Once we've dealt with these messages, I suggest you be on your way. You'll be home in time to see the outcome on TV."

Whilst I was out, Jean had clearly had a whale of a time feeding the secretarial grapevine but I knew I could rely on her to say nothing about Liz's role. She had taken down a small change Pat wanted to my quote and phoned it through to the DTI.

I was rather relieved that there was no invitation to a last-minute briefing. There would be no point in shoving my oar in at this stage. I called DTI to check that there were no problems with Pat's change, and then Roberta to explain that I, as well as Liz, would be very late. There was, as I had expected, no problem at all in Jenny staying overnight. She was such a lovely little girl. She had a word with 'daddy' before I disposed of some other work.

By twenty to five I was on my way to the department's large conference room. In the corridor outside, a private secretary was arguing with John Willis.

"The Secretary of State is very clear, John. No reporters inside the building."

"So he wants them hearing it all from the people outside. We must give our briefing straight after."

"We'll brief when we've worked out our line and not before."

The room seated about fifty people round a large table, and more below the windows looking over Millbank. I joined Ed at a side table there. Soon after I sat down the continuing murmur from the crowd outside broke into a roar. To the background of phrases such as 'Sort them, Joe!' and 'With you all the way', I commented to Ed on the view nearby.

"If Martin wanted a small meeting, he hasn't got it. Who are all those people over there?"

"Officials of the Scottish and Welsh Departments, who have junior ministers attending. The Treasury and Employment Department have declined to attend."

"That's very sensible of them. I reckon an enterprising reporter not known to John could blag his way into here. Everyone would think he's from another team."

A few minutes later the Secretary of State led the ministerial team in, followed by the Permanent Secretary, Julian, Martin and various private secretaries. They took the seats on our side of the table. John took a seat to one side, with two of his staff. The Coal Board's people and the two smaller unions arrived together. They took seats opposite us and their mutual bonhomie rather gave the game away. Last of all, the NUM team filled the remaining places opposite us. Joe Gormley, Mick McGahey and Lawrence Daly were accompanied by various officers and support. Liz pulled a chair round to where she could sit behind the Big Three. We avoided eye contact. The man I knew to be the Coal Board's Secretary recognised her. He wouldn't recognise me.

At two minutes past five, the Secretary of State launched off. He welcomed this chance for a frank discussion of the issues. He hoped we could get away from some of the exaggerated stories which had appeared in the press. Those had caused unnecessary worry and agitation to thousands of people employed in the industry. He was sure that this initial meeting could be followed by others which could develop the issues further. And so on, and so on. I couldn't see his face but he sounded like a man who knew he had lost already.

The reason for that soon became apparent. No doubt it had been discussed earlier in the afternoon. On came Sir Derek Ezra, Chairman of the National Coal Board. His rather growling, bleating delivery didn't assist him but, after some preamble, he came out with the killer words.

"The Treasury has set this financial straitjacket in which we have to operate. Given the impact of the recession on the demand for coal, we have to take measures to bring the supply of coal more in line with demand." I saw Martin Thomas wince. No doubt he had tried to persuade the Board not to come out with this line.

Then it was Joe Gormley's turn. He sounded bewildered but to a purpose.

"Derek, what's this all about? Last year, you said how good it looked for coal, how we all had a great future working together. What the heck's going on?"

Ezra mumbled something. Gormley didn't wait for more but turned to John Moore. As he did so, Liz put a note in front of him.

"And you, John – should I call you John? I don't really know what to call you."

"Oh, of course, yes," said John Moore, defensively and almost inaudibly.

"Time and time again, right through last year, only a few months ago, you were saying how well things were going." He looked down at the note. "You said that coal was a most exciting energy industry on the brink of an outstanding future. But now we have *this*! I hope you know how angry the men are. They've been deceived."

Again, Gormley did not wait for an answer but turned his fire.

"Secretary of State, what are *you* going to do about it? And don't say there's nothing you can do. We're importing millions of tons of coal that we needn't import. Make proper use of our exciting energy industry."

"To be clear," said Mick McGahey, "unless you do something about it, and fast, the men will all be out by Monday."

After all that, the representative of the deputies' union NACODS supported Gormley in a rather incoherent speech. Then the man from the British Association of Colliery Management chipped in, with an appeal to all in our great industry to work together in a more flexible financial framework than the government was presently allowing. He also reminded us of the virtues of making oil from coal.

Meanwhile, John Moore, the Permanent Secretary, Julian and Martin vied to put notes in front of the Secretary of State. Perhaps encouraged by these, he tried to play for time.

"I think we all recognise that pit closures are inevitable in an extractive industry. The Plan for Coal certainly anticipated that they would continue, alongside massive investment in continuing pits as well as in new pits. Nearly £300 million is being invested in continuing pits this year. What I would like to suggest is that the Board and the unions discuss a pattern of closures consistent with Plan for Coal and the economic realities, standing back from the financial constraints which you've argued the industry cannot sustain. At the same time, the Board should discuss with the industries which are currently importing coal what can be done to reduce these imports. I know they are already on a falling trend and we need to know what can be done to accelerate that trend. On oil from coal, I propose that we ask a technical sub-group to meet, and to report to us. I hope all that can be done quickly, and then I can come back to you with proposals as to what the government can do to help."

"So, are you telling us that the Board is withdrawing its list of closures?" asked McGahey, grimly.

"I'm saying that the Board can discuss with you what could be done, standing back from the financial constraints."

Lawrence Daly had earlier removed his jacket and tie. Now he leaned forward over the table, breathing heavily.

"Secretary of State, I don't think you understand. We've come here to hear that list withdrawn. We've come here to be told that imports will stop. The men outside have come here to hear us tell them that. The men all over the country are waiting to hear that – tonight!"

There was a silence.

"It's for you to answer, Secretary of State," said Gormley.

There was an even longer silence. Ezra took his moment.

"I think that what you're asking us to do, Secretary of State, is to withdraw our closure proposals and re-examine the position in consultation with the unions, with a view to movement. We'll do that, including looking at the scope for reducing imports. Those could be much lower than now, though there is an irreducible minimum comprising special coals which simply can't be found here."

There was no dissent. The NUM trio conferred in murmurs but not for long. Liz gave Gormley another note and he continued with a smile.

"That's a very sensible way ahead that Derek has suggested. We're still booked to meet next Wednesday. Let's stick with that and see how we're getting on."

McGahey and Daly tried to look not wholly satisfied. There were nods from the Coal Board and the other unions. It remained only for the Secretary of State to close the meeting. As soon as he could decently do so, he left the room with the other ministers and officials. The Coal Board and union teams followed.

I sat in silence while Ed jotted down more points in his notes. Suddenly there was a cheer from outside, doubtless as the miners there received a message. Then a chant began.

"*We want Joe. We want Joe…*"

"I think they'll be carrying him shoulder high, not tearing him limb from limb," said Ed.

"Yes, what an act that was. The three of them knew exactly what to say and when. Gormley has preserved his image of the moderate, under pressure. The other two played along."

"The lady who was hovering behind them is your partner, Pete?"

"Yes."

"You must be very proud of her."

"I certainly am."

"It must be very odd for you, being on both sides."

"I'm on the side of common sense. You fight to win. You don't fight to lose. By the way, what was that business between Gormley and Moore about?"

"It was a pay-off for what happened at the end of June. Ministers had a meeting with the whole of the NUM Executive about the Coal Industry Bill. John Moore tried to show off. As soon as the union people came into the room, he went over radiating friendliness. 'Oh, hello, *Joe.*' Gormley's face said it all. For a Conservative to do that in front of the whole Executive…!"

"Whatever he felt about that, Joe Gormley has been handed a triumph. He'll have no problem in getting the Exec to recommend that the men go back pending discussions."

As I said that, louder cheers from outside confirmed it.

"I'd better stay and write the meeting note," said Ed.

"I wouldn't do much until you see the account for No. 10 that's doubtless being concocted in the Secretary of State's office right now. The key thing for us is to be able to say something about redundancy terms at next week's meeting. Why don't we argue that in the light of this meeting, improved terms are necessary to obtain agreement to any closures at all? That will keep the estimates of cost down."

"I've been having another idea about making the short-term costs look lower, too." He explained.

"That sounds good but we need some accountancy advice on it – proper accountancy advice from someone who knows the score. I know who to talk to. I'll get back to you on Friday. Until then, Jean knows where to find me if necessary."

A few minutes later I was strolling down Millbank, past groups of miners dispersing cheerfully. The Morpeth Arms was crowded but I spotted Carol with Brian and an older, stockier version of Brian.

"So yer'll the bugger I've been talking ter," said Alan Smitham. "In t'*Post* a year back, but dain't like it, oop North. What's wrong with oos, then?"

"I'm running my own company now. Brian is a director."

"Yeah, you know that, Dad, stop ribbing. What a day for you, eh?"

"'Twas a day for Joe. Mick and Lawrence just had to do their part. And Arthur – he'll just 'ave to like it. Now, sup oop time. Sorry to leave yer so fast but some of t'lads are to go down on t'afternoon shift tomorrer. Great to meet yer, Pete; heard so much about yer. Brian weren't be where he is without yer."

Alan made for the gents' on the way to his coach as the crowd thinned out. What he had said about Brian was quite true, though neither he nor Brian knew why.

Brian looked at his watch.

"I can just make the 7.20 from Charing Cross. See you Tuesday, Pete."

"I'll be calling you at the weekend, Brian."

"God, I'm starving," said Carol. "I bet you are, too, Pete. Come back to my place for a bite. You cook, I type. Then we eat and read through. I should be at the House for nineish, but first I've a slot in the *Courier* tomorrow. I'm not trying to pump you. I've enough of the story from union people, though I wasn't able to catch Liz. I won't mention David Owen!"

"Gormley used the title of your article."

"He doesn't need to watch his back right now."

We grabbed a taxi and by eight o'clock were nearly through spaghetti bolognaise and a bottle of Chianti. I chipped in while Carol jotted some amendments onto her first draft.

"That's a better way to refer to what Ezra said. But what you're describing at the end hasn't happened yet!"

"I know I'll get into the debate and I think I know how it will go. If necessary, I can phone a correction through any time before midnight. Now, Pete, I'll whizz this off while you wash up, then if you can drop it at the *Courier* office in Fleet Street that would be great. Sorry to rush you along."

"Not at all, and thanks for the meal, or rather, the non-meal. This meeting didn't happen, like lots of other meetings and discussions I've had recently. I'm glad you've picked up this opportunity."

"It was your suggestion, Pete. You've done me two good turns today. We must have a more leisurely meal together sometime."

Carol leaned towards me in a way that would have given me a good view down her cleavage if she had had one. More importantly, there was a look in her eye that I knew.

"That's an interesting suggestion, Carol. Perhaps that wouldn't be a non-meal."

"It might not be."

"Just remember what I told you about Greg. In all practical ways, Liz and I are married."

"Paul and I are married in all ways, and happily despite our arguments about politics. I understand, Pete. Now, we'd better get on."

Ten minutes later, we were reading through her retype. "You're certainly quite a fast typist," I said.

"I can do forty words per minute. That certainly helps when you're on deadlines. Now, I'll just ring the *Courier* so they expect you."

As I sat next to Carol on the Underground, I reflected that she wasn't changing as a person, whatever was happening to her politics. She had always enjoyed making a pass at me, though she didn't mind being fended off, at least for the first time. She looked very tempting. For a moment I recalled good moments of the past.

I wondered how Liz was doing at recreating good moments of the past. She had told me once that they had usually done it early on, before having too much to eat and drink. Today he would want to unwind in triumph. Liz could be riding him right now after enjoying the feel of his hands bouncing her breasts. If there had been more time with Carol this evening…

Could Carol have been dropping a hint that she knew about Liz, from the past if not now? As far as I knew, the secret was very tight but you never could tell.

Carol alighted at Westminster. I continued to Temple and found the *Courier* offices. By half past nine I was back at the Houses of Parliament. The DTI officials waiting around the Box entrance were relieved when I introduced myself.

"Thank goodness you're early. Norman Tebbit is coming out in ten minutes. It's on the press tapes that the miners have won game, set and match. Keith Joseph's office has sent over what's just come in."

They waved in front of me the letter to the Prime Minister that had been concocted in the Secretary of State's office.[56]

"I was at the meeting. The miners have won this game but there are at least six games in a set and three sets in a match."

"You'd better talk it through with him."

Ten minutes later, I did so. Norman Tebbit's conclusion was definite.

"God, what a mess. How's David going to get out of it?"

"Immediately, we need to take two steps, both of which affect your department. The redundancy terms need to be improved and there needs to be a visible attempt to reduce imports. Fortunately, we can draw up a package of improved terms which will deliver exits without creating serious comparability problems with steel or shipbuilding. Also fortunately, it's clear that any switch back to British coking coal can only follow trials taking several weeks, so as yet there can't be a definite commitment. We're in touch with your people."

"Keith has been handling this himself. I'd better try to take it over. It needs fast decisions. Thanks for explaining so clearly. What's up?" He had noticed my involuntary start when the name on the display screens changed.

"Sorry, Carol Milverton is speaking now. She's a friend of mine from Cambridge."

"She has more sense than most of them. Don't I remember your name from that campaign she fought in '74?"

"Yes, that's right."

"And weren't you with International Electronics? No doubt that's how you provided that good quote from Pat O'Donnell. I

---

[56] The voluminous ministerial correspondence relating to these events, including this letter, is in No. 10 correspondence file PREM19/539, entitled 'The Financial Position of the Coal Industry. Mineworkers' Pay. Part 2'. This file is downloadable from the National Archives or at the Margaret Thatcher Foundation website.

had some briefing on IE's Sunderland plant in connection with getting Nissan to set up there. What are you doing now, apart from being an industrial advisor?"

"I'm running my own company, which is developing specialist computer software to support commodity trading."

"That's Ken Baker's area. Are you getting any help from his people?"

"I made enquiries but I didn't get the impression that there was any available."

His face hardened. "There is. We're not just about the past. I'll have a word with Ken in there, right now. Call his office tomorrow."

Tebbit went back in and a couple of minutes later a private secretary buttonholed me.

"The Minister was very grateful for your briefing on coal. Michael Marshall is winding up, though. He'll be out soon for the conference. It would be very good if you could give him the same briefing and then stay around for any follow-up."

"If I'm to stay after eleven o'clock, you'll need to get me a car back to Bellinghame."

"We'll do that."

"I'd better ring home."

Actually, I gave Roberta a further, basically truthful update.

"Liz called me earlier. She was feeling very tired and was going straight to bed. She hoped that on my way back I could look in on you to see how Jenny was. But now, I'm still needed at the Houses of Parliament. I won't be back until after midnight."

"Jenny is fine and it's thrilling that you're both so involved. I spotted Liz with Joe Gormley and the others on TV as they came out of your department's building. I do hope that you can help to sort all this out."

If Roberta suspected anything about how Liz was helping to sort all this out, she kept it to herself. She knew that we knew what we were doing. She believed in us.

Daily Courier Thursday 19 February 1981
MINERS' NIGHT OF VICTORY

by **Carol Milverton**

I was with the miners last night. Hundreds of them, from Yorkshire, from South Wales, from Kent, were waiting to hear whether the threat to their jobs was lifted or not. They stood patiently along Millbank, not far from the Houses of Parliament. The minutes ticked by. Then a shout of 'We've won! The closure list's withdrawn.'

After cheers, the chant began for their hero of the day. 'We want Joe, we want Joe, WE WANT JOE.' And a few minutes later, though it seemed longer, they got him. Joe Gormley, President of the NUM, was the victor of two national strikes.

Now, he had won without a national strike. Just the threat of one had made the government change its mind. It was a great achievement to crown his career.

Smiling and perhaps with a tear in his eye, he passed through the crowd, thanking them for their support. It wasn't his victory, it was their victory. Vice-President Mick McGahey and Secretary Lawrence Daly were smiling, too. Whatever differences there might be on the union's National Executive sometimes, there were none last night.

When asked 'Should we stay out; can we trust them?' Joe Gormley replied, 'The Executive will be meeting in the morning.' But few left doubting what the decision would be. The union had shown its strength. There was no need to lose more pay.

And so the government is humiliated. It has agreed that the National Coal Board should withdraw its closure proposals and re-examine the position in consultation with the unions, with a view to movement. The government will have to respond very positively to this re-examination. Not just with a relaxation in the financial controls on the Coal Board, which Chairman Sir Derek Ezra described as a straitjacket, but also with improvements to the redundancy terms and a reduction in coal imports to the minimum of whatever special coals we simply can't produce here.

They'll have to do much more than they would have

needed to do if they had made a reasonable response earlier. For they forced the Coal Board to make pit closures an emotive issue, rather than the fact of life they really are; not too difficult to agree locally if the men who want to go on working can move to other pits where productivity is higher and working conditions are better. In the mines, emotion costs money. Had no-one in the government read the history books?

By last weekend the need for a tripartite meeting as soon as possible was clear. Yet the government havered around, pretending that the earliest everyone could be gathered together for a meeting was next Monday. On Tuesday, the realities finally sank in and the meeting was brought forward. But even then there seemed no plan. I'm told that all the unions at the meeting, not just the NUM, were astonished at the government's lack of understanding that the closure list had to be withdrawn. Eventually, it fell to Sir Derek Ezra to say that. Ministers just sat there, looking glum.

It was all so different later, when Parliament debated the need for additional finance for the steel industry. All of us – Ministers, Tory backbenchers and Opposition Members – agreed that the industry faced a crisis and tough decisions needed to be taken. Naturally, Members spoke out for their constituents. I did so myself. But no-one was sticking their head in the sand and assuming that if the industry followed an unrealistic plan then the nasty business would all somehow go away. Perhaps those responsible for coal should take a leaf out of their colleagues' book.

HOUSE OF COMMONS, 19th FEBRUARY, 1981

Mr Merlyn Rees. The government has not engaged in a U-turn: it is like a truck in a skid. Goverment policy has jack-knifed.

10. MONDAY, 23ʳᴰ FEBRUARY, 1981

"So the bills are coming in, big time," said Ronald.

Earlier, Jean had taken round my 'weekend note' and Julian had used it to brief our Ministers for a Cabinet committee discussion of how to respond to the NUM at Wednesday's tripartite meeting. However, the discussion had led to few decisions, and we had to sort things out by correspondence. Now, the National Coal Board had told Martin that it was likely to roughly treble its previous estimate of the cost of not going ahead with the twenty-three closures, from between £150 and £200 million to nearly £500 million annually.

"Does the Board have *any* kind of management accounting system?" I asked. "Before this adventure, was *anything* actually worked out? Or is this just another try-on?"

"You may well ask, Pete," said Julian. "But we're where we are now. Martin, you say that the Board haven't worked this out fully, yet. I assume that you and Ronald will organise some kind of check. I suggest therefore that, in the meantime, we keep this information to ourselves. The time to tell Ministers is soon after Wednesday's meeting. Any earlier communication will further cloud discussion of the tactics for then. As we've heard, the Prime Minister and colleagues are very reluctant for us to be at all definite on Wednesday. Also, this information is very likely to make the Prime Minister even angrier. By the time Wednesday's meeting finishes, she'll be in the air, on the way to Washington for her meeting with President Reagan. I am told, by the way, that she regards that meeting as of the utmost importance.[57] She is not going to be distracted from preparation, however unfortunate is our current predicament. So don't expect any decisions during the next two days."

"There's a meeting between the Board and the unions this afternoon. I hope the new figure won't be given out then," said Ronald.

"I did press the Board's team not to," said Martin, wearily. "But they feel they may be forced to."

"I don't see why," said Julian. "When is the meeting?"

"Three o'clock."

"I'll call Ezra before then. No, better, I'll ask the Permanent Secretary to call him."

"You're right to do that," I said. "The increased costs of not closing pits mean, though, that if improvements to the redundancy terms allow at least some closures, they are even more of a bargain than we thought. They make big sense even if the steel industry terms need to be improved so as to maintain comparability. It's a pity that despite my conversation with Norman Tebbit, Keith Joseph's rather theoretical approach is still driving things at DTI."

"Also, we've found a way to cut the immediate cash costs of improvements," said Ed. "Quite a lot of the costs would be for bringing forward pensions, like the costs we already pay towards benefits for deputies and staff. At the moment we pay the pension fund in advance for all these benefits. Instead, we could match our payments more closely to the actual cash flow. We could spread the costs over five or even ten years. There would be less impact on public expenditure now, though more later."

"How might that appear in the Coal Board's accounts?" asked Ronald.

---

57 It established an aspect of the 'special relationship' which has prevailed since then; the first overseas visitor to a new US President is the UK Prime Minister.

"They would probably decide to accrue the whole cost and create a special account for the grants. So, in the near future, they would appear to be receiving more grant than we're actually paying. As I say, that would be reversed later."

"What might their auditors think?"

"They seem a pretty compliant lot," I commented. "They've done the job for rather a long time. I've had a very informal word with a friend whose accountancy expertise I respect. She reckons it should be OK."

"It could be attractive to the Treasury's expenditure team. Ed, talk about it to them, and to our internal audit people. You can also give the Treasury the timetable for sorting out the financial controls now we have it agreed with the lawyers."

"Don't forget that that timetable is dependent on Ed keeping the two staff Douglas has lent us, or their equivalent," I said.

"I'll speak to Douglas about that," said Julian. "Now, what about imports?"

"They will fall but rather gradually," I said. "Only one British Steel import contract comes to an end this year. Fortunately, it's in South Wales where the concern about imports is greatest. Also, Welsh coking coal is as good as imported, only more expensive. So it's just a question of the subsidy needed. We must argue only for the opportunity to match import price and quality. DTI won't accept anything that smacks of controls."

"Then there's this long shopping list of other concessions that the NUM will be asking for on Wednesday, at least according to your sources, Pete."

"Yes, but the only critical items for Wednesday are redundancy terms and imports. The subcommittee on oil from coal is there because the managers' union wants it. Some of the others are just there so we can turn them down and pretend we've won something. Distributing surplus coal free to old-age pensioners is an example. None of the surplus coal is of a kind that could be burnt in domestic grates, even if smoke control legislation allowed it."

"They're good at negotiating, aren't they?" said John, in his first contribution.

"They're professionals at it. On redundancy terms, I think the bottom line is the same as it would have been last week. We need to commit to making improvements in next month's parliamentary Order, and say that those will apply to anyone departing as from when all this blew up. The NUM has some understanding of the Board's ideas, but Wednesday's meeting is no place for the detail and we shouldn't try to get agreement to that by then. On imports, the key is to show the maximum progress possible. The South Wales contract amounts to that."

Julian summed up. "So, Martin, your people can provide letters for the Secretary of State today on the basis of what Pete's just said, without waiting for the Board to tell us what happens at the meeting with the unions this afternoon."

"I've done most of a draft on redundancy terms," said Ed.

"I'll give DTI another call and get back to you on imports," I said.

The meeting broke up but Julian asked me to come with him for a word with Douglas Arnott. Once in Douglas's office, he came to the point, quickly.

"Pete, we're telling you this in strict confidence until it's announced, probably at the end of this week. Martin is being moved to a post in the Treasury."

"Lucky Treasury."

"His replacement will be Howard Larkin, on secondment from the Cabinet Office. He's a real high flyer. We're lucky to be getting him. It shows how important sorting all this out is seen to be, right at the top."

"I hope he can not only write polished memoranda but also take decisions, give clear advice and manage his staff."

"I think we'll notice a big difference," said Douglas.

"That's good news. There's only one bit of news that would be better."

"What's that?"

"That we were to have a new Secretary of State. Norman Tebbit showed me what we're missing. It was worth a late night to see him in action, for example how he dealt with his own backbencher, Matthew Parris. He's used to responsibility, used to being in charge. It comes of having been an airline pilot, I suppose. He's been an officer for the pilots' union, too."

"I don't know him. He had a row with Labour at the end of last month," said Julian.

"Yes, but they respect him for it. Everyone kicks our man around, not just the Opposition but his own colleagues, too. Thanks for telling me about Martin."

"We have a purpose, Pete," said Douglas. "It seems that Derek Morris won't be fit to return for some time. He'll understand that in present circumstances we need to fill his post. When he does return, there are some temporary assignments which he can take on until he retires next year. Julian has discussed the position with me. Would you be ready to take the post on for a period of time?"

"That would be full-time."

"Yes. You could meet Howard to get a feel for how the two of you might work together."

"I'm tempted, but it's not on, for two reasons. My company is at a critical stage of its development. There's a Board meeting tomorrow which is make or break. I've been on the phone or meeting people much of the weekend about that, as well as about coal. To declare an interest, my talk with Norman Tebbit led to the people in the DTI who deal with computers being more forthcoming than they were before. My company could be in line for an Innovation grant of £50,000 or so. That makes 'make' more likely. I can't spend more time here. Indeed, I may not be able to continue at all beyond my two-year contract."

"And what's your second reason?"

"As you both know, but isn't generally known, my partner works one day a week for the NUM, normally on Thursdays, though she came in last Wednesday. You may have noticed her, Julian, passing the papers and murmuring to Gormley."

"Yes, I did notice. She was very smart."

"I don't think it's in anyone's interest that she leaves the NUM, at least for another year. She's totally committed to those in the NUM whose aims are tough but realistic. The arrangement works as long as I'm the Industrial Advisor, standing outside the staff structure here. I don't think it could stand if I were part of the structure and dealing with the same issues."

"I was afraid you'd say that, Pete," said Douglas. "You'll have to look elsewhere, Julian. I've a couple of possibilities on my side that we could talk about."

"Why not promote Ed?" I asked. "He's experienced in his present grade. Last summer, he chose to move to the coal post because it was clearly so important, though his predecessor had made nothing of it whilst cruising towards retirement – witness the mess on financial controls. I'm sure you agree that Ed has made something of the post, Julian."

"It would need special agreement from the Cabinet Office to promote someone as young as him and it would put some others here out of joint."

"He's the same age as I am. He'll want to know where he's going. If he's to go on showing what he can do, he'll need careful management by whoever you put in."

"He'll have plenty to do," said Julian. "We're in really deep trouble now. Next autumn's pay negotiations will be very difficult indeed. The mood in the NUM will be for another victory over Thatcher, particularly if the economy doesn't improve. Gormley's successor will be looking over his shoulder. There's no doubt of his name."

"No doubt at all," I replied.

"I hope you can go on keeping in touch with coal, Pete, though clearly you have other duties here. In particular, the department traditionally sends an observer to the NUM's Annual Conference, early in July. Derek has attended the last few. This year's Conference is to be held in Jersey of all places. Would you be able to go?"

"It's in Jersey because it's Joe Gormley's last Conference. He was given the choice of location. They went there two years ago as a break from the tradition of moving around the coalfields, and he liked it. I must decline, though. I'll be looking after our little girl because Liz will be there for the whole week. Ed can represent the department. Ask him to book that now – before Derek's replacement arrives."

There wasn't much more to say. I was glad that my good reasons for not becoming a full-time civil servant had been accepted easily. I had left another unvoiced. The international meetings about coal that Derek had attended wouldn't be my cup of tea. I hadn't wanted to say that to Douglas, though. For him, no week was complete without a visit to Brussels, or to Paris, the headquarters of the International Energy Agency. I remembered the shock I had created over the lunch table when I had questioned the value of UK membership of that body, whose main achievement had been an agreement to share available oil 'fairly' in the event of a shortage. I had pointed out that now we produced more oil than we consumed, our 'fair' share was what we needed and had the heft to get from the oil companies. To the response that that would not be playing the game, I had said we were paid to play to win. It was very depressing that many of my colleagues did not share my view on that or on the priority of national interest over the need to be *communitaire*.

I sorted out a line on imports and made a few suggestions for Ed's draft on redundancy terms. By three o'clock, both drafts were with Martin. If he wanted to play around with the wording that was up to him. He might wait for feedback from the Coal Board on its meeting with the unions but I didn't expect that to require any changes.

I felt justified in spending the rest of the afternoon filling in a formal application for the DTI Innovation grant, which was the second piece of good news for Creators Technology within a few days. On Saturday, Sir Pat O'Donnell had agreed to become Chairman. He would increase his stake from £20,000 to £40,000, provided that we could show him a clear funding plan. With my extra £25,000, we would need no loan finance before the end of 1981, so then £75,000 of additional credit from New Hampshire would become available.

Altogether, we had possibilities for £170,000 towards the funding gap of £300,000 that we had discussed a month before. That left £130,000 to find. After my meeting with Pat, I had called my fellow directors with the good news and to see just how much more each of them was ready to put in.

I had been pleasantly surprised to hear that Paul could find another £10,000. That indicated his confidence in the project, as reflected in the effort he was making to market it to his colleagues at New Hampshire Realty. But, for differing reasons, none of Jenny, Sheila, Brian and Tony could commit more now. Maybe they could do so later in the year but it wouldn't add up to more than about £10,000 in all.

Other shareholders, including staff, had all come in quite recently and were unlikely to find any more money. The largest investment was of £30,000 from Waterhouse College. This had followed my rather guarded account of our activities to Nick Castle and to Graham Harcroft, the Bursar, given during a visit to address the Business Club about 'Striking Out on One's Own'.

As to new shareholders, Morag could now put in £10,000. Steph had been pleased to hear from me and also pleased to have heard already that New Hampshire could increase its commitment; but when you're at Corporate Director level, you can't invest personally in clients – sorry.

So the news was good but not good enough. There remained a gap of over £100,000. At the meeting in Crawley the next day, we had a stark choice to make. We could go on, and hope for the best, though that would depend on persuading both Pat and New Hampshire Realty that doing so formed an acceptable funding plan. We could accept a capital infusion which would much dilute our stakes and might amount to a takeover. Or we could delay the software project and go for contracts that brought in money quickly.

Sorting out Creators Technology involved thousands of pounds rather than millions but it was just as much make or break for me as sorting out the coal industry was make or break for the government. I could feel more confident of success if I had the full and enthusiastic support of all the other directors. But I did not have that. For nearly the last year someone had just been going through the motions.

At the same time as I had made an offer for the house in Bellinghame, Liz and I had told our friends and relatives that we were to live together, pending any changes in Greg's condition. We had made it fairly clear that if Greg recovered, I would go away, whilst if he died, we would in due time get married.

Contrary to my expectations, most relatives had been neutral to positive. Despite my mother's coolness when Liz had visited our home many years before, she and my father seemed relieved that I was at last settled with someone. Roberta and Frank were fine. Sir Stephen Partington was his usual uncommunicative self. Greg's parents rationalised acceptance in terms of giving a more settled environment for their grandchild.

Amongst friends, Carol was very supportive, and I now had a regular fortnightly duty to look after little Jenny on those Sunday mornings when Carol was in London, so that she and Liz could go swimming. Paul's attitude to us did not appear to have changed. The Smithams were happier than I had thought they might be, though I had to put up with matey remarks from Brian such as 'I could never make out whether you two were together or not'. Doubtless it was helpful that their house was better than ours and that Brian could invite us to the Down Golf Club, where he was making an impression as a sociable younger member. Jane thought it was super, though she had never met Liz.

Steph had accepted my explanation of why Fred had killed himself, which built on her own analysis of Fred and Melissa. She had also applauded my leaving IE to build up my own company; it was part of the great American dream. On hearing my further news, she wanted assurance that I was doing all this for me, as well as for Liz. Morag asked about that, too, though very much as a friend. Sheila was a little more negative than I had expected, considering her feminism. However, she had accepted that it was our business.

That had left Jenny.

I still winced as I remembered her call to me in Leeds on a cold Wednesday evening nearly a year before. How could I take such advantage of Liz? How could I betray Greg by carrying on with his wife while he was unconscious and incapacitated? What was she to say to little Jenny, her godchild? What was I to say to Katie, my godchild? And was this actually why I'd left IE? People kept asking her about that. She told them about Creators Technology but they didn't really believe that was the reason, and now she didn't believe it was, either. She'd put a lot of time and money into my venture. Now she was wondering if she'd made a mistake. No 'buts', Pete – you've messed this one up, someone has to say it. She would go to see Greg but I had damn well better not be around when she did. Down had thumped the phone.

Earlier that same evening, I had had some warning from Liz. Two days before, she and little Jenny had made the difficult drive from St Albans to Weybridge. Big Jenny had seemed to be under some stress, perhaps because of a crisis at work. She had a bruise on her face, which she had said was the result of her walking into a shelf at the office. Tuesday was her non-working day, and on that Tuesday Dick had been able to look after the children. So Liz and Jenny had gone to see Greg. On the drive back, Jenny had praised my support, and that had prompted Liz to break the news. A silence had been followed by a change of subject, and the rest of Liz's visit had been a little awkward.

Jenny's outburst was so unexpected. Her reaction might be born of frustration at seeing me forever out of her reach, but my suggestion to her mother appeared to have borne fruit. Two months before, Jenny had given me a very friendly call to wish me a Happy 1980. After some talk about what I would now be doing for Creators Technology, she had mentioned that her pre-Christmas break had begun not far from me, with a visit to John and Amanda. I had asked how they were and this had prompted her to say that the men had looked after the children whilst she and Amanda had had a most enjoyable visit to a ladies' sauna. I had licked my lips audibly. She had laughed and done the same. Until her call, she had gone on being helpful and professional, very much the friendly member of the Creators Technology team, and with no look in her eye.

The next call, two days later, had been irritating rather than distressing: Dick, in his worst public school mode. He knew Liz very well and was sure that she had a great part in this. He was trying to calm Jenny down but it *was* a bit *off*. He sounded remarkably cheerful and I could feel him enjoying the position. *He* could give *me* a friendly talking-to and use his good offices.

About a week later, Belinda's call had been more illuminating if not more helpful. She had said that it would be good for Jenny if I were with someone again. She had not anticipated that it would be Liz. I said that I had not anticipated that, either. She said that, although she understood how it had come about, she could also understand Jenny's surprise. Further talk had prompted her to describe the outcome of what I had suggested.

Jenny made periodic visits to a client based near Pontefract and had found a place to stay which had spa facilities. She had invited Amanda to join her there in the evenings. The second time, Amanda had stayed the night. The third time had been the week before Liz visited Jenny. Late in the evening, Amanda had returned home. According to John, she was in rather a state when Belinda had called a day or two later.

Jenny had also seemed to be in rather a state but had told her mother only that she and Amanda had fallen out. I commented that Dick's cheerfulness appeared to confirm that. Belinda said that she didn't blame me and all we could do now was wait for everyone to calm down.

Some calming down had taken place. Jenny would come up with answers to specific questions of mine that interested her, as she had done in connection with paying for miners' pension benefits; but she didn't want to talk to me, so she wasn't making the creative input of which she was capable. I also knew how she would react to Liz investing in Creators Technology the proceeds of the sale of the St Albans house. I had not even tried to factor it into my calculations.

Whilst changing for dinner, I reflected that I had done all I could, including making another call to Ana on Saturday. She had promised to help as much as possible, though she was somewhat distracted because Leopoldo Calvo Sotelo had not secured a majority vote of the Congress of Deputies. The vote was to be taken again this evening and was expected to be successful this time. I just had to hope that this evening would be successful for me, too. I returned to my office to find Jean putting her coat on.

"Wow, you do look smart, Pete. Where *are* you going?"

"I'm going to dinner with the Spanish Ambassador."

I was explaining why when John Willis turned up. He told me that the NUM 'shopping list' for Wednesday was as I had given in the morning, and then concluded cheerfully.

"Have a good evening. You and Liz both deserve it. Tomorrow will be easier here. We *won't* be the headline story. Bernard tipped me off just now."

On my way to Victoria, I left the grant application at the DTI offices. Fortunately Liz's train ran roughly to time and soon after 6.30 we were at the ambassadorial residence in Belgrave Square. We were received by a distinguished-looking Spaniard whom I had not met before, together with his wife.

"It is too sad, His Excellency cannot be with us tonight. He has the influenza. He has asked that I act as host. The lady Ana will be joining us shortly. Her aircraft was a little delayed. She is unaccompanied. Her husband has had to remain in Madrid, owing to an urgent business commitment."

We conversed for a few minutes, rather haltingly as the wife's English was poor and I dragged out some rusty Spanish. Fortunately, there was a ready-made topic.

"Is it true that your Prince of Wales is to marry at last? There are rumours of an announcement tomorrow."

"Maybe, but you must not believe all that is in the newspapers."

"The lady is of noble blood but so much younger than the Prince."

I suppressed my doubts, which were to be so unfortunately justified. "That is true but there are in history many examples of such royal marriages proving very successful. Equally, there are very successful royal couples close in age, such as your own King and Queen."

At that moment Jenny and Dick were ushered in. Jenny had dressed sensibly for what was Ana's party but with her mature beauty she caught the eye of most. I made sure that she caught my eye. Although I had not bought a new evening suit before I left Leeds, I had taken some trouble to ensure that my old one looked smart.

Then Ana was announced. Our host welcomed her, in Spanish and English, to applause that was both customary and deserved. Ana was slightly built, with a thin face under dark hair, and radiated character rather than beauty, but her gown rightly outclassed that of any other woman in the room. She greeted Jenny and Dick in a very friendly manner and brought them over to join Liz and me.

"Elisabeth – Liz – I am so pleased to meet you, at last. How do you find it, to have the same name as your Queen?"

"It doesn't make much difference. No-one calls her Liz, so far as I know. I've been that from childhood."

"By all accounts, as a child she was called Lilibet," I observed.

All this took the conversation along the same way as a few minutes before. After we had reached the same end point, Ana signed off quite loudly.

"Yes, King Juan Carlos and Queen Sofia, they are who Spain needs now. They combine tradition and progress, the old order and the new."

Her remark bought a momentary pause in the conversation in the room before our host and his wife took Ana to meet the other Spaniards there. Liz and I circulated and partook of *tapas* and Catalan champagne. One of the Spaniards bent my ear and Liz returned to Jenny and Dick. After a few minutes, I brought the Spaniard over.

"Jenny, you were in the States round about the time of the Presidential election. This gentleman has served in Washington and is interested in Mrs Thatcher's visit. I think it's clear what she wants of President Reagan. What do you think he wants of her?"

Once the Spaniard had introduced himself formally, conversation flowed, since Jenny had always been interested in American politics. After a while, Dick drifted away to join another Spanish couple, and Liz took me aside.

"Well done Ana – she's got us off to a good start," I began.

"Before you came over, Jenny noticed something odd. See the bald bloke who's with Dick now? When Ana made that remark about their King and Queen, he looked very alarmed. The man who is hosting noticed and said something quietly to him."

"Perhaps he thought the man was being disrespectful."

"Maybe, but something is odd about this whole gathering. There's Ana, us two couples, three Spanish couples and that guy you were talking to who's on his own. None of the Spaniards seem to know Ana very well. That's another reason why she came over to us. Why are they here?"

"Two of them must be replacing the Ambassador and his wife, and the single guy must be replacing Carlos, and all at short notice. I expect the table in the dining room is right for twelve. It's a pity the Ambassador isn't well. He's the family friend. I have the impression that Ana doesn't like our host very much. It's odd, though, that the most senior Embassy man at the meeting last month isn't here today. He seemed to know quite a lot about Ana. Perhaps he's away. The Spaniard who's now with Ana and our host was at the meeting. I'm going to join them, as they'll be talking in Spanish. You join Dick and our bald friend."

The conversation in Ana's group was mostly about children: the many grandchildren of the hosts, the teenage children of the man I had met and his wife, and Ana's description of the arrangements for her three whilst she was away from home. She remarked that she was quite often away these days, to places all over Spain. Talk of her travels was the closest anyone came to Spanish politics. That also seemed odd, considering the voting that was probably going on right now. Maybe the conclusion was foregone and the failure on Friday was just a piece of political play-acting or the result of some of Calvo Sotelo's supporters clearing off for the weekend.

Eventually, the Spaniard I had met addressed me, in English. Naturally, he assumed that since I had come with a companion, I was not interested in children.

"I am sorry, Mr Bridford. We are perhaps boring you."

"Not at all," I replied, in Spanish. "Children, they are the future of us all."

"Quite right," said his wife. "And your Spanish is still good. I believe that you improved it whilst assisting the lady Ana in preparing her book."

That led to Ana and I giving a rather cautious account of our photographic expeditions and to my giving Ana some background on the MPs Carol had told me were intending to attend the next day's reception. Then we were called to dinner, and sat down as shown in this plan.

DOOR FROM KITCHEN		SERVERY		GUEST ENTRANCE		
Bald Spaniard's wife	Me	Host's wife		Host	Ana	Dick

T A B L E

Single Spaniard	Jenny	Spaniard I'd met	Liz	Bald Spaniard	Wife of Spaniard I'd met

CURTAINED WINDOWS FACING BELGRAVE SQUARE

To have Jenny opposite was a stroke of luck but I was cautious. The first course was a small but flavoursome *Fabada*, an Asturian cassoulet. Whilst we ate that, I had polite Spanish conversation with our host's wife about the really splendid plates and tableware, which were the Ambassador's own property. I could hear Jenny continuing her conversation with the single Spaniard about America, and the bald Spaniard's wife chipped in, too; she could speak English well, because her husband had served here for many years. I wondered whether to ask about the vote but decided not to since Ana had not raised it.

With the main course came change-around time. Ana was talking to Dick, rather than to the bald Spaniard opposite her or to our host, who pulled his wife into a conversation with the man I had met and Liz. I joined in a discussion Jenny had begun about what was happening in Poland, where General Jaruzelski had become Prime Minister earlier in the month. He was expected to take a tougher line with the independent Solidarity union led by Lech Wałęsa. However, above them all was the immense influence of the Polish Pope, John Paul II.

I could sense some unease in the bald Spaniard's wife. Was she thinking that whilst as a good Catholic she should be supporting the Poles' struggle against Soviet domination, there were some disturbing parallels with the position at home? Was she finding it difficult to tackle the subject in a foreign language? Or was it simply that she wasn't accustomed to women taking part in serious discussions?

After a while, she had some relief. Jenny seemed to drop out of the conversation, and our neighbours engaged in Spanish. This was my moment.

"This really is one of my favourites, *Trucha a la Navarra*.[58] And the Rioja is excellent, don't you agree, Jenny? It's very much the food of Pamplona tonight and a very good choice in this cold weather."

There was a pause, during which my heart sank; but then she replied, turning to the single Spaniard as she did so.

"Yes, it is cold. I think there is a window open behind me. Could it be closed please? Women can easily feel cold, while all you men are warm in your jackets."

---

58 Trout stuffed with serrano ham and fried in olive oil.

The Spaniard got up and went round to our host, who beckoned to a waiter. Whilst all this was going on, Jenny leant forward and murmured to me.

"Look outside."

The waiter drew back the curtain to close the window and for a moment I could see past Jenny, out into Belgrave Square. Carol and Paul were standing under a lamp post, only a few yards away.

I nodded to Jenny. She thanked the Spaniard and began to reminisce about the meals her family had had whilst staying with Ana and Carlos the previous summer. As I took the last bites of my trout, there was another of those moments in my life when all the lemons on the fruit machine came up in a row.

Why had Carlos not come here with Ana?

Why was the Ambassador replaced as host by someone Ana seemed to dislike? Why was the room full of people whom Ana evidently didn't want to talk to? Why was the man I had spoken to last month, who had praised her, not here?

Why was dinner so early?

Why had the bald man seemed agitated when Ana praised King Juan Carlos? Why was his wife uneasy?

Why was no-one talking about the vote? And so...

Why were the Milvertons outside and what news could they have?

I could not wait long but was in luck. The bald Spaniard muttered an apology to Liz and went out. I gave him a few seconds, apologised to my neighbours and followed him to the entrance hall. 'Necesito ventilar' was not very accurate for 'I must have some air' but dealt with any suspicions the man at the door might have had.

I walked past the Milvertons, apparently ignoring them, and waited around a corner for them to join me. Carol had typed their message out. We did not need to say much.

I returned to the residence, murmured 'muy bueno' to the man and re-entered the dining room where plates were being cleared and two of the Spaniards had lit up; that more recent excuse for going out had not been available to me. Ana was speaking to our host so I observed brightly to Dick how good the meal was, slipped him the note and returned to my seat.

Ana turned back to Dick and read the note. Then she rose. Everyone fell silent as she faced our host, who also rose. She had the look of determination that her namesake in Mozart's *Don Giovanni* should display when pressing weaker people to continue with the search for her father's killer. The words following give the sense of the ensuing conversation, even if they are not a totally accurate translation.

"Sir, you are deceiving me. At this very moment an insurrection is taking place in Spain. Yet I have not been told of what is happening."

"Calm yourself, my dear lady Ana. It is nothing, some foolish hotheads who will be dealt with quickly. I did not wish this news to spoil your evening."

"*Nothing*? The Congress of Deputies held hostage at gunpoint? In Valencia, tanks on the streets? Talk of a provisional military government, a *pronunciamento*? You call that *nothing*?"

"There is certainly nothing we can do, here in London."

"I will decide about that. I, Doña Ana Guzman de Leon y Vasquez. My family were Grandees of Spain, entitled to remain covered in the presence of the King, when yours – I do not know what they were. How *dare* you pay me this disrespect. I am leaving this house this instant."

"I think that would be unwise, my lady. In these times of uncertainty I think you should continue to enjoy His Excellency's hospitality."

"When His Excellency hears of your insolence, you will never enjoy his hospitality again. When this matter is resolved, I shall be back."

I had understood enough of the conversation to react to it by moving past our host to stand between Ana and the door. Jenny picked up Liz, and Dick was right there. We passed through the room where we had had drinks, to the sound of an alarm bell and a shout behind us.

"¡Alerte! ¡No pasaran!"

We came into the entrance hall to find the man at the entrance, reinforced by two others, barring our way. Dick addressed them.

"Excuse me please."

There was no response so he didn't waste time. A swing with his six feet and twelve stone behind it brought one of them down. The other two were too amazed to block us and we poured out of the door. There was a scream from Liz, followed by a louder scream as she pushed past me. Carol and Paul rushed up to us as I slammed the door shut, to the sight of someone writhing on the floor.

It was cold outside, particularly for the ladies, but taxis passed frequently. A few minutes later, we were stamping up four flights of stairs to the Milvertons' flat. "News," yelled Carol, for it was one minute to nine.

Soon we were seeing the first reports, including a fuzzy still of what became the iconic image of the day, of Lt-Col. Tejero in the Congress of Deputies Speaker's podium brandishing his revolver. Ana watched and listened intently until the story was complete on the BBC. Then Paul, who had been fiddling with his radio whilst listening through headphones, made a gleeful announcement.

"Madrid on short wave."

He flicked a switch and a torrent of Spanish came through the loudspeakers. I could follow some of it and murmured to the others.

"Tanks in Valencia – we knew that; not a good place for them to start, that was the centre of Republican Spain... No tanks anywhere else... The President of the autonomous Catalan region is making it clear he wants to stay in a democratic Spain – he would, wouldn't he?"

Ana interrupted, suddenly.

"I have heard enough. Turn it off for now. I know what to do and, thanks to you all, I can do it. I believe you can dial Spain from here?"

"Yes, but it isn't very reliable. You often need to try several times," said Paul.

Ana went to the telephone, pulled a notebook from her bag and began to dial. The first two attempts failed to get through. The third obtained an engaged signal. She waited a few minutes and tried again. One failure, then another engaged. We all drank coffee, draped around the room in silence. Ana was clearly concentrating 100% on what she was trying to do.

What was that? Was she calling Carlos to find out what he was up to in all this or to check that he and the children were safe? That didn't add up with it having been regarded as important to get her out of the way and to stop her from doing anything. We had got her back into the way and she was doing something.

Another wait, three failures and then finally we could hear the phone ringing somewhere. After what seemed an interminable wait, someone answered. The following is a rough translation of Ana's end of the ensuing conversation, as I murmured it to the others.

"This is Doña Ana Guzman. I wish to speak with the King… I know what is happening but he will wish to speak with me. Please tell him now… Your Majesty, are you safe…? How will you respond to this act of treason?… Sire, you cannot wait to see which side the generals take. Milans del Bosch, he has acted in Valencia, but you know what a fool he is. You must speak to others and tell them you expect their loyalty… I know what the Generalissimo would have done, and you know, too, Sire. He would have acted decisively to condemn these acts. He knew that 1936 was long past. He knew that things had to change after him. He told you that to survive you would have to be part of that change. So support him now. As soon as possible tonight you must broadcast to the nation on television, in uniform, as Head of State and Commander in Chief, the designated successor of the Generalissimo... I know who to call at the television station. I will do so and give them this telephone number if I may... Yes, I am in London but I can do it from here... No, my husband is not with me and I fear I know why. But at these times, Sire, everyone needs to act in accord with their beliefs and be strong... Your Majesty, my highest regards and wishes for good fortune."

She rang off, consulted her notebook and immediately dialled again. At the fifth attempt, she got through. Rapid-fire Spanish conversation followed. Then another call and another. The rest of us continued to sit quietly. The room was not particularly warm and Ana's gown showed her slight figure well but we could see the sweat pouring off her. Quite a lot of sweat was pouring off us, too.

"It's good that my parents are staying overnight with the children," observed Dick. "I'd better call them when I can, to say don't wait up."

"It's the same for us. Jenny likes to stay with the Booths," said Liz.

Carol paused from making jottings in a notebook and got up to make more coffee.

"You're all welcome here as long as you want. Did you all have enough to eat?"

"I did. Desserts are always a bit of a let-down in Spain," said Jenny.

"Gosh, that makes me realise. Paul and I haven't eaten. Excuse me for a moment."

It was nearly eleven o'clock. For none of us was there any question of leaving to catch last trains. We were seeing and hearing history in the making.

Finally, Ana was off the phone. She stepped over to the sofa on which Jenny and Dick were sitting close together. Jenny moved aside and Ana tumbled in between them, looking quite exhausted and strained. Jenny put an arm around her and there was a look on Ana's face that reminded me of someone else beginning with A.

"That is all I can do. Put Madrid on again, Paul. I am sorry. I have been ignoring you all, after you rescued me from a plot to detain me, to prevent me from acting as I have now done, a plot involving the people you met tonight and perhaps the Ambassador."

"I think he's hedging his bets," I said.

"Yes, like many others. He will see who wins, and support them. I hope that I have persuaded the King that he cannot do the same if he wishes to remain King. He cannot wait. Now is the time for decision. Eventually, I found someone at the broadcasting station who was prepared to decide and to give the orders needed. Now, I must wait. Liz, I have scarcely spoken to you. Paul, I have not spoken at all to your wife, about whom I have heard so much."

A formal introduction took place after Carol had returned with two plates of baked beans on toast. Between mouthfuls, she explained her part.

"I was in the Chamber right through the debate on the Energy Conservation Bill and made a couple of interventions. None of it was controversial, which must have been a relief to the Tories after last week – we've been having a crisis with the coal miners, Ana. The debate finished soon after 7.30 and we were all pleased to be having an early night. As I was leaving, everyone was talking about the Spanish Parliament being held at gunpoint. So I grabbed what was on the Press Association tapes, called Paul, told him to listen up and hot-footed it back here. We didn't know when your dinner would finish but I thought that if I could meet you tonight, Ana, then I could phone round and make sure of a good turnout tomorrow. So I typed out what we'd heard, thinking you would want to know the latest, and we came along. We thought the dinner would be at the Embassy but the man at the door there was very unhelpful."

"Then I remembered that the residence was round the corner," said Paul. "So we walked along. We were asking each other which house it might be."

"I heard what sounded like your voices," said Jenny. "I realised that if the curtain were drawn back, Pete might be able to see you."

"Which I did," I continued. "So I came outside and the rest is history, as they say. It was an amazing moment when the host yelled '¡*No pasaran!*' – 'they shall not pass'. It was the right message to his men but a Republican slogan in the Civil War. Well done, Dick and Liz. Thanks to you both, we passed."

"I knew what I had to do," said Dick.

"It was bad luck on the guy who tried to grab me," said Liz. "The old trick works pretty well through trousers, though it's meant for when the guy is naked and hard. Sorry, Ana, I'd better explain."

She did so with entertaining detail, which didn't upset Dick as it once would have done. Then I had a chance to summarise.

"I think tonight's message from history is 'United we stand, divided we fall'. You have The Creators with you now, Ana. We think, and act, together, fast. We're rather a contrast to some of the people I've had to deal with during the last week. Don't quote me on that, Carol."

There were nods and laughter around the group, including from Jenny.

11. TUESDAY, 24TH FEBRUARY, 1981

We chatted on in a desultory way, three couples half dozing while Ana kept an ear to the radio. After about half an hour, she stiffened.

"Quiet... The King will speak in ten minutes."

They were a long ten minutes. Finally, music came on and Ana stood up.[59]

"The Royal March – the Spanish national anthem," I muttered.

There was an introduction, and a voice that I recognised as I watched Ana following every word. She began in tension as King Juan Carlos spoke. The rather turgid official translation of what he said does not bring out the drama fully.

"Addressing all Spaniards, with brevity and conciseness, in the extraordinary circumstances that we are currently experiencing, I ask of everyone the greatest serenity and confidence and I inform you all that I have given the captains general of the military, the navy and the air force the following order:

'Given the situation created by the events that took place in the Palace of Congress and to avoid any possible confusion, I confirm that I have ordered civil authorities and the Joint Chiefs of Staff to take all necessary measures to maintain constitutional order, within the law.

Should any measure of a military nature need to be taken, it must be approved by the Joint Chiefs of Staff.'"

---

59 This happened at 1.14 am Spanish time – 12.14 am UK time.

Ana was beginning to look happier, but the clincher was:

"The Crown, the symbol of the permanence and unity of the nation, cannot tolerate, in any form, actions or attitudes of people attempting by force to interrupt the democratic process; a process which the Constitution, voted for by the Spanish people, determined by referendum."

Ana's face told it all.

"He has spoken. The *coup* is finished."

She burst into tears. Jenny's arm was around her again and that look was back on her face. Carol went to the kitchen and returned with a tray, bottles and glasses.

"This calls for a celebration. I put this in the freezer, in hope, an hour ago. It's Italian but better than nothing. So, to democracy in Spain, to Ana and to The Creators."

Ana joined in, then burst into tears again. Eventually, she went on.

"As you say, Pete, many will have hedged their bets. If they have not shown themselves, they will escape retribution. What has Carlos done? I know that he is in Madrid tonight, but he is not at our house there. I fear that he knew this was to happen. He will not have hedged his bets."

"He is of the same family as you, Ana. Others will have hedged their bets. They will protect him, if only for the sake of your children," I said.

"You are right, Pete. I will call my father now. I must tell him what happened to me earlier. I have loved Carlos, and forgiven him, before. What is to happen between us now?"

She went to the phone and after a few tries was through. I could hear her speaking firmly, and had some of the sense, which Ana confirmed on rejoining us.

"Father says that he knew nothing and I believe him. But when he heard, he did nothing. Now, he will try to contact Carlos. Also, he will call the Ambassador at nine hours, to show his anger at the way I, his daughter, have been treated. No, Pete, he will not challenge anyone to a duel! He has no desire to share the fate of the 'Commendatore.'"

Her last sentences was a reaction to the feigned alarm on my face. As was my intention, it delivered laughter and relief.

"Ana, you look quite worn out," said Carol. "We can put you up in our spare room. After nine hours, which is eight o'clock our time, I'll take you back to the residence. By then I'm sure you'll be very welcome there. Also, we need to turn the reception tomorrow into a show of solidarity from all of British politics. I'll ring round in the morning. I'm sure we can involve a government minister. You should give an address there. I can help you work that out, too."

"Thank you so much, Carol," said Ana, with a slightly guarded look in her eye. "Thank you *all* so much. You are truly friends of Spain in this hour of need. If there is anything I can do to show my gratitude, you must let me know."

She came round and formally kissed us all. With Jenny, the kiss was quite long and greeted with a smile. With me, the kiss was formal, but I held on to her for a moment and could feel her getting less tense as she whispered.

"You supported me those years ago and you support me now, Pete."

"I'll call a minicab for you all, from the firm that takes MPs home after late debates," said Carol. "Liz, you know where the kit is for making up the spare bed."

"I'll give you a hand," said Jenny, in a practical voice. "It's always easier with two."

Liz soon returned from the spare bedroom, saying that Jenny was helping Ana to settle down. We talked on, still excited at what had happened.

After a while, the entry phone sounded and Carol called to Jenny, who took a moment to emerge from the spare bedroom. I glanced at her with interest as she, Dick and Liz started down the stairs. I hung back for a moment, first to speak to Paul.

"Are you in your office late tomorrow morning, or rather later this morning?"

"Yes, in fact I've had to give my apologies for the reception. There's a client lunch I can't miss. I may be a little late for the Board meeting, too, even with the 3.30 start."

"I suspect, or at least I hope, that there'll be a good reason for starting the meeting late; if so, I'll call you before your lunch, and you'll need to speak to Jim Schurman urgently."

"Hmm... Yes, I understand. Good thinking, Pete. Provided New Hampshire retains seniority, there shouldn't be a problem."

Carol came over to us. "The cab fare shouldn't be more than £15. Mention my name if they try anything on."

"Thanks, Carol. Now, do I detect a lady in search of her second by-line within a week? 'THE COUP HITS LONDON', perhaps?"

"I suppose you do," she replied with a grin.

"Don't get too keen. My guess is that there'll be a strong desire to hush up the numbers involved in the coup and to portray it as the work of a few nutters rather than as any real threat. Ana will go along with that. She won't want what's happened here to be in the papers. Anyway, tomorrow or Wednesday, you've no chance at all."

"Er... Oh. I would be courting trouble with the NUJ, too."[60]

In the minicab, Dick as the largest was in front with the driver and I was in between Liz and Jenny at the back. We all dozed, as much as the din from the driver's radio allowed. Jenny's smiling face was encouraging and along with what I had spotted in my glance fostered a very pleasurable imagination of what had happened before Carol had called her.

Half an hour later, we were pulling up in Bellinghame.

"Sorry, I'm bursting," said Dick. "Can I use your facilities?"

"I'll let you go inside with Liz," said Jenny, playfully. "Some wouldn't. Pete can keep me warm here until you get back. Don't get up to anything naughty."

---

[60] The National Union of Journalists, which did not welcome columnists becoming reporters without the appropriate apprenticeship on the local press.

"And don't you two, either," said Liz, equally playfully.

Jenny and I spread out at the back but our faces were close so that we could hear each other under the continuing racket.

"That was quite an evening. It was your reaction to hearing Paul and Carol that made the difference, Jenny."

"You took it on the way you do, Pete – fast and well."

"Mmm. We worked together sharply, as we've done before. That's the way it should be. Friends again? Brother and sister?"

"Friends again, the way we should be. Brother and sister."

We exchanged knowing but strictly friendly, sibling kisses.

"That makes me really happy, Jenny."

"Me too, Pete. I'm sorry I was so unkind to you."

"I should have told you myself about Liz. I knew how you felt after working with me."

"When Liz told me, something else had gone wrong in my life, something not to do with you, Dick or the children."

"I'm sorry to hear that. Is it still wrong?"

"No, it's back where it should be, now."

"I'm very glad to hear that. Talking of now, Ana asked if there was anything she could do. I've an idea. Paul thinks it might run."

A brief technical discussion ended with Jenny on an upbeat note. "So it could work, provided that old Pedro and Carlos do as she says. I guess they'll be rather under her finger."

"Precisely, and you do seem to get on very well with Ana." I licked my lips.

"Mmm, yes I do." She licked her lips and we both smiled.

"Could you come and see her with me, perhaps at 11.30?"

"I could set off once the children are at school."

"I'll speak to Carol and call you at about nine o'clock. I guess you'll need to be up at the normal time, however late you get to bed."

"Yes, and somehow I don't think we'll be going straight to sleep. Thumping that Spaniard turned Dick right on. He was turned on more by hearing what Liz did, though it was a repeat of what she'd tried out on him all those years ago. Feeling him earlier has turned me on lots, too."

"He made a difference tonight."

"Yes. That's so good for his self-confidence and so good for our relationship. Ah, here he is. Goodnight, Pete, and I'll see you later on."

Jenny and Dick weren't the only ones. "Upstairs," came the shout as soon as I was in the house.

"It's a good thing you wore that dress you can get out of without help," I said as soon as I came into the bedroom.

"Yes, though that was to make walking easier. Hurry up. Oooh, that's cold." She protested as I pulled the bedclothes back.

"If you're going to masturbate whilst watching me undress then I'm going to watch you doing it."

"I've been dying to do it since I got that man in the balls."

"That was clear by the way you told the story. It had me feeling hot, and the Sinclairs too, Jenny told me, though there's another reason why she's hot. There's no doubt what will happen as soon as they're home. Now then, my girl, you can use your hand on *me* – gently…"

A little later, we lay back, temporarily satisfied.

"It's nice we don't have to worry about how much noise we make," said Liz. "*Oooh*, I'm very sensitive there still. Hold on for a moment."

"This is a kind of repeat of our first night ever, when I came back with coffee and found you in my bed."

"Yes, though you're performing better now. Ow." Liz laughed as I smacked her.

"You said I'd done jolly well for a first-timer."

"And that you were going to be ace. You were ace, and you are ace, Pete. Gosh, here we are, in our mid-thirties, behaving as if we were students. I guess the whole evening was a kind of super student prank."

"It was more than a prank. It may have made a big difference. No doubt others were talking to Juan Carlos, too, but Ana's family carry some clout."

"What will she do now? Suppose Carlos is sent to prison."

"He won't be. Complicity in all this will be hushed up."

"She said that she'd forgiven him before."

"Yes, on what we've always called the 'Day to Remember' – the day we were in Cambridge for Katie's christening and heard that Harry Tamfield had been killed in the DC-10 crash. You helped to calm Dick down."

"That was the day when Greg told us it wasn't a bomb that had caused the crash."

We held each other very close, before I replied.

"That's right. Ana had found out that, ten years earlier, Carlos had had a homosexual adventure. When I was in Spain, I'd told Ana about Harry, Dick and Jenny. On the 'Day to Remember', she called me in the hope that I could ask Jenny to speak with her. So though Jenny and Ana had never met, they had a heart-to-heart talk on the phone. That helped Ana to realise she could go on with Carlos. In fact, later that day they did it all for the first time, luckily with no immediate consequences. Pedro dutifully appeared exactly nine months after the wedding. Ana didn't meet Jenny until 1978, when the Sinclairs stayed at the Guzman castle outside Pamplona. They went there again last summer."

"No wonder Ana feels close to Jenny. She was showing that lots. She still feels close to you, too. That was so clear when she kissed you."

"She was pleased at what she'd done but very upset and worried about Carlos. I started off the job of relaxing her. She likes the feel of my hands."

"I'm not surprised. Relax me now."

For a while, my hands worked over Liz's body. Eventually, she continued.

"Mmmm, great, Pete. Jenny and Dick must be back in Weybridge by now. How do you think they're doing it?"

"The way Jenny likes best, I guess. Her legs will be hooked over his shoulders and he'll be driving down into her. They are a handsome couple to imagine."

"When I put up Melissa's sketches, I was thinking that if things had turned out differently, I might have introduced Jenny and Dick to her last summer."

"We could still do that. She would jump at the chance of posing them. I think that they would enjoy it, too. Meanwhile, you'll just have to imagine them. Since that day in San Francisco, I have the advantage. You won't have seen Jenny naked since her infamous hen party."

"Yes I have. Greg and I went to stay with them for the weekend before Dick went off to Berkeley in '76. That was the very hot, dry summer, when we were being encouraged to share baths to save water. So after Katie and David were in bed, the two of us did just that. It was all fairly proper. We had some nice girls' talk about each other's bodies and just a little feel."

"You *are* bosom friends. I hope Jenny remembered what you liked."

"She did, and her nips were hard as could be by the time I'd finished. We both knew what we wanted afterwards. Jenny said, why bother to dress? Greg *was* a bit surprised when we came downstairs together but he had his hands working on me pretty fast."

"Dick was faced with wife and ex, on parade and hot. How did he take it?"

"He liked it lots, perhaps too much. He mentioned the act we put on at that Bump Supper on your last evening in Cambridge. Then he said that unlike then we were on our own, and took his shirt off before holding Jenny."

"Mmmm."

"I must admit I was hopeful and started to undo Greg. It would have been great to ride him whilst watching Jenny and Dick. I think Greg would have enjoyed it, too, just the once. But Jenny had us off to our separate bedrooms, quietly, so as not to disturb the children. She didn't want a repeat of the sunbath with John and Amanda on the day of the Moon landing."

"I'm not surprised. What happened then, or may happen now, with John and Amanda is in a private box as far as Jenny is concerned. That's why she's never tried to link them into The Creators. Amanda forgot that at the hen party and Jenny made that very clear. The year before, Dick had forgotten that when he told you and me about the sunbath."

"Jenny was annoyed then, though she said it was because she was cold."

"I was cold, too, Liz. First you jumped into that lake and then Dick, being a decent chap who'd been at a public school, followed you in. Jenny and I had no choice. You've reminded me of what I wanted to do then but couldn't as you were going with that cop."

"Ow... *Ow... Ow!* It was fun to take a refresher look at you all."

"I guess we all felt that, really, though I can tell you that California is a more suitable location for a refresher look than is County Durham. I've heard a lot about Amanda, though I've met her only three times, most recently on the 'Day to Remember'. As Angela said to me then, what Jenny wants, Amanda delivers."

"She certainly delivered what Geoff deserved. Mmmm, it's nice to think of her doing that."

"And for doing it, she had a nice sauna with Angela and Jenny. That's a reward she likes. She adores Jenny. What happened at the sunbath was part of keeping her with John."

"So Jenny didn't want it to happen with anyone else. I hadn't thought of that, and Dick hadn't thought of it, either, even after what happened in Durham."

"Jenny said to me tonight that, just before you told her about us, something else had gone wrong in her life, something not to do with me, Dick or the children."

"You mean she tried to use Amanda to get you out of her system and it went wrong, wrong enough that she had a bruise on her face."

"Yes, but apparently it's all fine now, and fine for her and Dick, too. Dick can look back with pride at what he's done tonight. He needs these boosts or he feels down because Jenny is doing so well."

"He knows you're not a threat anymore, Pete. I think I've saved their marriage or perhaps Fred Perkins saved it. Jenny knows that, too, and always did. She didn't know whether that was good or bad for her. Tonight, it looked very much like she's finally decided that it's good and we should all be chums again."

There was another silence, punctuated only by quiet, gentle kissing as I held Liz tight in my arms.

"Yes, and even more chums while we were waiting for Dick to come back to the taxi, though we didn't do anything naughty. It really is a huge relief. I know how well Jenny and I worked together on the IE rights issue. That's the way we should work together on Creators Technology, and I think it's now the way we will work together. She'll have the creative ideas on finance of which she's capable and she'll organise people in the loveliest sort of way."

"So if I sell the house in St Albans, and invest the proceeds in Creators Technology, Jenny won't shout foul. I'm sure Frank can sort out the power of attorney I'll need. Now I know that the tenants want to leave at the end of April, I can put the place on the market straight away. I should have the money by May."

"It's your money and your decision, Liz. I've said that and I'll say it again."

"Pete, I know you can make Creators Technology succeed. I want to be part of the success, for me, for little Jenny and for the other children we'll have, as well as for you. I want us all to be rich."

"You'd better tell Jenny before she sees me again. It's her non-working day. Call her at ten past nine, after I've called her at nine o'clock. We're going to talk to Ana before the reception."

"Ana will like that. There's definitely something of Amanda in how she regards Jenny. When they were sitting together, a couple of times she had a look in her eye that reminded me of Amanda at the hen party. Then after Jenny and I had made up the bed, and found her some pyjamas, she asked Jenny to help her out of her gown. She clearly didn't have much on underneath it."

"Mmm, and Jenny had made the same decision about her dress as you had – for the same reason, of course. She took her time to reappear. It's nice to think of them together."

"That's easier for you. You've seen both of them naked."

"Like Amanda, Ana will stay in Jenny's private box as far as Creators are concerned. But she's helped to sort Jenny out with me. Also, I've a practical way in which she and old Pedro can thank us for rescuing her. Jenny and Paul think it can work." I explained.

"So the man we saw on TV, brandishing the gun, has saved Creators Technology and given us the chance to be rich."

"Yes, now Jenny is back on board we have the chance. I hope she's now ready to put more money in. When she was promoted to senior audit manager she must have had a good rise."

"Back in October, at Katie's party, she did open up for a moment with me. She said they're resigned to paying school fees, as do most of their neighbours. The local comprehensive is pretty awful."

"That's the problem of living in Weybridge. It feeds on itself. A lot of children are sent to fee-paying schools, so the state schools don't have a quality input. They should be living around here, where there are good grammar schools and people use them. Her parents and Dick's will help with fees, though, and she could up the mortgage on their house. I need to sort out how to give all Creators more incentive to find equity."

"You know, Pete, you've never told me the whole story of how you made the money you've put into Creators Technology. You've told me about 'Plain Jane's' but how were you able to invest in that in the first place, as well as buy your flat in Aberdeen? Carol told me how flash that was. Jenny was mightily impressed, too. You must have done very well in Spain."

"I did. International Electronics, New Hampshire Realty and Banco Navarrese did even better. Harry Tamfield got wind of what we were up to. That explains why he was coming back when he did, on the plane that crashed. It's a long story, which involves Ana, Paul and Steph, and links up with Carlos's peccadillo. You should know it as part of my life, Liz. I'll tell you soon but not now. I need to go to work in four hours, and we haven't finished, have we?"

I began to stroke Liz again and for a few minutes we were quiet.

"Mmm, that's nice. You said that Morag is coming in with £10,000."

"Yes. She can do that now. For years she was supporting her invalid and widowed mother in Scotland, so she had little to spare from a university lecturer's salary. Now, she has a legacy. I'm pleased she's coming in. Back in '74, Sheila came in because she had the money and also because her research area was closer to the basis of what we were trying to do. More recently, though, it's Morag's research that has been closer. She pointed out how my own work might link in and persuaded me to go for it. Two weeks ago she spent a day at Crawley, giving people there a fresh view of my maths. Chris Rowan reckons that's taken a fortnight off the timetable."

"Morag believes in you. She always has done, since right back in Cambridge. She used to say that you were the only man she might have been able to go with."

"So I've heard, though she's never said that to me."

"How are things between her and Sheila, do you think?"

"They seem to be settled but sometimes I wonder. It has suited Morag financially to live in Sheila's house, though Sheila tends to dominate. Now, Morag is more able to think about where she's going. She led her relationships with Gill and Angela."

"And the times with me."

"She likes to be involved with the Pankhurst Centre but that's growing and changing as more grants are coming in. You've been to most of their Christmas parties but before last December I'd not been there since 1973. I was amazed at the difference. Two adjacent houses have been taken over and there are lots more facilities – a gym and even a massage room, I'm told."

"They have a masseuse who comes in twice a week and Sheila said that massaging each other helps the women to relax and makes them less tense after what they've been through."

"That's quite possibly true, in all sorts of ways."

"*Ooh… oooooh.*"

"Also, there are professionals on the staff, so there's less responsibility for volunteers. Sheila will need to make sure that it's a more equal partnership. I'm going to suggest politely that, once Morag is a shareholder, she might be Sheila's alternate on the Board of Creators Technology. Each of them has a contribution to make. Goodness, you've made me imagine you with Morag, though I've never seen her naked."

"I've a better idea than talking about Morag, with less imagination needed from you! I never had time to tell you about my chat with Carol after swimming a week ago Sunday. It began in the shower together with no-one else around. So some more girls' talk and just a little friendly contact."

"A nice bounce and stroke, eh? Sit up. I've a flat chest."

"Mmmm, yes… *mmmm.*"

"Did you think back to Jenny's hen party when you two followed Morag and Angela onto the couch? I had both your accounts soon after; and Angela told me how much she enjoyed watching the two of you as Morag went on gently touching her."

"What really got me going for it then was wriggling my legs astride Carol's bottom while watching Angela and Morag. This time in the shower was mostly about convincing Carol that she shouldn't worry about her weight. She's fully built but in the right places. Her bottom was always her best part. Now it's magnificent and her chest has filled out. That doesn't slow her down in the water, I can tell you. Over coffee, we were in the mood for confiding. She and Paul are very happy together. They won't split up, even if Carol decides to go with Owen, but some of the time they'll live their own lives. She wants to stay in the flat. It's convenient for all she does. Paul wants a house in the country, near London. He has his eye on Beaconsfield, of all places. Apparently he knows a couple of people in the local Labour Party there."

"You mean he knows the total current membership."

"Oh, there are a few more than that."

"Can they afford another place? They already own two."

"Not right now because last year New Hampshire was rather stingy with Paul's bonus. This year, he's hoping for better."

"He's finding £10,000 for Creators Technology. Clearly that's the current priority in his mind."

"I don't think even Carol knows what's in Paul's mind a lot of the time. Do you?"

"Not really. He's a quiet fixer. As we both know, he always has been, and that can cause trouble. When I tell you about Spain, I'll be telling you about how he nearly caused very big trouble indeed. But, at around the same time, he had the idea that's put Creators Technology where it is now."

"I'm glad you know to keep an eye on him, Pete."

"Sir Pat O'Donnell gave me the same advice."

"Coming back to Carol, her polite message was that she'll be looking out, as you noticed on Wednesday."

"Maybe she will be looking out but I have who I need, right here and now. It's so great that I'm not lonely anymore, Liz. I don't think I realised how lonely I was until I left Aberdeen. Laura had moved on. Jane was good fun but there wasn't any real feeling in it, just as there hadn't been with Carol or Angela. Working long hours with Jenny didn't help me, let alone her. I even began to fantasise about Melissa, whom I'd never met. Now, you and I have come together, when years ago we couldn't. I can come home to you and to little Jenny, *our* Jenny. And now big Jenny and I are back to being friends – just friends but *real* friends."

"Mmmmm… *Mmmmmm…*"

"Mmmmm…"

"Pete, for the moment we can really enjoy ourselves but our plan means I need to go off in good time for July. Later in the year, it *will* be different. If you find you need someone then, go again with Carol. She's a Creator and a very good friend indeed to both of us. Ooh, that's nice, now… Just there… *Oooh… Ooooooohh!*"

"You've got me thinking of Carol's bottom. Yours is pretty good, too, Liz. Turn over… I've no need to finger your arse. You've much better spots to finger."

"*Oooooh*, don't tickle."

"That reminds me. At the department, there's an attractive blonde called Nicola. That's a silly name for her parents, Mr and Mrs Tipple, to have given her."

"Nicola Tipple – tickle'er nipple… Ooh yes, that's turning me right on. Just a bit more after all… Great we're alone in the house… Aah… More… *Aah… Aaaaahh!*"

A few minutes of rhythmic squelching as groin met buttocks were accompanied by uninhibited yells of pleasure. Full satisfaction was followed by almost instant sleep; the blessed sleep of two people happy together, in a relationship that was deepening all the time. It would need to be deep to stand up to Liz's plan for making a difference.

She had come up with that on Thursday evening when we were comparing notes on the day and night before. Under Joe Gormley's leadership, the NUM had concentrated on keeping miners' earnings well above those of most industrial workers. However, Gormley was nearing retirement and his successor from April 1982 would be Arthur Scargill, whose declared objective was to use the miners' industrial strength to bring the Thatcher Government down. The government had to be in a strong position to face him. They weren't in a strong position now. We had reached the same conclusion as others had done.[61]

If what Creators had done a few hours earlier had been a super prank, Liz's plan would be the greatest prank ever.

---

[61] 'We would have to rely on a judicious mixture of flexibility and bluff until the Government was in a position to face down the challenge posed to the economy, and indeed to the rule of law, by the combined force of monopoly and union power in the coal industry.' – *The Downing Street Years*, p. 143.

ADDRESS BY Doña ANA GUZMAN[62]

Delivered at a reception to mark the publication in the UK of
'The Lost World of Old Castile'
Tuesday 24th February 1981

Minister, Your Excellency, Right Honourable and Honourable Members of the British Parliament and all others here today, I am honoured to be able to address you.

I am sure you all recognise that today is a great day for Spain and a great day for democracy. What you may not understand so well is that if the shade of Francisco Franco is looking down upon us, and if he is not looking down yet I am sure that he will be looking down soon, he would regard it as a great day, too. He would see that the trees he planted had taken firm root. He would see that the institutions he created, in particular the restored, constitutional monarchy, would survive threats and maintain order. He would see that those professing to maintain his ideals, but possessing less vision than he had, would not prevail.

You may think these are strange things to say. But to comprehend them, note that following the brief interruption, which has now terminated, the Congress of Deputies, our Parliament, will give today its approval to a new government, led by Leopoldo Calvo Sotelo. He is a man of the Centre Right but a moderniser who knows that the time for democracy has come, and come for good.

His uncle, José Calvo Sotelo, had the same hope but in vain. In the 1920s, during a period of authoritarian rule, he helped to modernise Spain. In 1936, though, he was the leader of the Opposition in a restored parliamentary system. Early in the morning of the 13th of July, police officers with what purported to be valid authority took him from his bed. A few minutes later, they murdered him. The complicity of men then in government was widely suspected. Certainly, attempts to pursue the murderers were half-hearted.[63]

---

62 As published in the *Sunday Courier*, 1st March 1981, with an introduction by Carol Milverton MP.
63 Although more recent accounts of the origins of the Spanish Civil War are less sympathetic to the Nationalist cause than those available at the time related here, all continue to agree that the impact of this murder on support for the government both within Spain and internationally was catastrophic.

To many Spaniards, that was the signal that democracy and the rule of law had finally broken down. Four days later, they saw the military uprising as the only hope of preserving order. That was the view of my family when they took part in the terrible struggle which followed. They were right to do so. They knew that, despite the many faults of the side they took, the alternatives of anarchy and Stalinist communism were worse.

So do not take last night's events lightly. I have already heard the words 'comic opera' applied to the image of Tejero brandishing his revolver. It was not comic at all. And as someone who shares a name with Mozart's great operatic character, I can say that it was not opera, either.

It could have turned out very badly indeed. It did not turn out so badly because our King acted with the authority he had been trained to show. He was trained by the Generalissimo, who knew that after him things should be very different. The Spanish royal family has cause for celebration today, just as does your royal family. The New Spain will go on, with the support of many who grew up and played their part in the Old Spain.

My book which is published here today was published in Spain in 1975, shortly before the death of the Generalissimo. It is a record of journeys through Old Spain nearly ten years ago. These journeys took me to places that had hardly changed for hundreds of years, to places that are the visual and cultural equivalent of the greatest sights in the United Kingdom, France or Italy, but which are hardly visited, indeed are scarcely heard of outside Spain. They remain, amidst a New Spain which is changing so rapidly.

So visit them before everybody does. Take the road to Santiago, through Estella and Sahagun, full of huge churches in which pilgrims rested on their way. Next, go to the cathedral of León. According to the experts, its stained glass is excelled only by that of Chartres. Perhaps back towards Madrid via Tordesillas, where nearly 500 years ago the Spaniards and Portuguese divided the world between them. Then to the castles and fortified towns such as Coca, Cuéllar and Penafiel, which marked the frontier with Moorish lands 800 years ago. You will not be disappointed.

On your way, along rapidly improving roads, you will find the New Spain, too. See how our country is emerging, to combine the best of the old and the new. That is what Spain is about, now. Our tourist office has a table here and can provide you with all the information you need. Wherever you go, our people will welcome you.

MINUTES OF THE 63rd BOARD MEETING OF CREATORS TECHNOLOGY, HELD AT THE COMPANY'S OFFICES, VAGGS LANE INDUSTRIAL ESTATE, CRAWLEY, ON 24th FEBRUARY 1981[64]

Present: Dr A.E. Higgins, Chairman
  Mr P.M. Bridford, Chief Executive
  Dr P.R. Milverton
  Mr B.G. Smitham
  Dr S.A. Yates
  Mrs J.I. Sinclair, Secretary
In Attendance: Mr C.L. Rowan, Operations Manager

The meeting opened at 4.35 pm.

1. The Chief Executive apologised for keeping the Chairman and other attendees waiting. The delay arose from recent events of which Board members were already aware and from the opportunity which had arisen to clarify financing issues with Banco Navarrese and New Hampshire Realty. Mrs Sinclair could now table the consequent paper MB 4/81, which set out the key issue for the meeting. He proposed that since all Board members were present, the meeting could consider this paper after a break of fifteen minutes to study it. This was agreed.

2. On resumption, Mrs Sinclair summarised the position which MB 4/81 seeks to address. The 62nd meeting had noted a likely shortage of funds amounting to at least £250,000 before significant revenues from product sales

---

[64] Both *Creators Unbounded* and *The Chicks come Home* append these minutes, in recognition of the crucial importance of this meeting to the company's development. The former describes it as 'the Key Meeting'. The latter speculates as to why Banco Navarrese appeared to be so generous. Research amongst Spanish sources which have been in the public domain since 2006 could have led its authors some way towards the truth.

could be expected. The note by the Chairman and Chief Executive, MB 3/81 already circulated, indicated that possible launches by IBM later in 1981 could accelerate the widespread availability of equipment on which the company's products could operate. However, this would require increased staffing to ensure that an initial version of the products was ready for demonstration on a minicomputer in the summer of 1982 and launch in the spring of 1983. In her view, the more rapid development timetable brought increased risks. She suggested that an additional contingency of at least £50,000 and preferably £100,000 would be desirable, making a total requirement for additional finance of at least £300,000 and very probably £350,000.

3. She continued by reporting that though details needed to be formalised, as set out in MB 4/81 there was a high probability that funds to meet and exceed this requirement could be available from the following sources:

a) A grant of £50,000 under the DTI's Innovation scheme;

b) Additional equity investment totalling £100,000, comprising £35,000 by Mrs E.J. Woolley, £25,000 by Mr Bridford, £20,000 by Sir Pat O'Donnell and £10,000 each by Dr Milverton and Dr M.T. Newlands; and

c) Additional loan funding of £200,000, comprising £75,000 of further funding by New Hampshire Realty and £125,000 by Banco Navarrese. The Banco Navarrese funding, though wholly subordinate to all New Hampshire funding,[65] would be on the same terms as the initial tranche of New Hampshire funding.

---

[65] That is, in the event of default, Banco Navarrese would receive nothing until New Hampshire had been repaid in full, so New Hampshire's exposure was not increased. Normally such subordinate debt would carry a very high charge.

4. The Chief Executive said that this package secured the funding necessary. The potential debt/equity ratio at 2:1 constituted high gearing but also gave high incentive. However, the doubling of the capital base of the company would substantially dilute the prospects for the four original investors who were not, at present, able to add to their existing £10,000 equity stake: that is, Dr Higgins, Mrs Sinclair, Mr Smitham and Dr Yates. He felt that this position would not adequately recognise either their historic or their continuing contribution to the company and would leave two-thirds of the equity in the hands of Sir Pat O'Donnell, Mrs Woolley and himself. He therefore proposed that these investors should receive an option to subscribe for further shares at par up to a value of £10,000, at any time preceding an offer of shares to the public. That would enable them to restore their proportion of the equity if they desired.

5. The Board unanimously welcomed these developments and congratulated those who had brought them about. In discussion, the following points were agreed:

a) Since the Banco Navarrese funding was to be on the same terms as the first £200,000 of funding from New Hampshire Realty, it would be desirable to draw on it before moving to the further £75,000 of funding from New Hampshire, which was on more costly terms. It was unlikely that there would be difficulty in this, but the matter should be checked;

b) Dr Milverton should also receive a stock option, to the extent of £5,000;

c) Arrangements for employees to receive stock options should be developed; and

d) The financing package would allow appropriate adjustments to staff salaries to ensure retention of key personnel and also the recruitment of a first-rate programmer whom Mr Rowan knew was dissatisfied with his present post and for whom Dr Higgins could also vouch. This addition to staff would make an accelerated timetable more secure.

6. The Chief Executive, Dr Milverton and Mrs Sinclair were authorised to formalise arrangements embodying the above for approval at the meeting to be held on 28th April. Following that, the agreement of shareholders would be sought at the Annual General Meeting, which was already provisionally arranged for 19th May.

7. The Chairman reported that the Chief Executive had spoken to him about a discussion with Sir Pat O'Donnell. Sir Pat was prepared to become the company's Chairman following his retirement from International Electronics. He recognised that this was a great 'catch' for the company and he would be ready to resign at the appropriate time to allow it. The Chief Executive, on behalf of all, thanked him for his contribution as Chairman and emphasised the value he could bring in a continuing non-executive role on the Board. Sir Pat expected to be able to attend the meeting on 28th April and to meet staff on that day.

8. The meeting closed at 6.15 pm.

JENNY SINCLAIR
Secretary
28th February 1981

BOOK VIII
THE DIFFERENCE MADE

12. TUESDAY, 8TH DECEMBER, 1981

The telephone woke us in the darkness. There was a barrage of coughing as Liz sat up. I staggered downstairs and answered. It was ten to six.

"Pete, it's Roberta. Have you seen what's outside?"

"No." I lifted the curtain. "Oh my God." Just the sight made me shiver.

"I know how important it is that you both get to work with as little trouble as possible for Liz. You should start before this gets worse, as it's forecast to do. I can come round as soon as you want."

"We'll need some breakfast before we go. Come round at half past. I hope the nursery runs OK."

"Don't worry, either of you. Frank and I will manage."

Shortly after 6.30 we trudged off towards the local station, through snow which was already two inches deep and coming down harder. If a bus heading for Morden had appeared we would have caught it, but none came along.

"You OK?" I asked Liz, after a few minutes of silence. She was not her sporty self, even allowing for being five months gone.

"Yup, I'm just walking a bit slower than usual. It's the wrong moment to have a bug but I think I'm getting over it. I'm glad you're carrying my bag, Pete."

I didn't hold out much hope of services running from the local station but in fact the 6.47 left on time and made reasonable progress to Balham. Major delays from there into Victoria were expected so we switched to the Underground. Luckily Liz found a seat. At Pimlico, I left her.

"Good luck, Liz. It's a good day for you not to be coming back. Look after yourself, and *ours*."

"Don't worry, Pete, I will. I'll call you if I can. Right now, to quote Han Solo, I've a bad feeling about this. Maybe something will turn up, though."

She continued to the NUM headquarters near Euston. As I walked through the thickening snow and slush, I knew what she meant.

It was very quiet when I arrived at the department but in those days it would have been quiet anyway – civil servants still tended to arrive and leave late. I had not been in since Thursday, and Jean Simmonds had left a good stack of papers for me. Soon after nine o'clock, she arrived.

"Wow, Pete, you made it."

"Yes, before it was coming down really hard."

"I set off earlier, too, but the District Line's completely stopped. I got a bus over to Leyton. The Central Line was just about working. I squeezed in, and couldn't breathe until Bank. All this snow, this early. What does it mean? Are we in for another Ice Age, like the papers say?"

"There was snow earlier than this in '62, which started the Big Freeze winter, and again in '67. I remember being so cold in Cambridge that I went home to Dorset."

"I can just remember 'em. Three years ago, at the New Year, was bad enough. This wasn't forecast. It's a big surprise."

She made us coffee and I worked on, trying to concentrate rather than wonder what was happening up at Euston. Everything was still very quiet. Even the traffic on Millbank was sparse and muffled.

At about half past ten the phone rang outside and I wondered. But – "Jenny Sinclair for you."

"Pete, just to let you know I've made it in. I'm glad you have, too. Dick's got some bug and is staying at home today but he could take the children to school. So this morning I'm doing my Christmas shopping."

"That's a good idea. There won't be crowds."

"I was darned lucky. Everything is stopped into Waterloo. People are getting out and walking along the tracks, so now they've turned the current off. Goodness knows when it will be sorted out."

"What happened to you?"

"I was on the train that came to a halt in Vauxhall Station." The old trains, with doors you could open yourself, had their advantages and disadvantages.

Douglas Arnott was in, since during the week he used a flat in Bayswater rather than attempt the journey from Eastbourne. His 11.30 meeting to consider the latest report about industrial energy prices had just about enough attendees to be worthwhile. In any case, it wasn't very important, as he admitted. Nigel Lawson, who had become Secretary of State in September, was ready to leave all this to the market.

Soon after midday I was back at my office. Ed Plunkett looked in.

"I'm just about the only coal guy in. I was on the last train from Ealing before everything froze. Have you heard anything, Pete?"

"No. The NUM Executive meeting won't end until one o'clock at the earliest. Liz may be able to call me then but she'll have to be careful about it. Why don't we have an early lunch?"

We settled on our own in the sparsely filled canteen. I had been at least half expecting what he said next.

"It's marvellous that Liz has been able to carry on. When's she going to finish?"

"She's planning to stop work at the end of January."

"It was good to meet her again at your place in October. I'd met her in July at the NUM Conference, of course. Who didn't meet her there? She really tried to be everywhere and know everybody. Her greatest moment was at the National Executive dinner on the Saturday before the conference began. It began with an hour's drinking organised by Lawrence Daly. He's a bit past it but he can certainly organise that. Then a five-course dinner, with a separate wine for each course, and refills offered and accepted by many. Brandy, liqueurs and a cabaret took us to five to twelve, when I saw her giving signals. At midnight it was July 5th, Joe Gormley's birthday, and so time for champagne, cake and 'happy birthday to you'. The party revived. I'm told Joe was up until four o'clock. Just before I tottered off to bed, I saw him and Liz in the midst of a lively group."

Ed was looking at me quite intently. I knew why.

"You sound like me, Ed. I've never been a late-night socialiser. I first met Liz at Cambridge. Even then, we sometimes disagreed about when to call it a night. Domestic responsibilities usually make our lives more regular now, but I know she enjoyed doing her own thing in Jersey. How's your friend Maureen, by the way?"

"Fine, when we have time to meet! She's in the Treasury's public expenditure team, dealing with the Home Office. She'll be at the Houses of Parliament all this evening for the big debate."

"I hope that in this weather they help her to travel home afterwards."

"She called earlier. It should finish soon after ten, so I'll work on here, have something to eat and meet her at the House. She lives in Clapham. We should be able to get back there OK."

"It should be a good debate. I know that another old Cambridge chum of mine, Carol Milverton, hopes to speak later on. She knows that she'll be overshadowed by the reappearance of Shirley Williams."[66]

---

[66] Shirley Williams had re-entered Parliament two weeks before and had become the finance lead for the Social Democratic Party (SDP), which had been formed late in March 1981 as a development of the Council for Social Democracy. About thirty Labour MPs moved to it, and in June 1981 it formed an alliance with the Liberal Party.

"You've kept up with a lot of your friends from Cambridge."

"I suppose I have. Several of them are involved in my company. We've a board meeting at 3.30. Carol's husband will be there, and Jenny Sinclair, too."

"She struck me as a very capable woman."

"She is. Within five years she could be a partner in her firm. I hope that the four of us didn't shut you and Maureen out when you came to dinner. We know each other as well as possible. Liz was Dick's girlfriend before she was mine. After Liz had moved on, I met Jenny and she was my girlfriend for a while. She met Dick through me."

"Maureen found it particularly good that she was expected to talk on equal terms with the men. Too often that's not so. I suppose there aren't that many women of our age with degrees, though it's changing fast for younger people."

"True enough, though neither Liz nor Jenny has a degree. Liz lived in Waterhouse College because her father was the Master. Jenny comes from a family in which the men are academic. She qualified as an accountant in the old-fashioned way. I'm glad you both got on with us."

I gave a suitably discreet account of the activities of Creators Technology and then it was back to my office, having left exactly the right impression.

"Howard Larkin is in," announced Jean on my return. "There's a meeting in his office at 2.15."

At 1.35 Liz called. I dictated a note and gave Ed a heads-up whilst Jean typed it. The meeting began by reading this. Outside, the snow was still coming down. Eventually, Howard broke the silence.

"So, just when things seemed to be going better than we could possibly have hoped a few months ago, we're completely buggered, by the *weather*. The NUM Executive members from Nottinghamshire and the Midlands would have voted for accepting the Coal Board's final pay offer. They hadn't too far to come so they left travelling until this morning and didn't make it. The militants from Scotland, Yorkshire and South Wales travelled yesterday and did make it. Therefore the Executive has rejected the offer and will recommend that the members vote for strike action in a ballot."

"But it hasn't called a ballot straight away," said Ed. "Instead, it's called this Special Delegate Conference for the end of next week. Why do you think that is, Pete?"

"My hunch is that people want it for various reasons. The militants want it so as to whip up enthusiasm for a strike. They don't want a repetition of what happened two years ago when the members didn't support the Executive recommendation to reject the pay offer. Also, the result of the election for President will be out tomorrow. Though everyone knows Scargill will romp home, he's not placed to say much today. At the conference, he'll have the definite authority of President elect."

"Why has Gormley gone along with having a conference?" asked John Willis.

"He may have felt that there was little point in opposing it. And along with the moderates on the Executive who were there, he would have seen that it means no ballot before Christmas and so more time for people to think."

"How soon in January could a ballot take place, Ed?" asked Howard.

"With no go-ahead until just before Christmas, the ballot couldn't be in the first week back at work in the New Year. They're always on Thursdays because that's the day of the week when absenteeism is lowest. So it looks to me like the 14th of January."

"If the 55% needed for a strike were delivered then, when could a strike begin?"

"If there were no more talks, notice could be given of a strike to begin on 25th January. If more talks were suggested that might hold it off for another week, but the Coal Board has said that its offer is final."

"And that's the way it must stay," I commented. "When the ballot takes place the men must know that if enough of them vote for a strike, there will be a strike, not some more money found to avoid a strike."

"You're right, of course, Pete," said Howard. "That's the very clear line the Board will take. But we've been very lucky indeed to get away with two months of Phoney War. The Board's final offer is several per cent lower than was feared would be necessary a few months ago. The Board has negotiated skilfully and the NUM, Gormley in particular, has been content to let things drag on, delaying the start of any strike. I've not understood why he's been content with that but one doesn't look a gift horse in the mouth."

He paused for a moment before continuing.

"Or, at least, one doesn't look until it's not a gift horse anymore. I suspect that, in a crunch, there will be voices around the Cabinet table saying that perhaps the original estimate of what would be necessary was right."

"The voices won't include our Secretary of State or the Employment Secretary,"[67] said John. "We can't be seen to repeat last February."

"The Prime Minister will agree with them but she didn't make a total clear-out of the 'wets.'"

"If I were Nigel Lawson, tonight I would want the timetable Ed has just set out, particularly if it could also include an estimate of how long the power stations could keep going after a strike began. Then I would have a perspective on the problem and could start thinking straight away about what I should say, to whom and when. That's the way he works. He's a journalist, remember."

"Estimates of endurance are the task of the interdepartmental committee I'm on. Sorry, forget I've said there's such a committee," said Howard.

---

67 Who was now Norman Tebbit.

"Is it so difficult to give an answer to within a week or two?" I asked. "We know how much coal is stocked at the power stations. We know roughly how much is being used. We know how much is being delivered, though we'll need some idea of how much the weather will slow deliveries. Presumably snow holds up coal trains as well as passenger trains."

"I think we can make a pretty good guess," said Ed. "A few weeks ago I was looking for something else in our registry and I noticed a file about coal deliveries during the bad weather three years ago. I pulled it out this morning. Someone did a note analysing what happened. Snow across the Midlands and Yorkshire roughly halves the rate of deliveries. The note also mentions that because the bad weather didn't last long, power station stocks never fell near the level it quotes as being that at which real difficulties in running the electricity system occur."

"I'm on for John's idea," said Howard. "Let's see what you can put together, Ed. Say how long we might keep going if this weather doesn't last and how long if it continues. I'll warn people that this is coming. If you have something to me by 4.30, I ought to be able to clear it with them in time to go to the Secretary of State this evening. I'll tell his office that that's what we're doing. I'll also speak to the Board, with the advantage of already knowing what's happened – thanks, Pete. I'll see at once which messages they're underplaying or overplaying. John, what's our press line?"

"No comment; the negotiations are between the Coal Board and the NUM."

"The line for Ministers to take with colleagues is that this is serious but they should stay calm and keep quiet."

After the meeting, Ed hurried off to put something together, but John seemed to have the time to talk. He began with a statement of the obvious.

"What a contrast between Howard and his predecessor. We had a crisp discussion, he recognised ideas from others and at the end there were clear decisions."

"Bill Armitage wasn't there. Is he still stuck in the snow?" Bill was Derek Morris's replacement.

"He's at a meeting in Luxemburg, but anyway he gives Ed plenty of scope. He knows a good'un."

"That's the way it should be, the way it was in IE and the way it is and will be in Creators Technology, whose Board meets in twenty minutes."

I could see that John might be about to make a confidential comment. For now, I didn't want that.

The snow was dying out as I headed for the Universal Assurance offices in Holborn. The normal cycle of meetings made the December meeting a short lunchtime discussion[68] but developments over the last few weeks required a full meeting and Pat O'Donnell would not be available for several weeks after Thursday. Since Pat had an early evening engagement in London, the location had been retained by courtesy of Universal Assurance, rather than being shifted to Crawley. That was fortunate in view of the weather.

On my way I had a reminder of the developments. An office equipment store proudly displayed an IBM PC in its window, for 'quick delivery'. The rumours early in the year had been true but formed by no means the whole story.

IBM had unveiled the new machine in August, though supplies were only now arriving in quantity. It was formally known as the IBM 5150 but was to give its more familiar name ('Personal Computer') to the 'desktop' machines of the next twenty-five years. There was a box with the works inside and two ports for floppy disks, a keyboard and a monitor screen using the cathode ray tube TV technology of the time.[69]

The PC appeared to be reliable and relatively easy for

---

[68] The cycle with which the company operated almost throughout its separate existence and growth was of full Board meetings in February, April, June, September and November; short discussions in January, March, May, July, October and December; and no meeting in August.

[69] The 'mouse' came into general use a few years later.

non-experts to use but so were the latest products of other manufacturers. In the USA, Apple and Hewlett-Packard were selling in volume. Atari was pressing ahead with machines dedicated to computer gaming, including a home version of the wildly successful 'Space Invaders' arcade game which had been developed in Japan. The next year was to see the appearance of the Commodore 64, the most successful 'home computer' of all time. British companies were also doing well; Clive Sinclair had been joined by Acorn, whose BBC Micro had been announced the week before but was not to be generally available for some time.

The key point was that IBM had made three dramatic reversals of its secretive corporate policies.

First, it had sourced most components of the machine from outside suppliers all over the world. The scale of its orders led quickly to the creation of suppliers capable of providing components not just to IBM but to any manufacturer.

Secondly, it had published full details of how the machine worked, with the specific intention that other manufacturers would build similar machines, and that outside software companies would create software that could run on its machine and on others.

Finally, it had adopted an operating system developed by Microsoft, then a small company based in Seattle.

IBM had set the standard. Its design was capable of almost unlimited development and would quickly dominate first the business and then the home market. Instead of a lot of efforts by individual enthusiasts, there was a new industry in being. In the 1980s, capital would pour in to force innovation and reduce costs, just as in the 1780s it had poured into the new industry based on the machine spinning and weaving of cotton. That had set off the Industrial Revolution.[70]

---

[70] The turbulent early days of the computer industry do recall the turbulent early days of the cotton industry – see the classic account in Mantoux, *The Industrial Revolution in the Eighteenth Century*.

At Creators Technology, we had anticipated all this in our decision two years before to quit constructing machines and to concentrate on software development. Now, the market was opening before us. The sky was the limit.

The IBM PC had an 8-bit Intel 8088 processor and up to 65,536 bytes of memory. Input of both data and software was from floppy disks (with cassette tapes as an option). Most programs therefore had to be loaded each time they were used. Our trading software would work only with the higher power of a 16-bit processor. To run fast and to support networks with other computers, it needed hard disk storage, giving several million words of memory. The question was, therefore, whether the next generation would deliver that. Tony Higgins and Chris Rowan had been using their contacts, and the main paper for consideration today set out their answer. The next generation, to appear in a year or so, would have a hard disk but still with 8-bit processing. The generation after would move to 16-bit processing but could be three years away.[71]

"Is it a busy day at the Ministry, Pete?" Brian asked, as we settled down.

"You could say that, at least for those of us who got in."

That prompted a few inevitable exchanges but Pat quickly had us in order. He was a Chairman with his own mind, as I had hoped he would be. Jenny and I knew what he would say.

"Thank you all for attending promptly on this difficult day. Tony and Chris, I won't pretend to understand the technical stuff in your paper but I am sure that two factors underlie the decisions it leads us to make. First, as always, Jenny, what's your latest financial assessment?"

"IBM has caused a remarkable change from earlier in the year. We're now the kind of business that people want to invest in, even if we're keeping fairly quiet about what we're doing. As

---

71 These were quite accurate predictions. The IBM 5160 (PC-XT) was introduced in March 1983 and the IBM 5170 (PC-AT) in August 1984.

you know, Paul, ten days ago Jim Schurman phoned me, quite off his own bat. He's the credit controller at New Hampshire. They're ready to up their credit limit to £300,000 and drop the penal terms on the last £75,000. In other words, though they're still pals with Banco Navarrese, they want to keep the lion's share of the action. Of course, they're expecting that before long, interest rates will start falling for good. MLR could be down to 10% in a year's time."[72]

"So we don't want to get locked into current rates for more than we have to," said Pat. "Have we had any contact with banks not connected with one or more of you good people? Pete, did Allied Proprietary contact you after my lunch three weeks ago?"

"They did. They would certainly match New Hampshire's terms. Also, they might accept a lower penalty for early redemption," I said, looking at Paul.

Brian came in. "Would it be worth finding out more about the new Investors' Startup Fund? Its great feature is that you don't pay interest until you register a profit." He went into a few details.

"Can you send me whatever detailed prospectus there is, Brian?" asked Jenny. "An accounting profit would need to reflect a deferred liability for interest. Does their definition of profit do so? Pat, I'm inclined to get a better package out of our present bankers. Carlos Casares of Banco Navarrese is visiting London later next week. Pete, why don't you and I meet with him and Jim Schurman, having researched the alternatives a bit more?"

After a few minutes of discussion of our line for that meeting, Pat moved us on.

"Two things have transformed our position over the last few months. First, we're now much more confident of our product. As we discussed fully at our last meeting and this month's progress reports confirm, development is on course and the likelihood of big snags is much lower than it was earlier

---

[72] It was then 14%.

in the year. That's a huge credit to Pete, Chris and the whole team. I'm very sorry that I won't be able to say that on Saturday. Secondly, as you say, Jenny, IBM's launch has transformed the funding position, so we can make decisions with an eye to the best outcome in two or three years' time. We can resource those decisions appropriately, though without being extravagant. I suggest also that we can make decisions with an eye to the date of a flotation when, naturally, we will want to raise new capital on the most advantageous terms and maximise the value of our own shareholdings and options. So, Pete, what decisions should we make now on the basis of the paper?"

"I can add to the paper what Neil Farnham told me at the weekend. This is not to go outside this room or for the minutes. As one might expect, International Consolidated is taking advantage of the component supply bottlenecks that are holding up PC deliveries. Every week, a freighter takes off from Manchester Airport, packed with stuff from Sunderland. So they're getting well used to making the bits fast and to quality. That will help them launch their clone, which they aim to do next May. The price will be about £2,000 for the full outfit, compared to IBM's £3,000. They hope for a good share of the European market. Elsewhere, there will be at least three more contenders, two US and one Japanese. Most importantly for us, IC hopes to launch a hard disk model early in 1983. It might even be available before the comparable IBM machine is delivered over here. Thus we could plan for a launch late next year, on the clear expectation that a hard disk 8-bit PC will be available then or very shortly thereafter. That launch could be of a Version 1, which will be effective on a stand-alone computer of that kind. We could market it as an interim version which will deliver profits for anyone with quick access to off-line trading data, for example frequent telephone or telex reports. We could also say that Version 2, for online data, is underway and will be ready when the 16-bit computers needed for fast networking are ready. So hurry along IBM, IC and competitors! That's it in a nutshell, so far as I'm concerned."

"Isn't there a risk of showing our hand too early?" asked Brian. "Once the big boys know that something like this is possible, they'll go for it themselves, with more resources than we can possibly throw at it. They could overtake us, to get to Version 2 from scratch."

"We're not going to publish the architecture of the software," said Chris. "Anyone wanting to develop Version 2 would first have to disassemble our Version 1. In my view that would take them several months. And, Morag, didn't you say that it would be very difficult for anyone to create the software without understanding Pete's maths?"

"That's right. Sheila and I make it our business to keep tabs on who's working on anything that might be related to what Pete has done, and Professor Kraftlein still has his ear to the ground enough to tip us off. There's no sign of activity."

"I've already written up my work for publication," I said. "On this plan, I would submit it and circulate preprints early in 1983, soon after the launch of Version 1. By the time people have understood it, it would be too late for anyone to catch up before Version 2 is launched, late in 1984. On normal journal timescales, publication would be in mid-1984, just in time for Version 2."

"And after?" asked Brian.

"If Version 2 is the success we hope for, we'll be able to afford the staff to keep ahead."

"I think customers will welcome Version 1," said Paul. "Even if they don't make any profit from it, their staff will have the opportunity to practise using it, so that when they do have Version 2 they can make good use of it quickly. We can take orders for Version 2, making it clear that they'll be fulfilled in strict rotation; no favours, to New Hampshire or anyone else."

"You're right, Paul," Pat chipped in. "Creators Technology will have customers who are fiercely competitive with each other. It won't succeed unless it's seen to be independent of all. So our order book must be confidential. I take it that that won't create difficulties for our balance sheet, Jenny."

"No. Auditors can confirm the validity of the total without disclosing details."

Discussion took in the detail of Chris's progress reports. After an hour, the provisional timings for launch were agreed. We had even concluded that spring 1985 could well be a good time to float the company. We were on the way to a pricing strategy, too. The availability of loan finance would allow Version 1 to be almost a loss leader, aimed at bringing customers in. Version 2 would be much more expensive but the price for Version 1 could be offset against it. Once traders could see that getting in first with Version 2 gave prospects of large profits, they would be ready to pay.

"So, Pete, the main action is for you," concluded Pat. "For our next meeting, on the 26th of January, we need a revised draft corporate plan, to include sales projections, the results of your discussions with bankers and staffing requirements. We'll have a short discussion then and you can finalise it for approval at the full meeting in February. I'm temperamentally suspicious of requests for more staff but I agree with you and Jenny about the compelling need for a qualified finance manager. It's a tribute to her that the company has come this far with just an accounts clerk. We also need to settle our thinking on office location. In the meantime, I wish you a Merry Christmas, a Happy New Year and Good Luck. From what I've heard, the country will need it. On Thursday, my wife and I sail for the West Indies, assuming that we can get to Southampton. We'll be back on the 19th of January, after the cruise of a lifetime. I'm going to enjoy it, which shows that I *am* slowing down. But now, I must be off to my next meeting. It's amazing how busy retirement is. However did I fit my job in? Pete, tomorrow I'll call you on a couple of things."

Pat left, to our best wishes. Chris had an important question for the rest of us.

"For the staff dinner on Saturday at the Copthorne Hotel, I presently have Pete, Jenny and Brian down to attend. I know you can't be there, Tony. Are any of the rest of you intending to come?"

"Carol and I are in the constituency, sorry," said Paul.

"I may be on by own," I said. "Liz is soldiering on with a nasty bug."

"I can come but Sheila can't get out of evening duty," said Morag. "I won't want to stay too late unless the weather improves and I can rely on the trains back."

"We could put you up if necessary, Morag," said Brian.

"Thanks Brian. Now, this year the Pankhurst Centre's party starts at six o'clock on Friday the 18th. It's not the best day of the week for our clients but it's better for the guests we want to attend and donate, and just before Christmas we tend to have fewer people turning up. Any who do turn up will just have to join in. Hands up for takers."

Most hands went up but not Paul's.

"Sorry, Morag, that evening there's the New Hampshire bash, and Carol will be in her constituency again. It may be that threatened women stick it out over Christmas but lots of people have other problems just before, mainly about paying for it. She's still their MP, despite change of party. Let me write you a cheque now."

"Drink, Pete?" said Brian, as we broke up. "In the City, they open at five o'clock. Later, I've a meeting of the Worshipful Company of Insurers social committee."

"Will people be staying for that, in this weather?"

"They need to. There's plenty to do on the arrangements for next year's banquet. I've not been told that anyone isn't coming. When it snows, people rush to cram on the early trains. Later on, there'll still be some trains. You'll wait but you'll get a seat. I learnt that lesson three years ago."

"Let me call Liz."

I actually called Roberta, to say that I would be late, though in time to pick up Jenny. Then Brian and I walked through the slush on Holborn Viaduct, passing newsstands whose placards alternated 'SNOW CHAOS TO GO ON' and 'MINERS' STRIKE LOOMS'. Once we were settled in a deserted pub, I began.

"I must say, I was pleased with today's meeting. We started this company nearly eight years ago without much idea of what we were doing at all. Today, we were a team. Everyone had something to contribute. I guess it's because we all have expertise. Jenny has the financial expertise. Whoever of Morag and Sheila comes along delivers maths research expertise. Chris has the technical expertise. Tony has engineering research expertise. You and Paul bring the business expertise of the man on the up in a big company, and Sheila has the expertise of someone running what's now another small business – the Pankhurst Centre. Over us all, Pat's chairmanship is great."

"Jenny is putting so much in now. How does she do it all? She has a big job, a family and Creators Technology."

"I guess it's through good management of her time and a husband who helps. As Dick said to me a long time ago, she is good at organising people, in the loveliest sort of way."

"I know, Pete, they're the couple of the future, not like Susie and me. Jenny had a rough patch last year, though."

"I know. It impacted on me as well as on Creators Technology."

"It's great that she ain't fussed about you and Liz anymore. It's greater still, what you've done for Liz."

"Liz has done lots for me, Brian. We've been close for over fifteen years, whether in a relationship or not. We used to say that we were the brother and sister neither of us had. But there seemed no way that we could live together and we went our own ways. Then this awful business with Greg somehow made something click. Now, I'm settled at home and my work benefits. Gosh, that went down fast."

I returned with the next round a couple of minutes later. I had a pretty good idea of how Brian would continue and indeed of the reason for the invitation.

"It's a busy time for Liz, I guess," he continued. "How's she bearing up? Sorry to hear she's got a bug."

"There are lots of them around. Jenny told me that Dick has been hit, too. As you know, Brian, Liz isn't one to give up. I'm going to coddle her a bit, if I can, for the baby's sake as well as for hers."

Brian paused for a moment before continuing.

"Pete, we're very old friends. I think the world of you and Liz. I always have done. That's why I need to tell you about a story that my dad says is going around."

"What story?"

"That – that Liz's baby isn't yours."

It was my turn to pause. Then I got out a response.

"*What*? Whose do they think it is, then?"

"People don't say, but they do say about the man she was with for so much of the time in Jersey, particularly on the Saturday before the Conference began. The National Executive dinner turned into quite a birthday celebration. Dad wasn't there, of course. He arrived the next day. He's going on what he's been told."

"Who told him?"

"There are those who think the Executive is too free with spending the union's funds on partying. They say that there will be some changes soon. I've said to Dad that I can't believe the story. It's absurd."

"Certainly it's absurd, as well as being very hurtful indeed. Brian, I'm grateful to you for warning me. I'll have to warn Liz. She'll be very upset. I just hope she hasn't picked it up during today. Perhaps she'll start her maternity leave sooner than expected. Maybe she won't go in tomorrow to help organise next week's conference. Or maybe she'll tough it out. That's her way, but it won't be because she's not upset. Can you please tell your dad that anyone who puts this round in writing will receive a formal letter from Frank Booth pretty sharpish, as well as perhaps a note from someone else's solicitor. You can also say that earlier this year Liz and I decided that we wanted a child together. Just before or after she was in Jersey, we succeeded. Our decision came out of knowing what we told you and other friends. Greg isn't going to recover. We're making our lives together, permanently. It's not what we expected to happen but it's what *has* happened. We're making the best of it."

"I'll do that, Pete. This is political, so it's a dirty business."

"I agree. Look at what some of your dad's jolly friends are doing to Carol."

"She must know that a miners' MP who defects to the SDP won't be popular."

"Her seat isn't NUM-sponsored and she's never been on the NUM parliamentary panel, though I know your dad put in a good word for her."

"She won't get in again there."

"Currently the polls put the SDP/Liberal Alliance well ahead of either Labour or the Conservatives but I agree that if she wants to continue as a Member of Parliament, she needs to find another seat."

"Why doesn't she go for your neck of the woods again?"

"The Lib won't want to stand down after only two tries. He's certainly an improvement on dear old Cyril. I think she'll quit politics and become a full-time journalist. Her *Clarion* column is already being syndicated in the States, as 'The Limey View'. She's writing for the *Express*, too. They wanted someone from the SDP."

Brian looked at his watch. "I'd better get going."

"Brian, tell your dad also that informal calls about the pay situation are welcome."

"His view will be simple. If he thinks a strike will win quickly, he'll support it. If he doesn't think it will win quickly, he won't support it."

I took the Underground to Balham and stood on the bleak platform there for some time. Eventually a train turned up that would get me somewhere near home, though by a long way round. We passed through an alpine-looking Crystal Palace station, down to Norwood Junction and through West Croydon after a long wait to view the Selhurst carriage sidings. From where I alighted, it was only about an hour's trudge.

Roberta was solicitous when, at a quarter past eight, I made it to her place. "Oh, Pete, what a long day for you both, but you did phone to warn us, thanks. How is Liz?"

"I spoke to her earlier. She's found somewhere to stay overnight because now she needs to be in to organise the conference you'll have heard about."

"Oh yes. It all sounds terrible. What *can* we do?"

"Nothing will happen until well after Christmas, so let's enjoy that first."

"That's the spirit; like when we enjoyed Christmas in '73," said Frank. "Now here's Jenny, who's been so good all day. A good roll in the snow at nursery helped, didn't it, Jenny? But here's Daddy to take you home."

"Snow – cold – wet," muttered a sleepy Jenny.

"I do hope Liz feels better soon," said Roberta. "If I were her, I wouldn't be so devoted to the NUM."

"I'm pleased she isn't struggling around outside in this weather. She said she was going straight to bed. The bug has rather got her but she's always been pretty determined. She knows that I'm staying home tomorrow. I've lots from today's Creators Technology meeting that I can do on the phone."

The little walk back home woke Jenny up. As I brought her into the kitchen for a late night drink, she had a natural question.

"Where's Mummy?"

"Mummy is away tonight but she'll be back tomorrow night. I'll look after you now and tomorrow."

"Mummy calls you Daddy, but you're not my daddy."

"No, I'm not your real daddy, Jenny. Your real daddy is very ill and can't look after you. I'm looking after you instead because I love your mummy and I love you."

"Mummy says I'm going to have a little brother or sister soon."

"Yes, and we'll love them too. But we'll go on loving you just as much."

Jenny was certainly precocious. I could only hope she understood the message. At four, she had to know, before someone else told her. Since Liz and I had been more open about ourselves, most people we knew locally had gone on accepting us; but a few people had not. We hoped that their children would accept her.

By a quarter past nine, after one of Peter Rabbit's adventures, Jenny was fast asleep and I could unwind over a drink and a meal. I had much to unwind from.

Liz's plan had been working out so well.

First, there had been the quiet persuasion to adopt a measured approach to the pay negotiations. Then, as crunch point approached, we had put on more pressure.

It had been so easy to start the rumours. Three weeks ago, a member of the NUM Executive who would be certain to talk had received an anonymous letter. The man who mattered had wanted to believe the rumours. He had not asked a direct question but he had become very receptive. He had swung some waverers on the Executive towards acceptance of the Coal Board's pay offer. Last night, all had seemed done and dusted.

We had accepted that the rumours would draw attention to the link between Liz and me. She would be suspected at the NUM offices and I would be suspected in the department. However, we had reckoned that our jobs on coal were in any case finishing. In January, Liz would begin maternity leave. I had plenty to occupy me during the last six months of my contract, which I would not be renewing. The demands of Creators Technology were increasing rapidly. There was more money available, so the revised draft corporate plan could include provision for me to draw a reasonable salary, pending what would hopefully be the jackpot from flotation. Liz and I had been expecting to withdraw from the coal field, sharing quiet satisfaction at the success of our prank.

But now the weather had intervened and the pay offer was rejected. I had not seen the note Ed had been putting together, but I was sure that a strike beginning in January would succeed before the spring, particularly if the weather continued to increase demand and disrupt deliveries. A union still led by Gormley would have support from the public and from other unions, just as it had had support in 1972 and 1974. The temptation on him to go for the hat trick would be strong, particularly if it were apparently being forced upon him by his Executive and a conference.

The government would have to decide whether to lose a strike or to concede a settlement which would wreck their policies. Whatever they decided, Mrs Thatcher would go the way of Mr Heath. The left of the Labour Party would be greatly strengthened. The prospects for successful business in Britain would be much weakened.

Liz and I had thought that we had foiled the NUM's best chance. Far more coal was being mined than was being used, so stocks would be higher next year and higher still the year after. By then, too, other measures would increase the ability to resist a strike. There was a lot of secrecy about those but I had seen papers occasionally. I chuckled to recall one produced by some general. If the trains moving coal from collieries to power stations were 'blacked', metaphorically as well as literally, then with practice 'his men' could drive them. So why not let them practise on a full-sized train set built in some remote corner of Salisbury Plain? Trains could run round it, loading and unloading coal or some less messy substitute. Fortunately, it had been realised that this 'secret' (and expensive) facility would be spotted very quickly and that such use of troops would force the power workers' union to bring its men out.

Provided no such silly mistakes were made, after this year it was very unlikely that the NUM would have real support from any other trade union. Arthur Scargill's abrasive and self-centred style would not go down well with their leaders. Ed had read some history before pointing out that Scargill had a personality very similar to that of A.J. Cook, the miners' leader in 1926. Then, the General Strike had lasted ten days. After that, the miners had been left on their own to lose, despite Cook having some public sympathy for the plight of those he represented. Scargill would have no public sympathy. He inspired fear and hatred, rather than respect. A government determined to resist him would have widespread support.

But that was all for the future. We were in the present. Liz and I had done our best but our prank had failed. We had not foiled the best chance. The prospects were as bleak as the view outside.

This was crunch time, unless something turned up.

HOUSE OF COMMONS, 8th DECEMBER, 1981

Mrs Carol Milverton (Holtcliffe). I will add briefly to the points made earlier by my Right Honourable friend the Member for Crosby,[73] whose return here is so welcome (*Interruption*).

We heard much this evening about the need for radical action. In fact, to some Right Honourable and Honourable Members, radical action seems to be an end in itself, whether it is to roll back the frontiers of the state or to extend them. But all action needs a purpose.

We have also heard this evening how much easier it is to blame the other side than to make constructive suggestions of your own. The Right Honourable Member for East Surrey[74] began this by pointing out that public spending as a proportion of GDP rose from 39% to 46½% between 1973 and 1975. He used this to criticise the previous administration. He omitted to say that the increase in spending was largely the result of commitments made between 1970 and 1974 when his party was in government.

Surely we can all agree that the priorities facing this country are to get economic growth going again and thus begin to catch up with our competitors or at least not to fall even further behind them. The question is, how? Clearly the present government's policies are not working. They boast only that real GDP is no longer actually falling. It's still 6% below what it was when they took over. That's 6% less wealth, 6% less money for anyone to spend and the cause of three million unemployed. What an achievement.

But what have the official Opposition made of it? Only to suggest that if we bring more industry under state control, everything will be better. That might make sense if the industries presently under state control were models of good management but clearly they aren't and nobody seems to be prepared to do anything about that.

---

73 Shirley Williams.
74 Geoffrey Howe, then Chancellor of the Exchequer.

Take as an example the coal industry, in which many of my constituents are employed. It's in the news again today, as it is so often. We all recognise the importance of investing in it in accordance with the Plan for Coal but the increased productivity that the Plan for Coal was supposed to deliver has been lacking. Productivity should have increased by 30% since 1974, but it has hardly changed. (*Interruption – Have yer bin darn a pit then, lass?*)

Mr Speaker. Order. Honourable Members are making too many sedentary interventions.

Mrs Milverton. I will answer the Honourable Member's comments. Yes, I have made several colliery visits. I was last underground on the 13th of November. I am not sure that 'lass' is parliamentary language but I will take it as a compliment. I am after all the Lass from up North who was elected in 1974 on a 20% swing. I was voted in by constituents who wanted common sense, just as the British people do now, according to the opinion polls.

To return to my point, the static productivity in coal is not the fault of the miners. It is the fault of their management. Neither the previous nor the present administration has addressed this. It is astonishing that, although it is known that Sir Derek Ezra will retire next summer, we have no indication of who will succeed him. The coal industry and its employees need to know who will lead them.

Mr Skinner. Who's going to be the leader of the SDP, then? Will it be Woy from Wawwington?[75] (*Laughter*)

---

[75] After being President of the European Commission, Roy Jenkins had attempted to re-enter Parliament at the Warrington by-election in July 1981 but narrowly failed. He succeeded at the Glasgow Hillhead by-election in March 1982. His father was a Welsh miner, NUM officer and MP but his Oxford education and later career eliminated any hint of that from his speech. This intervention appeared in the official *Hansard* as "We do not know who the leader of the SDP will be."

Mrs Milverton. The processes of leadership selection in the SDP will certainly be more democratic than those in the Conservative or Labour Parties.

Mr Brittan.[76] I was not expecting to have the Honourable Member for Bolsover in aid but here we have the SDP in glorious form; all things to all people. (*Interruption – Have it all ways, lass; best if yer do.*)

Mrs Williams. On a point of order, Mr Speaker, the sedentary interruption just made contains the most unfortunate and unfounded innuendos concerning my Honourable friend.

Mr Speaker. I repeat my request to Honourable Members to desist from sedentary interruptions. I did not hear the interruption clearly myself.

Mrs Milverton. I have made my point. If Honourable Members wish to ignore it, that is their loss. (*Hon. Members – Oooooh.*)

---

76 Leon Brittan was then Chief Secretary to the Treasury.

13. FRIDAY, 18TH DECEMBER, 1981

Jim Schurman leaned back contentedly and took another sip of his brandy.

"Don't thank us, thank New Hampshire. We all earned it this morning. You two have shown us how Creators Technology is on its way to being a world beater, and you've agreed not to go elsewhere for funding. Carlos, you came up with the right funding structure. We've done a lot more work than most people in London today."

Jim looked around the restaurant, which was crowded with large parties on their way through roast turkey with all the trimmings, as Carlos responded.

"This morning I was reading that your people are celebrating Christmas early and well because they are fearful of what will happen afterwards, with your miners on strike and continuing cold weather."

"Yeah, this commie McGahey, what makes him tick? Can't Margaret Thatcher have him put away somewhere?"

"Not unless he commits an offence or incites others to do so," said Jenny.

"Guess that's right. She can't do what Jaruzelski has done with *his* miners."

Earlier in the meal, we had discussed the previous Sunday's news of martial law in Poland. That had made the Cold War seem as cold as the morning had been.

A waiter approached Carlos. "Your taxi is here, sir."

"Thank you. It is time for me to be on my way. I have enjoyed my visit to London. Jim, it is good that our two banks are continuing to work together. Jenny and Pete, it is a particular pleasure to meet you both again. I think, too, that I have been lucky in my timing by arriving on Wednesday and leaving today."

"You're right," I said. "Last Saturday night was the coldest for a hundred years. On Sunday, snow closed most airports. Since then, it's been slightly milder in London, though not further north. Early next week, more snow is expected."

"Today, Madrid is also cold. I am meeting Ana there later. Now she is a politician she receives many invitations before Christmas. This evening we attend a reception at the Embassy of Argentina. *Madrileños* like the winter cold after the heat of summer. I am not so sure. The invitation makes me recall the warmth of Buenos Aires in December. I know it well. I spent a year there, and last month I visited for a week."

Carlos left with mutual felicitations of the season, and a few minutes later Jenny and I were walking briskly towards the Plender Luckhurst offices.

"Jim is right," I said. "We did damn well this morning, the pair of us. I'll put a note round. I won't bother Pat, though. It's really good that you were able to take most of the morning out of your job, and some of the afternoon, too."

"I've a meeting at 3.30 and another at 4.15. Next week, I'm in right through to Thursday lunchtime, including Tuesday. Luckily, our Christmas is local this year. Mum and Dad are with Amanda and John."

"I hope they get there but I suppose Sheffield is no colder than Cambridge."

"Dick and I begin with 'us' time. On Christmas Eve, his parents are looking after the children. Dick and I will have lunch up here and then we're going to the matinée of Strauss's *Silver Rose*[77] at the English National Opera."

"Marvellous. You do fit your life together so well, Jenny."

---

77 The English name for Strauss's *Der Rosenkavalier*

"I'm liking the Creators work more and more, Pete. I'm beginning to wonder if I want to be a partner in Plenders."

"Don't burn your boats until we know we have it made. Then we'll be expanding very fast and a fairly full-time Finance Director will be a must. I know who that should be, and so does Pat."

"Having him around takes me back to when we worked together on the IE rights issue. We did so well, then."

"Yes, but it was a strain for both of us, and for Dick. Now, we're working together just as well and it isn't a strain."

Jenny paused for a moment, before going on. "That reminds me of the odd comment Jim made. They knew we two could deliver for Creators Technology because two years ago we delivered on the rights issue. *Our* bit of that turned out well for New Hampshire. Then he stopped, as if he'd said something he shouldn't have said, and changed the subject. I wonder what he was talking about. I can't think of anything connected with the rights issue that turned out badly for New Hampshire."

"No, I can't, either."

"Though last year Carol told me they weren't going on as good a holiday as usual because Paul hadn't had a large bonus."

"Yes, she mentioned that to Liz, too. Perhaps some scheme of his went wrong. He's always been a man for schemes."

"It can't have happened again. This year it was Greece, and not backpacking."

"They have no children. They can afford it."

"And Paul's definitely buying this house near Beaconsfield, so they'll have two houses and a flat."

"That's not very socialist at all."

"Maybe not, though Carol told me that Paul is staying with Labour for the long haul."

"Carol is having rather a rough time just now. Last week, she was really done over in the House. Maureen Johnson, who you met over dinner in September, was there. I'm told the *Hansard* is rather bowdlerised. I hope Paul gives her some sympathy."

"I've never known Paul express any emotions at all. Right, here we are at my office, with twenty minutes to my meeting."

"Mine isn't until 4.30. That's a wash-up on what we've heard about the NUM conference. I won't be able to contribute much because Liz isn't there."

"It's good you can work at home, Pete, to take pressure off her."

"In this weather, I'm being saved a load of hassle. With what we've agreed today, I'm well on with the first draft of a revised corporate plan. It will be round to you all very early in the New Year."

"At the staff party on Saturday, Liz was soldiering on but she didn't look good. Come to think of it, she seemed tired when we met up three weeks ago. I'm glad you persuaded her to go to the doctor."

"I made it clear that I was worried about our baby. She was refusing to be got down. She's now on an antibiotic which won't hurt the baby and she must stay in the warm over Christmas. Luckily, we're at home, too, with parents, aunt and uncle nearby, and also cousin Gerald and family on Boxing Day."

"I wonder if Joe Gormley caught from Liz whatever is keeping him at home."

"If he did, he hasn't complained about it. I'll see you and Dick later. I'm glad he's over *his* bug."

"Actually, we can't come to the Pankhurst Centre party. Can you pass on our apologies? Almost as soon as I arrived at the office this morning, Dick called. Our sitter has fallen through. There's no chance of another. His parents are out so he can't come up. I don't fancy travelling back from Stratford late on my own."

"You won't need to. I'll come with you to Waterloo afterwards and change at Clapham Junction. I won't want to be too late myself, though Liz was keen that I go. This afternoon, she can rest because Roberta is looking after our Jenny for a while. I'll meet you here, when, 6.15?"

"Oh, *great*. Morag and Sheila make such an effort with this party. It would be a pity to let them down."

I had not been into the department since the previous Friday so there was a heap of work for me, mostly about the sale of state-owned oilfields and gasfields, on which subject my industry contacts, though rather out of date, were still useful. I piled papers into my briefcase, for attention before I was next in. That would be later on Monday, weather and Liz's state permitting. I would attend John Willis's press office party, to which Bernard Ingham was confidently expected to drop in. Even more important, I would give Jean her Christmas present.

Before Howard Larkin's meeting, Ed Plunkett came in to go over his follow-up to some ideas we had discussed on the phone. At the meeting, I raised a few eyebrows by explaining why I had no news. The best information about the conference was from John.

"The press was allowed in so I've had several calls. As expected, the conference voted almost unanimously for a ballot on January 14th, with a recommendation to vote for a strike. Not as expected is what McGahey did, with encouragement from Scargill. He allowed in a load of people who shouted the odds about overthrowing Thatcher, revolution and so on. Guess what the papers will say."

"Joe Gormley's absence sick appears to show how indispensable he is. I wonder if that was his plan," said Howard.

"The conference did pass unanimously a motion supporting Polish miners but that won't get many points."

"Whatever was Gormley's plan, we've ended up with more or less the timetable you set out last week, Ed," said Bill Armitage. "And your back-of-an-envelope predictions of what the current weather would do to coal deliveries have been spot on so far."

"I've updated them on these sheets. Taking account of the latest news about the railways, I assume a work to rule from early in January and frequent short strikes. A miners' strike from the 25th of January would lead to serious problems for electricity supply by mid-March; earlier, if the weather stays cold."

"John, do we have any information about what miners themselves think, not just the delegates at the delegate conference?" asked Howard.

"These Coal Board regional press summaries suggest that over 80% of miners in Yorkshire, Scotland and South Wales would vote for a strike, and nearly half of Nottinghamshire miners, too. But that's not all of the NUM. Ed, you were looking at how miners vote in different parts of the country."

Ed handed round what he and I had been talking about.

"This shows the local results of the last six ballots. The votes in individual parts of the NUM usually move quite closely in line with the national figure. Yorkshire Area is more militant and Nottinghamshire Area less militant but the percentage differences in militancy stay fairly constant. Sometimes there's a local issue that shifts the vote. That happened in South Wales last year, look. But if you strip those out, you have a fairly good idea of the way opinion is going nationally if you know what's happening in three or four parts of the union."

"I see what you mean," said Howard. "So, what's the conclusion from John's reports?"

"A ballot now would give a national strike vote of about 65%, well above the 55% that's needed to authorise a strike."

"What Christmas cheer. We have to tell Ministers that they're toast, and all because of the cold weather. You've been quiet, Pete. Have you any ideas?"

"Only that we should emphasise that the ballot isn't now. It's in four weeks' time, which is four long times in politics, according to Harold Wilson. Before then, something might turn up. We need to know more about opinion across the union. Apart from the NUM Areas which represent miners in particular parts of the country, there are several small groups whose names don't link them to particular localities – for example, the Power Group. Who are they, Ed?"

"They represent maintenance staff at collieries in the Midlands. In Jersey, I met their Secretary, Ray Ottey, and his wife. They were having a whale of a time. Ottey is one of the leading moderates on the Executive."

"With other small groups they add up to quite a few votes. Ed's table shows how we can predict the national result if we have information about their intentions. I wouldn't be surprised if their leaders have quite regular contact with the Board."

"We need regular reports from the Board, covering all Areas and groups," said Howard. "That way, we can at least say that we're monitoring the position. There's clearly nothing for Ministers to consider until the end of the first week in January. Until then, they should keep quiet, relax and enjoy the Festive Season as much as the weather allows. Ed, give me a short draft by 5.30."

My line at the meeting had reflected Liz's views. Resting whilst poorly had given her plenty of time to think and she had made one or two calls to the private number she knew. Consequently, the handling of today's conference was not a surprise to me. Joe Gormley's indisposition appeared to have provided Mick McGahey with a good length of strong rope.

Something might turn up, just as earlier in the year, when all seemed black for Creators Technology, something had turned up.

However, as I travelled east, first alone and then with Jenny, the newspaper headline I saw many times was clear:

MINERS TO TAKE ON MAGGIE
NUM strike vote: Scargill challenges government

The idea of the Pankhurst Centre's Christmas party was that the women who were staying at the time would organise a buffet for donors to and friends of the Centre. Morag and Sheila knew what dishes went well and could be made easily. Over the years, the party had got bigger. The place was heaving when Jenny and I arrived.

"When did you last go to a bottle party?" I asked.

"This time last year. As we've had lunch, let's have at least one glass of what we've brought ourselves, and circulate for now. What have you got?"

"Bulgarian Cabernet Sauvignon from an outfit called Majestic that's just opened up in Croydon. It's not bad; try it."

"Mmm, it needs a nibble. This Sancerre has been in the fridge in the office. I'll put it at the back, for the fish platter later. Hey, there's Brian, gosh, and his father!"

We moved through the crowd around them and Brian re-introduced us.

"Dad, you'll remember Jenny from our wedding, and Pete you met in February."

"So, what are you two doing, skulking off here withart t'other halves?"

We explained, doubtless putting Brian in mind of the difference from the party of twelve months before, at which two couples had tried to avoid each other.

"We're just as bad, Dad," he observed.

"Doris came down for t'shopping. Now, she's having a nice talk with Susie and t'kids over a coop of tea or two. Who's to win t'race, Susie or Liz?"

"Liz is due early in April," I replied.

"Oh yes, I should know that."

"Behave yourself, Dad. Susie's a head in front, then. She's one up, too."

"You and Susie are gluttons for punishment, Brian!" said Jenny, firmly.

I could see that the crowd around Alan Smitham was annoyed by this frivolous distraction from the serious political discussion they were trying to have with a real live miners' delegate. One of them got back in.

"You must be very proud to have been at the conference today."

"Yes and no."

"What do you mean, yes and no? Surely this is the first step towards securing a new government, in place of the Thatcher gang."

"No, it ain't. It's a step towards getting a good deal for t'members."

"But you can't get a good deal from the Tories," objected another.

"Can't we? We dain't do badly in Febry."

"All eyes are on you now. We've been waiting for this moment for a long time," said a third.

"Yer'll be waiting a lot longer if owt more happens like happened today. I've already had words with those who let all sorts into a private meeting. I saw with my own eyes two members of t'National Executive threatened – *threatened* – by these idiots. What message will they give to their members? What will members think when they read 'boot this in t'papers and watch it on TV? Don't forget, t'members will decide. Not t'national officers, not t'National Executive, not delegates – t'members."

"But aren't the miners proud to lead decisive action?"

"Miners are proud to be miners, proud to work with thar friends in a dirty and dangerous job. They expect good pay and they expect respect. They don't like layabouts. Remember t'riots in soommer?"

"Lord Scarman's report shows they happened because of unthinking police brutality towards black people."

"His report was 'boot the Brixton riots in April. Early in July, there were copycat riots all over the country, including in parts where there ain't many black people."

"Yes, deprivation and unemployment caused by the Tories led to them."

"Whate'er the causes, they 'appened. Soom 'appened during Annual Conference. As there are ladies present, I won't repeat what most thar thought of the rioters and what should be done with them."

"There aren't many black miners, are there?"

"We're all black enoof when we come out t'pit."

Jenny came to the rescue before this got worse. "I was glad to hear that your conference pledged its support to Polish miners."

"Mick made sure that was unanimous. How he stays in t'Party I don't know, boot he stayed through Hungary in '56, through Czechoslovakia in '68 and now he's staying through this."

"Perhaps he realises that it's all a question of priorities. To achieve long-term good, you need to accept some things that are disagreeable on the way there."

I couldn't resist the temptation to lob one in. "Who are you paraphrasing – Margaret Thatcher or Joseph Stalin?"

"Er, neither, but you have to realise that Jaruzelski is in a very difficult position. The CIA has been stirring things up and the influence of the Catholic Church is everywhere in Poland."

"I agree he's in a very difficult position. He probably had to do what he did or else the Russians would have moved in. Like all patriotic Poles, above all else he wants to stop that from happening. And like all patriotic Poles, he's hugely proud of the remarkable accident of John Paul II."

"That's not an accident. It's a CIA plot. They had John Paul I murdered[78] to get their man in."

---

[78] Following deadlock between 'conservative' and 'liberal' forces in the first papal election of 1978, a compromise candidate emerged: Albino Luciani, Patriach of Venice, who took the name John Paul I after his two predecessors. He died suddenly after thirty-three days in office. The same deadlock was then resolved by the election of Karel Wojtyła, Archbishop of Cracow, to be John Paul II, thus creating in strongly Catholic Poland an untouchable symbol of peaceful resistance to Soviet domination. All sorts of conspiracy theories have been ranged regarding John Paul I's death (for example, in the film *Godfather III*).

"Oh, the story I've heard is that he was murdered by the KGB. If so, that's one of the great 'own goals' of history."

Alan and Brian sneaked off whilst Jenny further distracted the crowd. "At lunchtime, Pete and I were talking to a business colleague from Spain. He's a rather unreconstructed Francoist, and a Catholic of course. He was saying that in Jaruzelski's position, Franco would have done just the same."

That set off a few minutes of mayhem until Sheila rescued us. She looked rather worried. There was no sign of Morag to share the hosting. Was she unwell, too?

"Jenny, Pete, sorry not to have spoken to you earlier. Let me take you over to meet someone from the London Docklands Development Corporation."

We inched our way across the room. "Who are those people we've just been talking to?" I asked.

"They're from the Borough council's Social Work Department."

I knew why Sheila wanted us to be in contact with the LDDC. An industrial estate in Crawley had been a good location for putting together computer kits. It continued to have the advantages of being unobtrusive and of providing the opportunity to take additional space as we needed it. However, by the time Creators Technology began marketing, either we needed a separate office in or near the City, or we needed to transfer our whole business there. Docklands might offer a way of doing so at reasonable cost.

Sheila introduced us, and hurried on. The man told us a lot about the exciting future prospects. As I said, they could hardly but be an improvement on the situation at the time. I recalled a high point of a visit to London with my parents in the late 1950s. On a boat trip from Westminster Pier to Greenwich, we had passed a hive of activity on both sides of the river. Cranes were loading and unloading ships and there were continual arrivals and departures. On a visit to London in the summer of 1975,

I had a fine afternoon free, and repeated the trip. It had been one of the most depressing experiences of my life, a passage through silent desolation that had seemed like the aftermath of a war – as in fact it was, of an economic war which London had lost to ports on the Continent such as Rotterdam, Antwerp and Hamburg.

It was good to hear that there was a plan to begin reconstruction. However, it would be some time before transport links would allow either staff or visitors to reach easily any offices located in Docklands.[79] So it wasn't for Creators Technology just yet. Eventually, we gave our thanks and moved on.

"We'd better find some food, Jenny. But first, there's somewhere I must go."

I went in search, and opened what seemed a likely door. It wasn't the right door. It led into the administrative office. Amidst desks and filing cabinets, Carol and Morag were seated on a sofa, each with a glass and a two-thirds empty bottle beside them. Morag was delivering a very long kiss and had a hand inside Carol's blouse. Carol looked pleased to see me; Morag less so.

After a pause, I spoke brightly. "Hello, you two. I didn't think you could make it, Carol."

"We're drowning our sorrows, Pete. People are being shitty to both of us. We can't take any more," said Morag.

"Can I help? I was just about to pick up some food. It looks very good – well done, Morag. I'll get some for you both, too, and another bottle."

I dashed out without waiting for a reply, and found the right door. Two minutes later I was back with provisions, having told Jenny that something was up.

Carol had evidently persuaded Morag to let me help. She moved, to let me sit between them. I put an arm around each and gave both a friendly kiss.

---

[79] The Docklands Light Railway began operations in 1987. The Jubilee Line extension opened in 1999.

"Now, you're very old and valued friends to whom I owe a great deal. I know what's up for you, Carol, so let's start with you, Morag."

"It's finally boiled over with Sheila. I suppose that was going to happen sometime. I went with her because she offered me a settled life and a worthwhile purpose. Also, I was left with the money to help Mother. After she passed away, I put her money into Creators Technology. I trust you, Pete. I know that eventually I'll have something for all the work I've done; but, meanwhile, I still have nothing."

"I was very pleased that you came in, Morag, and I was very pleased that Sheila agreed that you should attend some board meetings. Your contribution ten days ago was great."

"The Pankhurst Centre has changed - because it's so successful, of course. The paid staff can't ignore Sheila. This house is hers and she does a lot of fundraising. But they can ignore me, and they do. In the summer, I suggested that she should allow the Centre to take over the top floor and we could find somewhere else nearby to live. It's now possible for people like us to obtain a mortgage together. But there's not much 'we' about decisions here. It all festered on. Things came to a head about three hours ago. Someone dropped something in the kitchen and Sheila took it out on her. I kept quiet but, when we were alone, I said she shouldn't behave like that towards people who are here because they couldn't take it from their men anymore. We had quite a row. I said I couldn't stay here any longer and I couldn't be at the party. That shook her; but before she could say anything Carol arrived – early, not expected and upset. 'Just look after *her*, then' Sheila said, so that's what I'm doing."

"Yes, things have come to a head for me, too, Pete. You probably know what happened in the House ten days ago."

"Yes. I'm told that the *Hansard* doesn't give the whole story. The girlfriend of someone I know at the department was there. I don't think Shirley Williams helped you at all. She gave quite the wrong message."

"You're right, but I made a real mess at the end. I was so upset that I stopped thinking and then I made it worse for myself by not staying to vote. I just couldn't face going through the lobby with these people. So I was in trouble with our whip. Whips are all men. They don't like young women members. That's a cross-party view. So for most of Thursday, and Friday, I concentrated on my column."

"A good one it was, too."

"On Saturday, there was an evening do involving MPs from across West and South Yorkshire – an all-party event. Paul and I went up in the morning. He did some jobs round the house in his overcoat. I drove round, calling on people who had written to me at the House. People thought it was great I'd come to see them despite the snow and ice. I got back to Paul full of tea and feeling I'd done something useful and could manage without a constituency office. So I was looking forward to the evening. But the Labour people wouldn't speak to me, and nor were the Tories keen to chat, though they were all chumming away together. Fortunately, the weather meant people didn't stay long. We decided to drive straight back to London rather than stay in the cold house."

"So you missed the next lot of snow, though it must have been a cold drive."

"Paul's car can cope with that. This week I kept my head down but mugged up on the Social Security Bill that had its Committee Stage on the Floor last night. I thought I could get in usefully, and there wasn't much argument between SDP and Labour on it. Then I'm taken aside by the whip and told that it's been agreed that no-one from the SDP will speak. These things happen as part of deals to manage time, so I accepted it. But what happens? The debate finishes before eight o'clock. The man moving the adjournment debate said he wasn't expecting to come on so early. It seems that my own people think I'm a liability. Today was the last straw. I was to go up this evening, to take constituency surgeries tomorrow. I'd booked them all myself, in various halls and public libraries. The adverts say nothing about my party, just that I'll be there if you have problems. I'm rung up twice today, to say my venue isn't available. One excuse was the weather and the other that an unexpected staff absence means it won't be open. Maybe these are genuine but all these places are run by the local authority. They can make it impossible for me to do my job as a constituency MP, and then they can say I'm not doing it. Now my first surgery is at 12.30, so I decided to take the first train up and have some 'me' time here."

"And now I'm looking after Carol," said Morag, with a smile. "She's had a rough time with men, and her husband isn't caring enough. She needs female sympathy. We're going off to her flat. When he's back from his party, he can use the spare room."

"Paul gave you plenty of help last week, Carol," I said. "Look, I've a better idea. I can feel how tense you both are. Before you decide what to do, you ought to be less tense. I can help. Jane Sandford taught me lots about massage. Where's your table?"

"Mmm, *yes please*," said Carol, as a look I knew came into her eye.

"Do you mind if Morag watches, to see what I can do?"

"Mmm, *no*."

"Would you like to watch, Morag, before deciding whether it's for you?"

"Well, yes," she replied, rather uncertainly.

Five minutes later, Carol was laid on the table, face down and wearing just her glasses. She was beginning to look more cheerful. I took my shirt off, oiled my hands and slid them gently over her back and bottom, the way I knew she liked. Then I worked on her swimmer's thigh muscles and next down her legs before moving up her back.

"Why don't you call up the leader of your local Council? They must allow you proper facilities."

"They'll deny anything is wrong. Oooh that's nice; more there."

"You don't have to say that anything is wrong, just that the constituents expect your service and you expect to be able to provide it. And talk to your dad. What happens to Conservative MPs in Manchester?"

"Good ideas, Pete. Perhaps I shouldn't be so worried. I won't be standing there again. It's only forty minutes' drive from Mum and Dad's place. I could visit from there… We could sell the house… Mmmm… *Mmmmm*, that's really good. Lessons from Jane haven't lost you your old touch."

"Time to turn over."

I ran my hands gently across her chest until her nipples were really hard. Then I worked round her belly.

"You're like Liz, you get tense there… Ah, that's better. How's your work for the *Express*?"

"It's going well. They want something from me about once a month."

"I'm glad that they still want a variety of political views in their articles, though it's not the paper it was when Lord Beaverbrook ran it."

"Yes, that's where Michael Foot made his name… Oooh… *Ooooh*… Yes, just there. Pete, you remember!"

"I always remember things I enjoy doing. Now, this is new. Jane taught me, and had me practise on her until I got it right. Left hand outside, right fingers inside and squeeze a bit – good?"

"Just a little up… There… *Great*… Aah… *Aaah*… *Aaaaah*! Time to turn over again."

"I wonder why, bottom girl. Just say when."

I slipped a pillow under her, gave a few gentle smacks and moved her legs apart. There was a pleasant squelching as one, and then two, right fingers did their work inside her, whilst a well-oiled left finger moved up and down her back and further and further between her buttocks.

"Oooh, harder inside... Harder... Now... Aaah... Aaaaah... Aa – aaaaah... Aaa – aaaaaa – aaaaaaaaah!"

"Ow, you're not swimming now."

I said that as a flailing leg caught me and the table creaked as she thumped into it. Finally, there was calm as I returned to gently fondling Carol's magnificent bottom.

"Oh Pete, that was marvellous, the best for ages and ages."

I had been concentrating on the job in hand but had been pleasantly aware of rustlings behind me. I turned my head to see Morag stepping out of her pants. She smiled at me and bent to kiss Carol.

"Looks like you've got this right, Pete. Ow."

"That's for trying to seduce a straight woman. And so is that."

"*Ow.*"

"My turn to watch, Morag," said Carol, grinning and kissing back briefly.

Morag settled on the table face up. I washed my hands and re-oiled. Her left shoulder was quite bruised and I worked gently round it.

"You've been in the wars."

"It was at a basketball match two weeks ago. I fended off their lead shooter. She's six foot two."

"Wow, quite an Amazon."

"I had to fend her off in the showers afterwards, too. She gives that team something of a reputation. She could move to a better team but she stays because she can take any of them she fancies."

"Trying for you was a compliment, then, Morag. I'm not surprised."

"She was attracted because, like her, I have my works on view. Every few weeks Sheila and I shave each other and then it's great to lick away any soreness. It's an idea we had years back after hearing from Steph about her time with Beth."

"Steph was neatly trimmed but you've gone the whole hog. Isn't it a bit ticklish?" I used a finger, playfully.

"Ooh! Not yet! There's a place in my right shoulder that's always aching... Ah yes, there... Mmm, much better."

"You're such a helpful and sensible person, Morag. It's easy to take you for granted. I've done that myself."

"I've always liked working with you, Pete. That's great..."

"I'm told you like it here." My hands had moved to her cleavage and just below.

"Mmm, yes, super... *Oooh*... Do my legs now... Yes, there... You've given me more ideas for research, too. They're nothing to do with trading but eventually there can be a cross-reference to what you've done. I've a sabbatical semester coming up, with no lecturing from mid-February until the end of September. I hope to do enough to have a good chance of Derek Hadfield's readership at Essex. He retires in 1983. I know the people there quite well."

"I suppose you could commute to Colchester from Stratford but it would be much better to live nearer."

"That's right, Pete. I want to move my career on, if I can. Sheila isn't doing much research now. She's concentrating on building this place up."

"That's not surprising. She's created it."

"I need some space to think but I don't want to lose her. It's still so good a lot of the time. But it's 'you' time now, Pete. I've waited a long while for this."

She moved her legs apart and raised one.

"When's your next shave due? I can feel some hairs."

"When I get back from meeting friends in Glasgow for the New Year... Ooh... Ow, not so hard yet. I'm not used to this nowadays. Sheila likes using a vibrator... That's much better... Harder now... Up a bit inside; stay where you are outside… Mmm… Just right, Pete… Harder… *Harder*… Aye… Aye… Aaah… *Aaaah… Aaahhhhh… Aa – aaa – aaaaa – aaaaaahhhh!*"

"You look as if you're about to burst out of your trousers, Pete," said Carol, a few minutes later.

"That's a credit to you both. Perhaps I should pop under the shower for a moment."

Morag sat up and reached for my belt. "No, I'm going to do what I've always wanted to do with you, Pete – what I nearly offered to do that one time we went out."

"It *was* a first date."

"Yes, but there you were, the Senior Wrangler, unattached. I wondered whether to have a last try at going straight, but I didn't. Mmmm, you look really good, Pete. Carol, you fondle, I'll suck."

So it was my turn to lie on the table and yell with delight, to the accompaniment of satisfying yelps as my hands found where each of them was still sensitive. Afterwards, we squeezed together under the shower, sliding our bodies around each other like the three good friends we were.

"Liz has always liked being close in the shower. She'll really enjoy hearing about this. She's not so up for it herself right now, so you had quite a mouthful, Morag."

"Aye, it tasted good, to the last drop. For a man, you're *very* special to me, Pete."

"If you'd done that before, Morag, Pete wouldn't have rescued me from the police."

"And he wouldn't have fucked you, Carol."

"And I wouldn't have been a Member of Parliament. Oh well, I am."

"It goes much further than that," I said. "If Morag had become my girlfriend, Liz wouldn't have invited me to Archie Frampton's party, which is where I met Jenny. So Dick would never have met Jenny. I might still be at Cambridge. There could be no Creators and no Creators Technology."

"That's the stochastic world. One decision can change everything," said Morag.

I came out of the shower first, dried myself and began to dress.

"I've rather stood up Jenny, and must get back to her. Are you both ready to join the party? Alan Smitham is with Brian. He ought to know why you're here, Carol."

"I can tell him now. You've helped me to pull myself together, Pete. Morag, do come and stay in our spare room. You can stay there over Christmas, if you still want to be alone then. We'll be in Manchester."

They stepped out of the shower, a handsome but contrasting pair. Carol was now quite chubby but in the right places. Morag was tall with short cropped black hair and had freckles all over her hairless body. We had been together in body, and together in mind, as Steph had once suggested could be the motto of the Creators.

I left them for the party, which was still going strong, and helped myself to cheese and a stiff one. Jenny joined me, looking very cheerful indeed.

"You were a long time. You've missed all of my Sancerre."

"I've been sorting out Carol and Morag." Below the hubbub, I explained.

"Wow! I hope for your sake that Liz takes it in good part."

"She will. Along with you, those two are still her closest friends. She'll know that I've stopped them from rushing into something they might come to regret."

"I've a better idea for Morag. She can come and stay with us."

"That's quite something for you to offer, over Christmas."

"Not really. We've no-one else staying. Dick's parents will be with us for lunch. The bed is made up in the spare room. Dick and I haven't forgotten how helpful Morag was on the Day to Remember."

"Morag's huge quality is to be calm and sensible. Tonight, that snapped. I may have helped temporarily but more needs to be done to settle her."

"Yes, we don't want her going the way of Anna Karenina, sorting everyone else out but ending in a hopeless mess herself. The children will like having Auntie Morag around, and that will do her good. There they both are. One each, I think. Carol is heading for the Smithams. You join her."

I did so, without appearing too anxious. "Carol, we didn't think you were able to come," said Brian.

"This is always such a great party, and I'm going up early tomorrow, now." She repeated what she had told me about Holtcliffe, but this time calmly.

Brian looked at his father. "Dad, that's bad. It shouldn't happen again, should it?"

"No, it mustn't happen again. Yer needs to be able to do yer job, Carol." There was enough in Alan Smitham's tone to make clear that he would see to it.

We talked more about the NUM conference, this time uninterrupted by local social workers. "What do you think the mood is, then?" asked Carol.

"In Yorkshire, it's strong for a strike, hitting 80%. I couldn't say about others, 'cept for one. I know how t'Power Group will go, once Ray Ottey gets back to Stoke and talks about what happened to 'im today. They're small, though."

"It sounds like you're in for a tough time in your other job, Pete," said Brian.

"Ministers are being advised to keep quiet, relax and enjoy Christmas."

"That's sense. We'd better be going, Dad. Happy Christmas, Carol, and sorry we can't make your people's New Year party. We're at home, with Susie's parents coming down. Ah, there are Morag and Jenny. I must thank Morag and give my best to them both."

I told Carol of Jenny's offer. Her look of relief prompted me to ask a question. "Were you worried about what Paul might do with Morag in your absence?"

"Rather the opposite. He would have ignored her. He's all the time out at meetings or playing with his radio. As Jenny says, being an auntie is what Morag needs now. I'm looking forward to being an auntie with my sister's kids. It's a horrible thing to say, Pete, but you're a very lucky man and Liz is a very lucky woman. Anyone who knows the two of you can't believe for a moment the nasty story that's going around."

"We know that, Carol. Another drink, and some pud?"

While fetching those, I reflected that Carol had said the right thing to me, but I wondered whether she believed it. What I had just done could have been read as a reaction to what Liz had done. Indeed, back in February Liz had encouraged me to go with Carol if I needed relief.

I also wondered about what Alan had said. 'Hitting 80%' for a strike in Yorkshire sounded impressive but it wasn't the same as the 'over 80%' in the Coal Board's press summary. It was only a few percentage points above the Yorkshire vote in recent ballots. If that were the pattern elsewhere, the national vote would be around 60%, not so much over the 55% needed to sanction a strike. And it sounded as if the message from the NUM office in Stoke-on-Trent would not be wholly in accord with the national line. Other small groups could go with that, and they could add up. There was plenty to play for in the New Year. On Monday, I would speak to Ed.

By the time I was back from the buffet, Morag was speaking to Sheila. Jenny had joined Carol and was organising us nicely.

"Morag will circulate for a while and then pack a few things. I want to catch the 10.17 from Waterloo, and Morag will need to buy a ticket. If we all share a taxi, Carol can take it on to Kensington."

"I'll call a taxi for a quarter to ten. That should be plenty of time."

I did so, and thanked Sheila with the promise of a phone call the next day. I returned to find Jenny alone, relaxing on a settee with her shoes off.

"So, Pete, you've seen another of us Creator girls naked. Are there any left?"

"I've not seen Sheila or Susie but I've caught up with your tally from the hen party. I'm ahead if you count Ana in as an overseas associate Creator."

Jenny grinned. "No you're not, Pete. The summer before last at their house, she suggested a dip in the pool on our own in the early morning Spanish time; that's about nine o'clock. I said that one of my swimsuits was torn so I had only one usable. I didn't want to wear it and later put it on again, wet, but I didn't need to if we were on our own, did I? She looked surprised but went with it."

"Were you really down to one swimsuit?"

"Don't ask silly questions, Pete." She licked her lips.

"Mmm, yes. On a cold evening, it's nice to think of Ana."

"She was lithe and went through the water like a little mermaid. That was only three months after Fernando was born. We did it again a couple of times."

"And you got a nice kick out of how she was looking at you." I licked my lips.

"Mmm, yes." Jenny licked her lips again.

"And any more?"

"Just a little gentle touching. Neither of us needed more to be *very* happy."

"So, for you, Ana is Amanda the Second. She admires you for what you did for her and she admires your body, too. Back in February, that was very clear. You were both very quiet about it when you were on your own, though outside we were all jolly and certainly not listening."

Jenny leaned back, her face a picture of contentment as she remembered. She wasn't minding my rather obviously leading her on.

"She needed my help to get out of her gown. It was just so clear what she wanted then. I'd travelled up in an outfit which wasn't meant to compete and so didn't take a moment to slip off.

I let her unclip my bra. How she looked at me as she did that – pure yearning. I could feel that in her hands, too. There was a tall mirror to face as I worked over her. After five minutes I just had to touch her slit and she came very nicely but quietly – we were mouth to mouth."

"I noticed that when you finally responded to Carol's call your dress was on slightly differently from before. You spot these things if you've helped in a drapery store. I don't think anyone else noticed."

"Oh, dear." Jenny giggled, with at least feigned embarrassment.

"Judging by Carlos's mood today, he knows nothing of any of this."

"He certainly knew nothing after our time over there. If Ana told him after February, it would strengthen her hold on him. He would face total ridicule if it came out."

"It certainly helped to get the money for Creators Technology, and left you very ready for Dick."

"Yes, it was another time when my little bit of bi helped with him. And Ana helped sort me out, with you and with Amanda."

"With Amanda?"

"I'd better tell you now, Pete. As you said earlier today, two years ago I found working with you something of an emotional strain. Then you said you would be living down here and doing more for Creators Technology. We were bound to see more of each other. To pull me away from you, I needed more than Dick. Amanda and I hadn't done anything since Louisa was on the way but, when I gave her something of a come-on, she came on.

"I remember you telling me about going to a sauna again with her."

"Yes, off we went. Soon afterwards I invited her to the spa at the hotel I use when I'm in Yorkshire on business and then we went to my room. I fingered her up, and this time I let her do the same to me. We ended the evening both very happy. A month later we did the same, slept together, and in the morning were ready to do what we had seen Morag and Angela, and then Liz and Carol, do at my hen party. So we were going on, and without John there. But we both said we were having friendly fun, not a relationship, and we were very happy with our husbands."

"You were pretty cheerful when I met you around then."

"That was before it went wrong. When I was there again in March, she came along with a dildo. She wanted us to use it on each other. I wasn't ready for that then, and said so. She said I always wanted things my way but this time it was going to be her way. For a moment she tried to hold me down and force it in, and she's strong. Eventually we calmed down but we were left in rather a state."

I put my arm round Jenny, who now looked in rather a state herself, as bare emotionally as when, many years before, we had seen each other naked for the first time and she had told of the scarifying end of her first relationship.

"In February you said that you'd had a bad time but that it was fine again."

"I realised that I had been rather selfish with Amanda, perhaps as Sheila has been with Morag. I still felt pretty down when we went over to Spain in the summer. Two years before, Ana had given me one or two looks but there had been no chance to do anything. When she suggested that morning dip, I made a try. That made me realise that I can live with my feelings for her and could also live with my feelings for Amanda. By September last year, Amanda and I were back to where we should be. Since then, we've gone on together. It's two way now, and caring."

"I'm very glad to hear that."

"The bad time with Amanda was a few days before Liz told me about you both. I was so mixed up that I didn't know how I felt about you anymore. That went on until January, when Ana called to say she was looking forward to seeing you and me again, and we got talking about you. That didn't sort me out but it set me thinking. In February, you and I worked together to help Ana, and I saw how she felt about you, as well as about me. I was dressing quickly, with Carol calling outside, when she said that I'd made her happy just as you did when you were in Spain. You and I were her best friends in England. That finally brought me back to my senses."

"I thought I understood you, Jenny, but I didn't."

"That's because I didn't understand myself fully. I hadn't worked out how to live with my little bit of bi."

"Judging by those I know, many successful women have a little bit of bi. They need it to succeed in a man's world. They need a private corner to express it. Thank you so much for showing me your private corner. I won't be telling anyone else about it, not even Liz. We're right back to where we should be, very close and special friends, like brother and sister. I think I understand you now, Jenny."

"Thank you, Pete."

"I've one piece of brotherly advice. I don't know Amanda well but I know Ana very well. Whatever form your relationship with her takes, it must be two way."

"Mmm, yes, and it will, when it happens again. We'll be visiting her next summer."

For a minute or so a passer-by might well have gained a false impression of us. But our kiss though long was the knowing kiss of two who knew they were as smart, and as bad, as each other. Then Jenny continued, brightly.

"So after all these years of Morag talking about you being the only man she might go with, she actually went with you. Tell me *exactly* what she did."

"First, she licked the tip very gently," I began. Soon, Jenny was even brighter.

"Do you mind if I tell Dick all about it when I get home, perhaps as I try it out? That's if he's not too tired. He's over what he had ten days ago but it did rather hit him."

"Of course you can. Won't there be a hint of a reminder of, er, his past?"

"That's part of the fun. We joke about his past, even about Harry Tamfield, and certainly about the little fling he had in San Francisco. It's like talking about my hen party or about Amanda or Ana. It helps us to get going. He knows I'm right for him and certainly he's right for me. That late night in February really helped. Once we'd finished, I told him why I'd been so turned on. He thought it was great."

"I'm surprised he didn't put you across his knee and give you a good spanking."

"He's a gentleman, Pete. It sounds like you're speaking from experience."

"Not recent experience, but it happened with Steph and before that with Carol. It got us going for Carol's way. A red bottom is a big turn on."

"That night it wasn't needed, nor since. When we were in Sheffield last September, one afternoon Dick took the children out, leaving Amanda, John and I together. Later on with Dick was one of the best."

"Might Dick find someone for another little fling?"

"He hasn't found anyone yet, though once or twice he's said that some bloke he's met gave him a kick. If he does find someone, we can handle it. We understand ourselves, and each other, better. We both know we've got a little bit of bi but just a little bit. We both know the other matters more, and the children, too."

"There are Carol and Morag. It's twenty to ten; shoes on time." I reinforced any false impression by tickling a foot.

"Oooh. Pete, thanks so much for persuading me to come along with you. We've followed your advice up the line – relax and enjoy Christmas. I hope that in the New Year we don't have as much to worry about as the government looks like having."

14. THURSDAY, 7TH JANUARY, 1982

"Have you heard the latest weather forecast, Howard?" asked John Willis.

We were waiting to meet Nigel Lawson. Outside, it was grey and raw, but dry. Around London, there had since Christmas been a slight thaw, resulting in some flooding.

"No," answered Howard Larkin.

"There's the granddaddy of blizzards forming up in the Atlantic. It will hit the west this evening and come right across the country overnight."

"Just what we need," said Julian Street. "So what do we tell him? That we haven't a hope in hell or that something might turn up? After what happened last February, we need to be honest."

Before anyone could say anything more to that, we were ushered in. Lawson began in his usual upbeat manner.

"There are two questions I need to have answered before I meet the Prime Minister and the Chancellor later today. First, what's the best assessment we have of the way the miners will vote in a week's time? Secondly, on Monday I'm due to give a speech at the Coal Industry Society lunch. What, if anything, should I say about the vote?"

We began with the first. All sorts of snippets of information and anecdotes were to hand, including some I had gathered up for a note dictated to Jean over the phone the day before. After ten minutes or so, Lawson moved to a conclusion.

"So, let's go round the table. What's each of your best guesses for the strike vote? Julian?"

"It could be over 70%, I'm afraid. Miners have a great deal of team spirit. It they think they can beat the government, they'll have a try."

"John?" asked Lawson, sounding a little surprised.

"I put it lower, though still over 60%. The local press reports show that people in some of the moderate areas were incensed by what happened at the conference last month. For example, the Power Group's Executive has made a unanimous recommendation to its members to vote no. But these small areas won't swing the result."

"I agree. 60% plus," said Howard. Bill Armitage went for 65%.

"What about you, Ed?" asked Lawson.

"Based on what I've heard of the mood around the country, I would put it slightly below 60%. But we've not heard much about some NUM Areas, including Nottinghamshire, North Derbyshire and Durham."

"Pete?" I made myself concentrate.

"If I were asked for a spot number, I would say 60%, but there's a big range of uncertainty in interpreting what we're told. For example, the expected Yorkshire vote is said to be holding steady at 80% or just below. What does 'Yorkshire' mean, though? If it's just the NUM's Yorkshire Area, then the vote is consistent with a national vote not much above 55%. If 'Yorkshire' also covers other union members based there who tend to be more moderate, then the vote is consistent with a national vote around 60%. I suspect the answer is somewhere in between."

"So, you're all telling me that present predictions are uncertain, but the NUM is very likely to get its strike authority, though not by such a large majority as was expected before Christmas. For it not to, something has to change quite a lot of minds. What could? The weather? Next week's railway strike? I can't see those doing anything but hardening the vote. So, unless something happens, we're up against it."

No-one disagreed with that. Julian turned to me. "Pete, have you any more information about what Gormley thinks of the position? He was supposed to be a calming influence."

After a moment I felt myself speak, rather than hearing myself speak.

"He's been keeping out of it. He's retiring in less than three months. If this were to go right for the NUM, it would be his last triumph. Otherwise, he'll say it's a good first lesson for his successor."

"So we need otherwise to happen," said Lawson, with the hint of a chuckle. "Now, my speech for Monday."

"There's plenty you can say about what we've spent on coal, and are continuing to spend," said Howard.

"We've said all that before. What will other people be saying on Monday?"

"Ezra, who's speaking before you, will be repeating that if NUM members vote for a strike, there will be a strike. There won't be a further offer to avert it. There'll be no painless gain for the miners."

"It's vital that they hammer away at that over the weekend," said John. "I'm in touch with the Board's chief of press."

"Scargill is trying to counter that line," said Ed. "The *Yorkshire Miner*, which goes to all Yorkshire Area members, is suggesting that a strike mandate will result in more money being offered, without a strike being needed."

"Make sure that the Board deals with that at pit level," said Lawson. "They must call his bluff, very firmly."

"I'm afraid the *Mirror* will run a story that you'll prefer to fight the winter than fight the miners," said John. "Their industrial correspondent says he knows you. Do you want to call him yourself?"

"No. Is there a date?"

"Early next week."

"Stall them. Suggest that they wait for what Ezra and I say on Monday."

Ed came in again. "Why don't you say that we're offering the miners a chance to work in a modern, forward-looking industry? Their vote is about whether they want to work in that kind of industry or whether they want to be trapped in the past."

There was silence for a few seconds and then John responded. "I like that. It gives just a hint that a strike would lead to reduced investment. You would have no comment, of course."

"We'll need a very careful line on that," said Howard.

"It sounds good to me," said Lawson. "Let me have a draft speech and follow-up questions and answers, for the weekend. As from Monday, we could use it across government. Meanwhile, we go on making no comment. I know that Bernard has stressed that round the interdepartmental net but make sure that all your contacts know it. Fortunately, Parliament isn't back until the week after next. Finally, is there anything new on stocks?" [80]

"No," said Bill. "Rail disruption was already factored into our calculations. We're in trouble from early March if this weather keeps up, a week or two later if it improves.

Julian had another meeting but the rest of us went back to Howard's office and settled down in a rather resigned manner.

"Lawson the journalist is to the fore, eh, John?" Howard observed.

"Yes. He knows that if we lose the public and the media, we've lost outright, however large coal stocks might be. We must get the message right. He's certainly not lost hope. Oddly enough, I think Julian giving his ridiculously high guess of over 70% rather heartened him. It shows there's a wide range of uncertainty."

"It shows that Julian hasn't understood Ed's paper on regional variations in voting," said Bill. "Over 70% nationally

---

[80] One request not made was for a note to send round other departments. Those perusing the Margaret Thatcher Archives will find very little ministerial correspondence covering this period, in contrast to the previous February.

would imply over 90% in the militant areas. It's happened only once, in 1974, when the yes vote was a no-brainer."

"John, why don't I start by drafting the press notice for Monday, basing it on what I said just now?" said Ed. "I'll talk to your people and put something round tonight. If we all agree what the notice should say then the speech will be easy."

"That's a good idea, Ed," said Howard. "John, it will be your job to make sure the Board's notice fits in with it."

It was getting dark outside as we dispersed. I went to Ed's office so that he could try out on me a couple of ideas for the notice. I knew he couldn't keep me for long. I certainly didn't want to stay for long. In fact, I hadn't wanted to come in at all but Liz had insisted. She said she wouldn't be alone. She had Jenny for company. I kept on trying to take my mind off her.

"You're certainly on top of the job, and appreciated," I said, a few minutes later.

"I'm enjoying it. It's obviously important. Right now, there's a lot of waiting around for things to happen. I've been using it to corral the lawyers into finalising the rules about social grant payments, including the changes consequent on last March's improvements in the redundancy terms."

"Good. Is the Board being more co-operative about that?"

"Yes, thanks to a push from Howard, though still with bad grace. Yesterday, I had this from their head of finance."

He showed me a letter which began:

'Dear Ed,
I was extremely surprised to receive your letter asking for a repayment of sums legitimately claimed in grant and certified as such by the Board's Auditors...'

"That's encouraging for you, in two ways," I commented. "He wrote back to you, rather than taking it up with Bill or Howard.

Unlike in the past, he realised there would be no change from either of them. Also, he wrote 'Dear Ed' not 'Dear Plunkett'. They're no longer treating you as if they were in a Billy Bunter book. You're carrying more weight. I'm sure that will be noticed."

"I guess so. The Treasury people have noticed. They know we're taking a grip on the financial details. Later this year or early next, that will help. The better redundancy terms have already allowed half of the infamous twenty-three pit list to be closed by local agreement, with little fuss. When we're ready to propose further improvements, they'll play along."

"The DTI won't see so many problems now the big wave of steel reorganisation has come to an end."

"That's right. It depends on what happens next week."

"Everything depends on that."

On that note, I extricated myself, settled with Jean when I might be in during the next week, packed my bag with papers about North Sea privatisation and set off for Victoria. The rail drivers were working to rule though not, as yet, refusing to drive trains without speedometers. That additional twist was still in reserve. Eventually, I was able to cram onto a train that the rules apparently allowed the driver to drive.

My involvement in coal was coming to a natural end. Whatever happened during the next week, there would be little more I could do to help. The regular civil service team was transformed from a year before. That was fortunate, since for me the old saying that problems come in threes had certainly turned out to be true.

When we returned from the hospital that morning, there had been an airmail letter on the doormat. At least I had found some distraction in reading it on the nearly empty train into Victoria that I caught after twenty-five minutes on the cold platform. Once there was room to pull it out again, I did so. It began in a way that was irritating, particularly from a German, but then it came to the point.

Dear Peter,

I trust that the New Year finds you well, though I see that your unions continue to create problems. I hope for all your sakes that Frau Thatcher can resolve these and provide some improvement for your country.

A colleague in the United States has sent me this preprint. It appears to contain work very similar to what you have done, except that the author has not made the final step to the conclusion you have reached. As I am sure you will agree, that is puzzling, since once the earlier work is done and fully understood, the final step is relatively simple to make. Perhaps the author is trying to make two published papers out of one, as so many do. If so, he is taking a risk. A good referee might cause delay by commenting that the paper is incomplete and could be improved. He could even (quite improperly) prepare his own completion.

Perhaps the author aims to claim the ground without immediately giving away the conclusion which you have recognised as being of such potential commercial value. In that respect, it is interesting that the preprint appears to have had rather limited circulation. I have not received a copy directly. It is also interesting that the author acknowledges funding from the Richard Horstmann Foundation. There is, I believe, an American bank by the name of Parker Horstmann.

My compliments,
Siegmund Kraftlein

On the way up, I had read enough of the paper sent with the letter to agree with Kraftlein's conclusions. I had had Jean make three copies, to her cheerful comment: 'Wow, Pete, you do read some funny stuff'. I had brought stamped envelopes with me so that I could post the copies to Paul, and separately to Morag and Sheila, though I knew that they were together again in Stratford. I hoped that they would receive them before the weekend, despite the weather. Then we could try to work out what to do, if I could think straight.

Now, I noticed a footnote on the first page of the paper. 'Submitted to *Statistica*, 4th December 1981.' The name of the journal rang a bell from the past. It was something to do with Kraftlein… Yes, got it.

When I arrived home, Liz was eventually able to gasp out a greeting amidst a barrage of coughs.

"Oh good Jenny, here's Daddy now. There's a *Mr. Men* programme for you to watch on the TV while I pack your things and talk to Daddy."

"Hello Daddy. Auntie Brenda asked Mummy if I can stay the night. I like her and Uncle Alan and Stephanie."

"Oooh, what a lovely surprise. You didn't see them over Christmas but, now, twice the same day. You've been having such fun playing with their present."

"Stephanie likes yours, too," said Liz.

I took Jenny into the lounge and settled her in front of the TV. There was a minute or so before the programme began.

"Auntie Brenda says she's going to have another baby soon, like Mummy."

I could hardly reply. Eventually, I managed to say something.

"Yes, but not so soon as Mummy."

"How do mummies have babies?"

"I'll tell you another time. Here's your programme."

Liz was sitting in the kitchen, coughing and crying. I put my arm round her and for a minute or two we said nothing. Then she spoke.

"What are the prospects for the vote next week, Pete?"

"They're pretty grim."

"I thought so. I've been telephoning, starting with *him*. He's dreadfully put out. He's desperate to see me."

"He could have stuck up for you against the others at the NUM offices."

"He knew it was best I left there after the story started going round. This doesn't change that. He was looking forward to seeing the baby. He really thinks it's his. He wants me to go round to his home this evening, just to talk. His wife is away."

"That's a lot to ask."

"Pete, *think* a moment. What have we been told? An immediate operation gives some chance. Of course, the baby would be lost. Or we can wait for the baby to be born normally. There would be a good chance for the baby but no chance for me. I know how he feels. He would do *anything* for that to happen. And, if anything could make a difference, *so would I!*"

After another minute or two she explained her plan, quite calmly, with pauses for coughing. Then it was time for me to take Jenny over to the Murtons' house.

While Brenda settled Jenny down, Alan Murton took me aside. He was typically diffident.

"Brenda told me, Pete. What awful news."

"Yes, it's difficult to take in."

"She's asked me to say that we'll do whatever we can to help. It's because of you that we're so happy now, and the way Liz has borne what she faced before, let alone now, has been an example to us all."

"That's good to know, Alan, thanks. I'm sure that, when they're back, Roberta and Frank will be doing lots, too."

Alan took the opportunity I had provided to change the subject. "Yes, they made a good move, didn't they, by going off to Jamaica on Tuesday? Apparently everything is priced in dollars there. That makes it cheap, right now."

"Yes. Also, at this time of year it's not too hot and there are no hurricanes."

"Have you heard the latest forecast for tonight? There'll be heavy snow from about eleven o'clock. I hope you're back by then."

"We should be."

"We're so glad you've both had this surprise invitation and that Liz is still ready to go. She's got so much spirit and guts."

"Yes, she has. One just has to carry on, as much as possible."

By the time I was home, Liz had something from the freezer ready to eat. We had just finished when the phone rang in the hall.

"I'll go. It may be Carol," said Liz.

It wasn't Carol. A minute later, I was on the line.

"I will try not to detain you for too long, Pete. Liz said you were about to go out but this is very urgent."

"We understand, Ana. Happy New Year."

"I am quite alone. Carlos is away and it is the evening the servants are now allowed off. I need your advice as to whom to contact in your government."

Her explanation took a few minutes. Eventually, I got in.

"That's astonishing, or perhaps not from their point of view."

"A minister attended my reception in February. Could he help?"

"I doubt it. Our country should be very grateful for this warning, but governments do not believe warnings. No-one in government believed our story about the Egyptians and Professor Kraftlein."

"The Spanish Government did."

"Later this evening or tomorrow, I could speak to Carol Milverton. She is not of the government party but not now of the Labour Opposition, either."

"Can you trust her, Pete?"

"Yes. I have known her for many years."

"She must not tell her husband. He knows Carlos."

"No, she will not tell her husband."

"Thank you, Pete. I will telephone you tomorrow at about nineteen hours your time. I hope that your evening out is enjoyable. Please pass my salutations to Liz. She did not sound well. I hope that she has not a chill."

"No, she hasn't a chill. I will tell you more tomorrow."

The raw wind was strengthening as I got Liz into the car and we set off. In the past, she would have been asking what Ana had wanted that was so urgent. She wasn't doing that now. She was thinking about what lay ahead. She wanted to save her voice and not provoke her chest. The days of 'Lively Liz' were over for good.

Thanks to Ana, we had set off later than Liz had hoped, but the suburban roads were quiet, doubtless because people had heard what was coming. We were on time for a 9.15 pickup of Carol outside Wimbledon Station. Even then, there were few greetings. Clearly, they had unburdened themselves on the telephone.

It might or might not have been a surprise to Carol to hear that there was some truth in the stories we had so emphatically denied. She was here as a journalist, but Liz's plan would not give her any public opportunity. She would be joining in out of friendship rather than political inclination. Whilst she had no reason to be friendly to the NUM militants, others in the union like Alan Smitham had helped her out. Certainly she had no reason to help rescue the Thatcher Government. She might not be displeased if Liz's plan failed.

They were sitting at the back, and now I could hear them talking quietly, through barrages of coughing. I concentrated on finding my way through Kingston and on, with several stops to consult a map.

"That's the place. Go just past and stop," said Liz, eventually.

She climbed out and I helped her on her way to a large bungalow. She rang the bell and, as I returned to the car, the front door opened to let her in. I got in beside Carol. She gave me more of a hug than she had given Liz.

"Oh, Pete, what can I say?"

"Not much, I guess, Carol."

"It all seems to happen to you."

"No, it all happens to people I know."

"How will you cope?"

"I'll find a way. Let's talk about other things. That's really easier for me, and probably for you, too. Also, there's something else up. Ana rang me. You know that since last February's business she has Carlos very much under her thumb."

"Yes. The morning after, before she gave that marvellous speech, she was *very* clear what she was going to do when she got back to Spain. I've never met him. From what Paul has told me about him, he sounds like a rather weak man."

"He's in his job only because of his family. One of his concerns at the Banco Navarrese is its interests in Argentina. He knows the country. He was out there for a year or so before they were married, which was why I could spend so much time with Ana."

"That was before the military junta took over in Argentina. It's a pretty nasty place now. People the junta don't like just disappear.[81] They keep making threatening noises about their claim to the Falkland Islands. David Owen thinks the Foreign Office and MoD are being sleepy about those. He says that the withdrawal of the patrol vessel *Endurance* from the area will be further encouragement to them."

"There's no need for further encouragement. Carlos went out there in the autumn. No doubt he was pleased to be off the leash. He had good times with some of the people running the place. He *can* sell himself. He gave them the impression that the old families still had some influence in the New Spain, and that in return for favours he and Ana could help promote Argentine

---

81 Some details of this had emerged then; more emerged later. A favoured method of 'disappearing' people was to throw them out of an aircraft, well out to sea.

interests. It could still be like the old days, when Franco relied on food imports from Argentina. Carlos told Ana all this when he got back and she, I suppose, took note. The first thing it led to was an invitation to a pre-Christmas reception at the Argentine Embassy in Madrid."

"I'm sure they're invited to plenty of bashes like that."

"Yes. They do have a house in Madrid, and staff to look after their children when they're away from Pamplona."

"The New Spain isn't completely new, then."

"You could say that. At the reception, there was mutual commiseration about British occupation of the Falkland Islands and of Gibraltar, in which Carlos played along and Ana kept quiet. That's pretty standard stuff out there, of course. Then, someone asked Carlos whether he might be in Madrid on the evening of 5th January. There was to be a private dinner with a few Spanish friends of Argentina, to discuss some plans for 1982. Ana gave a little nod and Carlos agreed. So on Tuesday they arrived, to some embarrassment. All the other guests were men. Though nothing was said at the reception, they had been expecting Carlos to be on his own. Ana had guessed that. Before Carlos could say anything, she said she knew why they were there. She agreed with their objectives. She was a friend with the right contacts, at the top."

"What happened then?"

"Then, or at least later in the meal, the discussion got going. The Argentine junta is in big trouble. They need a distraction and they see us off our guard. They're planning to occupy the Falklands during their autumn, our spring, which would make it difficult for us to do anything about it during the winter months following. That would be hugely popular with their people. Ana sounded sympathetic. She made some quite genuine suggestions for influential contacts and offered to make introductions. By the end of the meal, she was part of their group."

"And…"

"And she wants to know the best way of keeping our government informed and warned. She doesn't see supporting Argentina as the way ahead for Spain. She's very grateful for the help we've given her – last February, and before."

"Won't they find her out?"

"There's no reason why they should. On the face of it, she has little connection with the UK. She never came here before February, and what happened then was hushed up pretty effectively. Some of us have visited her over the years but they have a stream of guests at their castle. The only man who may guess is Carlos, who'll do exactly as she says. No, the problem is getting people here to believe her, which is where you, and perhaps David Owen, come in. You can ask questions in the House. You can put things in your column. If that generates any suspicion in Spain, they'll think you're getting information via Carlos and Paul. That won't be true, so it can easily be denied."

"Yes, it won't be true. Paul won't know anything about this. Pete, you've given me some work for the rest of the recess, starting with learning all I can about the Falklands."

"Here's Ana's telephone number. Don't call her yet, though. She's calling me tomorrow evening. I'll say you're ready to help and ask what time you can call her, when Carlos isn't around. I'll let you know that."

"Over the weekend I'm down here, fortunately it seems on the weather forecast. A long break in Manchester was helpful. Paul came back on Saturday but I stayed until Tuesday. I borrowed Mum's car and did lots in the constituency from there. Dad weighed in with some of my local councillors. He doesn't agree with what I've done but he'll fight for my right to do it. He's always coming up with odd facts. When Stanley Baldwin was Prime Minister, one of his sons was a Labour MP – real Labour, not National Labour.[82] Baldwin senior

---

[82] That is, not someone actually supporting the 'National', effectively Conservative, government of the 1930s.

took it in his stride, saying that his son was entitled to his own views."

"I can't imagine Mark Thatcher as a Labour MP."

"No. Anyway, thanks to the dads, mine and Brian's, there's now acceptance that for this Parliament I've a job to do. So it was great that you calmed me down, Pete. I talked sensibly to Alan, rather than making a scene. It was great that you calmed Morag down, too."

"She's back with Sheila, following her New Year in Scotland. The Christmas break with the Sinclairs was good for her. That was very generous of Jenny."

"I gather that the day after the party you gave Sheila quite an earful."

"I wouldn't put it that way, Carol, but I did telephone her. She knows now that she's been too domineering in the relationship and has taken advantage of Morag being self-effacing. I hope that no-one was listening in when I gave some account of what the three of us did."

"Mmm, yes. You helped both Morag and Sheila to work things out, and me, too – lots of ways."

"What *do* you mean by that, Carol?"

"Paul was away last night, so I invited Morag over. We had a nice meal and carried on from there. Morag had brought along what turns her into a man and I had my pot of Vaseline. So she did me just how I like. I said it could have been you. Then I licked her off."

"I guess she liked that from you more than if I'd tried it."

"Probably, but you have more impact on her than you realise, Pete."

"I know she likes me. She likes Liz, too. They slept together for a few months, before she met Sheila and Liz met Greg. Telling Liz what we did cheered her up lots. I assume you told Paul. Was he amused?"

"I think he was. You never can tell with Paul. I'm saying

that, though I've been married to him, and happily married, for nearly ten years. When he's back, he'll know that Morag and I will be exploring each other for a while. Sheila already knows that, and now you know. Thanks again for stopping us from rushing into it. We've begun when we'd both had time to decide it's what we wanted to do. It will be a genuine two-way effort which enhances our main partnerships. So it'll be like our times together, Pete."

"That's right. It's important to look at it that way."

There was a pause before Carol responded.

"Oh, Pete, how *do* you manage to keep thinking straight at times like this?"

"There's no point in *not* thinking straight. You know that, Carol. You've known that for a long time. Remember your first great speech, in Waterhouse College Hall, the day after Paul was attacked?"

"Yes. We've both come a long way since then."

Again, we were silent for a moment. Carol would remember what had happened between the attack and the speech. It couldn't help crossing my mind that her grief was mixed with anticipation.

"I'll just have to face up to things and carry on, just as you've been doing."

"There's Liz now."

We made our way through the bitter wind towards the porch of the bungalow, feeling rather than seeing occasional flakes of snow beginning to come down. I put my arm round Liz as she greeted us with a barrage of coughs. Eventually, she was able to tell us what had happened.

"He's wavering but I've persuaded him to speak to you, Carol. He needs to know how an article might appear."

"He's worth centre page, with a front-page trailer."

"You'd better wait in the car, Pete. I hope we won't be too long."

"Good luck."

I left Liz with a long kiss, and returned to the car. I noticed that Liz and Carol remained in the porch for a minute or two before going back in. It was nearly half past ten. The wind was so strong that it was not easy to see whether snow was coming down but flakes were flashing past street lights. As I sat there, they flashed past more frequently.

We had both half expected to hear what the consultant had told us that morning. Liz had even joked about it beforehand, almost as she had joked years before when I pointed out to her the risks of smoking. That hadn't reduced the numbing hit of reality. To distract myself, I ran through our days of Christmas.

On the evening of December 23rd, Jenny gave me a cheerful call. Dick had picked up another bug and didn't feel up to *The Silver Rose* at the London Coliseum, so would I like to come instead? Liz insisted that I should accept, saying that she thought the antibiotic and staying in the warm was doing her some good. There wasn't very much to do in the way of getting ready because my parents, who had arrived that afternoon, were staying with Roberta and Frank 'in view of Liz's delicate state'; and they would certainly be interested in time with their surrogate grandchild.

So, on Christmas Eve, I drove into central London through the snow showers. Then, one could park under cover, not far from the theatre. Jenny and I had a good lunch, before a splendid performance conducted by Sir Charles Mackerras. For the afternoon, I was able to forget the miners, the weather and the gnawing worry about Liz that was already there inside me. It wasn't a dressy event but Jenny looked every inch the attractive woman moving to full maturity. During the intervals, she turned eyes. I was proud to be with her. I was celebrating the renewal of a friendship which was so important to me, and to Creators Technology.

When we met, she had seemed worried and there had been a hint of something unsaid, though she reassured me that it was really great to have Morag around and that preparations for

Christmas at her home were going well. I wondered whether she regretted her frank and alcoholic talk with me the week before. However, by the last scene of the opera, any tension seemed to have gone. She slipped her hand into mine, I massaged it gently and could feel a response. I wondered whether she saw a parallel between my giving her up to Dick and the on-stage action of an unhappily married woman of thirty-five giving up her seventeen-year-old paramour (played by a woman) to an heiress of his own age. The parallel didn't seem close but perhaps our talk had taken her mind back, as well as mine. Had her 'little bit of bi' unconsciously sent her to Dick? It certainly explained much else that had happened over the years. She and Dick now understood it and so understood each other better. I could also celebrate that and the part I might have played in bringing it about.

After the opera, I took Jenny back to Weybridge to exchange parcels and more greetings. There was a hint of something unsaid in the air there, too. It was affecting Dick, and also Morag, despite what Jenny had said earlier.

I forgot about all this on returning to a happy household. The cheerful mood continued during the next day when I cooked lunch at Roberta's house whilst she and Frank went to see Greg, and into that Christmas evening when Liz and I celebrated quietly the second anniversary of our coming together again.

Boxing Day was busy, too, because we were all at our house and my cousin Gerald and his family, who lived not far away, joined us. I had been rather insistent with Roberta about inviting them.

Her feud with her son by her previous marriage stemmed from eight years back when she had climbed into Frank's bed and a year later married him. Its continuation was certainly not Roberta's fault. Gerald and even more his wife had not been mollified to know that Roberta's new will left the bulk of her money to him and his sister – 'Frank has his own'. However, I had not wanted a repetition of the thirty-year family feud that had begun before the War, with Roberta's dismissive, big sisterly remarks to my mother about the man who later became my father. So I had invited Gerald and his family to my house where they would have to put up with Roberta and Frank, and also with expectant Liz, who was not married to me. They could take us or leave us. They had taken us, and the day was a success.

Contributing to the success had been the family conference that took place whilst Liz rested, Gerald's wife looked after Jenny, and their two teenage children plugged into our TV the video game I had bought them.

My maternal grandfather had unwisely left a majority interest and the management of the family business, a drapery store, to his son. My mother and more particularly Roberta, the oldest child, had been side-lined. My uncle and his son had never been very enterprising and from the mid-'60s the store had been visibly failing to keep up with competition. The thirty-year feud had prevented the two sisters from taking a common line until it was too late. The business had staggered on somehow through the '70s but now it was a final curtain for curtains in our home town. My mother and Roberta had both received letters from their sister-in-law saying how difficult it would be for them to manage and suggesting that some Yuletide assistance would be well received. Responding firmly to these created some useful bonding.

The next day, I saw my parents off and then took Jenny over to see Greg. She was old enough to begin to understand what had happened to her father. We explained that Liz was still unable to visit, for fear she would spread an infection. Though we noticed no response, the nurses still thought he was hearing what we said.

We returned to find that Liz had coughed up blood.

Another visit to the doctor had led to breathing tests, more antibiotic and also to a referral. An X-ray on the first Monday of the New Year was followed by a bronchoscopy using the latest, flexible instrument so that only mild sedation was needed, not a general anaesthetic. This morning, we were faced with the result.

The choice was hers and, she had said, mine.

Her way, I would be left with a child and a baby to be looked after.

The other way, there would only be little Jenny, for whom Greg's parents might be prepared to take responsibility. And there would be some chance for Liz, at least for a while, though realistically she would be only a shadow of her former self.

This was a consequence of Liz having smoked since she was fourteen. Since her marriage, she had smoked less but the damage was already done. Even if nothing had happened to Greg, this would have happened to her now. Then, it would have been his problem. But something had happened to Greg, so it was my problem.

It was best to think back to the good times we had had over the past two years. Liz and I had made the right decision. The couple who had felt they could never live together had become the couple happy together.

The snow was whirling down now and accumulating round the kerbs. I started the engine so as to be able to run the demister and wipers. We would want no delay when Liz and Carol returned. I tried to concentrate on something else. What was I to do about the preprint?

At five to eleven, two figures appeared through the snow. Carol got in at the back and I helped Liz in beside me.

"He's on," Carol murmured.

"Well done."

"It took quite an effort to swing him."

Liz said nothing as I set off. Main roads were still fairly clear, though the grit and salt were clearly on a losing battle. The real problem was in seeing ahead. The next words were spoken by Carol when we dropped her off at Wimbledon.

"I'll call after I've spoken to the *Express* tomorrow. I hope you both get back OK."

"I hope *you* do, Carol," I replied. "Thanks so much again for turning out on a night like this. I'll wait for a moment. Come back if nothing is running."

She didn't return and we set off, Liz silent beside me, indeed seemingly asleep. I had to make sure that I didn't jerk her about.

Now the snow was settling all over the roads. The 1978/79 winter in Aberdeen had given me some experience of driving in these conditions, but in a better car and often using wheel chains. I decided to go via Mitcham as the flattest route. Keeping in second or third gear, I did well enough until I reached the roundabout at the north end of Mitcham Common. There, the road south was blocked. I guessed that someone had become stuck on the climb to the railway bridge by Mitcham Junction Station, so without stopping I took the Croydon road. What next? Through Beddington was shortest, but narrow. The A23 'Croydon by-pass', then past industrial premises rather than warehouse stores, was the best bet for avoiding anything that was stuck. I could take it to Purley. From there, the gradual climb to Bellinghame should be all right.

This worked out well enough until the next upslope to a railway bridge, near Waddon. A jack-knifed articulated lorry forced me to turn right, towards Sutton. As I inched over the junction, I remembered Merlyn Rees's comment in February. Was the whole country jack-knifed? The combination of the weather and the NUM looked unstoppable. The Argentines were waiting in the wings for the opportunity to solve their problems at our expense. The *Argentines…*

Suddenly, I realised why our man was now on.

Unlike Liz or me, Carol was a professional politician. Unlike Liz or me, she had grown up in a world which understood the 'working class patriotism' of many older people.

That attitude had a bad side. It could spill over into racism and xenophobia. Enoch Powell had exploited it. Alan Smitham's rather flippant remarks about black miners reflected it, as did what he had said about miners' views on urban disturbances. I knew, too, that the NUM's declaration of support for Polish miners was somewhat theoretical. Ed Plunkett had shown me the manuals of national agreements between the Coal Board and the unions. Those confirmed something my father had told me. During the War, he had met many Poles who had escaped from the Germans or Russians and had joined the Eighth Army. After the War, it was accepted that they had earned the right to remain in this country rather than be returned to their fate under Communism. Some of them were skilled miners who were much needed at the time. However, their employment had been restricted by agreements with the NUM concerning 'foreign labour' that were blatantly discriminatory.

But our man would show the good side to 'working class patriotism'. Whatever his views on how this country should be run, he wouldn't want to see it humiliated, particularly by a nasty dictatorship. He would want the government to stand up to the Argentines.

He would realise that a government that had lost again to the NUM would be a sitting duck. It wouldn't have the strength or will to resist. Public opinion would be fatalistic. Everyone would urge acceptance of the inevitable.

Carol had told him what Ana had told me and I had told her. Perhaps she had applied a little journalistic embellishment. She had finished the job that Liz had begun. Together, they had swung him over.

It was safe enough. He wouldn't tell anyone else. They wouldn't tell Ana that they had told him. Indeed, they wouldn't tell me.

If I had been thinking straighter, maybe I would have suggested telling him, or maybe not. Carol had spared me that decision. She was a Creator. She had thought, and decided. Quite possibly, she had not decided until some way through talking to him, though clearly she had given Liz a few words of warning.

Liz stirred when I turned left, ahead of a blockage before Wallington.

"Where are we?"

"I'm not quite sure but this is a Road, not a Close, so it shouldn't be a dead end. There's a sign, low bridge ahead, which means we can get under the Croydon to Sutton railway. The houses are sheltering us, er, most of the time!"

I said this as we came to a gap in the terraced houses and a whiteout of horizontally driven snow. At least in those days the road was fairly clear, rather than being effectively a single-track road owing to continuous parked cars on both sides. So we skidded to a halt against the kerb, rather than running into anything.

"Very gently now into reverse," I said to myself.

Fortunately that worked and we ploughed forward again. Under the railway bridge, another few hundred yards, and we were on a road I knew. Soon we were turning left at Wallington onto the gentle climb up to Bellinghame. I just had to hope that we could keep going steadily.

Some hope. Half a mile on, a mile from home, two cars had collided. Their occupants were standing around, wondering how to separate them and get on their way. They waved me down, doubtless hoping that I could help, but I wasn't having any of it. There was room to go through on what I recalled was a level verge under the snow. I kept going at a steady 15 mph with a muttered "hold tight".

With a bump I was over the kerb. I waited for the sickening jolt as I dropped into a hole or hit an obstruction but it didn't come. Fifty yards further we were back on what seemed to be the road. The rest of the run home was without incident. With palpable relief I turned into the entrance drive to the Bishop's

Park Estate, passing over where ten years before Roberta's house had stood.

I half carried Liz inside and got her into bed, with a cup of hot cocoa. Eventually, between coughs, she was able to say something.

"I'm all right, Pete, as much as I can be. I think I've made a difference."

My arms around her, we heard the wind outside and the snow rustling down. This was the perfect blizzard. Someone had to make a difference. Unless they did, it would finish Britain off.

15. WEDNESDAY, 13ᵗʰ JANUARY, 1982

"So, let's begin. What have we found out about the author of this preprint?"

Morag answered my question.

"Jack Diechenbach, aged twenty-nine, is currently an assistant professor at the University of South Illinois, where he obtained his PhD just over three years ago, after taking his first degree and Master's at the University of Chicago."

"Why did he move there? Wasn't he good enough to stay at Chicago?"

"In 1976 his research supervisor, Hank Lechynski, moved there from Chicago to become a full professor."

"I remember Lechynski's name. Back in Cambridge, Carl Obermeyer passed me a couple of his early papers. Eighteen months back, I caught up with some of his more recent stuff."

"He's had an interesting career," said Sheila. "Here's his list of publications. He started off in fairly pure theory. That's what you first saw, Pete. Then he did some more applied stuff for a few years, but since moving to South Illinois he seems to have become purer again."

She passed over a sheet copied from a universities yearbook. She had written in the most recent publications.

"What's his rating?" I asked.

"He's well respected. His 1974 paper on ergodic flows has over a hundred citations in other papers. That's not so far short of your 1970 paper, Pete... Pete?"

"Oh sorry, I was looking at the photo of Lechynski on

this sheet. He has a distinctive beard. I've seen him before somewhere."

"Perhaps he visited Cambridge when you were there."

"I don't remember him, do you, Morag? He would have looked different nearly fifteen years ago. I don't see how I can have met him. It must have been someone who looked like him. Or maybe his photo was with one of the papers I've read. Well, no matter. I remember this paper, and this one. They don't suggest any move towards our stuff. What about Diechenbach?"

"I've made copies of his papers that I can find – six in all," said Morag. "There are two more in US journals that our library doesn't take, but they date back three or four years and their titles suggest they're based on his PhD work so they aren't likely to be relevant. The key point is that these papers don't suggest any move towards what he's now done. They're quite unconnected. To begin with, none of them cite your paper."

"When did the last one appear?"

"In June. It was submitted for publication in March 1980."

"So he might have moved onto this work any time since then. Well, I suppose I did the work in three months or so."

"Yes, but you're you, Pete. Even though you'd been out for twelve years, you had your earlier work ingrained in you. This guy's earlier papers don't suggest that he's up to much. They're all a bit of a churn-out. So it's rather a mystery how he got into the problem."

Sheila came back in. "Another mystery is that his list of references is quite short. You're there, of course, and also Kraftlein's late '50s stuff, which is basically historic now. But some papers are missed that he ought at least to have said he looked at, even if they weren't essential to the argument."

"Yes, I noticed some were missing. Perhaps the referee will ask for them to be noted."

"Also, he cites some papers which though well regarded

aren't really very relevant at all – for example, Carl Obermeyer's 1972 paper."

"The circulation of the preprint seems sporadic, too," said Morag. "It would be normal to send a copy to anyone active and cited. You're the missing man, of course, Pete, and Kraftlein hasn't published for several years, so perhaps it's not surprising that neither of you received it. Carl Obermeyer is still active, though. His latest paper was last April."

"He used to receive floods of stuff from all over the world. Remember his office in Cambridge?"

"He still does, and he looks at it all, I'm told. So I rang him and pretended that Diechenbach was interested in coming over here for a sabbatical year. Did Carl know anything about him? Eventually, Carl recalled a couple of his earlier papers, of which he thought much the same as we do. The preprint wasn't sent to Carl."

"So, what we've seen, at third hand, is a badly written and incomplete paper ostensibly by someone obscure, which has had a rather limited preprint circulation and has recently been submitted to *Statistica*, a journal which is really about statistics applied to biology. That suggests to me that someone, not necessarily Diechenbach, is trying to make sure of priority for the work without alerting very many people to what's going on. *That* suggests that someone has realised the commercial potential in exactly the same way as we have done. So, Paul, what have you on the Richard Horstmann Foundation?"

"Richard Horstmann died in 1963. He was the founder of Parker Horstmann, a middle-tier Chicago bank. The Foundation owns 28% of its shares. Parker Horstmann is much into the Chicago futures market, though not forex or oil trading."

"How fast is trading on the Chicago futures market?" asked Sheila.

"It's all by shouting – the original bear-pit model."

"How many commodities are traded?"

"Loads; almost anything, in fact."

"What's the average interval between trades?"

"For a lot of the business, it's quite long."

"So, how would this work, or Pete's work, actually relate to Parker Horstmann's interests? The application of the work is to commodity trading which goes on all the time so that there's a continuously fluctuating price. It's not to commodities whose price jumps around in steps, set by widely separate trades. We're looking towards the records of transactions being available instantly through computer networks, rather than being put out minutes or hours later on a ticker tape."

"That's the key question for us," I said. "A month ago, we had no sign that anyone was onto the maths. Now, we have a sign that someone is, and that they're financed by a Foundation with links to this Chicago bank. Can we find out whether the grant to Diechenbach is a one-off or part of a pattern of funding?"

"It's not mentioned in any of Diechenbach's earlier papers, or in Lechynski's papers, though as he's tenured he wouldn't need a grant," said Morag.

"That's another point. Diechenbach is still reliant on grants because his appointment isn't tenured. Can we find out if the papers of others in Lechynski's group are also funded by this Foundation? If they are, but cover quite different subjects, then perhaps we're reading too much into this."

"Let's go along to the library, then."

Over a rather long lunch break, we were meeting in Morag's office at King's College. The Maths Library was nearby. After half an hour of perusing the most well-known journals, we had our answer. Lechynski was fairly prolific. During the previous year, he had published four papers on his own, and five others jointly authored with research students and colleagues at the University of South Illinois. Those included the paper of June 1981, of which he and Diechenbach were authors. There were also some solo papers by those whose joint papers identified them as being in Lechynski's group. None of these papers acknowledged funding from the Foundation and none of them had anything to do with my work, which was apparently also now Diechenbach's work. When we were back in Morag's office, Sheila put the point which was already in my mind.

"It's almost as if it's deliberate. Someone has put this round in a way that means little to most but says to anyone like us: 'Hey, you guys, we're on to this, too.'"

"Why should they do that?" I asked.

"To tell us that there are two things we can do. Either we can press on as fast as possible and hope to hit the market first or we can come to an arrangement with them. Beat them or join them, them being Parker Horstmann, of course."

"I was thinking the same way," said Paul. "We could make contact with Parker Horstmann through New Hampshire. In fact, speaking with an interest, under the terms of the loan agreements, we would have to involve New Hampshire."

"Yes," I said. "But we've no idea at all of how far Parker Horstmann might have got in developing trading software based on Diechenbach's work. Indeed, we don't know if they've got anywhere. We don't think this paper is Diechenbach's unaided work but whose is it, then? Lechynski is up to it but why should he then let Diechenbach pass it off as a solo effort, even as part of this exercise?"

"Perhaps the idea is that *Statistica* rejects the paper, or doesn't get back to Diechenbach for some time because it's not really in their field," said Morag. "In due course a better paper is submitted, with the right author or authors. Meanwhile, there's evidence of priority. Parker Horstmann might feel that that puts their foot in the door."

"Who might *Statistica* ask to referee the paper?" I asked.

"They'll be in some difficulty. It isn't really in their area.

Carl would be an obvious choice, but about three years ago he had a big row with someone on their editorial board and said he would never do anything for them again."

Sheila came back to her point. "The fact, though, Pete, is that you've lost your priority in terms of submission to a journal. If you contacted Diechenbach and pointed out how the work could be extended, you could get joint authorship of a better paper."

"True enough, Sheila, if they're trawling for other academics, but I'm not an academic. Of course, for all we know, there could be other banks, and academics, out there."

"That's why we would go to Parker Horstmann if we made contact. Others would be likely to go to Diechenbach," said Paul.

"I understand that, Paul. I understand also that whilst it would be nice to have academic priority for my work, in itself that has no effect on Creators Technology. Neither we nor anyone else can patent the research. We need to take a view on whether Parker Horstmann or anyone else might be setting up to compete with us. If they are, then we have two options. As Sheila said, beat 'em or join 'em."

"We'll need to discuss this at the next Creators Technology board meeting, on Tuesday week."

"Certainly we shall. By then, too, I hope I'll have found out who sent the paper to Kraftlein. I've called him three times but he must be on his usual winter break. Meanwhile, Jenny and I made it to Crawley for some of yesterday. I told Chris that there might be someone else on the same track. There were two messages for him. First, he and everyone else had to be even more careful about confidentiality: no idle chatter."

"Very right, Pete," said Sheila. "It's easy to say more than one intends. Morag and I are careful but both of us have had to fend off inquisitive questions about what we spend some of our time on. It's good that very few people know what you're doing. It's also good that we engaged Kraftlein as a consultant, rather than

Carl or anyone else in this country. They would have talked. I have to admit that now."

"My second message was, can we speed up? The answer may be yes. Chris is optimistic about the progress being made on debugging, despite the difficulties people have had in getting in this week. He reckons that we could bring forward to July the launch of a version that could be run on the most common minicomputers. That would be Version 0, to stimulate interest and obtain customer feedback. At the same time, we might trail Version 1 for hard-disk 8-bit micros but leave its launch until around May 1983, by which time there should be several brands of such machine available. To develop Version 0 for July would need another minicomputer, and three or four more staff. We would need about another £80,000 over the next six months. Jenny reckons we can find that, provided New Hampshire and Banco Navarrese agree. I would rather not talk with them until after Tuesday week, though."

"I guess that's right. Pat will have views," said Paul.

"I'll have views, too, on how much I can do. I'm grateful to you all for realising that I don't want to be reminded continually, but the position is this. Liz and I saw three consultants on Monday. To go through with the baby, she'll need to be in hospital from early next month. So from then I'll be looking after little Jenny. It's best not to ask when Liz might come home after the baby is born. I'm about to turn into a single parent. I'm sure that my uncle and aunt will do their best to help but they're getting on and there's a limit. There's also a limit on what I can ask of some friends of ours who are themselves expecting. I'm going to have a new first priority."

There was a silence. Eventually, Paul spoke.

"I think we all understand your position, Pete. We'll do all we can to help. You are pretty essential to our success. This does mean, though, that we may need to give the 'join them' option more consideration."

"Join what? We just don't know," said Morag.

"We may need to find out. Sorry, Pete, I must go now. Do pass Liz my very best wishes. Carol was aiming to call her this afternoon. I wouldn't be surprised if she asks what Liz thinks of the article in the *Express*."

"I saw someone reading it on the Tube this morning, and bought a copy," said Morag. "It's quite incredible. Will Liz have seen it, Pete?"

"We heard about it on the radio, first thing. She wanted to take Jenny to nursery today and was going to buy one while she was out. I expect that some on the NUM Executive will have something to say about it."

"I should think so, too, starting with the Vice-President and the President elect. God, what's got into the man? Perhaps it's the weather."

"Perhaps it is. This morning it was at least ten below. I know because I walked most of the way to South Wimbledon. The queue for tickets at Morden was so long that there was simply no point in waiting there."[83]

"It's worse in South Wales," said Paul. "Some people who got stuck on the M4 on Friday were only rescued on Monday. The whole place is at a standstill. The miners' ballot there is postponed until next Tuesday."

"I must go, too," said Sheila. "I'm lecturing at 4.15. See you later, Morag."

"Yes, I'll be back by six o'clock."

"Great. We're both on duty tonight. Alex's husband is poorly."

They exchanged kisses, and Sheila followed Paul out. Morag turned to me, with almost the same friendly smile as I remembered from when I had first met her nearly fifteen years before.

"Stay for a coffee, Pete, if you can. You look as if you need it."

"I certainly do but I want to be back onto the Tube fairly soon. That way I might be able to get a bus from Morden."

---

[83] At that time, there was no interchangeability of season tickets between most British Rail routes and the Underground.

Whilst Morag made us coffee I picked up the paper and turned to a centre page, with its headline, photo and key points highlighted.

A MESSAGE TO THE MINERS
from JOE GORMLEY

I and others negotiated hard for what is now on the table. I think it is as much as we can get.

Some people are trying to turn this into a political argument. That creates dangers that I don't think any trade union ought to be involved in.

I'm not telling you how to vote but I know which way I would vote.

It was a very clear message. It confirmed that a strike vote would be followed by a strike rather than, as Arthur Scargill continued to maintain, by the painless extraction of more money.

But the article had quite a difference to make.

Before coming over to King's, I had been into the department for a short time. Lawson's speech on Monday had been well reported in the more serious papers and might help with public opinion; but it had made little impact in the coalfields. The information that had come through yesterday and overnight included a few calls to me. It was not significantly changed from last week. All was pointing to around a 60% vote for strike action, perhaps just below that but almost certainly over 55%.

The blizzard overnight on Thursday and into Friday had dumped two feet of snow onto South Wales and several inches onto most of England. It had been followed by a weekend even colder than that after the first snow a month earlier. Sunday 10th January 1982 remains the coldest day on record in England and Wales, with a lowest of -26°C or -15°F. All the forecasters were saying the weather would continue very cold and attempts by less cold air to move in would cause further blizzards.

Now, the train drivers were on strike for two days each week, stopping all passenger services apart from the London Underground, as well as any deliveries of coal to power stations on those days.

Faced with all this, would Margaret Thatcher's Government be as united or resolved as they might be? Ted Heath might still resurface as the man of the moment, despite his inglorious record.

Surely enough miners would know that they would never have a better chance of winning. Arthur Scargill certainly knew that. At the Special Delegate Conference, he had said that if they didn't obtain the strike mandate they would live to regret the day. I wondered whether as a Yorkshireman he mused on a predecessor to whom Shakespeare attributed words which have become a figure of speech.

'Now, York, or never, steel thy fearful thoughts,
And change misdoubt to resolution;' [84]

Morag settled down beside me, and after a few sips began.
"I can see that you're not in favour of joining them, Pete."
"Not without knowing a great deal more."
"You need to watch Paul. He always has his own agenda."
"He's had his own agenda since I first knew him. More than once, I've had to face the consequences of not watching him closely enough."
"That's right. He had a long talk with Sheila yesterday."
"They did have something to talk about."
"Sheila said the conversation ranged."
"I'm glad there's still a role for you at the Pankhurst Centre,

---

[84] *Henry VI Part 2,* Act III Scene 1. That 'resolution' led to thirty years of civil war.

Morag, even if only in emergencies. I'm also glad that you and Sheila are on again."

"Yes, my time out, first with Jenny and Dick and then friends in Scotland, made us both feel we missed each other. It was so great that Jenny invited me."

"I think they enjoyed having you there."

"Yes, I was able to help." Morag paused, suddenly.

"How is Sheila taking you and Carol?"

"It's working out. Actually, Paul has helped. He pointed out to Sheila that Carol was on and off with you for about seven years. You'd helped to sort out her frustrations and keep her with him. He couldn't see why it should be different this time."

"I guess it brought home to Sheila that Carol is straight and will stay straight. You know that already."

"Yes, Carol told me that it was great to crouch and think of me as a man. That was great for me, too. When I took my thing off, just a few licks from Carol and I was there. I took Gill and Angela that way sometimes and I've been missing it. It's helped with Sheila, too. On Sunday we shaved each other and had the best time for ages."

"Will Sheila let you take her that way, sometimes?"

"Maybe. Certainly she now realises that our relationship has to be of equals. She can't dominate it the way she's been doing. She's grateful to you for pointing that out. She also admitted that whilst the Centre gave her plenty to do over Christmas and the New Year, she took a couple of breaks to get over being uptight about you and me. If I have more times with Carol, she'll take more breaks."

"Oh, and what are the breaks?" I managed a smile as I asked, though I could guess.

"She knows a masseur who's very gay. When he gives her all the trimmings, it's very professional but very good. So thanks, Pete. You stopped me from dashing at Carol in a way we would have both regretted the next day. It's much better for happening after we both had time to think."

"And after I'd reminded you what Carol really likes. She's a pretty forceful woman, but she's always wanted her partner to drive. I've always thought it a good thing you didn't meet her before you were settled with Gill."

Morag put her arm round and kissed me.

"You're such a friend, Pete. You came to Liz when she and little Jenny needed you. Now, this awful thing has happened to her."

"That's the way it is."

"By deciding to keep the baby she's showing guts that the rest of us wouldn't have."

"At least there'll be a new life. That's how she puts it."

"But, as you've said, it leaves you with a big problem."

"I'll sort it out."

"You can't do everything on your own, Pete. Practical Morag has a suggestion. Think about it, and talk to Liz. I told you about my sabbatical semester. After the middle of February, I've no lectures or other jobs here until September. I'm not going away. Like you, I can work on research almost anywhere. So I can come and keep house for you. I've met little Jenny several times. She seems to like me."

"You're offering to come and stay to look after Jenny, and the new one when they arrive, while I'm doing my job. That's a great offer, Morag, really great."

"It would be for most of the week. Weekends are for Sheila, the Pankhurst Centre, and basketball. There could be an away night with Carol during the week, depending on Parliament and when Paul is around."

"I've an idea for making clear that you're a housekeeper. You've met Roberta and Frank, who live two hundred yards away. I think they would be pleased for you to stay with them, though I can't ask them until they're back next week. Look at this card they sent as soon as they got to Jamaica. It arrived this morning."

"'Do hope Liz is better.' Oh, Pete."

We sat there for a minute or so. Then it was time for me to go.

At Leicester Square Underground, the southbound trains which went only to Kennington were leaving with plenty of room because people knew they would have no chance of continuing south from there. The few through trains were impossible even for me to join. So I went north to Euston and found a seat on a southbound train through the City. It was then just a matter of staying put until we reached Morden, where I was onto the second bus that left after I arrived.

Jenny rushed into the hall as soon as I came in. "Mummy is very tired and I'm hungry."

Liz was slumped in an armchair. "I'm knocked out but all right, Pete. I'm glad you're back. I'll tell you more later."

"I'll get your tea, Jenny. What did you do at nursery today?"

"We built a snowman."

"Ooh, was it cold?"

"Yes, and it was wet. Why is snow wet, Daddy?"

"It's wet because it's frozen water. When you make water cold, as it is outside now, or in the freezer, it turns to ice."

We went into the kitchen and I took an ice cube from the freezer.

"Feel it. It's cold, and as you touch it with your warm hand it starts to melt. See, your hand is wet."

"But snow is white. It's not like ice."

"It *is* ice, but lots and lots of very little bits of ice, with air between them. That makes it look different and makes it lighter. Now, what would you like for tea?"

"Baked beans on toast. Daddy, why is Mummy so tired?"

"It's what happens to mummies when another little brother or sister is on the way. We need to look after Mummy."

"It was boring here after nursery. She was too tired to play with me."

"Tomorrow, I'll be taking you to nursery and I'll be here

in the afternoon. You're looking forward to being at school all day, aren't you, Jenny? That's not until September, the ninth month of the year. We're only in January. That's the first month."

After tea it was again time for *Mr. Men*, and I had a few minutes with Liz. That was just for sitting with an arm around her. It wasn't until Jenny was read to and in bed, and we had eaten, that she had the strength to talk between coughs.

"Taking and collecting Jenny meant I showed my face to the other mums at nursery. A couple of them offered to pick Jenny up if I was still poorly. I've taken that up for Friday, as I know you're busy then."

"Yes. I'm clearly wanted for when the results start to come in."

"How did it go down?"

"The main reaction was astonishment. Yesterday afternoon, John Willis had a tip-off and was able to warn Bernard Ingham. John thinks it will make a difference but doesn't know how much difference. The Coal Board is doubtful about impact. It wasn't invented there, of course."

"Is anyone guessing about me?"

"It's up to them what they make of the rumours about the baby. As we agreed, I've not said anything about you yet, except to Ed and Jean, who both know not to pass it on. The others just think you've started your maternity leave early."

"Carol called this afternoon."

"Yes, Paul said she would. He didn't give the impression he knew, but then he wouldn't, would he?"

"I'm sure Carol hasn't told Paul. She worked darn hard over the weekend to get the article as punchy as it is, but mostly at *his* home. Before yesterday afternoon, only two people at the *Express* knew about the article. Only they will ever know about her hand in it. And even they know nothing about me."

Liz couldn't continue for a few minutes. Eventually, she was able to go on.

"Taking Jenny to nursery was just the start of my day. I went on to Coulsdon. I apologised for coming over with a cough but no-one had been over for ten days because of the weather. They wheeled Greg into a side room so I wouldn't spread it round. I had over an hour with him. I told him about me and that I wasn't sure how many more times I could come to see him. I told him about the baby, and the article. I can't be sure but I think he understood, somehow I do. So now there are five of us who know. Him, you, me, Carol and Greg. That's the way it will stay, forever."

I held her tight while she coughed for what seemed forever and the pile of blood-spotted tissues grew higher.

"Someone who definitely won't know is Morag. She was shocked by the article, but Carol doesn't talk in her sleep."

"Mmm yes, it's nice that's worked out well. You did them both a good turn."

"It was a very enjoyable good turn for me, especially how it ended. To come back to now, she's made a most remarkable offer."

I described it, and Liz's eyes lit up, though she could say nothing for a minute or so.

"That's marvellous, Pete. I'm sure Roberta and Frank will put her up. It answers the question, when do we tell Jenny?"

"Yes, when we can say that Morag will be helping. She needs to know. She's growing up fast."

"And whatever you say about Morag being just a housekeeper, perhaps more than helping, Pete?"

"I don't think that's her idea."

"Oh Pete, don't throw away a chance if it does happen. You're going to need someone after I'm – gone."

"I know that. I've always liked Morag and she likes me but, despite last month, I think she's set in her ways."

"I'm going to bed happy. There could be a way ahead for the people I love."

"I'll be up before long. I need to call Ana."

As I had expected, Liz made no response to that. She had not asked what my calls to Ana were about. To me, that confirmed she knew already. Now, perhaps Greg 'knew' too.

Before I could pick up the phone, it rang. I recognised the caller's Yorkshire accent.

"Pete – Alan."

"Happy New Year. You must be busy. Can you actually get around up there?"

"We're more used to this than yer southern buggers but t'was rough over the weekend. We had a late start on Monday because not all weekend maintenance were done – nowt to do with t'union. I'm glad yer've answered. Doris and I are right coot up to hear 'boot Liz. It's easier to say that to you. I've not met her that often but I've thought mooch of her guts and now I think even more."

"Thanks for saying that, Alan. I'll pass it on. She's gone to bed, very tired."

"When Brian told me, he was almost in tears – not like our Brian at all."

"In his first year at Cambridge they were very close. She taught him a lot."

"Yes, he remembers those great times. What'll yer do?"

"Carry on."

"That's all yer can do, I guess. While I'm on, d'yer want what I've heard 'boot Joe's article?"

"It must have been quite a surprise."

"Yes and no. We all knew how Joe would vote. Cooming out in public, though, that was a shock, a big shock. There's soom very angry about it."

"I can imagine that."

"But there's others who in private ain't as angry as yer'd think. Four in a row for Joe – what's that leave for anybody else?"

"I see your point. How do you think it'll hit the men?"

"Frankly I don't know. He's a Lancashire man. They're not always heard in Yorkshire. P'raps a bigger effect oother parts. Well, I mustn't keep yer. Chin oop, I guess."

"That's right. Thanks for calling, Alan. I'll tell Liz in the morning. Oh, and to say that Carol now seems much happier about dealing with her constituency for the rest of this Parliament. I guess you've had something to do with that."

"I did tell soom to stop being silly. Most work an MP does locally is nowt to do with thar party. People took t'lass though she's from Manchester. They can still take her, for now. Mind you, I'm glad she's to go for journalism. Her oosband's right. The SDP's got no future 'cause it's no Party. It's a load of parties. Thars Roy Jenkins Party, David Owen Party, Shirley Williams Party, and so on. P'raps Carol Milverton Party, too."

Hardly had I put the phone down than it rang again.

"Pete, it's Belinda. Is this a good time to speak?"

"Yes."

"I spoke to Simon. He was amazed to hear you'd been in touch with me. As far as he and everyone else in statistics are concerned, you'd just disappeared. He'd never realised even that you knew Jenny. He was away both for Jenny's wedding and for Katie's christening, so he's never met you or even seen you on TV."

"Good. My chums still working in the area have been careful not to mention me."

"Yes, and I was careful. I said that you'd gone into business but had kept an interest and still receive preprints sometimes. This one turned up and you leafed through it. You could follow it as a development of what you did years ago but you'd noticed some things that were wrong with it. You would be pleased to have a word with whoever was refereeing it. Well, as you'd guessed, they were in some difficulty about finding a referee but he wondered if he could send the paper to you."

"Well done, Belinda – *well done!*"

"I said you would call him tomorrow. Here's his number… But I hope that's all right still, Pete? Jenny gave me this terrible news about Liz. When you called on Friday you didn't say anything about that."

"Liz wanted to speak to her closest friends herself first. They include Jenny."

"I understand, Pete. What's it going to do for you? How will you cope?"

"I'll work something out. Morag Newlands has offered to help with the children. She has some sabbatical coming up."

"Oh *yes*, she was *so* helpful at Katie's christening when Dick was upset by the news about his friend, and before that she was *such* a good influence on Angela. Even Jane came round to liking her. She's a very understanding woman. But does she still, er, prefer the company of other women, Pete?"

"Since soon after she and Angela split, she's been in a settled relationship. Her partner couldn't be at the christening because of the charitable work they both do."

"I'm sure that all your friends will rally round," said Belinda, who had for a moment sounded as if something was worrying her, but now seemed quite relieved.

"I know they'll help as much as they can but most of them are already very busy. Jenny certainly is, with four days a week in her regular job, much of the fifth day and some of the weekend on Creators, and bringing up two children."

"Ah yes, it was while she was with you, all those years ago, that Jenny became interested in accountancy. She's doing so well at it. Women do so much more now than in my time. It's so nice to speak to you, Pete. Just let me know if there's anything else I can do. I must go now; Harold will be back soon."

Finally, I got to talk to Ana. On Friday I had told her that Carol was ready to help and then, quite separately, I had given her the news about Liz. I had said that I would call this evening to check that she and Carol were in touch, and to update her. Indeed they were in touch and Ana accepted that I should duck out of any further involvement in passing on information.

Somehow the conversation got onto how those who achieve could end up paying for it. Ana recalled how, to great profit, we had overheard Anwar Sadat's strategy to recover Sinai being set out. On the previous October 6th, exactly eight years after he had put it into effect, and three years after he had been rewarded through the 1978 Camp David Accords, he had been assassinated. I wondered whether Ana meant any parallel with Liz.

When I climbed in beside Liz, she was already sleeping deeply and peacefully, whether because of her mood or because of some medicine to control her cough at night I did not know. I lay awake for a while.

Ana's serious mood had somehow pointed up a contrast with the previous conversation. Belinda had seemed very matter of fact about Liz. The day before, Jenny had been rather the same whilst we were travelling to Crawley, though when she picked me up she had been very sympathetic to Liz. Admittedly, she was concentrating hard on driving. The roads, though cleared and gritted, were still slippery in the intense cold and we passed enough accidents to bring that message home. I wanted to focus on the work in hand and she had the message that I didn't want continual harping. We returned quite early in the afternoon and I welcomed thus having the opportunity to look after little Jenny. That had prompted Jenny to say that Dick would welcome not having to look after Katie and David for long after collecting them from school. He was still suffering from the after-effects of two bugs and was going into the university only when he had to. The weather was very lowering for him.

Once again, I had had the impression that there was something Jenny wasn't telling me. Was she worried that she would feel bound to give me help? As I had said to her mother, I knew she had little time to do so. Could she see any help she could give leading to our friendship becoming awkward again? But that didn't fit with her seeming *less* worried yesterday than on Christmas Eve. Morag's offer would reduce any pressure to help that Jenny might feel. Perhaps that was why Belinda had seemed so pleased to hear about it, though I wondered why she had then been so interested to know that Morag was still with Sheila. Belinda did not appear to know about Morag's Christmas stay. Most likely, that reflected Jenny's sensible discretion, but Morag hadn't wanted to say much about her stay, either. I was sure that Jenny had not got up to anything with Morag, in the family home or anywhere else. Her little bit of bi was in a private box with a tight-fitting lid, and quite separate from her friendship with other Creators; I was privileged to know of it. What else could be causing her reticence?

Other thoughts drifted round in my mind aimlessly.

Liz, Carol and I had our reasons for doing all we could to prevent the miners from voting for a strike, though we weren't natural supporters of the Thatcher Government. Liz was the nearest to being such a supporter but she had never been very interested in politics. Carol had made her views clear enough in Parliament. If I thought the SDP/Liberal Alliance would succeed, I would support it, despite misgivings that it would not be tough enough with our partners in the EEC. But like Alan Smitham, and like Paul, I did not think it would succeed.

I thought back to May, when we had given the Milvertons dinner. Carol was full of her move to the SDP. Paul was firmly for staying with Labour, which needed support from members with business experience. In March, 364 academic economists had written to *The Times* to condemn the government's policies, which seemed to have moved the UK further down the economic league, to the extent that the Italian government was often boasting of *il sorpasso*. I asked Paul whether, if he were an academic, he would have made it a signatory for every day of the year. He said that the 364 were mostly Keynesians, whilst he was a monetarist. He didn't say that he was a Labour supporter of the government's policies but he was clearly closer to them than was Carol. He did not share Mr Foot's vision of the Labour Party.

My mind drifted on over well-tilled ground but away from the awful present. How had I got here? It all went back two years... Why had I left IE?... What had been going on in Fred Perkins' mind that last weekend in November?... How would Melissa Copehurst do on stage? She seemed a natural Lady Macbeth...

Going back much further, if I had exposed Fred for his brutal attack on Paul, things would have been very different... Fred would never have become a doctor but nor would he have been the potent symbol that led people at Waterhouse to fight back and achieve... Not exposing Fred had meant not exposing Paul's role in the wrecking of Harry Tamfield's concert, so Paul had gone on... You had to watch him but he had achieved a lot for IE, and now for Creators Technology... We had avoided disaster from his scheme to boost Labour Party funds... He had done well for New Hampshire, perhaps with one exception that no-one wanted to talk about... As Morag had said, we lived in the stochastic world.

Sleep drifted up, but pointless reflections continued. Five people knew how the *Express* article had come about and they didn't include Paul. Most other secrets of my life did involve Paul. How many knew of those? From a few years before, more than five knew about the profits from oil trading and probably more than five knew about the Labour Party funds. Going further back, to my time in Cambridge, more than five knew that Fred Perkins had attacked Paul – Paul himself, Carol, Liz, me, Brian, Susie, Melissa and probably Jack Unwin. Also, more than five knew of Paul's role in wrecking Harry Tamfield's concert – Paul, Carol, Liz, me, Arthur Gulliver and at least two Framptons. So, in comparison, the *Express* article was a real secret.

Rambling on, I wondered how much Paul had told Steph about his time in Cambridge. I had always been careful in what I said, right up to when I put Steph up to dealing with the bogus clinic, and Steph had never said anything which implied that she knew. Surely Paul wouldn't have got a job at New Hampshire

Realty if Steph had known more about him. But what did she actually want him for, and what might he have wanted to say he could deliver...? And they had been together for some time, here and in the USA...

Suddenly, I was wide awake. Once again, the lemons were in a row.

I remembered where I had seen Hank Lechynski before. Everything fell into place and I knew what was happening now.

16. FRIDAY, 15TH JANUARY, 1982

"It's just a question of waiting, now," said Howard. "Any bets?"

"It'll be closer than we thought a week ago," said Bill.

"I've heard it said that the bad weather will make it closer. People have enough problems. They don't want a strike as well," said John.

"That might affect the South Wales result, but they'll know what everyone else has done before they vote. There's no suggestion that the rest of the NUM should keep their results quiet until after Tuesday, is there, Pete?"

"As you know, I've no direct information from their HQ anymore. However, I can't believe that that would be possible. Each NUM Area or group is responsible for its own result. The local press will be on to them. We'll have most results later today."

"There could be a suspenseful weekend," said John. "Suppose that the vote for the rest of the NUM is, say, 52% and the challenge on South Wales is to push the national figure over 55%. What vote would do that, Ed?"

"About 80%, if enough men get to the pits to vote. They're certainly capable of delivering that, though their performance in recent ballots hasn't been very consistent."

"So there's a credible scenario that the hacks who aren't looking for Mark Thatcher in the Sahara will be fighting their way through the snow to get down there."

"Good luck to them," said Howard. "Ed, you'll brief on what South Wales vote is needed, if it turns out that way. Our job here would be to hold the line on no comment before the full result. No doubt you'll be speaking to Bernard during the day, John."

"It would be good if you could speak to the Welsh Office, Howard. They've a lot on just now and questions may be asked of someone who isn't properly briefed."

"I know someone there who was in the Cabinet Office a couple of years back. Ed, get the Secretary of State's office to impress the message on the Welsh Secretary's office, too. Any hint of compromise would be all over the papers by Tuesday and would give the South Wales men the feeling that they just have to vote for victory. Now, have we any more information about reactions to Gormley's article?"

"We've no real information about voting intentions more recent than Tuesday," said Ed. "That, as you know, was suggesting a slight lessening of support for a strike, but only very slight. Over 55% is still much more likely than not. Anything over 55% is enough. Don't forget, the 1972 strike started with 58%. It was solid and effective."

"That fits with what Paul Routledge is saying in the *Mirror*," interjected John.

"About the clearest view on the effect of the article is what Pete put round yesterday, after his call on Wednesday night," said Bill.

First thing the day before, I had dictated a note to Jean over the phone. Now, it informed some discussion of the real positions of the main players in the NUM.

Eventually, Howard called a halt.

"I'm sure that if any of us hear anything they'll let the rest of us know. The Coal Board has clear instructions. Anything they get is to be passed to me immediately or, if I am not available, to Bill or Ed."

"Whilst you're speaking to the Secretary of State's office, Ed, let them know I'll provide later a sitrep on how coal movements are doing today," said Bill.

"If this morning's performance of the trains is anything to go by, not well," said Howard. "And from next week the railmen are striking on Tuesday and Thursday so as to maximise disruption throughout the week. Bill, you're fairly relaxed about the impact. Is that because you live in Rickmansworth, which is on the Underground as well as British Rail?"

"The Underground trains aren't underground out there. In this weather, they can be rather sparse. The current impact on coal movements does look like being less bad than we feared, though. The drivers who've been out during the week seem quite interested in making up lost pay over the weekend, on plain time, and the people at the pits who supervise the loading of the trains are some of the least militant in the NUM. If there's no miners' strike, then short of an all-out railway strike, which seems unlikely at the moment, we'll get through the winter, even with the present weather."

"Is there any forecast of the weather better than what's on TV?"

"Not really. The Met Office thinks the pattern is stable. It will continue very cold but there's no immediate prospect of more snow, except in Devon and Cornwall where Atlantic and Arctic streams are fighting it out."

Back at my office, Jean placed calls whilst I went through the latest draft of briefing on a parliamentary Bill to facilitate the sale of state-owned oilfields and gasfields. Then it was on to industrial energy prices and how to convince business that these were market-related despite the suppliers' monopolies. At a quarter to twelve, I called Liz. She was resting, before Jenny was brought back from nursery. I had no news other than that my early start in the car had let me park not far from Morden and there hadn't been much of a queue for tickets there. Those with British Rail season tickets had perhaps been hoping that services would not take too long to resume after the two-day strike. I suspected that their hopes had been in vain. The work to rule was still on and doubtless lots of careful checks would have had to be made before anyone could actually do anything, particularly in this weather.

Ed had asked to see me at noon, and he arrived with some handwritten tables and graphs.

"Pete, it's gone on that I've not had much to do whilst we wait. So I've been thinking more about how the redundancy terms might be improved over the next couple of years so that enough men are ready to go that sufficient closures can be achieved. I'd like to try this out on you."

"The problem is that we don't know which pits are losing the big money. The Coal Board don't tell us that, and with good reason. There isn't a list of pits to be closed."

"For each of the Board's Areas, we have the financial results and figures for manpower, with age distribution. Here they are. So we can see how many men would find the present terms attractive if offered to them now, and how many more will do so during the next few years. Suppose that the result of reductions is split fifty-fifty between reduced output and higher productivity, for example a 10% reduction in manpower leads to a 5% reduction in output and 5% higher productivity. What does that do? This table estimates the results for each Area. By this time next year, most Areas will be running out of miners that the present terms attract. If we then introduce something like the rest of the Board's package of a year ago, we'll get another year's progress. But after that it's no longer possible to move younger men from closing pits to vacancies created by people going voluntarily at continuing pits. We'll need to offer redundancy terms which make it easier for younger men to leave."

I looked through the figures.

"Yes, I see. The most economical way to restructure the industry is to improve the redundancy terms step by step, not all at once. So when last year we only agreed some of the

Coal Board's proposals, we were unwittingly doing the right thing."

"That's right. By improving the redundancy terms in steps, we could have the industry making a profit again within four or five years, for a total cost in redundancy payments of about £1,500 million."

"That's the figure we talked about last February, for part of the package."

"It's higher because it's on top of what has already been committed, but it's less than two years' losses at the current level. What's more, quite a lot of the payments would be through the pension funds and hence the government needn't put the money in straight away. Effectively, the pension funds would provide off balance-sheet financing."

"That's provided the funds' trustees, who include the unions, agree."

"How many of them understand the figures, Pete?"

"Also, don't forget that your definition of 'making a profit' assumes that the electricity industry and other customers go on paying higher than the world price for coal and that that price stays high, along with the oil price."

"Those are reasonable assumptions[85] but even without them you get an industry that's in a much better state than now."

"This is very interesting but it's dynamite. You're actually saying that *if* we survive now, then we can probably get through to the spring of 1984 without a crunch with the NUM, because anyone who wants to remain a miner will be able to do so, and good enough terms can be offered to those who are ready to leave. But after then, some people will be made redundant against their will. We have two years to get ready for the crunch. Have you shown this to anyone else?"

---

85 They were reasonable until 1986, when OPEC lost control of the world oil market and the oil price fell by two-thirds.

"No, and I'm not going to. It's best if Howard and Bill don't know I've done this work. It will stay locked in my security cabinet. It won't be on any file. It's just a guide to me. No-one can understand it without my explanation. When the Coal Board comes up with proposals, I'll know the questions to ask."

We talked through some details, and after half an hour he had a list of points to look at further. I brought us back to earth.

"So, whether we can deal with the NUM and sort out the industry depends on whether we survive now. We'll know that soon enough."

"Yes, but thanks for letting me talk that through with you, Pete."

"I'm always pleased to talk with someone who's clearly on top of their job, is enjoying it, with all the stresses involved, and has worked out what needs to be done. You've moved on from a year ago."

"Now, my management value me, so I have the confidence to think strategically, and to talk confidently to the people I need to deal with. A lot of the change is down to you, Pete. You stood up for me, found me the staff I needed, made sure I had enough help from the lawyers and showed me how to make an effective contribution. You've made a difference for me and you've given me the opportunity to make a difference myself. Thanks."

"You've done it for yourself, Ed."

"I suppose I have, but you've shown me how. I'm not even so wound up about Bill coming in as I would have been. I've a big role. I want to see this through and I think I can. For thinking clearly under stress, you're quite an example, especially now."

"I've learnt that it's best to take things as they come and to work out carefully how to react. Just now, it's easier that only you and Jean know about Liz. She didn't want me to tell anyone here but you've met her and Jean needs to know that she may have to find me very fast."

Ed locked his papers away and we called at Howard's office, where there was no news. Down in the canteen, we joined others in foreboding mood, relieved only slightly by the news that Mark Thatcher had been found after his car had gone missing from the Paris-Dakar rally and his father had joined the search for him. After another hour or so on industrial energy prices, I left the office with a loaded briefcase.

I was a little behind time but fortunately I jumped straight into a passing taxi, traffic was light and the central London roads seemed clearer of snow than they had been earlier. At five to three, I was in the reception of New Hampshire Realty's offices, asking for Dr Milverton with whom I had a meeting at three o'clock. A few minutes later, I began.

"Thanks for finding time, Paul. After our meeting on Wednesday, I worked out what we needed to do, but there are some points to talk through with you."

"I'm pleased to help but I've a meeting in an hour. I expect you've plenty happening today, too."

"I certainly have, though there won't be any immediate decisions. So, let's make a start. What were you doing on the evening of Thursday, October 25th, 1979?"

Paul was very good at not looking surprised but this time, perhaps unsurprisingly, this skill failed him.

"Pete, how should I remember what I was doing on a particular day over two years ago?"

"Let me refresh your memory. It was just before the Creators reunion in Yorkshire that Carol and you kindly hosted. Steph was over here already. That evening, she would have particularly enjoyed telling you what she'd been up to. Indeed, she would have made clear what her reward should be. It was most convenient that Carol was already on her way to Holtcliffe, earlier in the week than usual."

"What *are* you talking about?"

"Come on, Paul, you remember and we haven't all day. I'd put Steph up to persuading Fred Perkins and his practice nurse, Melissa Copehurst, that they should close down the bogus clinic they'd set up for his, and more importantly her, gratification. In fact, Steph had an extra reason for persuading them, which I'd not given to her. When I was with Steph I'd told her a lot about Cambridge, including what Fred had done to the Secretary and members of the Socialist Society, but I never told her that Fred had attacked you. She might have asked why he hadn't been prosecuted and you might not have wanted her to know the answer to that question."

"That's very thoughtful of you, Pete."

"You'll be pleased to know that both before Steph did her stuff and when she entertained me on the Sunday morning at your place, she was careful to refer only to what I'd told her. However, I realise now that there's an explanation of everything else that happened only if she *did* know about Fred attacking you. Perhaps back in 1973 you wanted to convince Steph of your credentials as a schemer, so as to convince her that you were the man to get New Hampshire oil trading winnings into the Labour Party. So you told Steph what you had got up to with the Framptons, to Harry Tamfield's cost. That could have been the night before she and I gave Harry dinner, after which he rehearsed to me some of the remarks he made later on TV. I *was* quite surprised that Steph didn't quiz me after hearing my end of a telephone conversation in which I reassured Carol that Harry couldn't have found out about you, and perhaps I should have guessed that she already knew the story. Anyway, once you'd told her that story, there was no extra risk for you in telling her about Fred."

"Maybe I did tell her sometime back and maybe we did meet on the Thursday. What of it? Steph said to me, and no doubt to you on the Sunday morning, that she and her husband were open outside America. Carol and I are tolerant, as you know very well. Where's this going, Pete?"

"It goes next to just after our Sunday lunch near Stocksbridge. Thanks to Carol, we handled Dan Worsley smartly and he sent me two sets of prints of the photos his chum had taken. I passed one set on to you and Carol, with my note of thanks for the weekend."

"So?"

"The prints included a good shot of Steph, Liz, Greg and me together, which wasn't published in the *Yorkshire Post*. Ten days later, Liz had to take little Jenny to her doctor, who was in the same practice as Fred. Whilst she was waiting to see him, Melissa came by and gave her a very odd look, odd enough that she wondered if there was any way that Melissa and Fred could have seen a picture that linked Steph to her. I was reassuring. Even if somehow they had seen the *Post*, the published pictures gave no clue. But, of course, I'd neglected another possibility – *that they had seen the unpublished picture.*"

"What on earth are you suggesting? That Carol or I sent the picture to Fred Perkins? *Fred Perkins*, who but for Brian might have *killed* me? Pete, I've the most enormous respect for you, I always have had, and I do realise that what's happening to Liz is a terrible shock. But I think this conversation is rather weird."

"Paul, I've the most enormous respect for you, too. You like to control things without seeming to do so. You do your homework, you spot opportunities and you keep them in mind, ready to use them. Those are your strongest qualities. I saw them at Cambridge and I've seen them since. Two years ago, you were fascinated by Steph's account of the nurse, and of how she seemed to have Fred under her control. Perhaps you recognised a kindred spirit. I think I know what you did but do correct me if I have anything important wrong. First, you consulted the telephone directory. Yesterday, I did just that in our local library. Perhaps because of Thatcher cuts, its set is not fully up to date. The one for the St Albans area is still the 1979 edition. There are details of the practice, listing Fred Perkins and giving the name of the nurse – Melissa Copehurst. There's only one with her unusual name in the residential directory. So, you had her address. A week or so after our weekend, you sent the photo, anonymously, not to Fred but to her. You said you would call her to arrange a meeting. Melissa must have just received your letter when she saw Liz in the waiting room."

"You should be writing thrillers, Pete."

"So you had told Melissa and Fred that someone was on to them. You could let them stew whilst you decided how to use them."

"Use them – how?"

"You weren't yet sure but you had a possibility in mind. You knew that Roy Delaval, then the Number 2 at Consolidated Electrics, very much wanted to be Number 1 there as a prelude to being Number 1 at a company that had absorbed IE. You knew that, before Linda Flitton killed herself, she had written Morag a letter that would finish Don Flitton if it came out."

"What letter? This is ridiculous."

"When I called Morag yesterday, I asked her if there was any way that you might have known about the letter. She told me that, at the Pankhurst Centre's 1977 Christmas party, she was interrupted whilst talking to you. One of the women who was staying there had had too much to drink. She'd been at the Centre before, at the same time as Linda Flitton, and they had kept in touch. She asked Morag what had happened to the letter and gave some description before Morag was able to shut her up. You didn't seem to pay much attention but no doubt you put the information neatly away in your mind. So you knew that if you could get hold of the letter and pass it to Roy Delaval, Don Flitton would have disappeared from view *very* quickly."

"Maybe he would have done. Why might I have wanted that to happen?"

"For about two weeks, you didn't want anything to happen. You wanted the IE rights issue to succeed, and that was more likely if IE's share price held at least steady. Ructions at Consolidated would lower short-term expectations of a bid for IE and hence force the price down. So you held off. But as the closing date approached, you saw the picture change. IE's share price was going up, but on rumours of what eventually happened, an agreed merger with Consolidated rather than a takeover. Roy Delaval would have seen time running out for him. He could not be Chief Executive of a merged company without first being Chief Exec of Consolidated. So you contacted him and explained what might come his way. You may have been surprised at how receptive he was. No doubt he gave some tangible promise of gratitude."

"Such as?" said Paul, sarcastically.

"He promised enough for you to make a plan. Liz had told me, and I had told Steph, that Melissa was good at amateur dramatics and had encouraged Fred to take part, too. No doubt Steph passed this on. Melissa could play the abused wife, so as to get inside the Pankhurst Centre. Fred would play the husband and distract Morag and Sheila whilst Melissa hunted for the letter and took a copy. The office at the Centre is quite near the entrance. I found it by mistake only last month, but you've been to the Centre more often and could have told her where it was. A Friday evening, when the Centre was busiest, would be the best timing for this plan."

"Go on," said Paul dispassionately, apparently listening intently, in characteristic pose with his head tilted to one side.

"Suddenly, the plan became urgent. On Thursday 29th November, the rights issue closed. I think it was then, and at your prompting, that New Hampshire decided to buy shares not taken up at the closing price on Monday 3rd December. Exposure of Don Flitton in that day's papers would reduce the perceived chances of an early merger. So it would push the IE price down, which would benefit New Hampshire and your reputation there. So you called Melissa and asked her to meet you that evening, on her own. When you met, you told her what she and Fred had to do the next evening, Friday 30th November. That was the price for your keeping quiet about their bogus clinic."

"Pete, this is all nonsense. None of it happened," Paul said, gently.

"Yes, it did happen. During our journey to Cambridge on the Saturday morning, you must have been amused to hear Morag's account. On the other hand, you must have been worried to hear that she was going to the hockey final, though as usual you didn't show it. Liz had told Carol that Fred was planning to be there – you and Carol stayed to lunch only when you heard that he would be late. Would Morag and Fred recognise each other? In fact, Morag did recognise Fred, but he wasn't paying much attention to anyone. He looked very worried and distracted."

"Now you remind me, I remember Morag's account. She only met this man outside, in the dark. Maybe he looked rather like Fred Perkins."

"She recognised him clearly enough that she went back to London straight after the match because by then she knew that Sheila was worried that someone had been at the files. She found that their file copy of the Linda Flitton letter had been moved, which suggested that a copy had been taken. During the next morning, Sunday, there was a lot of press interest in Don Flitton, stirred up by Roy Delaval's chum Luke Allnutt. There were hints of a big story about to break. However, at lunchtime this faded away. By then, of course, Fred Perkins had killed himself."

"You know very well that press stories can appear out of nothing and then disappear as quickly. For example, I remember now that, on that same Sunday morning, Carol was faced with a barrage of press enquiries about her time as a leader of student protests in Cambridge. Those fizzled out by lunchtime, too. I certainly remember being shocked when you told me later that day what had happened to Greg and how Fred Perkins couldn't face up to it. I'll say again, Pete, how great it's been that since then, and especially now, you're looking after Liz and young Jenny."

"It's been great for me, too. What happened then sent my life in the direction it needed to go. It prompted me to make the right decision – to leave IE and concentrate on Creators Technology. So I'm not angry with you, Paul; indeed I'm very grateful to you, for reasons I'll explain. It's time, though, that you heard the whole story, for there are lessons to learn. To begin, why was Consolidated so passive during the rights issue? In particular, why did Don Flitton seem so weak?"

"Everyone was saying he'd not been the same man since his wife died."

"Don knew that if Consolidated went for IE the letter would come out. Morag had passed me a copy, for use if necessary. Necessity arose on the day we launched the issue. Nigel Thompson told me that, if I didn't come quietly, my involvement in 'Plain Jane's' would be all over the papers. So I gave him a copy of the letter to show that if attacked I could retaliate. He would have shown it to Lord Cunliffe. Neither of them would have shown it to Roy Delaval. However, rumours would have caught Roy's ear by the time you contacted him. He would have been very pleased to hear that you might be able to get him a copy."

"If Fred Perkins and this woman did do what you say, I guess we'll never know why. Perhaps they knew Roy Delaval. If he'd heard of the letter, he could have put them onto it himself."

"That's what I encouraged Morag to believe. However, Roy would have got them moving earlier in November in the hope that he could blackmail Don into showing some spine. Let's move on. Later on the day of the match, I stayed in Waterhouse and there met Clive Salzburger. Do you remember him?"

"No."

"Somehow we got to talking about James Harman and that he rarely laughed. Clive showed me a photo he had of one occasion when James did laugh. In 1975, you and Steph were at a party New Hampshire threw at the end of a conference in New York. Clive had won a place at the conference. James was one of the speakers and Steph cracked a joke. The photo shows Clive with Steph, James and you."

"I remember that party, too, now you say. What of it?"

For the first time, there was a hint of unease in Paul's face. I knew that he had two reasons for unease.

"Clive told me he had passed the photo round after the Bump Supper the previous June, when there was a lot of ribaldry concerning some remarks James had made about rowing. Then, early in November, someone wrote to Clive, asking to borrow it for a few days – *someone who had been invited because years before he had done very well rowing for Waterhouse but hadn't been able to attend the Bump Supper then.*"

Paul was still just about in control of himself. "You mean…"

"Yes, Paul. The *Yorkshire Post* photo suggested to Fred and Melissa that Liz, Greg and I were involved with the woman who'd wrecked their game. But Liz and Greg were friends of theirs, and how could I be involved? Fred would have told Melissa that there was someone else who might take any chance to get at him. Back in 1968 he felt lucky that you hadn't identified him but he knew that lost memories could return, perhaps years later. Suddenly, a bell rang. Fred contacted Clive and asked to borrow the conference photo. When it arrived, snap. *You* – and the woman. They weren't going to take this lying down or, perhaps more accurately, Melissa wasn't going to take Steph's kick up the crotch lying down. So, whilst waiting for whoever it was might contact her, they worked out how to get their own back on you."

"I know from experience that Fred Perkins liked to get his own back but I don't recall him or anyone else trying to get back at me, Pete."

"You work behind the scenes, Paul. Your head isn't often over the parapet. They couldn't find any way of getting their own back on you directly but they spotted how to get at Steph. The frame of the photo refers to New Hampshire Realty Bank, so they looked up your Report and Accounts. Those confirmed that Steph and you were senior employees, showed them another picture of Steph and referred to her shareholding in 'Plain Jane's'. They could have found out what business that is. Perhaps someone Fred knew from his time at Guy's then practised in Aberdeen. They might have told him of Jane's strict no drugs policy, which keeps her out of trouble. So if Melissa could visit 'Plain Jane's' as a client and plant some drugs, and Fred perhaps via his colleague could tip off the local police and press, there could be a high-profile raid. Then, Steph's involvement could be publicised."

"That's an ingenious idea, Pete. As I say, you should be writing thrillers. I don't remember you or Steph saying that there'd been any trouble for 'Plain Jane's.'"

"There wasn't any, for reasons I'll come to in a minute. Melissa and Fred set their plan up for Saturday, 1st December. That way, news could be coming south on the Sunday and would link up with another plan of theirs. I'm sure you recall that at Cambridge Carol knew Cathy Slater, who was the source of so much bad feeling between Fred Perkins and Jerry Woodruff. Fred would have remembered what Cathy had told him about Carol, and some research in the press files of the time would have yielded more. On the Saturday, before travelling to Cambridge for the hockey match, Fred would present a dossier to various newspapers. It might include some information about you as Carol's husband now working for this American bank. When it came out alongside the stuff about 'Plain Jane's' and Steph, with any luck the two stories would feed on each other."

"You're suggesting that Fred Perkins might have inspired the press interest in Carol. Whoever inspired it, Carol handled it."

"Yes, but that's running ahead. By Thursday 29th, Melissa and Fred were ready to go with their two plans for the weekend. Then Melissa had a call from the person who had sent her the *Yorkshire Post* photo. They didn't know who that might be, other than that it was probably someone Fred had met, since she rather than him had been contacted; and now they knew it was a man. Melissa must have been surprised to recognise you from the conference photo but I'm sure she gave no sign. She was already a pretty accomplished actress. She decided to play you along, so she and Fred did what you wanted at the Pankhurst Centre. Their aim must have been to keep you quiet until their own stories burst and made anything you put round about them much less credible. I think that unwittingly you helped them with their aim. You asked them to hold on to the copy of the Linda Flitton letter during Saturday and to pass it to Luke Allnutt on Sunday morning. You expected to be driving back from Yorkshire then, so your hands would be quite clean. And so, on the Friday and Saturday, they carried through all that you and they had separately planned. However, two things went wrong for them."

"What do you suggest those were?"

"First, after the hockey match I moved fast. Morag thought she recognised Fred and her description of the wife fitted what I'd heard of Melissa. What could all this be about? Were they working for Consolidated? If so, could they have further assignments, directed at me? Nigel Thompson's earlier efforts had reminded me of my weak spot. I called Jane. Guess what? She'd just enjoyed herself lots, bringing off someone who answered to Melissa's description. Jane got rid of the planted drugs in the nick of time, before the cops arrived. Phew! So if you hadn't set up the business at the Pankhurst Centre for the Friday, then on the Saturday there would have been huge damage to 'Plain Jane's'. There would probably also have been huge damage to me when some reporter spotted my links with the place. That wasn't part of anyone's plan because Melissa and Fred didn't know of those links. It would have been unintended consequence number one. Fortunately, and thanks to you, Paul, it didn't happen. I'm very grateful."

"I'm glad you foiled them, Pete. I'm sure Steph would be, too. This all confirms that Fred Perkins was a pretty unpleasant type and frankly no loss to the world."

"As you can imagine, I was left pretty worried, and puzzled because Nigel Thompson, and presumably others in Consolidated, knew that if hit I could retaliate. I was very relieved when later that Saturday evening I saw the conference photo, which suggested that I wasn't the target. Then on Sunday, Carol was pestered, and Luke Allnutt set off press speculation about Don Flitton. So I guessed that Melissa and Fred had been going for you and Steph as best they could and had separately been working for Roy Delaval to get the Linda Flitton letter. Perhaps they knew him or perhaps they thought that removing Don Flitton would somehow be bad for New Hampshire. It was a rather muddled explanation. I could perhaps have puzzled it all out fully, but by the end of the Sunday I had other preoccupations and was certain nothing more would happen. That, of course, was because of the second thing that went wrong for Melissa and Fred – unintended consequence number two, which *did* happen."

"You mean, what happened to Greg."

"And what happened to Fred, too. He was just as much a victim as was Greg. After Fred left Cambridge, he kept himself under control and took forward his career. He realised that fucking every girl in sight wouldn't benefit that and maybe he came to grips with his sexuality. If he had found the right partner, he might have been able to go on, happily. Instead, he met Melissa, who dominated and used him. The bogus clinic was to gratify her. I expect that he was inwardly relieved when they had to close it down. Then the photo turned up. I'm sure that Melissa drove their response. In doing the tricky bit at the Pankhurst Centre, and the whole Aberdeen operation, she showed her stage skills and her determination. Fred did what he was told. On the Saturday morning after surgery he delivered the dossier on Carol to the press whilst Melissa was travelling to Aberdeen. In the evening, he had to meet her plane. He had promised Liz and Greg that he would be at the hockey match. He thought that he could just fit it in. He was hoping to have some break in the normal world. Then Greg was hurt. Fred should have insisted on a hospital check but that would have delayed him so he took a chance. Once it was shown to be the wrong chance, he could see only one way out. Melissa said as much to me."

"You've met her – this woman?"

"On the Sunday, she came to give Liz the apology that Fred couldn't give. She also gave another fine demonstration of her stage skills, even more than I realised at the time. I knew what she'd been up to, and had guessed the link to what had happened to Greg, but of course I didn't know that she knew that Liz and I knew Steph. I was able to suggest that if she wanted to move on she should try to become a professional actress and that she might well be able to pay for drama school by selling the sketches at which she is such a dab hand."

"Did she do the sketches we saw when we came over to your place?"

"Yes. The sketch of me was done while we talked that day. That of Angela Frampton was done after I put Melissa in touch with her for advice about selling work. The sketch which we said was being framed is back in place now. It's of Fred Perkins. Melissa had given it to Liz before all this happened. I've not seen Melissa since and I'm not going to contact her now but I know that she and Angela have become quite good friends, and that drama school is going well. I'm glad that Melissa is on the way to a career that could use her talents to good rather than harm.

I'm certainly glad, too, that she drew a thick line under what had happened. I guess she tore up her copy of the Linda Flitton letter. So that was the end of the story, and one of your failures, Paul. On the Monday, the IE share price went up rather than down. No wonder that the next April your bonus wasn't so good."

"Pete, I'm glad to hear what you and Angela Frampton have done for this woman Melissa but I'm really astonished that you've had time to build up these fantasies about what might have happened over two years ago. I know that you're under great stress so I'm listening politely, and I won't think any more of it."

"Oh yes you will, Paul. I've not come to my real point, yet. Dr Johnson said that the prospect of being hanged concentrates the mind marvellously. If awful things are pressing in on you, you need to concentrate on something else. That's what I did on Wednesday evening. I finally worked out almost all of what happened. The one missing piece went into place yesterday when Morag told me about the Pankhurst party. But that's all history. What you did in 1979 goes along with what you did to fund the Labour Party in 1974 and what you did to Harry Tamfield in 1967. It's done and can't be undone. As Pat O'Donnell said to both of us once, what's in the past stays in the past. I'm not interested in raking it over, except for how it tells me what's going on now."

"How does it tell you that?"

Paul was trying to sound disinterested but I knew he was following every word of mine intently.

"Who is in the conference photo, besides James, Steph, you and Clive Salzburger?"

"I don't remember. It was a big reception. There were lots of people there."

"Colin Mackay's office at Waterhouse told me that Clive is now in the Economics Department at the University of Maryland. Yesterday evening our time I got hold of him after a couple of tries. Yes, the other man in the photo is Hank Lechynski, who was then still at Chicago and had given some lectures on maths for economists. At the conference, Hank had spoken about developments in maths and computing, and Clive had spotted him at the reception. *Then Hank had noticed Steph. He told Clive that she had invited him to speak and had previously given him a research contract. He took Clive over to meet Steph, and so they were in the photo. That's where I had seen Hank Lechynski before.*"

"What are you suggesting, Pete?"

"I'm not suggesting, I'm *saying* that the Diechenbach paper is a fake – not just a plant, a fake. It's not a fairly crude fake like Carl Obermeyer's 'thesis', remember that? But it's a fake, nevertheless. Someone with a copy of my work has been careful to change the presentation and the notation thoroughly. They've even made a few variations of method. With guidance from Lechynski, Diechenbach was quite able to do that for a modest fee. The fake paper hasn't been circulated widely, because its authors don't want publicity for the same reasons as we don't. But Kraftlein received it from someone, probably a chum of Lechynski's at another American university. The idea is clear enough. We contact Parker Horstmann and discover what seems to be work in progress comparable to ours. So we decide to link up. Then, Parker Horstmann sells its stake to New Hampshire, or maybe it's taken over. One way or another, New Hampshire ends up in control."

"This is very fanciful, Pete. If people plotted with everyone they met years ago, there would be a lot of plots going on."

"True enough. If on Wednesday you had referred to meeting Lechynski, I might not have picked this up. But you didn't do that, for you wanted to conceal New Hampshire's connection with him. So there it is, Paul. New Hampshire *won't* bag Creators Technology. There *won't* be a big feather in your cap and a big bonus for you. This time, I've spotted your plot whilst I can do something about it."

"Such as?"

"There's been a lapse in your homework, Paul. It was a good idea that the paper wasn't sent to a mainline journal in the subject area but you didn't take proper account of the fact that the Editor of *Statistica* is Professor Simon Frampton. I can use my connections when I need to, which isn't very often. So I'm refereeing the paper. I'll be polite but I'm sure we'll see nothing further of it and nor will anyone else. At the Creators Technology board meeting on Tuesday week, I'll refer to a further talk with Kraftlein, whether or not I've been able to contact him before then. I'll say that we should ignore the Diechenbach paper and foil any other challenges by bringing forward the Version 0 launch to July. You'll support that and make sure that Sheila agrees with you."

"Will you have the time to lead the work for an earlier launch?"

"Yes. The main reason I called Morag yesterday was to accept her offer to keep house for me over the next few months."

"So Morag has a soft spot for you, Pete, as well as for Carol."

"Paul, I want to keep this conversation calm. Don't say things that make me want to hit you. I know that you haven't a soft spot for anyone. To continue, at the end of the meeting on Tuesday week, you'll resign from the Board. You might quote possible conflict of interest but I don't really care what you say. You're welcome to continue as a shareholder and to exercise the option you have to buy more shares. So, financially, you won't lose. That's right, in view of your intellectual contribution to where we are. But when Frank Booth is back I'll ask him to draw up a confidential document for you to sign. By doing so, you'll undertake to follow any request I make as to how you cast your vote at any general meeting. So you'll be right out of the running of Creators Technology – for good."

"What if I don't do what you want?"

"As I've said, your game of two years ago is all history to me. I suspect, though, that you never told either Steph Coolidge or Louis Demaire about it. I know where you would be if they knew the truth. And you know. And you know I know."

Paul remained silent, so I went on.

"I said earlier what your strongest qualities are, Paul. Well used, they achieve plenty, like the oil trading profits, but they tempt you into complicated schemes which don't always deliver what you planned. That's your big weakness. In Cambridge, your deal with the Framptons led to you being badly hurt and then running the Waterhouse JCR very differently from your original plan, though perhaps better. You could have got there with a lot less trouble. No-one will ever know what difference the Labour donations made in 1974 but if Harry Tamfield had exposed them whilst Heath was still Prime Minister, goodness knows what would have happened. Two years ago, you were almost scheming for scheming's sake. There was clearly an element of fun in manipulating your enemy. The objective of depressing New Hampshire's buy-in price turned up only as you went along. Now, you've tried to bag Creators for New Hampshire in this complex way, rather than making an offer to buy us out at, say, five times par. Well, I've had enough of your schemes. I want to stay friends but I don't want to do business with you anymore."

"I know that some of the things you say I've done have hit you pretty hard, Pete."

"That isn't the point, Paul. Really, it isn't the point. You've touched off changes in my life which were brewing up in my mind and which have turned out right for me. At Cambridge, I seemed to be on a kind of golden escalator but it was taking me on a road to nowhere. You sparked my decision to join IE. I became a director of IE at thirty-three and seemed well set. Actually, though, I was realising that my real talent was in building things up, as I'd done in Spain and in Aberdeen, rather than in running an established, large operation with thousands of employees. I was also feeling lonely. What you did put Creators Technology onto its way and gave me a happy personal life. What's happened to Liz now would have happened anyway. So I'm not angry or resentful about anything you've done that affects me. I would have been very angry and resentful if your latest scheme had succeeded, but it hasn't succeeded."

There was a knock, and Paul's secretary came in.

"I'm sorry to disturb you but there's an urgent call for Mr Bridford. Shall I put it through?"

I nodded, full of fear as to the most likely reason for the call. "Of course," said Paul. I picked up the phone, to a cheerful voice.

"Ed here, Pete. Jean told me where you'd gone. We have several local NUM results. They all point to a national strike vote well below 55%."

"That's without South Wales."

"South Wales would have to go over 90% to get the national vote over 50%. It's being said that with the mess they're in down there, the Fed[86] will be lucky to get over 55% themselves."

"Yorkshire?"

"It looks to be around 70%. You see what I mean?"

"Yes, I do. We're saved. Very well done, Ed."

There was a pause before Ed replied.

"Thanks, but your help was invaluable, Pete."

Ed's was the confident voice of someone whose career was right on track. It wouldn't be forgotten that at the crucial meeting with Nigel Lawson he had been closest to what the actual result would be.[87] And he was ready. He had worked out the strategy that would be needed to win, perhaps in two or three years' time.

"Thanks for letting me know, Ed. Have a good weekend. I'm in next on Tuesday. Meanwhile Jean can find me, but I think my involvement with coal is coming to an end."

I rang off. "That sounds like interesting news," said Paul.

---

86 The historic term for the South Wales NUM.
87 The final figure for the strike vote was 45%.

"Yes, many people will be very relieved. They certainly include me, if only because I'll be able to cut my time at the department back to the day and a half a week I'm paid for."

"I guess the news will be out pretty quick. Carol and I are going up to Yorkshire early tomorrow."

"There's no problem about passing it on."

"Pete, what you were saying actually fits with how I now need to spend my time out of the office. Within a few weeks I'll have my main residence in Beaconsfield and I may have much to do in the Labour Party there before long. Rumours are flying about the Tory MP. Will his dicky heart or his extramarital affairs get him first? We need to be ready. There's no prospective candidate and I've spotted just the man. He's young, energetic, articulate, presentable and a great admirer of the novels of P.G. Wodehouse. I think he could go a very long way."

"How did you meet him?"

"New Hampshire put some legal business to a new set of chambers. At its Christmas party, this man and his wife sought us out. They're both interested in standing. They knew that Carol won in '74 through picking up a lot of people who had never voted Labour before. They were both pleased to have some inside stuff from her."

"Not *too* much inside stuff, I hope, Paul."

"The wife comes over as more committed to Labour than he is. In fact, Carol tried to recruit him but like me he's absolutely sure that it's right to stay with Labour and update its policies. So he's the man for a first try in Beaconsfield and it will suit me to cut down my involvement with Creators Technology."

"Good. Your departure can be announced as part of changes in Board structure, to cope with growth. Before he went away, Pat called me with some suggestions which I think are right. Chris Rowan now has a big enough shareholding to be on the Board. With me, Chris and Jenny should form an executive group. The other directors should be more clearly non-executive and focussed on the inputs they can make. Brian is there to bring independent business expertise and so is Sheila."

"Sheila?"

"She's created a successful small business. The budget of the Pankhurst Centre is now nearly £100,000 and is growing fast. On Wednesday, I was impressed by a couple of her insights."

"She won't like you calling it a business."

"The fact that it's helping people doesn't stop it from being a business."

"It's interesting you say that. My man for Beaconsfield wants to see more social help provided through funded voluntary activity."

"You'd better introduce him to Sheila. Going back to our Board, we already have Tony Higgins to bring academic and research expertise, and we need Morag, too. Her research interest is now close to what we're doing. Sheila is doing less research because of the amount of time she spends on the Pankhurst Centre. I wouldn't be surprised if she leaves academic life in a year or two."

"Those all seem good ideas to me. I assume they are in confidence."

"Yes, though I'll be talking them through on the phone over the weekend. Paul, I'm glad we're ending this way. I'd better give you a few minutes before your next meeting." We shook hands.

I came outside to find that something felt different. By the time I reached Moorgate Underground, the change was evident. The wind had backed round and was mild, not cold. My drive home from Morden was through slush, though I had to avoid cascades of wet snow from trees.

Six weeks before, an unexpected blizzard had brought on the crisis. Now, an unexpected thaw marked its end for the country, though not for Liz.

To save us, something had needed to turn up, and it had.

"It's good news," were my first words to Liz.

"Yes, I know; it was on the six o'clock news."

There was brightness, even happiness, certainly pride, showing on her face, strained as it was.

"Well done, well done so much, Liz. You've made the difference that you always wanted to make."

"Well done you, too, Pete, and well done Carol. We can link her with a celebration. Jenny is over with Stephanie for tea. You need to collect her in ten minutes. On the way, buy something bubbly and good. Once Jenny is in bed, I've had one glass and some food, and we've watched *Fame is the Spur*, I think I'll be up for it, Carol's way."

And so she was, crouched across the bed in the position where she coughed least. Afterwards, memories drifted back as I held her in my arms.

Over fifteen years, we had come together, moved apart and come together again. We had been the sister and brother neither of us had. Then, for two years, we had been fully together. *Our*[88] child would mark that.

The TV serialisation brought to mind once again an eventful evening in Cambridge, long ago – the evening that had ended with Morag missing her last chance to go straight and my rescuing Carol. Earlier in the evening, Liz had said that none of the characters in *Fame is the Spur* actually wanted fame in itself. They wanted to achieve and to make a difference, some for themselves and some for others. That was what drove people forward in real life.

She had been right. Those were the qualities of Creators. She was a Creator, and was demonstrating that now, to the greatest extent possible.

She was giving her life for our future.

She had been my first. Would she be my last?

---

[88] As in due course DNA testing confirmed.

HOUSE OF COMMONS, 2nd APRIL, 1982

Dr Owen. Surely if any Argentinian soldier, sailor or air force man has landed on the Falkland Islands the House must be recalled. That is the assurance that we need and it has not actually been given by the Leader of the House. The government must accept that many of us have exercised great restraint on this issue, which has been running since the end of February. Clear warnings have been given of a dangerous situation.

HOUSE OF COMMONS, 3rd APRIL, 1982

The Prime Minister. Before indicating some of the measures that the government has taken in response to the Argentine invasion, I should like to make three points. First, even if ships had been instructed to sail the day that the Argentines landed on South Georgia to clear the whaling station, the ships could not possibly have got to Port Stanley before the invasion. (*Interruption.*) Opposition Members may not like it, but that is a fact.

Secondly, there have been several occasions in the past when an invasion has been threatened. The only way of being certain to prevent an invasion would have been to keep a very large fleet close to the Falklands, when we are some 8,000 miles away from base. No government has ever been able to do that and the cost would be enormous.

Mrs Carol Milverton (Holtcliffe). Will the Right Honourable lady say what has happened to HMS *Endurance*?

The Prime Minister. HMS *Endurance* is in the area. It is not for me to say precisely where, and the Honourable Member would not wish me to do so.

Dr Owen. There is no question of anyone in the House weakening the stance of the government but the Prime Minister must now examine ways of restoring the government's authority and ask herself why Britain has been placed in such a humiliating position during the past few days. The Right Honourable lady said that it would have been absurd to send forces but I do not agree. It would have been the right decision a month ago. The absence of that decision has meant humiliation. The House must now resolve to sustain the government in restoring the position.

HOUSE OF COMMONS, 14th JUNE, 1982

The Prime Minister. On a point of order, Mr Speaker. May I give the House the latest information about the battle of the Falklands? After successful attacks last night, General Moore decided to press forward. The Argentines retreated. Our forces reached the outskirts of Port Stanley. Large numbers of Argentine soldiers threw down their weapons. They are reported to be flying white flags over Port Stanley. Our troops have been ordered not to fire except in self-defence. Talks are now in progress between General Menendez and our deputy commander, Brigadier Waters, about the surrender of the Argentine forces on East and West Falkland. I shall report further to the House tomorrow.

Dr Owen. Further to the point of order, Mr Speaker. May I join the leader of the official Opposition and the leader of the Liberal Party in conveying the congratulations of the whole House to the Royal Navy, the Army, the Royal Air Force and the Royal Marines, and to the government and all the ministers who played a crucial role in the achievement of an extremely successful outcome? I wish all well, especially – thinking of those who have lost their lives – those families who are currently grieving tonight for their sacrifice. The sacrifice of their loved ones was a sacrifice which was necessary for all.

HOUSE OF COMMONS, 15ᵗʰ JUNE, 1982

Mr George Gardiner. In the light of today's marvellous news, will my Right Honourable friend study the precedent set by the Prime Minister and the Monarch in May 1940 and consider the designation of a Sunday very soon as a national day of prayer and thanksgiving for our success in freeing the Falkland Islands?

The Prime Minister. Of course we shall consider that, but I believe that throughout our land this day and the coming Sunday everywhere there will be thanksgiving.

Concluding celebration of Liz and Greg's lives
Tune: Maccabeus

Hail, we salute ye, bonded evermore,
As we share our mem'ries, face what is in store;
Those of us remaining, re-affirming life,
Theirs to leave together, now the end of strife.

As we commit them, to eternal rest,
Each and all of us here, know they were the best;
In this tragic moment, it is to us plain,
Rare is climb to glory, without struggles main.

From selfless efforts, boundless triumphs flow,
For us an example, of the way to go;
As inspiring story, both their parts were played,
Long to be remembered, for the diff'rence made.

Hail, we salute thee, bonded evermore,
As we share our mem'ries, face what is in store.

Commendation and Farewell
Blessing
Final Music: *Spitfire Fugue* (Walton)

Liz and Greg's families are grateful for your support at this time, and invite you to refreshments at the Red Lion Hotel. Many of you will recall that as the location of the reception which followed their wedding in this church in 1974.

The Committal will take place at 3.30 pm, at Hendon Crematorium, North Chapel. It will be taken by the Revd. Timothy Woolley, Greg's father. You are welcome to join us if you wish.

During her last weeks, Liz followed avidly the developing success of HM armed forces in the Falklands. She requested that music be played here which is a tribute to them. Donations to service charities are invited in memory of Liz and Greg.

EPILOGUE

TUESDAY, 15TH JUNE, 1982

Liz died early on 5th June, a Saturday. So I had not been able to do anything about the funeral straight away. As it turned out, that was fortunate.

Later that day, I visited Greg. I didn't stay for long but said just that I knew so well how happy Liz had been with him. The next morning, the hospital called me. Greg had died, peacefully, during the night. Perhaps that was final confirmation that, though unable to respond, he had understood what he had heard. He had known that people still cared about him but, now, he had nothing left to live for.

So it became clear to me where we should say farewell. The minister was new, but the organist was unchanged from 1974 and was ready to repeat his bravura contribution to Liz and Greg's wedding. He had begun with 'O God, our Help on Ages Past', a favourite for both Liz and Greg. At the end, I could sense some surprise when Handel's great tune blazed out, but the numbers there drove the line along and by the third verse the organist was able to let rip on the trumpet stop.

The minister's final words were slightly interrupted by gurgles from two-month-old Joseph, held comfortingly in Morag's arms. Then the front row began to file out. First, Lorna and Timothy Woolley, who both looked worn but perhaps relieved that the long drawn out tragedy in their lives had come to an end. Sir Stephen Partington followed, looking as vague as ever; and then Timothy's older sister and her husband. Finally, Morag and I turned to leave, little Jenny holding my hand. Only children have few relatives.

The two hundred or so people facing me encompassed almost all of my adult life. Only Steph was missing – really sorry, but a big meeting in Los Angeles. My original plan had been to put all Creators in the second row, so that they would follow the families out, but Jenny hadn't wanted that because her mother and all her Frampton cousins would be there; also, Ana was coming over and would be with them. I could just see them all together, grouped in a rather dark part of the church. I was impressed that Amanda and presumably John had taken the trouble to attend. John had known me at Cambridge, but they had not met Liz often and had met Greg only once. I could not see John but I noticed another face in the group and was relieved that it showed no sign of surprised recognition.

As soon as we were outside, Timothy was spelling out the message I intended.

"That was so comforting, Pete. How you and Morag must have worked, to arrange it all in the time. Your words so marvellously reflected Greg's determination to win that match, and Liz's determination to bring your child into the world."

"They're very right for today, too," said Frank, looking smart in his RAF blazer. "Liz was brave. We've seen that fortune shines on the brave."

"There weren't many dry eyes when the coffins came in to the *Spitfire Prelude*," said Roberta. "For those of us who lived through the War, that music means a lot. I know the plot of the film is rubbish but it's wonderful rubbish. It's so right for now, in every way. Liz gave up any chance so that Joseph could live."

"It's good enough rubbish that the Germans murdered its star,"[89] said Frank.

Only three people there understood the true significance of the words I had fitted to the tune but most agreed that its triumphant E major much suited the day. That was pure luck. I had settled the order of service on the previous Thursday, when news of the Argentine air strike at Bluff Cove had just come through. The result remained not in doubt, but looked to be delayed. The final cave-in had come as a pleasant surprise to our forces, and indeed to Mrs Thatcher.

"Yes, Pete, we're both so proud of you," said my mother. "We're so grateful to you, too, Morag, for being so helpful over all this time."

Roberta had doubtless primed my parents to be welcoming to Morag. Their fairly obvious expectation was one which until three days before I had come to share.

Early in February, Liz had gone into intensive pre-natal care in hospital. There was discussion of an induced early delivery but Liz insisted on going to term, as best for the baby. She went into labour whilst we listened on the radio to the emergency debate precipitated by the invasion of the Falklands. We had wondered whether Carol would get in but she waited for the longer debate three days later.

With support, Liz was able to feed for the first few crucial weeks but from early May she was failing. She was moved to a hospice and little Joseph came home. Until then, Morag had been staying with the Booths during the week. She had looked after little Jenny, whilst I combined visits to Liz with being an industrial advisor and leading work towards the launch of what was now called 'Tradeit Version 0'. But a four-week-old motherless baby needs day and night attention, including making up the proper feeds with scrupulous

---

[89] The 1942 film *The First of the Few* is a very fictionalised account of the life of R.J. Mitchell, and of his early death, supposedly through over-work on the design of the Spitfire. Its star, Leslie Howard, was killed when the unarmed plane he was travelling in was intercepted and shot down by German long-range fighters sent out for that specific purpose.

care. Morag had to move in. She offered to have Joseph's cot in the bedroom she was using, so that I had proper sleep.

Three days before, we were both up in the small hours; Morag for Joseph and I for Jenny, tearful because she would never see her parents again. I assured her that I would look after her. 'You and Auntie Morag? I like her', was the response. I was back in bed just a week after Liz had died. Then Morag crept in.

Half an hour later, we were much more relaxed as, head on my waist, she tasted the last few drops and I continued to enjoy the view of her athletic back whilst fingering gently between her legs. She was the first to say anything.

"That was good. We both needed it."

"We can do even better, Morag. I'm not the only one to hope for that."

"I know what Roberta would like to happen, yes."

"Jenny would like it, too."

Morag turned over and kissed me. "Pete, you're the only man I could ever go with, but it can't be."

"I know you don't want to let Sheila down."

"This has been all over your face for the last week. I know that Liz would have liked it to happen, and I'm sure you know that, too. I've talked it through with Sheila, and she wouldn't stand in the way. But it wouldn't work."

"Why wouldn't it work?"

"I've promised not to say, but you'll find out on Tuesday. I'd better go now."

There had been no time since then to talk further or for me to contemplate how I was to carry on when Morag's sabbatical ended. Each day was another day.

"Very uplifting, Pete, thank you. When I heard the little one, I offered up another prayer."

A soft voice behind me brought me back to the present. I knew it well enough. Six weeks before, its owner had made a quiet visit to Liz, held Joseph in his arms for a few minutes, and left. Again now, he was gone.

"Good heavens, was that –?" said my father.

"Yes. Liz did work for the NUM for several years. Some others from there are here. I guess he didn't want to be recognised too widely, especially now he's a peer.[90] Ah, he won't escape so easily. The Secretary of the Coal Board is catching him up."

"He seemed almost in tears," said Frank.

"By all accounts, he's an emotional man. Gosh, where are Jenny's party? Perhaps they're still in the church. Dick may want a little time with Liz's coffin. He was her first and he didn't get to see her much near the end. He kept getting bugs which meant he couldn't visit. Well, they know the way. I'll take the three Sirs along."

"Morag, we'll look after the children so you can go round, too," said Roberta. "There are so many here. Gerald can help Timothy with Lorna."

I joined Arthur Gulliver and Pat O'Donnell, who were being helpful by looking after Stephen Partington. Once inside the Red Lion, I was swept around the room, trying to thank as many as possible for attending. Fortunately most had found something to talk about to others. 'How did you come to know the deceased?' is a reasonable opener on these occasions but others are possible, as evinced by Susie and Brian being with Ed Plunkett and Maureen Johnson. Susie was most interested in the engagement ring Maureen was now wearing but the two couples would have fallen into conversation through Ed and Brian noticing each other's interest in the early leaver. It didn't matter what they now put together. I had taken accumulated holiday to finish at the department by the middle of May.

"Great stuff, Pete. You done 'em proud." Jane was with Laura, Claire and a couple of others from the Sales Office. They had flown down together from Aberdeen.

---

90 That had been announced in the Birthday Honours on 11th June.

"I promised Liz a good send-off. I guess I'm not the first, or the last, to get through bereavement by throwing myself into funeral arrangements."

Carol buttonholed me. Paul and Ana were with her. "Pete, so well done, but I must dash. The Prime Minister's statement is at 3.30."

"Are you hoping to be called?"

"There's not much chance, but no chance at all unless I'm in a decent place by 2.45. See you later, Ana."

"Carol has obtained a gallery ticket for me," explained Ana. "Pete, I have so admired Liz's fortitude. I met her only once but she played her part then and I owe her much for that. Your words about making a difference are quite right."

"Liz always wanted to make a difference."

"As you all do. Jenny also has made a difference for me and is also showing such fortitude. Pete, there is a tall woman looking at me. She seems very startled. She has seen a ghost, I think are the words. I do not recall meeting her."

I was wondering what Ana meant about Jenny's fortitude, but I glanced round.

"No, you've never met her, Ana. She must have been looking at someone else. I think she's leaving now. I'm glad that Carol has got you in for the statement. During the last few weeks, responsible Spanish opinion has been very important."

"You've had your own preoccupations," said Paul. "It was a surprise when Felipe Gonzalez[91] won the Andalusian regional elections."

"Yes. I am not a supporter of Señor Gonzalez but his victory is of assistance to those of us who wish for the formation of an effective, constitutional conservative party in Spain. It will also be very useful for me to return saying that I was present to hear *la señora Thatcher* on this day. She has astonished our people,

---

91 His party, the PSOE (Spanish Socialist Workers' Party), had won these late in May. It went on to a convincing victory in national elections in October.

perhaps in the same way as did your first Queen Elizabeth. So I am sorry that I cannot stay here very long, and I must now make a comfort visit. When shall we leave, Paul?"

"In about fifteen minutes."

"If before we leave you could introduce me to Liz's father, I shall pay my respects."

Ana moved away. "Good luck to her," said Paul.

"Paul, your coolness never ceases to amaze me. Melissa Copehurst was looking at *you*, not at Ana. I'm sure she remembers meeting you very clearly, and much more clearly than she remembers meeting Morag, Sheila or Jane. But enough of that – despite all your efforts, and Bell's heart and affairs *both* catching up with him, your man lost his deposit!"[92]

"It was inevitable, given the war and the SDP people going with the Libs. He's done well and will have a decent seat for the general election. Labour won't be back for a while, but when they are back, he'll be on top, or at least on his way there. He's the future for Labour."

Whilst he waited for Ana, Paul made across to a Cambridge group, including Nick Castle and a frail-looking Tom Farley, but I was not alone for long.

"Oh Pete, how are you bearing up? It's been so dreadful for you."

This was Brenda Murton, with Alan, young Stephanie and a babe-in-arms, and amidst a crowd of friends we had made in Bellinghame. After them, there were some I remembered from the hockey match in Cambridge. That led me to thanking more of Liz and Greg's friends from St Albans days. Next to several youngsters in the Creators Technology team, one of whom compared the frantic pace of building Spitfires, which is what

---

[92] The Beaconsfield by-election was held on 27th May, following the sudden death of the sitting MP, Sir Ronald Bell, whilst in the arms of his mistress in his Commons office. The result: Blair (Labour) 3,886; Smith (Conservative) 23,049; Tyler (Liberal) 9,996.

the Fugue accompanies on screen, with the frantic pace of work towards our launch. They left so as to be back in Crawley in time for plenty more work that day. I went on or, in terms of my career, back to another International Consolidated group, and did not omit Albert Simpson who had split off to reminisce with Frank. I had a few words with Roy Brampton; in January, he had intervened with the management of our local hospital, to mention that there were reasons not to stint on Liz's treatment. Then it was on, and on, and on...

Brian and Susie had joined the Cambridge group but now they cut across to me.

"Pete, I'll catch up in a day or two but, sorry, we can't stay now. Leninspart[93] won't allow a Victory Parade through London, but his word doesn't go in the City. The Corporation will have its own. There's a meeting later. If I play my cards right, I'll be on the organising committee."

"I'm sure that Liz and Greg would have wanted a good parade, Brian."

"It's more than that, Pete. The opportunity can't be missed. Remember the impact of that overbump on people at Waterhouse. We made more effort and got better results. It was a turnaround for us at Waterhouse. Winning this war could lead to a turnaround for the whole country."

Brian had said more than he knew. In 1968, Liz had urged on the crew who made the overbump. Now, her sacrifice had allowed victory. One day, that would need to be recognised and commemorated.

I joined the Cambridge group. After the usual condolences Nick had an unexpected question.

"How did Liz come to know Melissa Copehurst?"

---

[93] The usual nickname then for Ken Livingstone, who became Leader of the Greater London Council in May 1981 through a *coup* that deposed the moderate leader under whom Labour had obtained a majority. 'Dave Spart' was a character from the *Private Eye* of the 1970s – a student activist who made very lengthy and convoluted speeches.

"She was a nurse at the doctors' practice Liz and Greg used when they lived near St Albans. Fred Perkins was one of the doctors. I expect you all remember him."

"Yes, he was a very tragic loss," said Tom, rather vacantly and with less tact than I recalled him having. Nick continued, quickly.

"I've met Melissa only once but she made an impression on me, and on about five hundred other people. In April, Helen was playing Lady Macbeth at Coventry. As usual I went over for the last night, so as to bring her home afterwards, but I arrived to find that she'd scratched, with laryngitis. So she, I and the rest of the audience heard the understudy, straight out of drama school. Melissa won't lack work in her new career. Helen gasped that a Star was born, and she doesn't say that often."

"I've also only met Melissa once but she made an impression on me then. Having seen her act, I encouraged her to think about going professional."

"Well done. I'm sorry to have missed talking to her but it's a good sign that she's dashed off. She must be needed."

So it had happened again. Harry Tamfield had died and Carol Milverton was born. Fred Perkins had died and Melissa Copehurst was born. How would it go on? Liz and Greg had died. Who would now be born?

After a few more farewells I had a moment to grab some refreshment and contemplate the crowd. Some of Jenny's party were now here, though not her or Dick. A good sign for Morag's relationship with Sheila was that both of them were talking to Angela, though their conversation looked to be rather earnest. I wondered whether they had noticed Melissa, That didn't seem likely; three years before they had met her only briefly in the semi-darkness outside the Pankhurst Centre. Nevertheless it was a good thing that Paul had scared Melissa away before Angela had had any opportunity to introduce her, or before Jane's memory was stirred.

I also wondered whether Jenny and Dick were being detained by their children. Jenny had once or twice intimated at problems with them as another reason for visiting alone. Indeed, Jenny herself had not visited the hospice often and I had not seen her since the Creators Technology AGM, three weeks before.

Another from Jenny's party disturbed me. "Pete, my condolences."

"Thanks, Geoff. I'm glad you were able to come."

"Although it didn't work out between me and Liz, I thought a lot of her."

"I know you did."

"Belinda said that you were running a small computer company."

"That's right. It's small but expanding."

I moved quickly to offering belated congratulations on his election to the Royal Society three years before. For a couple of minutes we circled around each other, in conversational terms. I noticed Belinda enter the room with Penny Frampton, David and Katie. There was still no sign of Jenny or Dick. Belinda left the children with Penny and joined us.

"Pete, you need to be ready for a shock."

"I'm rather used to those, one way and another."

"Just before Christmas, Dick had a letter from Russ Halstrom."

"Who's he?"

"He *was* the man you met on the beach at San Francisco nearly three years ago. He was writing to everyone he could remember being with, to say that he was dying, of something awful which broke out there last year. It seems to be passed on when men have flings with each other, though as far as we know it doesn't spread any other way, thank God. It takes some time to develop but then your resistance to almost any disease breaks down."

"It's called GRID – Gay Related Immune Deficiency," said Geoff, rather unpleasantly.

"Around that time, Dick started going down with a series of bugs which he couldn't throw off easily. Jenny and he decided not to tell people very much, in the hope that someone would come up with a cure. But now, Dick has something called Karposi's Syndrome. He's been to a big London hospital, the best in the country for this, but they don't know what to do. Nor does anyone Geoff has spoken to. Over the last few weeks, it's got much worse. Dick wanted to stay at home, so Amanda came down to look after him. He was determined to come along today and we sat where we wouldn't be seen. Then, at the end of the service, he just couldn't move. Angela noticed that Greg's mother was being wheeled over here so she came over and borrowed the chair. We've brought him across, but into a small room, over there. He doesn't want to be seen here. Amanda has to go back to Sheffield later today – John has been so good at looking after their children but tomorrow he's going to a conference in Vienna. She said that Dick must go into hospital now and Angela's friend Melissa, who used to be a nurse, said that, too. They called the hospital and an ambulance is on its way. I'm going to stay with Jenny for a few days so she can carry on with her job while she works something out. Dick wants to meet you, Pete, but you'll hardly recognise him."

Belinda took me into the room. Jenny was sitting beside Dick. She had taken care to be well turned out, in a new black outfit which set off her blonde hair very well. She gave me a glance of silent recognition.

There is no point in my describing the wreck of the handsome man I had known. You can look up pictures on the Internet of early cases of what was shortly afterwards renamed AIDS (Acquired Immune Deficiency Syndrome). The identification of the HIV virus and the beginnings of effective treatment were a year or more into the future.

After a pause, I did my best at a greeting.

"Dick, I'm really sorry you're so poorly but thanks so much for making the big effort to come. Liz and Greg would have appreciated it."

After another pause Dick just about managed to respond.

"Thanks, Pete, for everything you've done for me. You and Jenny won't save me this time, though. I'm sure you'll look after her."

Then, he dropped off to sleep.

Jenny and I looked at each other. Neither of us said anything for what seemed a very long time. It all fitted together in my mind.

Russ Halstrom's letter must have arrived on Christmas Eve. The night before, Jenny had been cheerful. At the opera, she had seemed worried. There, and back at Weybridge, I had had the impression that something was being held back.

In January, after the news about Liz, Jenny had seemed less worried but had still left something unsaid. Morag had told me that over Christmas she had been able to help Jenny and Dick, and then she had paused abruptly. Belinda had seemed quite matter of fact and positively relieved to know of Morag's continuing inclinations. She had not appeared to have known of Morag's Christmas stay. Ana had said how those who achieved could end up paying for it.

By the last Saturday, Morag would have known of how Dick's condition had worsened, and what I would find out today.

A tear ran down Jenny's face. A tear of what?

My mind raced back to 1968, when Jenny and I had saved Dick from his attempted suicide. I had given Jenny up, to him. Then, her tears had been of happiness.

I moved on to 1979 and a conversation with Steph. Dick's 'fling' in San Francisco had probably arisen from frustration at Jenny's welcome to my visit. It had condemned him to this lingering death.

Jenny knew that. I knew that. We each knew the other knew that.

I recalled saying to Belinda that she was underestimating her daughter's intellect and ruthlessness. I was right then, but she certainly understood Jenny now. That was evident in the message she had just given me – a coded message, for she did not want Geoff to understand it, but a clear message nonetheless.

Amanda was standing behind Dick, looking quite impassive. Last night, she and Ana would have shared the spare bedroom at the house in Weybridge. I wondered how much they had found out about each other.

Tonight, Belinda would take the spare bedroom. There was no doubt where Ana would and should be. In a two-way relationship between Creators, it was her turn to support and console.

On Saturday, I would visit Weybridge. Belinda would look after children whilst Jenny and I came together for good, in body and in mind.

Jenny would have her private corner. Indeed, I could follow the example of her brother John and sometimes join her in it. Ana would certainly relish that. I could have my private corner, too. Carol and Morag might well be found there, separately or quite possibly together.

For fourteen years, Jenny and I had taken our separate ways. Each way had been the right way. Now, the right way was our way, for both of us, for our children and for Creators Technology. We had come to understand each other fully. We were as smart, and as bad, as each other. Together, we would be two Stars.

This was the first day of the rest of our lives.

BUSINESS FM – your station for facts

TRANSCRIPT OF BROADCAST OF 'MUSICAL MEMORIES'
3.30 pm – 5.00 pm SUNDAY 22 NOVEMBER 2015

JOYCE LAIDLAW (*presenter*): On this programme, people who've made their names in business choose music associated with events in their life and you, listeners, can ask them questions by text, Twitter or email. Today, my guest is Sir Peter Bridford, founder of Creators Technology, which was worth £5 billion when in 1999 it became part of ICC. Yet, Sir Peter, you were good enough at maths to become a Fellow of your Cambridge College when you were only twenty-one. What made you move from academic to business life?

SIR PETER BRIDFORD: I wanted to make a difference in the real world. Then, that meant a move. Fifty years ago, Cambridge wasn't the hi-tech powerhouse it is now. It was very pleasant but it was deliberately cut off from the real world. Local industry was discouraged.

JOYCE LAIDLAW: You weren't tempted to go to the USA, as many others did at the time. I remember talk of the 'brain drain'.

SIR PETER BRIDFORD: A few years later, I might have done. A close friend was returning there and wanted me to go with her, but by then I was doing well at International Electronics, the company which contributed the I to ICC. At age thirty-three, I became a director. That involved much more effort than had winning a Fellowship at twenty-one. Creators Technology began as a side-line business, owned by several friends. I only left IE, and took the lead, when I saw that the maths I'd done in Cambridge could be used to develop trading software. In 1999, the formation of ICC brought me back.

JOYCE LAIDLAW: To become, it is said, the richest man in the country who was working for someone else.

SIR PETER BRIDFORD: Will Sanders proved that he was the right choice to lead ICC into the new millennium. Being Director for Technology and Development suited me. After thirty years of working absolutely flat out, I wanted to spend a little more time with my family, and on music.

JOYCE LAIDLAW: So you've been able to do that.

SIR PETER BRIDFORD: Yes. Music has always been important to me, mostly as a listener. I play the cello at a moderate, and I really mean moderate, level. My greatest boast must be that I've played in a quartet led by Bill Latham.

JOYCE LAIDLAW: That doesn't sound moderate at all.

SIR PETER BRIDFORD: This was long ago at Cambridge. Despite Bill's valiant efforts, we played Beethoven and lost.

JOYCE LAIDLAW: One piece you played is your first musical memory, the Quartet Opus 95.

SIR PETER BRIDFORD: Yes, here played properly, by Bill and others.

[Beethoven Op. 95 first movement, played by the Latham Quartet.]

JOYCE LAIDLAW: How did you come to be in that quartet?

SIR PETER BRIDFORD: One of the orchestras Bill led was managed by Harry Tamfield, who was at Waterhouse College with me. Harry played the violin about as well as I played the cello and we enjoyed playing in a quartet. The leader left and Harry persuaded Bill to take over for a few sessions. Talking of the orchestra Harry managed leads to my next memory.

JOYCE LAIDLAW: That's the first movement of Haydn's Symphony Number 102, and you've made a special request.

[Haydn Symphony No. 102, first movement, breaking off after two minutes.]

JOYCE LAIDLAW: We heard the Philharmonia Hungarica, conducted by Antal Dorati, but they do go on to finish it. Why did you ask to break it off?

SIR PETER BRIDFORD: Because that's what I heard at the last concert given by Harry's orchestra. Some radical students objected to the orchestra going on tour to Portugal, which was a dictatorship then. They burst in and smashed the concert up.

JOYCE LAIDLAW: Good heavens.

SIR PETER BRIDFORD: The orchestra folded and Harry gave up his plans to be a musical administrator. For a few years he did very well in the property business but in 1974 that, too, went wrong. Before he could sort it out, he was killed in the Paris air disaster, along with over 300 others.

JOYCE LAIDLAW: So, he was a might-have-been?

SIR PETER BRIDFORD: Yes. I've known several of them. They deserve to be remembered. I'm one of the lucky ones.

JOYCE LAIDLAW: You left Cambridge with a very good first degree but not with the doctorate you'd been working for.

SIR PETER BRIDFORD: I was already beginning to wonder where I was going. Then IE offered me a very good job. After I decided to accept, I needed to relax, so I went to watch the inter-college rowing races. I never rowed myself but I knew Liz Partington very well. Her father was Master of Waterhouse and she was a kind of mascot for the College Boat Club. That afternoon, the crew of a boat named after her made an overbump, taking it up three places in the order. I'd not then ever heard my next piece. When I did hear it, I recalled rushing along the bank with Liz, shouting encouragement.

JOYCE LAIDLAW: The last movement of Shostakovich's Tenth Symphony? Most people associate it with rejoicing after the death of Stalin.

SIR PETER BRIDFORD: It's good enough music to inspire all sorts of interpretations. In particular, this passage building from *piano* to *forte-fortissimo* conjures up for me a rowing eight coming into sight round a bend in the river and then battling through stress and pain to chase a nearly impossible target, with the final strokes as they succeed.

[Shostakovich Symphony No. 10, figures 176 to 184 in the score.]

JOYCE LAIDLAW: That was the now classic version of the USSR Symphony Orchestra, conducted by Yevgeny Svetlanov. You say in particular that passage, but perhaps there is more in it, for you.

SIR PETER BRIDFORD: The movement's opening *Andante* reflects my state of mind on that day. There were also personal reasons for my decision to leave Cambridge. I've rarely done anything important for only one reason.

JOYCE LAIDLAW: So, you went off to work for International Electronics.

SIR PETER BRIDFORD: I was thrown in at the deep end but I survived, and a few years later I was building their business in Spain. There I made another good friend – Ana Guzman, who eventually became Minister of Economic Development in the Aznar Government of a few years back. That leads straight on to my next piece, for I first met her quite by chance, at a performance of *Don Giovanni*. Even then she had the force of personality that her namesake displays, for example in this aria. *[Donna Anna's Act I aria.]*

JOYCE LAIDLAW: There we heard Birgit Nilsson, with the Vienna Philharmonic conducted by Erich Leinsdorf. That's an unusual piece of casting.

SIR PETER BRIDFORD: It probably reflects whom Decca had under contract, but Nilsson suits my view of the part. Anna is putting some spine into her useless fiancé, Ottavio. She's probably about nineteen. Obviously her mother is dead. She is sexually assaulted, her father is murdered, and soon she realises that the criminal is a man she had trusted. In my view, the opera is about her response and growth. She builds a team from those available, to wit, Ottavio, scatty Elvira and an enterprising couple from a different social class. By the end, she's strong enough to hold Ottavio off for a year in the hope that, as a wealthy heiress, she'll attract someone better.

JOYCE LAIDLAW: You seem to like women with strong personalities.

SIR PETER BRIDFORD: I like people with strong personalities. Ana Guzman certainly qualifies. She comes from an aristocratic family but she played a crucial role in the transition to democracy in Spain. I've been lucky enough to have met several women who were determined to get on, at a time when that was far more difficult for women than it is now.

JOYCE LAIDLAW: Thank you, Sir Peter. After the break, we'll be back with more of your musical memories. Stay tuned, listeners, and keep those questions coming in.

[Resuming] Sir Peter, you returned to this country in 1973, I think?

SIR PETER BRIDFORD: Yes, and to two bits of good news. I was assigned to selling IE products into the rapidly expanding North Sea oil and gas industry. That kept me very busy for the next six years, right up to when I became a director. Also, I found that several of the people I'd known at Cambridge had kept up, and other interesting people had come to know them. So I had an instant social life. The American friend I mentioned, Steph Coolidge, called us 'The Creators' because of our desire to make a difference. Creators Technology was named after us.

JOYCE LAIDLAW: Was there bad news, too?

SIR PETER BRIDFORD: Yes. For Britain, things were going from bad to worse. We have problems now but they're far less serious than those we had then, which could be summed up in two words – Ted Heath. He was a talented man, a fine musician of course, but he was the worst Prime Minister of my lifetime.

JOYCE LAIDLAW: Are you saying that because he took us into Europe?

SIR PETER BRIDFORD: He was obsessed with taking us in and accepted the disastrous terms imposed by the existing members, particularly France. As one Creator said then, they saw him coming and skinned him alive. But I'm thinking more of his mismanagement of the economy and industrial relations. By the start of 1974, he had industry on a three-day week. Then he called an election on the question 'Who Governs Britain?' A Creator was standing for Labour – Carol Milverton, whose husband Paul had been at Waterhouse. She wasn't expecting to win but we piled in to support her as the candidate for common sense and for getting rid of Ted Heath. Some unexpected revelations about the sitting Tory helped but there was plenty of hard work, organised by Brian Smitham who was moving up fast in the insurance industry. After a long night, Carol won by seven on the third recount, with a 20% swing.

JOYCE LAIDLAW: I'm sure you all had quite a celebration.

SIR PETER BRIDFORD: Once we had caught up on sleep, we certainly did, but then came a tense wait to see whether Ted Heath would actually resign. He was still there two days later, when we met up again. The first Creators to start a family were Jenny and Dick Sinclair. Liz Partington and I were godparents at the christening of their second child. We heard my next piece as an anthem.

JOYCE LAIDLAW: This is Thomas Tallis's 40 Part Motet. Perhaps unsurprisingly, you've asked for the classic recording of the time – the Choir of King's College, Cambridge conducted by Sir David Willcocks.

[Tallis 40 Part Motet.]

SIR PETER BRIDFORD: Ted Heath resigned the next day. The electorate's answer to 'Who Governs Britain' was 'not you, mate'. But we remembered our day for a quite separate, and tragic, reason. It was the day of the Paris air disaster, and several of us knew Harry Tamfield.

JOYCE LAIDLAW: Brian Smitham is now Sir Brian, and was Lord Mayor of London a few years ago. Carol Milverton is the political journalist. As Lord Crumpsall, Paul Milverton became one of Tony Blair's key Ministers and is now Master of Waterhouse College.

SIR PETER BRIDFORD: Three out of three, Joyce, but if you're giving the full list of Creators with big gongs, you must include Dame Sheila Yates. She, too, began as an academic before she became Chief Executive of the charity that her ceaseless voluntary activity and energy had created. Last year, Action for London's Women helped over 150,000 individuals, many of them immigrants, to face the challenges of life and avoid abuse.

JOYCE LAIDLAW: Clearly the strong personalities you like go with success.

SIR PETER BRIDFORD: Yes, each in their own way, and for those who've made it. The Milvertons grew up in political families. Both of them were student activists. Carol moved to the SDP when that was formed but dropped out of Parliament in 1983, by which time her journalistic career was taking off. Paul stayed with Labour whilst pursuing a successful career in banking. He left the Milverton name for Carol. His title refers to the Manchester suburb in which they grew up. They've always been a power couple.

JOYCE LAIDLAW: It's rumoured that you were invited to be Master of Waterhouse but turned it down.

SIR PETER BRIDFORD: The Fellows made the right choice, especially as Carol makes it two for the price of one. Within weeks of arriving, they passed the hat round for the new buildings which have rightly won a load of awards. And there wouldn't have been room for my family in the Master's Lodge.

JOYCE LAIDLAW: You've not said anything about your family, yet.

SIR PETER BRIDFORD: No, because they didn't appear until well on in my life, and then only because not all Creators made it. Liz Partington married a splendid man and they had one child. At a hockey match, her husband took a knock on the head. He was determined to play on, and scored the winning goal. He seemed OK but that night he lost consciousness and never recovered. Liz needed my help, I found myself seeing more of her and one thing led to another. After a few months, we were living together. Two years later, early in 1982, Liz was diagnosed with lung cancer. She refused treatment which might have saved her so that the child she was carrying, my child, could be born. She was cheered by reports of the success of our forces in the Falklands War and wanted something reflecting their sacrifice and success to be played at her funeral, which became a double funeral, for her husband died the day after she did – you can make what you like of that.

JOYCE LAIDLAW: Your next choice, Walton's *Spitfire Prelude and Fugue*.

SIR PETER BRIDFORD: It was very appropriate, since the funeral was on what turned out to be the day of victory in the Falklands. That led to a remarkable change in national mood. By then, our standard of living had fallen far below that of our Continental neighbours. We had a long way to climb back up but suddenly we felt we could do it, and we did it. Despite recent ups and downs, the gap is small or non-existent now, depending on how you make comparisons. 1982 was Year Zero, the year of turnaround for the UK.

[Spitfire Prelude and Fugue.]

JOYCE LAIDLAW: That was played by the English Northern Philharmonia, conducted by Paul Daniel.

SIR PETER BRIDFORD: Some of the staff of Creators Technology were at the funeral and said they felt like the workers at the Spitfire factory in a scene the music accompanies in the film *The First of the Few*. They were getting ready for the first launch of the software package that was to become a world beater. So, for me, 1982 was a year of tragedy and triumph.

JOYCE LAIDLAW: It's difficult to believe that you took these blows and continued to push your company ahead.

SIR PETER BRIDFORD: One just has to keep going. There's no point in letting fate get you down. There was more to come. Three weeks later, Dick Sinclair died. Jenny was another very old friend of mine from Cambridge days, in fact more than a friend, but she had plumped for Dick, who was the viola in the quartet I told you about. The next step was pretty obvious, I suppose, and indeed Dick had given it his blessing. But it needed the agreement of three people who were in quite a state – Jenny's children David and Katie, and young Jenny, Liz's child for whom I took responsibility. Joseph, my child with Liz, was only a few months old. Fortunately, Ana Guzman had come to know Jenny as well as me and she invited us to stay with her family at her grand place near Pamplona. It had started off as a castle but by then had modern conveniences including a swimming pool. After a fortnight, the children were friends with Ana's three and, even more important, Jenny and I were Mum and Dad to all of ours. In less than three years, I had changed from apparently confirmed bachelor to father of four. By Christmas Eve 1982, we were settled in together. Late that day, Jenny and I listened to my last but one choice, which has a double significance.

JOYCE LAIDLAW: The final scene of Richard Strauss's *Der Rosenkavalier*.

SIR PETER BRIDFORD: We were marking the end of our Year Zero and recalling its start. Exactly a year before, Jenny and Dick were to attend a matinée performance at the Coliseum. Then Jenny had called me to say that Dick wasn't well, so could I come? We had enjoyed the afternoon together, though each of us was feeling worried about their other half. The scene also reflects the help I had from another of my oldest friends who kept house for me through the worst time earlier in 1982 and so allowed me to keep going. I might have gone on with her but she made it very clear who my choice should be. She stepped aside. I'm sure she's listening now and I want to thank her again for everything she did.

JOYCE LAIDLAW: This is the scene where the Marschallin steps aside so that her young lover, who is sung by a woman, can marry someone of his own age. We hear what you heard – Régine Crespin, Yvonne Minton and Helen Donath, with the Vienna Philharmonic conducted by Sir Georg Solti.

[Excerpt from final scene of 'Der Rosenkavalier'.]

SIR PETER BRIDFORD: Thank you. For the next two years money was tight because Jenny gave up her good accountancy job to become Finance Director of Creators Technology as well as mother of four. Then, in March 1985, came the launch of Tradeit Version 2, which was the world's first software to support trading online, using computers which were becoming available and precursors of the Internet. The timing was just right, with 'big bang' in the City coming up. The order book went through the roof and the company was floated soon afterwards. Jenny and I were well rewarded, along with all those who had risked their money in Creators Technology. So we could move to where we still live, and in due course to add to our family. I don't mean any disrespect by saying that our youngest child is not named after Her Majesty the Queen.

JOYCE LAIDLAW: That's Elizabeth Bridford.

SIR PETER BRIDFORD: Yes. All our children are doing well, in their own careers and on their own merits. Jenny and I always said to them that they must do their own thing. We sent them to the local state schools, which are generally very good. David Sinclair is well known to you here. Katie has beaten her mother, to become a partner in her accountancy firm. Young Jenny is the only one who joined the family firm; she's now one of ICC's top systems analysts. Joseph is the academic, with already over fifty publications on solid state physics. I was very pleased, though, to hear that Bill Latham had asked Liz to join him in recording the three Brahms sonatas. There's only one reason why a musician of Bill's standing makes such a request.

JOYCE LAIDLAW: So, as your last piece, we're to hear from a recording only just released: the last movement of Brahms's Second Violin Sonata, Opus 100, played by Bill Latham and Elizabeth Bridford.

[Movement played.]

SIR PETER BRIDFORD: As you heard, like all Brahms sonatas it's actually a duo. The piano part is as important and difficult as the violin part. If you pressed me to name my favourite composer, I would probably say Brahms. That sonata marks the apex of his career. The two opuses before are the Fourth Symphony and the Second Cello Sonata, and immediately following are the Third Piano Trio and the Double Concerto – which, by the way, is my favourite concerto involving cello. A very fine vintage recording features David Oistrakh and Pierre Fournier, whom I regard as the greatest cellist of my lifetime. The Dvorák and Elgar Concertos are too emotional for my taste, at least as they're usually played these days. I don't believe in wearing my heart on my sleeve.

JOYCE LAIDLAW: We take another break now but keep tuned for the second part of the programme. Sir Peter will begin by answering your questions about music. Then I'll take a wider range of questions because we're about musical interests as part of a total personality.

[Resuming] Sir Peter, we've had many questions about your views on *Don Giovanni*. Listeners point out that it can be played as a black comedy, in which the most important characters are Leporello and Zerlina, or as a tragedy of psychological disintegration, with the Don himself central. How does your interpretation relate to either of those?

SIR PETER BRIDFORD: As I've already intimated, I don't rate Mozart above all other composers; but, to me, *Don Giovanni* is the greatest opera ever written – a 'classic' with many interpretations possible. As with all operas, a production should suit the cast. For example, if you had Sir Geraint Evans as Leporello, you went for the 'black comedy' version, and that's what it used to be at Covent Garden. Recently, they've tried the disintegration version. My interpretation is nearer 'black comedy' in that I believe that the last scene, with all the team on stage, is an essential resolution.

JOYCE LAIDLAW: Would you have the same interpretation in mind if you'd not met Ana Guzman at a performance?

SIR PETER BRIDFORD: Perhaps not, but I did meet her. She was with her father, who was very much alive and a director of one of the largest Spanish banks. I picked up the opportunity that gave me early in my career. It's important to react quickly but thoughtfully to chance events, even if they change your previous plans. We live in the stochastic world. For Christmas, I recommend the recent book of that title by the only Creator who stayed in academic life – Morag Newlands, Professor Emeritus in Applied Probability at the University of Essex. As she says in her preface, the book grew out of a conversation we had with Carol Milverton many years ago.

JOYCE LAIDLAW: Moving on, listeners have asked what music you *don't* like.

SIR PETER BRIDFORD: There are some composers who excite me less than others. For example, Schumann strikes me as rather worthy and insipid, compared either to Brahms, or to Mendelssohn who is underrated because a few of his works are overplayed whilst we hear far too little of his chamber music. Much French music is also not for me; and though I now have more listening time, I'm less taken by Wagner than I was once. He's good stuff for home listening if you've had a long day. You can sit back, have a few drinks and wallow in the bath of sound, but his words are rubbish, as you find out if you see what they mean in English. Wagner wanted to write very long pieces of orchestral development and he span out the words to fit. For example, in the second act of *Tristan and Isolde*, the illicit lovers meet, fired up by the Dark Ages equivalent of Viagra, but all they do for about half an hour is spout quasi-philosophical claptrap. Then doddery old King Mark surprises them and witters on for about another ten minutes, perhaps because otherwise he wouldn't have any kind of decent part. Another of Wagner's fill-in games is to give frequent and lengthy reminders of what's already happened. Without those, the four 'Ring' operas would be about half the length they actually are.

JOYCE LAIDLAW: I'm sure that listeners will have something to say about those forthright comments. Wagner is always controversial, of course.

SIR PETER BRIDFORD: An advantage of being retired from executive roles, as I've been since 2007, is that you feel free to make forthright comments.

JOYCE LAIDLAW: So, now that you're retired, what are your priorities?

SIR PETER BRIDFORD: I'm not fully retired. I'm on all sorts of committees and working parties, and so is Jenny. We do have more time for music and for the expanding family. Being a grandparent provides plenty to do. I doubt that we'll catch up with Susie and Brian Smitham, though. You've heard about several career women. Susie decided that her career would be to support Brian and raise a family. She's been very successful at that. Brian told me recently that he has about fourteen grandchildren. I reminded him that when I taught him maths at Cambridge, he could be rather careless with numbers. However, that didn't stop him from taking Universal Assurance forward so successfully, as well as becoming Lord Mayor.

JOYCE LAIDLAW: Do you Creators keep up? Do you have reunions?

SIR PETER BRIDFORD: We try to meet up about every two years, with as many of our families as can join in. It was our turn to host after we made some improvements to our house. Liz repeated her first Wigmore Hall recital in our new music room, and Angela

Frampton joined us to open the two rooms she had designed to display the largest private collection of her ceramic art. There have been grander occasions when space has permitted. Brian and Susie had the Mansion House, of course. Ana Guzman, who's a kind of overseas associate, held open house for a week. Paul and Carol marked the opening of the new buildings at Waterhouse with a very good bash. But perhaps the best reunion was nearly ten years ago, when Morag and Sheila became civil partners.

JOYCE LAIDLAW: I think you said there's a transatlantic connection, too.

SIR PETER BRIDFORD: There hasn't been since my private phone rang early one fine September afternoon. Steph Coolidge had about five seconds to say goodbye before her phone, and she, went dead. Her first meeting of the day had been near the top of the World Trade Centre. She had already spoken to Paul Crumpsall, who worked with her for several years.

JOYCE LAIDLAW: So she was another Creator who didn't make it.

SIR PETER BRIDFORD: She was sixty-two and had done a lot in her life. The others were much younger. We remember them all and they have tangible memorials, too.

JOYCE LAIDLAW: We'll take our last break now. We already have a record postbag. Keep those questions coming in, but questions, please, not long statements and assertions.

SIR PETER BRIDFORD: On this wet afternoon, perhaps more people are listening than usual. If you forward on to me those questions we can't deal with today, I'll answer them.

[Resuming]

JOYCE LAIDLAW: There's been a rush of comments on your views about Wagner, ranging from 'Why do you let this ignoramus spoil our Sunday afternoon' to 'Great to hear someone prick the inflated balloon of adulation'.

SIR PETER BRIDFORD: I was only saying what Rossini said at the time. 'Wagner has magnificent moments, and very dull quarters of an hour.'

JOYCE LAIDLAW: I think we'll say that the comments cancel one another out, and move to the very many questions we've had about your wider life. I've left out some rather loaded allegations and divided the rest into four main topics. The first won't surprise you. Do you think your company's products encouraged the speculation which led to the financial crash of 2008?

SIR PETER BRIDFORD: Before I answer, can I ask you a question, Joyce? You've just referred to 'two thousand and eight' rather than the briefer 'twenty o eight.' Why has this style appeared? No-one says that the Battle of Hastings was in 'one thousand and sixty-six', or Waterloo in 'eighteen hundred and fifteen'.

JOYCE LAIDLAW: It seems to be what people say. Perhaps listeners have views.

SIR PETER BRIDFORD: The only explanation I can think of is that in twenty o one, people recalled the full title of Stanley Kubrick's film, which *is* 'Two Thousand and One', and they've continued with that style. To return to your question, my answer is that, on the contrary, I've always discouraged rash and unthinking speculation. Long before 2008, I saw the harm that it could do. When I became a director of International Electronics, the company had just lost a packet. I was much involved in organising recovery. All Creators Technology products and, since 1999, all ICC products have carried very specific guidance and warnings. Unfortunately, some competitors suggested that their products could be used more aggressively than ours, to deliver more profits. Guidance of similar quality to ICC guidance should be mandatory. In 2010 I said all this to a parliamentary select committee, which accepted my view. No doubt you can put links to the record onto your website, Joyce.

JOYCE LAIDLAW: Of course. There have also been many questions about the formation of ICC, International Consolidated Creators. You had said that your company should be independent of larger groups but then you supported a takeover at a price which was certainly good for you but wasn't maintained in later valuations. How do you justify that?

SIR PETER BRIDFORD: When Creators Technology was the only supplier of software used by banks and traders all over the world, we couldn't be linked to any of our customers. As I've said, eventually competitors appeared, including larger IT and software corporations. A takeover by a bank might then have been seen as not impeding competition. An agreed merger with another company, operating outside the finance area, seemed a good way to stay independent in practice. In 1981, International Consolidated was formed by agreed merger of IE and its erstwhile rival, Consolidated Electrics. I'd left by then but I kept in touch with people I knew and with new faces like Will Sanders. Creators went in at a valuation that was realistic at a time of boom in almost any Internet-related stock. Since 1999, ICC has been stronger than the sum of its parts. On a personal note, I was pleased to be back with my old employer and even more pleased that Sir Pat O'Donnell lived to see this outcome. For over forty years he built up IE; then for ten years he was Chairman of Creators Technology. His name lives on. In 1996, we opened O'Donnell House, our corporate HQ building in Crawley. It was designed by a good architect, with scope for some extension. That made it just right to house the HQ of ICC.

JOYCE LAIDLAW: So you were instrumental in creating what's now the largest British electrical and electronics company.

SIR PETER BRIDFORD: I'm glad you put it that way, Joyce. In 1999, we did not expect that distinction. ICC was rightly seen as a strong second force but very much second to the company which had dominated the industry for thirty years. Then, foolish decisions by that company's new management destroyed it. In the stochastic world, think carefully about what's best to do next, and then do it. Don't stick to plans which have been overtaken. Don't succumb to megalomania. In 2008, we had even worse examples of people ignoring that advice. The country is still paying for them.

JOYCE LAIDLAW: What do you say to listeners' views that you and your friends are a very privileged group, mostly from a privileged university, who have enriched themselves but done nothing for society?

SIR PETER BRIDFORD: That's a lot to answer. In fact, most Creators grew up in comfortable but modest homes. My father was a bank manager in a small country town. His father was a farm labourer, so he came a long way to get that far. Some of us were from what used to be called working class homes. Brian Smitham's father was a miner. Only one of us went to a fee-paying school and that was because his father worked for an oil company so his parents spent much time abroad. Half of us got into Cambridge University – on merit. They were mostly men. Three of the women Creators lived in Cambridge but didn't go to university. I told you about Liz Partington. Susie Smitham was a shop assistant. Jenny grew up in a background which was academic, and perhaps privileged – for the men. Her father was a reader and her brother was a research student but she was working for the University Press. She became a chartered accountant by night study. It was the same for others I've met. Angela Frampton's brother was given all the early chances. He became Sir Geoffrey Frampton, President of the Royal Society, but it's Angela who is now famous worldwide. I've done well out of spotting her talent. I also spotted the talent of a nurse called Melissa Copehurst and encouraged her to work her way through drama school. It was good that our Mansion House reunion could include seeing her famous interpretation of Lady Macbeth at the National Theatre. We think of the 'swinging sixties' as a time of sexual liberation, but actually a negative attitude to women getting on was still very widespread – not just amongst men but amongst women, too. When I first met Carol Milverton she was at what is now Murray Edwards College. She told me that some people she knew there didn't want to get better examination results than their boyfriends. By example, as well as by backing Action for London's Women, Creators have helped society to move on from that attitude.

JOYCE LAIDLAW: And, in one minute, what on enriching yourselves?

SIR PETER BRIDFORD: We could have chosen safer careers, making perhaps a little step up from our childhood environment. We could have had quiet lives. Instead, we drove ourselves hard and risked a lot, not just to build Creators Technology and create good jobs for thousands of people, but in the other ways

I've mentioned. We're part of the turnaround that happened in the UK from 1982 – Year Zero. Many people don't remember, or are too young to know, what a mess the country had got itself into by the '70s. After the War, too many British people wanted quiet lives and so we had no world-class industry capable of dominating the European market and on that basis competing worldwide. I remember Paul Crumpsall saying that we wouldn't recover without one, and he was quite right. Fortunately we have one now. It's driven us back up, and we risk it at our peril. Financial services employ millions of people, not just in the City but all over the country. Creators Technology grew as part of that industry.

JOYCE LAIDLAW: We're out of time but we've also had many questions about your reference to tangible memorials.

SIR PETER BRIDFORD: If you go to the Waterhouse College website, you'll find Carol Milverton's guide to the new buildings, including the memorials.

JOYCE LAIDLAW: Sir Peter Bridford, you've given us your memories, of good things and bad, and have told us how some pieces of music are special for you. And you've answered some questions which have ranged much wider than music. I think listeners now understand a little more about you. Thank you very much.

CREATORS COURT – A GUIDE TO THE NEW BUILDINGS

By Carol Milverton

This guide is intended for visitors to the College and also for those whose time here suffered from the inevitable disruption of building work, though we tried to keep the worst of this to the long vacations. Do return now to see what we have achieved – the best appointed of Cambridge's smaller Colleges, fully equipped to go on rewarding the efforts of its members with top results.

This College was built during the 1860s to the designs of Alfred Waterhouse, of whom our founder was a fervent admirer. However, there were not sufficient funds to complete what was then called Cobden Court. During the late 1960s, when Paul was an undergraduate here (and I was a frequent visitor!), there was a proposal to complete it with a more spacious library. This would have been a very limited improvement and it is not surprising that another College's scheme proved more attractive to the benefactor. Furthermore, the designs for the library would have been unsympathetic to Alfred Waterhouse's work.

Soon after Paul and I came here in 2007, he applied persuasive skills honed during his ten years in government. Within weeks, sufficient funds were pledged that detailed designs could be commissioned. There was no drawing back on account of later economic difficulties, which indeed promoted more competitive bidding from contractors. Construction began in July 2010 and was completed, to time and cost, in August 2013.

Who were the creators?

Whom did Paul persuade? Mostly, a group of friends made when we were here, or soon thereafter. One of us had called the group 'The Creators' and when we started a company, we called it 'Creators Technology'. That company was worth £5 billion in 1999 when it became part of ICC (International Consolidated Creators). We were now ready to join with the College (which had wisely taken a shareholding in 1980) in applying some of the value of our holdings in ICC. Accordingly, the College has renamed Cobden Court, to be Creators Court.

Alfred Waterhouse's Vision Realised

The exterior of the College is now exactly as originally proposed and is recognised to be amongst Alfred Waterhouse's greatest works. It stands alongside the Natural History Museum, and also Manchester Town

Hall, which Paul and I know well, for we both grew up in Manchester and my father was a City councillor for many years.

Inside, of course, it is a different matter. Eighty new rooms on five new staircases provide the most up-to-date facilities, including superfast broadband access. Below ground is where most of the work (and expense) has been. A large basement underlies the new buildings and extends under almost the whole of Creators Court. This provides a new library (at last), twenty teaching rooms, squash courts, staff offices and a substantial extension to the Crypt bar, the recognised social centre of the College. This now has proper access for those of limited mobility and full fire certification for use by up to 400 people.

A rolling programme of refurbishment of all other rooms in the College is now complete. We now have 420 rooms on our main site, which will allow all undergraduates to spend at least two years in College. Redevelopment of the Gilbert Lodge hostel has provided a peaceful location for eighty graduate students within ten minutes' walk.

Paul and I are very happy that all this has come about during our time here. We are even happier that the view from the Master's Lodge is no longer of a building site!

The Creators Memorial Fountain

This is the gift of Sir Peter Bridford (undergraduate 1964-67, elected Fellow 1968, Chief Executive of Creators Technology 1980-99, Director of ICC 1999-

2007). It occupies the centre of Creators Court and is the work of John Nemon RA. It commemorates, primarily, Liz Woolley (1945-82), who was the daughter of Sir Stephen Partington, Paul's predecessor but two as Master. She is depicted rushing along the riverbank, yelling support for the boat named 'Lively Liz' after her. She gave Pete Bridford the strength he needed at a critical stage in the development of Creators Technology. On falling seriously ill, she refused treatment which would have cost the life of their unborn child. The memorial's inscription 'she gave her life for our future' reflects that.

On the panels below the fountain are inscribed the names of other members of the College who were Creators or linked with them. As the memorial's inscription states, 'they all played their part, and more'. Though in some cases their careers were controversial, the good well outweighed the bad.

> Andrew Grover (1923-68) was Bursar from 1958 until within three months of his death. He was responsible for placing the finances of the College on a sound footing and for the most important improvements in facilities prior to the recent work.

> Harry Tamfield (1947-74) launched a property business which within five years was worth nearly £1 billion in present-day money. The economic crisis of 1973 put it into difficulties, which he was unable to resolve before in March 1974 he was killed with over 300 others in the Paris air disaster.

<u>Fred Perkins (1947-79)</u> was one of the finest sportsmen of his time at Waterhouse. In 1968 he was a key figure in the crew of 'Lively Liz' which achieved a very remarkable overbump, thereby setting an example of effort and direction which later generations of undergraduates have followed.

<u>Dick Sinclair (1945-82)</u> was the first husband of Lady Jennifer Bridford. A popular figure during his time at Waterhouse and later, he was capable of very decisive and quick action when necessary. He died only a few weeks after Liz, having expressed the hope that Jenny and Pete, who knew each other well and each had two children to look after, would come together. That partnership has been right not only for all of them; it was hugely important in securing the growth of Creators Technology, since Jenny is a financial manager of genius.

There is space for other names to be inscribed in due course.

The Chapel and the Coolidge Memorial Window

The founder was of free-thinking views, so the College Chapel is small, and many have passed through Waterhouse hardly aware of its existence. However, the College now attracts students from all over the world and of many religious persuasions. The refurbished Chapel is available for those on their own or in groups who wish to observe there any religion which is based on tolerance and the rejection of violence. That includes the mainstream forms of all major world religions.

The Chapel is therefore an appropriate location for the Coolidge Memorial Window, which is the gift of Lady Jennifer Bridford, Doña Ana Guzman and several donors from the USA. It commemorates all victims of intolerance and terrorism, and in particular <u>Stephanie Coolidge</u>, the originator of the term 'The Creators'. She was killed in the terrorist attacks of 11th September 2001.

The Chapel is fully licenced for marriages and civil partnerships, and for these can seat up to seventy. The College is an ideal location and photographic background. The excellent facilities of the new Crypt bar, with catering by our kitchen staff, are available for private use between 2 pm and 6 pm daily, and for longer periods during vacations, when in addition we can provide overnight accommodation. Rates are competitive, with a 10% reduction for Waterhouse graduates and their children, and an <u>additional</u> 5% off for those who were in residence between 2010 and 2013 and faced the disruption of the building work. Go to the College website for more information and to make bookings.